HANDS AND FEET

HANDS AND FEET

GHASTLY, SPECTRAL, AND FOREBODING LIMBS AND DIGITS IN CLASSIC SPECULATIVE FICTION

EDITED BY
CHAD ARMENT

COACHWHIP PUBLICATIONS
GREENVILLE, OHIO

Hands and Feet
Edited by Chad Arment
© 2024 Coachwhip Publications
Cover: Hands © Sabelskaya

CoachwhipBooks.com

ISBN 1-61646-582-4
ISBN-13 978-1-61646-582-7

CONTENTS

THE SPECTRE HAND
Anonymous
(1800s)

Do the dead ever revisit this earth?

On this subject even the ponderous and unsentimental Dr. Johnson was of opinion that to maintain they did not, was to oppose the concurrent and unvarying testimony of all ages and nations, as there was no people so barbarous, and none so civilized, but among whom apparitions of the dead were related and believed in. "That which is doubted by single cavillers," he adds, "can very little weaken the general evidence, and some who deny it with their tongues confess it by their *fears.*"

In the August of last year I found myself with three friends, when on a northern tour, at the Hotel de Scandinavie, in the long and handsome Carl Johan Gade of Christiana. A single day, or little more, had sufficed us to "do" all the lions of the little Norwegian capital—the royal palace, a stately white building, guarded by slouching Norski riflemen in long coats, with wide-awakes and green plumes; the great brick edifice wherein the Storthing is held, and where the red lion appears on everything, from the king's throne to the hall-porter's coal-scuttle; the castle of Aggerhuis and its petty armoury, with a single suit of mail, and the long muskets of the Scots who fell at Rhomsdhal; after which there is nothing more to be seen; and when the little Tivoli gardens close at ten, all Christiana goes to sleep till dawn next morning.

English carriages being perfectly useless in Norway, we had ordered four of the native carrioles for our departure, as we were resolved to start for the wild mountainous district named the Dovrefeld, when a delay in the arrival of certain letters compelled me to remain two days behind my companions, who promised to await me at Rodnaes, near the head of the magnificent Rans-fiord; and this partial separation, with the subsequent circumstance of having to travel alone through districts that were totally strange to me, with but a slight knowledge of the language, were the means of bringing to my knowledge the story I am about to relate.

The table d'hôte is over by two o'clock in the fashionable hotels of Christiana, so about four in the afternoon I quitted the city, the streets and architecture of which resemble portions of Tottenham Court Road, with stray bits of old Chester. In my carriole, a comfortable kind of gig, were my portmanteau and gun-case; these, with my whole person, and indeed the body of the vehicle itself, being covered by one of those huge tarpaulin cloaks furnished by the carriole company in the Store Standgade.

Though the rain was beginning to fall with a force and density peculiarly Norse when I left behind me the red-tiled city with all its green coppered spires, I could not but be struck by the bold beauty of the scenery, as the strong little horse at a rasping pace tore the light carriole along the rough mountain road, which was bordered by natural forests of dark and solemn-looking pines, interspersed with graceful silver birches, the greenness of the foliage contrasting powerfully with the blue of the narrow fiords that opened on every hand, and with the colours in which the toy-like country houses were painted, their timber walls being always snowy white, and their shingle roofs a flaming red. Even some of the village spires wore the same sanguinary hue, presenting thus a singular feature in the landscape.

The rain increased to an unpleasant degree; the afternoon seemed to darken into evening, and the evening into
night sooner than usual, while dense masses of vapour came
rolling down the steep sides of the wooded hills, over which
the sombre firs spread everywhere and up every vista that
opened, like a sea of cones; and as the houses became fewer
and further apart, and not a single wanderer was abroad, and
I had but the pocket-map of my "John Murray" to guide me,
I soon became convinced that instead of pursuing the route
to Rodnaes I was somewhere on the banks of the Tyri-fiord,
at least three Norwegian miles (*i.e.* twenty-one English) in
the opposite direction, my little horse worn out, the rain
still falling in a continual torrent, night already at hand, and
mountain scenery of the most tremendous character everywhere around me. I was in an almost circular valley (encompassed by a chain of hills), which opened before me, after
leaving a deep chasm that the road enters, near a place which
I afterwards learned bears the name of Krogkleven.

Owing to the steepness of the road, and some decay in
the harness of my hired carriole, the traces parted, and then
I found myself, with the now useless horse and vehicle, far
from any house, homestead, or village where I could have the
damage repaired or procure shelter, the rain still pouring like
a sheet of water, the thick, shaggy, and impenetrable woods
of Norwegian pine towering all about me, their shadows rendered all the darker by the unusual gloom of the night.

To remain quietly in the carriole was unsuitable to a temperament so impatient as mine; I drew it aside from the road,
spread the tarpaulin over my small stock of baggage and the
gun-case, haltered the pony to it, and set forth on foot, stiff,
sore, and weary, in search of succour; and, though armed
only with a Norwegian tolknife, having no fear of thieves or
of molestation.

Following the road on foot in the face of the blinding
rain, a Scotch plaid and oilskin my sole protection now, I

perceived ere long a side-gate and little avenue, which indicated my vicinity to some place of abode. After proceeding about three hundred yards or so, the wood became more
open, a light appeared before me, and I found it to proceed
from a window on the ground floor of a little two-storeyed
mansion, built entirely of wood. The sash, which was divided
in the middle, was unbolted, and stood partially and most
invitingly open; and knowing how hospitable the Norwegians
are, without troubling myself to look for the entrance-door,
I stepped over the low sill into the room (which was tenant-
less) and looked about for a bell-pull, forgetting that in that
country, where there are no mantelpieces, it is generally to
be found behind the door.

The floor was, of course, bare, and painted brown; a high
German stove, like a black iron pillar, stood in one corner
on a stone block; the door, which evidently communicated with some other apartment, was constructed to open in
the middle, with one of the quaint lever handles peculiar to
the country. The furniture was all of plain Norwegian pine,
highly varnished; a reindeer-skin spread on the floor, and
another over an easy chair, were the only luxuries; and on
the table lay the "Illustret Tidende," the "Aftonblat," and
other papers of that morning, with a meerschaum and pouch
of tobacco, all serving to show that some one had recently
quitted the room.

I had just taken in all these details by a glance, when
there entered a tall thin man of gentlemanly appearance, clad
in a rough tweed suit, with a scarlet shirt, open at the throat,
a simple but *degagé* style of costume, which he seemed to
wear with a natural grace, for it is not every man who can
dress thus and still retain an air of distinction. Pausing, he
looked at me with some surprise and inquiringly, as I began
my apologies and explanation in German.

"Taler de Dansk-Norsk," said he, curtly.

"I cannot speak either with fluency, but—"

"You are welcome, however, and I shall assist you in the prosecution of your journey. Meantime, here is cognac. I am an old soldier, and know the comforts of a full canteen, and of the Indian weed, too, in a wet bivouac. There is a pipe at your service." I thanked him, and (while he gave directions to his servants to go after the carriole and horse) proceeded to observe him more closely, for something in his voice and eye interested me deeply.

There was much of broken-hearted melancholy—something that indicated a hidden sorrow—in his features, which were handsome, and very slightly aquiline. His face was pale and careworn; his hair and moustache, though plentiful, were perfectly white-blanched, yet he did not seem over forty years of age. His eyes were blue, but without softness, being strangely keen and sad in expression, and times there were when a startled look, that savoured of fright, or pain, or insanity, or of all mingled, came suddenly into them. This unpleasant expression tended greatly to neutralize the symmetry of a face that otherwise was evidently a fine one. Suddenly a light seemed to spread over it, as I threw off some of my sodden mufflings, and he exclaimed—

"You speak Danskija, and English too, I know! Have you quite forgotten me, Herr Kaptain?" he added, grasping my hand with kindly energy. "Don't you remember Carl Holberg of the Danish Guards?"

The voice was the same as that of the once happy, lively, and jolly young, Danish officer, whose gaiety of temper and exuberance of spirit made him seem a species of madcap, who was wont to give champagne suppers at the Klampenborg Gardens to great ladies of the court and to ballet-girls of the Hof Theatre with equal liberality; to whom many a fair Danish girl had lost her heart, and who, it was said, had once the effrontery to commence a flirtation with one of the royal princesses when he was on guard at the Amalienborg Palace. But how was I to reconcile this change, the appearance of many years of premature age, that had come upon him?

"I remember you perfectly, Carl," said I, while we shook hands; "yet it is so long since we met; moreover—excuse me—but I knew not whether you were in the land of the living."

The strange expression, which I cannot define, came over his face as he said, with a low, sad tone—

"Times there are when I know not whether I am of the living or the dead. It is twenty years since our happy days—twenty years since I was wounded at the Battle of Idstedt—and it seems as if 'twere twenty ages."

"Old friend, I am indeed glad to meet you again."

"Yes, old you may call me with truth," said he, with a sad, weary smile, as he passed his hand tremulously over his whitened locks, which I could remember being a rich auburn.

All reserve was at an end now, and we speedily recalled a score and more of past scenes of merriment and pleasure, enjoyed together—prior to the campaign of Holstein—in Copenhagen, that most delightful and gay of all the northern cities; and, under the influence of memory, his now withered face seemed to brighten, and some of its former expression stole back again.

"Is this your fishing or shooting quarters, Carl?" I asked.

"Neither. It is my permanent abode."

"In this place, so rural—so solitary? Ah! you have become a Benedick—taken to love in a cottage, and so forth—yet I don't see any signs of—"

"Hush! for godsake! You know not *who* hears us," he exclaimed, as terror came over his face; and he withdrew his hand from the table on which it was resting, with a nervous suddenness of action that was unaccountable, or as if hot iron had touched it.

"Why?—Can we not talk of such things?" asked I.

"Scarcely here—or anywhere to me," he said, incoherently. Then, fortifying himself with a stiff glass of cognac and foaming seltzer, he added: "You know that my engagement with my cousin Marie Louise Viborg was broken off—beautiful though she was, perhaps *is* still, for even twenty years could not destroy her loveliness of feature and brilliance of expression—but you never knew *why?*"

"I thought you behaved ill to her—were mad, in fact."

A spasm came over his face. Again he twitched his hand away as if a wasp had stung, or something unseen had touched it, as he said—

"She was very proud, imperious and jealous."

"She resented, of course, your openly wearing the opal ring which was thrown to you from the palace window by the princess—"

"The ring—the ring! Oh, do not speak of *that!*" said he, in a hollow tone. "Mad?—yes, I was mad—and yet I am not, though I have undergone, and even *now* am undergoing, that which would break the heart of a Holger Danske! But you shall hear, if I can tell it with coherence and without interruption, the reason why I fled from society, and the world— and for all these twenty miserable years have buried myself in this mountain solitude, where the forest overhangs the fiord, and where no woman's face shall ever smile on mine!"

In short, after some reflection and many involuntary sighs—and being urged, when the determination to unbosom himself wavered—Carl Holberg related to me a little narrative so singular and wild, that but for the sad gravity—or intense solemnity of his manner—and the air of perfect conviction that his manner bore with it, I should have deemed him utterly—mad!

"Marie Louise and I were to be married, as you remember, to cure me of all my frolics and expensive habits—the very day was fixed; you were to be the groomsman, and had selected a suite of jewels for the bride in the Kongens Nytorre;

but the war that broke out in Schleswig-Holstein drew my
battalion of the guards to the field, whither I went without
much regret so far as my fiancée was concerned; for, sooth
to say, both of us were somewhat weary of our engagement,
and were unsuited to each other: so we had not been without
piques, coldnesses, and even quarrels, till keeping up appearances partook of boredom.

"I was with General Krogh when that decisive battle was
fought at Idstedt between our troops and the Germanising
Holsteiners under General Willisen. My battalion of the
guards was detached from the right wing with orders to advance from Salbro on the Holstein rear, while the centre was
to be attacked, pierced, and the batteries beyond it carried at
the point of the bayonet, all of which was brilliantly done.
But prior to that I was sent, with directions to extend my
company in skirmishing order, among thickets that covered
a knoll which is crowned by a ruined edifice, part of an old
monastery with a secluded burial-ground.

"Just prior to our opening fire the funeral of a lady of
rank, apparently, passed us, and I drew my men aside to
make way for the open catafalque, on which lay the coffin
covered with white flowers and silver coronets, while behind
it were her female attendants, clad in black cloaks in the
usual fashion, and carrying wreaths of white flowers and immortelles to lay upon the grave. Desiring these mourners to
make all speed lest they might find themselves under a fire
of cannon and musketry, my company opened, at six hundred
yards, on the Holsteiners, who were coming on with great
spirit. We skirmished with them for more than an hour, in
the long clear twilight of the July evening, and gradually, but
with considerable loss, were driving them through the thick-
et and over the knoll on which the ruins stand, when a half-
spent bullet whistled through an opening in the mouldering
wall and struck me on the back part of the head, just below my bearskin cap. A thousand stars seem to flash around
me, then darkness succeeded. I staggered and fell, believing

myself mortally wounded; a pious invocation trembled on my lips, the roar of the red and distant battle passed away, and I became completely insensible.

"How long I lay thus I know not, but when I imagined myself coming back to life and to the world I was in a handsome, but rather old-fashioned apartment, hung, one portion of it with tapestry and the other with rich drapery. A subdued light that came, I could not discover from where, filled it. On a buffet lay my sword and my brown bearskin cap of the Danish Guards. I had been borne from the field evidently, but when and to where? I was extended on a soft fauteuil or couch, and my uniform coat was open. Some one was kindly supporting my head—a woman dressed in white, like a bride; young and so lovely, that to attempt any description of her seems futile!

"She was like the fancy portraits one occasionally sees of beautiful girls, for she was divine, perfectly so, as some enthusiast's dream, or painter's happiest conception. A long respiration, induced by admiration, delight, and the pain of my wound escaped me. She was so exquisitely fair, delicate and pale, middle-sized and slight, yet charmingly round, with hands that were perfect, and marvellous golden hair that curled in rippling masses about her forehead and shoulders, and from amid which her *piquante* little face peeped forth as from a silken nest. Never have I forgotten that face, nor shall I be *permitted* to do so, while life lasts at least," he added, with a strange contortion of feature, expressive of terror rather than ardour; "it is ever before my eyes, sleeping or waking, photographed in my heart and on my brain! I strove to rise, but she stilled, or stayed me, by a caressing gesture, as a mother would her child, while softly her bright beaming eyes smiled into mine, with more of tenderness, perhaps, than love; while in her whole air there was much of dignity and self reliance.

"'Where am I?' was my first question.

"'With me,' she answered naïvely; 'is it not enough?'

"I kissed her hand, and said—'The bullet, I remember, struck me down in a place of burial on the Salbro Road—strange!'

"'Why strange?'

"'As I am fond of rambling among graves when in my thoughtful moods.'

"'Among graves—why?' she asked.

"'They look so peaceful and quiet.'"

"Was she laughing at my unwonted gravity, that so strange a light seemed to glitter in her eyes, on her teeth, and over all her lovely face? I kissed her hands again, and she left them in mine. Adoration began to fill my heart and eyes, and be faintly murmured on my lips; for the great beauty of the girl bewildered and intoxicated me; and, perhaps, I was emboldened by past success in more than one love affair. She sought to withdraw her hand, saying.

"'Look not thus; I know how lightly you hold the love of one elsewhere.'

"'Of my cousin Marie Louise? Oh! what of that! I never, never loved till now!' and, drawing a ring from her finger, I slipped my beautiful opal in its place.

"'And you love me?' she whispered.

"'Yes; a thousand times, yes!'

"'But you are a soldier—wounded, too. Ah! if you should die before we meet again!'

"'Or, if you should die ere then?' said I, laughingly.

"'Die—I am already dead to the world—in loving you; but, living or dead, our souls are as one, and—'

"'Neither heaven nor the powers beneath shall separate us now!' I exclaimed, as something of melodrama began to mingle with the genuineness of the sudden passion with which she had inspired me. She was so impulsive, so full of brightness and ardour, as compared to the cold, proud, and calm Marie Louise. I boldly encircled her with my arms; then her glorious eyes seemed to fill with the subtle light of love, while there was a strange magnetic thrill in her touch, and, more than all, in her kiss.

"'Carl, Carl!' she sighed.

"'What! You know my name?—And yours?'

"'Thyra. But ask no more.'

"There are but three words to express the emotion that possessed me—bewilderment, intoxication, madness. I showered kisses on her beautiful eyes, on her soft tresses, on her lips that met mine half way; but this excess of joy, together with the pain of my wound, began to overpower me; a sleep, a growing and drowsy torpor, against which I struggled in vain, stole over me. I remember clasping her firm little hand in mine, as if to save myself from sinking into oblivion, and then—no more—no more!

"On again coming back to consciousness, I was alone. The sun was rising, but had not yet risen. The scenery the thickets through which we had skirmished, rose dark as the deepest indigo against the amber-tinted eastern sky; and the last light of the waning moon yet silvered the pools and marshes around the borders of the Langsö Lake, where now eight thousand men, the slain of yesterday's battle, were lying stark and stiff. Moist with dew and blood, I propped myself on one elbow and looked around me, with such wonder that a sickness came over my heart. I was again in the cemetery where the bullet had struck me down; a little grey owl was whooping and blinking in a recess of the crumbling wall. Was the drapery of the chamber but the ivy that rustled thereon?—for where the buffet stood there was an old square tomb, whereon lay my sword and bearskin cap!

"The last rays of the waning moonlight stole through the ruins on a new-made grave—the fancied fauteuil on which I lay—strewn with the flowers of yesterday, and at its head stood a temporary cross, hung with white garlands and wreaths of immortelles. Another ring was on my finger now; but where was she, the donor? Oh, what opium-dream, or what insanity was this?

"For a time I remained utterly bewildered by the vivid-
ness of my recent dream, for such I believed it to be. But if
a dream, how came this strange ring, with a square emerald
stone, upon my finger? And *where* was mine? Perplexed by
these thoughts, and filled with wonder and regret that the
beauty I had seen had no reality, I picked my way over the
ghostly débris of the battlefield, faint, feverish, and thirsty,
till at the end of a long avenue of lindens I found shelter in a
stately brick mansion, which I learned belonged to the Count
of Idstert, a noble, on whose hospitality—as he favoured the
Holsteiners—I meant to intrude as little as possible.

"He received me, however, courteously and kindly. I found
him in deep mourning: and on discovering, by chance, that I
was the officer who had halted the line of skirmishers when
the funeral *cortège* passed on the previous day, he thanked me
with earnestness, adding, with a deep; sigh, that it was the
burial of his only daughter.

"'Half my life seems to have gone with her—my lost darling! She was so sweet, Herr Kaptain—so gentle, and so sur-
passingly beautiful—my poor Thyra!'

"'Who did you say?' I exclaimed, in a voice that sounded
strange and unnatural, while half-starting from the sofa on
which I had cast myself, sick at heart and faint from loss of
blood.

"'Thyra, my daughter, Herr Kaptain,' replied the Count,
too full of sorrow to remark my excitement, for this had
been the quaint old Danish name uttered in my dream. 'See,
what a child I have lost!' he added, as he drew back a curtain which covered a full-length portrait, and, to my growing
horror and astonishment, I beheld, arrayed in white even
as I had seen her in my vision, the fair girl with the masses
of golden hair, the beautiful eyes, and the *piquante* smile
lighting up her features even on the canvas, and I was rooted
to the spot.

"'This ring, Herr Count?' I gasped. He let the curtain fall from his hand, and now a terrible emotion seized him, as he almost tore the jewel from my finger.

"'My daughter's ring!' he exclaimed. 'It was buried with her yesterday—her grave has been violated—violated by your infamous troops.'"

As he spoke, a mist seemed to come over my sight; a giddiness made my senses reel, then a hand—the soft little hand of last night, with my opal ring on its third finger— came stealing into mine, unseen! More than that, a kiss from tremulous lips I could not see, was pressed on mine, as I sank backward and fainted! The remainder of my story must be briefly told.

"My soldiering was over; my nervous system was too much shattered for further military service. On my homeward way to join and be wedded to Marie Louise—a union with whom was intensely repugnant to me now—I pondered deeply over the strange subversion of the laws of nature presented by my adventure; or the madness, it might be, that had come upon me."

"On the day I presented myself to my intended bride and approached to salute her, I felt a hand—the same hand—laid softly on mine. Starting, and trembling, I looked around me; but saw nothing. The grasp was firm. I passed my other hand over it, and felt the slender fingers and the shapely wrist; yet still I saw nothing, and Marie Louise gazed at my motions, my pallor, doubt and terror, with calm, but cool indignation.

"I was about to speak—to explain—to say I know not what, when a kiss from lips I could not see sealed mine, and with a cry like a scream I broke away from my friends and fled.

"All deemed me mad, and spoke with commiseration of my wounded head; and when I went abroad in the streets men eyed me with curiosity, as one over whom some evil destiny hung—as one to whom something terrible had happened, and gloomy thoughts were wasting me to a shadow.

My narrative may seem incredible; but this attendant, unseen yet palpable, is ever by my side, and if under any impulse, such even as sudden pleasure in meeting you, I for a moment forget it, the soft and gentle touch of a female hand reminds me of the past, and haunts me, for a guardian demon—if I may use such a term—rules my destiny: one lovely, perhaps, as an angel.

"Life has no pleasures, but only terrors for me now. Sorrow, doubt, horror and perpetual dread, have sapped the roots of existence; for a wild and clamorous fear of what the next moment may bring forth is ever in my heart, and when the touch comes my soul seems to die within me.

"You know what haunts me now—God help me! God help me! You do not understand all this, you would say. Still less do I; but in all the idle or extravagant stories I have read of ghosts—stories once my sport and ridicule, as the result of vulgar superstition or ignorance—the so-called supernatural visitor was visible to the eye, or heard by the ear; but the ghost, the fiend, the invisible Thing that is ever by the side of Carl Holberg, is only sensible to the touch—it is the unseen but tangible substance of an apparition!"

He had got thus far when he gasped, grew livid, and, passing his right hand over the left, about an inch above it, with trembling fingers, he said—

"It is here—here now—even with you present, I feel her hand on mine; the clasp is tight and tender, and she will never leave me, but with life!"

And then this once gay, strong, and gallant fellow, now the wreck of himself in body and in spirit, sank forward with his head between his knees, sobbing and faint.

Four months afterwards, when with my friends, I was shooting bears at Hammerfest, I read in the Norwegian "Aftenposten," that Carl Holberg had shot himself in bed, on Christmas Eve.

THE SEVERED HAND
Wilhelm Hauff
(1826, trnsl. 1869)

I was born in Constantinople; my father was a dragoman at
the Porte, and besides, carried on a fairly lucrative business
in sweet-scented perfumes and silk goods. He gave me a good
education; he partly instructed me himself, and also had me
instructed by one of our priests. He at first intended me to
succeed him in business one day, but as I showed greater aptitude than he had expected, he destined me, on the advice of
his friends, to be a doctor; for if a doctor has learned a little
more than the ordinary charlatan, he can make his fortune
in Constantinople. Many Franks frequented our house, and
one of them persuaded my father to allow me to travel to
his native land to the city of Paris, where such things could
be best acquired and free of charge. He wished, however,
to take me with himself gratuitously on his journey home.
My father, who had also travelled in his youth, agreed, and
the Frank told me to hold myself in readiness three months
hence. I was beside myself with joy at the idea of seeing
foreign countries, and eagerly awaited the moment when we
should embark. The Frank had at last concluded his business
and prepared himself for the journey. On the evening before our departure my father led me into his little bedroom.
There I saw splendid dresses and arms lying on the table. My
looks were however chiefly attracted to an immense heap of
gold, for I had never before seen so much collected together.

My father embraced me and said: "Behold, my son, I have procured for thee clothes for the journey. These weapons are thine; they are the same which thy grandfather hung around me when I went abroad. I know that thou canst use them aright; but only make use of them when thou art attacked; on such occasions, however, defend thyself bravely. My property is not large; behold I have divided it into three parts, one part for thee, another for my support and spare money, but the third is to me a sacred and untouched property, it is for thee in the hour of need." Thus spoke my old father, tears standing in his eyes, perhaps from some foreboding, for I never saw him again.

The journey passed off very well; we had soon reached the land of the Franks, and six days later we arrived in the large city of Paris. There my Frankish friend hired a room for me, and advised me to spend wisely my money, which amounted in all to two thousand dollars. I lived three years in this city, and learned what is necessary for a skilful doctor to know. I should not, however, be stating the truth if I said that I liked being there, for the customs of this nation displeased me; besides, I had only a few chosen friends there, and these were noble young men.

The longing after home at last possessed me mightily; during the whole of that time I had not heard anything from my father, and I therefore seized a favorable opportunity of reaching home. An embassy from France left for Turkey. I acted as surgeon to the suite of the Ambassador and arrived happily in Stamboul. My father's house was locked, and the neighbors, who were surprised on seeing me, told me my father had died two months ago. The priest who had instructed me in my youth brought me the key; alone and desolate I entered the empty house. All was still in the same position as my father had left it, only the gold which I was to inherit was gone. I questioned the priest about it, and he, bowing, said: "Your father died a saint, for he has bequeathed his gold to the Church." This was and remained inexplicable to me. However, what could I do? I had no witness against the priest, and had to be glad that he had not considered the house and the goods of my father as a bequest. This was the first misfortune that I encountered. Henceforth nothing but ill-luck attended me. My reputation as doctor would not spread at all, because I was ashamed to act the charlatan; and I felt everywhere the want of the recommendation of my father, who would have introduced me to the richest and most distinguished, but who now no longer thought of the poor Zaleukos! The goods of my father also had no sale, for his customers had deserted him after his death, and new ones are only to be got slowly.

Thus when I was one day meditating sadly over my position, it occurred to me that I had often seen in France men of my nation travelling through the country exhibiting their goods in the markets of the towns. I remembered that the people liked to buy of them, because they came from abroad, and that such a business would be most lucrative. Immediately I resolved what to do. I disposed of my father's house, gave part of the money to a trusty friend to keep for me, and with the rest I bought what are very rare in France, shawls, silk goods, ointments, and oils, took a berth on board a ship, and thus entered upon my second journey to the land of the Franks. It seemed as if fortune had favored me again as soon as I had turned my back upon the Castles of the Dardanelles. Our journey was short and successful. I travelled through the large and small towns of the Franks, and found everywhere willing buyers of my goods. My friend in Stamboul always sent me fresh stores, and my wealth increased day by day. When I had saved at last so much that I thought I might venture on a greater undertaking, I travelled with my goods to Italy. I must however confess to something, which brought me not a little money: I also employed my knowledge of physic. On reaching a town, I had it published that a Greek physician had arrived, who had already healed many; and in fact my balsam and medicine gained me many a sequin. Thus I had at length reached the city of Florence in Italy.

I resolved upon remaining in this town for some time, partly because I liked it so well, partly also because I wished to recruit myself from the exertions of my travels. I hired a vaulted shop, in that part of the town called Sta. Croce, and not far from this a couple of nice rooms at an inn, leading out upon a balcony. I immediately had my bills circulated, which announced me to be both physician and merchant. Scarcely had I opened my shop when I was besieged by buyers, and in spite of my high prices I sold more than any one else, because I was obliging and friendly towards my customers. Thus I had already lived four days happily in Florence, when one evening, as I was about to close my vaulted room, and on examining once more the contents of my ointment boxes, as I was in the habit of doing, I found in one of the small boxes a piece of paper, which I did not remember to have put into it.

I unfolded the paper, and found in it an invitation to be on the bridge which is called Ponto Vecchio that night exactly at midnight. I was thinking for a long time as to who it might be who had invited me there; and not knowing a single soul in Florence, I thought perhaps I should be secretly conducted to a patient, a thing which had already often occurred. I therefore determined to proceed thither, but took care to gird on the sword which my father had once presented to me. When it was close upon midnight I set out on my journey, and soon reached the Ponte Vecchio. I found the bridge deserted, and determined to await the appearance of him who called me. It was a cold night; the moon shone brightly, and I looked down upon the waves of the Arno, which sparkled far away in the moonlight. It was now striking twelve o'clock from all the churches of the city, when I looked up and saw a tall man standing before me completely covered in a scarlet cloak, one end of which hid his face.

At first I was somewhat frightened, because he had made his appearance so suddenly; but was however myself again shortly afterwards, and said: "If it is you who have ordered me here, say what you want?" The man dressed in scarlet turned round and said in an undertone: "Follow!" At this, however, I felt a little timid to go alone with this stranger. I stood still and said: "Not so, sir, kindly first tell me where; you might also let me see your countenance a little, in order to convince me that you wish me no harm." The red one, however, did not seem to pay any attention to this. "If thou art unwilling, Zaleukos, remain," he replied, and continued his way. I grew angry. "Do you think," I exclaimed, "a man like myself allows himself to be made a fool of, and to have waited on this cold night for nothing?"

In three bounds I had reached him, seized him by his cloak, and cried still louder, whilst laying hold of my sabre with my other hand. His cloak, however, remained in my hand, and the stranger had disappeared round the nearest corner. I became calmer by degrees. I had the cloak at any rate, and it was this which would give me the key to this re-markable adventure. I put it on and continued my way home. When I was at a distance of about a hundred paces from it, some one brushed very closely by me and whispered in the language of the Franks: "Take care, Count, nothing can be done to-night." Before I had time, however, to turn round, this somebody had passed, and I merely saw a shadow hov-ering along the houses. I perceived that these words did not concern me, but rather the cloak, yet it gave me no explana-tion concerning the affair. On the following morning I con-sidered what was to be done. At first I had intended to have the cloak cried in the streets, as if I had found it. But then the stranger might send for it by a third person, and thus no

light would be thrown upon the matter. Whilst I was thus
thinking, I examined the cloak more closely. It was made
of thick Genoese velvet, scarlet in color, edged with Astra-
chan fur and richly embroidered with gold. The magnificent
appearance of the cloak put a thought into my mind which I
resolved to carry out.

I carried it into my shop and exposed it for sale, but
placed such a high price upon it that I was sure nobody
would buy it. My object in this was to scrutinize everybody
sharply who might ask for the fur cloak; for the figure of
the stranger, which I had seen but superficially, though with
some certainty, after the loss of the cloak, I should recognize
amongst a thousand. There were many would-be purchasers
for the cloak, the extraordinary beauty of which attracted
everybody; but none resembled the stranger in the slightest
degree, and nobody was willing to pay such a high price as
two hundred sequins for it. What astonished me was that on
asking somebody or other if there was not such a cloak in
Florence, they all answered "No," and assured me they never
had seen so precious and tasteful a piece of work.

Evening was drawing near, when at last a young man appeared, who had already been to my place, and who had also
offered me a great deal for the cloak. He threw a purse with
sequins upon the table, and exclaimed: "Of a truth, Zaleukos,
I must have thy cloak, should I turn into a beggar over it!"
He immediately began to count his pieces of gold. I was in
a dangerous position: I had only exposed the cloak, in order
merely to attract the attention of my stranger, and now a
young fool came to pay an immense price for it. However,
what could I do? I yielded; for on the other hand I was delighted at the idea of being so handsomely recompensed for
my nocturnal adventure.

The young man put the cloak around him and went away,
but on reaching the threshold he returned; whilst unfastening a piece of paper which had been tied to the cloak, and

throwing it towards me, he exclaimed: "Here, Zaleukos, hangs something which I dare say does not belong to the cloak." I picked up the piece of paper carelessly, but behold, on it these words were written: "Bring the cloak at the appointed hour to-night to the Ponte Vecchio, four hundred sequins are thine." I stood thunderstruck. Thus I had lost my fortune and completely missed my aim! Yet I did not think long. I picked up the two hundred sequins, jumped after the one who had bought the cloak, and said: "Dear friend, take back your sequins, and give me the cloak; I cannot possibly part with it." He first regarded the matter as a joke; but when he saw that I was in earnest, he became angry at my demand, called me a fool, and finally it came to blows.

However, I was fortunate enough to wrench the cloak from him in the scuffle, and was about to run away with it, when the young man called the police to his assistance, and we both appeared before the judge. The latter was much surprised at the accusation, and adjudicated the cloak in favor of my adversary. I offered the young man twenty, fifty, eighty, even a hundred sequins in addition to his two hundred, if he would part with the cloak. What my entreaties could not do, my gold did. He accepted it. I, however, went away with the cloak triumphantly, and had to appear to the whole town of Florence as a madman. I did not care, however, about the opinion of the people; I knew better than they that I profited after all by the bargain.

Impatiently I awaited the night. At the same hour as before I went with the Cloak under my arm towards the Ponte Vecchio. With the last stroke of twelve the figure appeared out of the darkness, and came towards me. It was unmistakably the man whom I had seen yesterday. "Hast thou the cloak?" he asked me. "Yes, sir," I replied; "but it cost me a hundred sequins ready money." "I know it," replied the other. "Look here, here are four hundred." He went with me towards the wide balustrade of the bridge, and counted out

the money. There were four hundred; they sparkled magnifi-
cently in the moonlight; their glitter rejoiced my heart. Alas,
I did not anticipate that this would be its last joy. I put the
money into my pocket, and was desirous of thoroughly looking at my kind and unknown stranger; but he wore a mask,
through which dark eyes stared at me frightfully. "I thank
you, sir, for your kindness," I said to him; "what else do you
require of me? I tell you beforehand it must be an honorable
transaction." "There is no occasion for alarm," he replied,
whilst winding the cloak around his shoulders; "I require
your assistance as surgeon, not for one alive, but dead."

"What do you mean?" I exclaimed, full of surprise. "I
arrived with my sister from abroad," he said, and beckoned
me at the same time to follow him. "I lived here with her at
the house of a friend. My sister died yesterday suddenly of
a disease, and my relatives wish to bury her to-morrow. According to an old custom of our family all are to be buried
in the tomb of our ancestors; many, notwithstanding, who
died in foreign countries are buried there and embalmed. I
do not grudge my relatives her body, but for my father I want
at least the head of his daughter, in order that he may see
her once more." This custom of severing the heads of beloved
relatives appeared to me somewhat awful, yet I did not dare
to object to it lest I should offend the stranger. I told him
that I was acquainted with the embalming of the dead, and
begged him to conduct me to the deceased. Yet I could not
help asking him why all this must be done so mysteriously
and at night? He answered me that his relatives, who considered his intention horrible, objected to it by daylight; if only
the head were severed, then they could say no more about it;
although he might have brought me the head, yet a natural
feeling had prevented him from severing it himself.

In the meantime we had reached a large, splendid house.
My companion pointed it out to me as the end of our nocturnal walk. We passed the principal entrance of the house,

entered a little door, which the stranger carefully locked behind him, and now ascended in the dark a narrow spiral staircase. It led towards a dimly lighted passage, out of which we entered a room lighted by a lamp fastened to the ceiling.

In this room was a bed, on which the corpse lay. The stranger turned aside his face, evidently endeavoring to hide his tears. He pointed towards the bed, telling me to do my business well and quickly, and left the room.

I took my instruments, which I as surgeon always carried about with me, and approached the bed. Only the head of the corpse was visible, and it was so beautiful that I experienced involuntarily the deepest sympathy. Dark hair hung down in long plaits, the features were pale, the eyes closed. At first I made an incision into the skin, after the manner of surgeons when amputating a limb. I then took my sharpest knife, and with one stroke cut the throat. But oh, horror! The dead opened her eyes, but immediately closed them again, and with a deep sigh she now seemed to breathe her last. At the same moment a stream of hot blood shot towards me from the wound. I was convinced that the poor creature had been killed by me. That she was dead there was no doubt, for there was no recovery from this wound. I stood for some minutes in painful anguish at what had happened. Had the "red-cloak" deceived me, or had his sister perhaps merely been apparently dead? The latter seemed to me more likely. But I dare not tell the brother of the deceased that perhaps a little less deliberate cut might have awakened her without killing her; therefore I wished to sever the head completely; but once more the dying woman groaned, stretched herself out in painful movements, and died.

Fright overpowered me, and, shuddering, I hastened out of the room. But outside in the passage it was dark; for the light was out, no trace of my companion was to be seen, and I was obliged, haphazard, to feel my way in the dark along the wall, in order to reach the staircase. I discovered it at last and descended, partly falling and partly gliding. But there was not a soul downstairs. I merely found the door ajar, and breathed freer on reaching the street, for I had felt very strange inside the house. Urged on by terror, I rushed towards my dwelling-place, and buried myself in the cushions of my bed, in order to forget the terrible thing that I had done.

But sleep deserted me, and only the morning admonished me again to take courage. It seemed to me probable that the man who had induced me to commit this nefarious deed, as it now appeared to me, might not denounce me. I immediately resolved to set to work in my vaulted room, and if possible to assume an indifferent look. But alas! an additional circumstance, which I only now noticed, increased my anxiety still more. My cap and my girdle, as well as my instruments, were wanting, and I was uncertain as to whether I had left them in the room of the murdered girl, or whether I had lost them in my flight. The former seemed indeed the more likely, and thus I could easily be discovered as the murderer.

At the accustomed hour I opened my vaulted room. My neighbor came in, as was his wont every morning, for he was a talkative man. "Well," he said, "what do you say about the terrible affair which has occurred during the night?" I pretended not to know anything. "What, do you not know what is known all over the town? Are you not aware that the loveliest flower in Florence, Bianca, the Governor's daughter, was murdered last night? I saw her only yesterday driving through the streets in so cheerful a manner with her intended one, for to-day the marriage was to have taken place." I felt deeply wounded at each word of my neighbor. Many a time my torment was renewed, for every one of my customers told me of the affair, each one more ghastly than the other, and yet nobody could relate anything more terrible than that which I had seen myself.

About mid-day a police-officer entered my shop and requested me to send the people away. "Signor Zaleukos," he said, producing the things which I had missed, "do these things belong to you?" I was thinking as to whether I should not entirely repudiate them, but on seeing through the door, which stood ajar, my landlord and several acquaintances, I determined not to aggravate the affair by telling a lie, and acknowledged myself as the owner of the things. The police-officer asked me to follow him, and led me towards a large building which I soon recognized as the prison. There he showed me into a room meanwhile.

My situation was terrible, as I thought of it in my solitude. The idea of having committed a murder, unintentionally, constantly presented itself to my mind. I also could not conceal from myself that the glitter of the gold had captivated my feelings, otherwise I should not have fallen blindly into the trap. Two hours after my arrest I was led out of my cell. I descended several steps until at last I reached a great hall. Around a long table draped in black were seated twelve men, mostly old men. There were benches along the sides of the hall, filled with the most distinguished of Florence. The galleries, which were above, were thickly crowded with spectators. When I had stepped towards the table covered with black cloth, a man with a gloomy and sad countenance rose; it was the Governor. He said to the assembly that he as the father in this affair could not sentence, and that he resigned his place on this occasion to the eldest of the Senators. The eldest of the Senators was an old man at least ninety years of age. He stood in a bent attitude, and his temples were covered with thin white hair, but his eyes were as yet very fiery, and his voice powerful and weighty. He commenced by asking me whether I confessed to the murder. I requested him to allow me to speak, and related undauntedly and with a clear voice what I had done, and what I knew.

I noticed that the Governor, during my recital, at one time turned pale, and at another time red. When I had finished, he rose angrily: "What, wretch!" he exclaimed, "dost thou even dare to impute a crime which thou hast committed from greediness to another?" The Senator reprimanded him for his interruption, since he had voluntarily renounced his right; besides it was not clear that I did the deed from greediness, for, according to his own statement, nothing had been stolen from the victim. He even went further. He told the Governor that he must give an account of the early life of his daughter, for then only it would be possible to decide whether I had spoken the truth or not. At the same time he adjourned the court for the day, in order, as he said, to consult the papers of the deceased, which the Governor would give him. I was again taken back to my prison, where I spent a wretched day, always fervently wishing that a link between the deceased and the "red-cloak" might be discovered. Full of hope, I entered the Court of Justice the next day. Several letters were lying upon the table. The old Senator asked me whether they were in my handwriting. I looked at them and noticed that they must have been written by the same hand as the other two papers which I had received. I communicated this to the Senators, but no attention was paid to it, and they told me that I might have written both, for the signature of the letters was undoubtedly a Z., the first letter of my name. The letters, however, contained threats against the deceased, and warnings against the marriage which she was about to contract.

The Governor seemed to have given extraordinary information concerning me, for I was treated with more suspicion and rigor on this day. I referred, to justify myself, to my papers which must be in my room, but was told they had been looked for without success. Thus at the conclusion of this sitting all hope vanished, and on being brought into the

Court the third day, judgment was pronounced on me. I was convicted of wilful murder and condemned to death. Things had come to such a pass! Deserted by all that was precious to me upon earth, far away from home, I was to die innocently in the bloom of my life.

On the evening of this terrible day which had decided my fate, I was sitting in my lonely cell, my hopes were gone, my thoughts steadfastly fixed upon death, when the door of my prison opened, and in came a man, who for a long time looked at me silently. "Is it thus I find you again, Zaleukos?" he said. I had not recognized him by the dim light of my lamp, but the sound of his voice roused in me old remembrances. It was Valetti, one of those few friends whose acquaintance I made in the city of Paris when I was studying there. He said that he had come to Florence accidentally, where his father, who was a distinguished man, lived. He had heard about my affair, and had come to see me once more, and to hear from my own lips how I could have committed such a crime. I related to him the whole affair. He seemed much surprised at it, and adjured me, as my only friend, to tell him all, in order not to leave the world with a lie behind me. I confirmed my assertions with an oath that I had spoken the truth, and that I was not guilty of anything, except that the glitter of the gold had dazzled me, and that I had not perceived the improbability of the story of the stranger. "Did you not know Bianca?" he asked me. I assured him that I had never seen her. Valetti now related to me that a profound mystery rested on the affair, that the Governor had very much accelerated my condemnation, and now a report was spread that I had known Bianca for a long time, and had murdered her out of revenge for her marriage with some one else. I told him that all this coincided exactly with the "redcloak," but that I was unable to prove his participation in the affair. Valetti embraced me weeping, and promised me to do all, at least to save my life.

I had little hope, though I knew that Valetti was a clever man, well versed in the law, and that he would do all in his power to save my life. For two long days I was in uncertainty; at last Valetti appeared. "I bring consolation, though painful. You will live and be free with the loss of one hand." Affected, I thanked my friend for saving my life. He told me that the Governor had been inexorable in having the affair investigated a second time, but that he at last, in order not to appear unjust, had agreed, that if a similar case could be found in the law books of the history of Florence, my punishment should be the same as the one recorded in these books. He and his father had searched in the old books day and night, and at last found a case quite similar to mine. The sentence was: That his left hand be cut off, his property confiscated, and he himself banished for ever. This was my punishment also, and he asked me to prepare for the painful hour which awaited me. I will not describe to you that terrible hour, when I laid my hand upon the block in the public market-place and my own blood shot over me in broad streams.

Valetti took me to his house until I had recovered; he then most generously supplied me with money for travelling, for all I had acquired with so much difficulty had fallen a prey to the law. I left Florence for Sicily and embarked on the first ship that I found for Constantinople.

My hope was fixed upon the sum which I had entrusted to my friend. I also requested to be allowed to live with him. But how great was my astonishment on being asked why I did not wish to live in my own house. He told me that some unknown man had bought a house in the Greek Quarter in my name, and this very man had also told the neighbors of my early arrival. I immediately proceeded thither accompanied by my friend, and was received by all my old acquaintances joyfully. An old merchant gave me a letter, which the man who had bought the house for me had left behind. I read as follows: "Zaleukos! Two hands are prepared to work incessantly, in order that you may not feel the loss of one of yours. The house which you see and all its contents are yours, and every year you will receive enough to be counted amongst the rich of your people. Forgive him who is unhappier than yourself!" I could guess who had written it, and in answer to my question, the merchant told me it had been a man, whom he took for a Frank, and who had worn a scarlet cloak. I knew enough to understand that the stranger was, after all, not entirely devoid of noble intentions. In my new house I found everything arranged in the best style, also a vaulted room stored with goods, more splendid than I had ever had. Ten years have passed since. I still continue my commercial travels, more from old custom than necessity, yet I have never again seen that country where I became so unfortunate. Every year since, I have received a thousand gold-pieces; and although I rejoice to know that unfortunate man to be noble, yet he cannot relieve me of the sorrow of my soul, for the terrible picture of the murdered Bianca is continually on my mind.

THE MUMMY'S FOOT
Théophile Gautier
(1840, trnsl. 1908)

THE SHOP OF CURIOSITIES

I had entered, in an idle mood, the shop of one of those curiosity venders who are called *marchands de bric-à-brac* in that Parisian argot which is so perfectly unintelligible elsewhere in France.

You have doubtless glanced occasionally through the windows of some of these shops, which have become so numerous now that it is fashionable to buy antiquated furniture, and that every petty stockbroker thinks he must have his *chambre au moyen âge*.

There is one thing there which clings alike to the shop of the dealer in old iron, the ware-room of the tapestry maker, the laboratory of the chemist, and the studio of the painter: in all those gloomy dens where a furtive daylight filters in through the window-shutters the most manifestly ancient thing is dust. The cobwebs are more authentic than the gimp laces, and the old pear-tree furniture on exhibition is actually younger than the mahogany which arrived but yesterday from America.

The warehouse of my bric-à-brac dealer was a veritable Capharnaum. All ages and all nations seemed to have made their rendezvous there. An Etruscan lamp of red clay stood upon a Boule cabinet, with ebony panels, brightly striped by lines of inlaid brass; a duchess of the court of Louis XV.

nonchalantly extended her fawn-like feet under a massive table of the time of Louis XIII., with heavy spiral supports of oak, and carven designs of chimeras and foliage intermingled.

Upon the denticulated shelves of several sideboards glittered immense Japanese dishes with red and blue designs relieved by gilded hatching, side by side with enamelled works by Bernard Palissy, representing serpents, frogs, and lizards in relief.

From disembowelled cabinets escaped cascades of silver-lustrous Chinese silks and waves of tinsel, which an oblique sunbeam shot through with luminous beads, while portraits of every era, in frames more or less tarnished, smiled through their yellow varnish.

The striped breastplate of a damascened suit of Milanese armour glittered in one corner; loves and nymphs of porcelain, Chinese grotesques, vases of *céladon* and crackleware, Saxon and old Sèvres cups encumbered the shelves and nooks of the apartment.

The dealer followed me closely through the tortuous way contrived between the piles of furniture, warding off with his hand the hazardous sweep of my coat-skirts, watching my elbows with the uneasy attention of an antiquarian and a usurer.

It was a singular face, that of the merchant; an immense skull, polished like a knee, and surrounded by a thin aureole of white hair, which brought out the clear salmon tint of his complexion all the more strikingly, lent him a false aspect of patriarchal *bonhomie,* counteracted, however, by the scintillation of two little yellow eyes which trembled in their orbits like two louis-d'or upon quicksilver. The curve of his nose presented an aquiline silhouette, which suggested the Oriental or Jewish type. His hands—thin, slender, full of nerves which projected like strings upon the finger-board

of a violin, and armed with claws like those on the termina-
tions of bats' wings—shook with senile trembling; but those
convulsively agitated hands became firmer than steel pincers
or lobsters' claws when they lifted any precious article—an
onyx cup, a Venetian glass, or a dish of Bohemian crystal.
This strange old man had an aspect so thoroughly rabbinical
and cabalistic that he would have been burnt on the mere
testimony of his face three centuries ago.

"Will you not buy something from me to-day, sir? Here
is a Malay kreese with a blade undulating like flame. Look
at those grooves contrived for the blood to run along, those
teeth set backward so as to tear out the entrails in withdraw-
ing the weapon. It is a fine character of ferocious arm, and
will look well in your collection. This two-handed sword is
very beautiful. It is the work of Josepe de la Hera; and this
colichemarde with its fenestrated guard—what a superb specimen of handicraft!"

"No; I have quite enough weapons and instruments of
carnage. I want a small figure,—something which will suit
me as a paper-weight, for I cannot endure those trumpery
bronzes which the stationers sell, and which may be found
on everybody's desk."

The old gnome foraged among his ancient wares, and finally
arranged before me some antique bronzes, so-called at least;
fragments of malachite, little Hindoo or Chinese idols, a kind
of poussah-toys in jade-stone, representing the incarnations
of Brahma or Vishnoo, and wonderfully appropriate to the
very undivine office of holding papers and letters in place.

I was hesitating between a porcelain dragon, all constel-
lated with warts, its mouth formidable with bristling tusks
and ranges of teeth, and an abominable little Mexican fetich,
representing the god Vitziliputzili au naturel, when I caught
sight of a charming foot, which I at first took for a fragment
of some antique Venus.

It had those beautiful ruddy and tawny tints that lend to Florentine bronze that warm living look so much preferable to the gray-green aspect of common bronzes, which might easily be mistaken for statues in a state of putrefaction. Satiny gleams played over its rounded forms, doubtless polished by the amorous kisses of twenty centuries, for it seemed a Corinthian bronze, a work of the best era of art, perhaps moulded by Lysippus himself.

"That foot will be my choice," said to the merchant, who regarded me with an ironical and saturnine air, and held out the object desired that I might examine it more fully.

I was surprised at its lightness. It was not a foot of metal, but in sooth a foot of flesh, an embalmed foot, a mummy's foot. On examining it still more closely the very grain of the skin, and the almost imperceptible lines impressed upon it by the texture of the bandages, became perceptible. The toes were slender and delicate, and terminated by perfectly formed nails, pure and transparent as agates. The great toe, slightly separated from the rest, afforded a happy contrast, in the antique style, to the position of the other toes, and lent it an aerial lightness—the grace of a bird's foot. The sole, scarcely streaked by a few almost imperceptible cross lines, afforded evidence that it had never touched the bare ground, and had only come in contact with the finest matting of Nile rushes and the softest carpets of panther skin.

"Ha, ha, you want the foot of the Princess Hermonthis!" exclaimed the merchant, with a strange giggle, fixing his owlish eyes upon me. "Ha, ha, ha! For a paper-weight! An original idea!—artistic idea!—Old Pharaoh would certainly have been surprised had some one told him that the foot of his adored daughter would be used for a paper-weight after he had had a mountain of granite hollowed out as a receptacle for the triple coffin, painted and gilded, covered with hieroglyphics and beautiful paintings of the Judgment of Souls," continued the queer little merchant, half audibly, as though talking to himself.

"How much will you charge me for this mummy fragment?"

"Ah, the highest price I can get, for it is a superb piece. If I had the match of it you could not have it for less than five hundred francs. The daughter of a Pharaoh! Nothing is more rare."

"Assuredly that is not a common article, but still, how much do you want? In the first place let me warn you that all my wealth consists of just five louis. I can buy anything that costs five louis, but nothing dearer. You might search my vest pockets and most secret drawers without even finding one poor five-franc piece more."

"Five louis for the foot of the Princess Hermonthis! That is very little, very little indeed. 'Tis an authentic foot," muttered the merchant, shaking his head, and imparting a peculiar rotary motion to his eyes. "Well, take it, and I will give you the bandages into the bargain," he added, wrapping the foot in an ancient damask rag. "Very fine? Real damask— Indian damask which has never been redyed. It is strong, and yet it is soft," he mumbled, stroking the frayed tissue with his fingers, through the trade-acquired habit which moved him to praise even an object of such little value that he himself deemed it only worth the giving away.

He poured the gold coins into a sort of mediaeval almspurse hanging at his belt, repeating:

"The foot of the Princess Hermonthis to be used for a paper-weight!"

Then turning his phosphorescent eyes upon me, he exclaimed in a voice strident as the crying of a cat which has swallowed a fish-bone:

"Old Pharaoh will not be well pleased. He loved his daughter, the dear man!"

"You speak as if you were a contemporary of his. You are old enough, goodness knows! but you do not date back to the Pyramids of Egypt," I answered, laughingly, from the threshold.

I went home, delighted with my acquisition.

With the idea of putting it to profitable use as soon as possible, I placed the foot of the divine Princess Hermonthis upon a heap of papers scribbled over with verses, in themselves an undecipherable mosaic work of erasures; articles freshly begun; letters forgotten, and posted in the table drawer instead of the letter-box, an error to which absent-minded people are peculiarly liable. The effect was charming, bizarre, and romantic.

Well satisfied with this embellishment, I went out with the gravity and pride becoming one who feels that he has the ineffable advantage over all the passers-by whom he elbows, of possessing a piece of the Princess Hermonthis, daughter of Pharaoh.

I looked upon all who did not possess, like myself, a paper-weight so authentically Egyptian as very ridiculous people, and it seemed to me that the proper occupation of every sensible man should consist in the mere fact of having a mummy's foot upon his desk.

Happily I met some friends, whose presence distracted me in my infatuation with this new acquisition. I went to dinner with them, for I could not very well have dined with myself.

ASTONISHMENT

When I came back that evening, with my brain slightly confused by a few glasses of wine, a vague whiff of Oriental perfume delicately titillated my olfactory nerves. The heat of the room had warmed the natron, bitumen, and myrrh in which the *paraschistes,* who cut open the bodies of the dead, had bathed the corpse of the princess. It was a perfume at once sweet and penetrating, a perfume that four thousand years had not been able to dissipate.

The Dream of Egypt was Eternity. Her odours have the solidity of granite and endure as long.

I soon drank deeply from the black cup of sleep. For a few hours all remained opaque to me. Oblivion and nothingness inundated me with their sombre waves.

Yet light gradually dawned upon the darkness of my mind. Dreams commenced to touch me softly in their silent flight.

The eyes of my soul were opened, and I beheld my chamber as it actually was. I might have believed myself awake but for a vague consciousness which assured me that I slept, and that something fantastic was about to take place.

The odour of the myrrh had augmented in intensity, and I felt a slight headache, which I very naturally attributed to several glasses of champagne that we had drunk to the unknown gods and our future fortunes.

I peered through my room with a feeling of expectation which I saw nothing to justify. Every article of furniture was in its proper place. The lamp, softly shaded by its globe of ground crystal, burned upon its bracket; the water-colour sketches shone under their Bohemian glass; the curtains hung down languidly; everything wore an aspect of tranquil slumber.

After a few moments, however, all this calm interior appeared to become disturbed. The woodwork cracked stealthily, the ash-covered log suddenly emitted a jet of blue flame, and the discs of the pateras seemed like great metallic eyes, watching, like myself, for the things which were about to happen.

My eyes accidentally fell upon the desk where I had placed the foot of the Princess Hermonthis.

Instead of remaining quiet, as behooved a foot which had been embalmed for four thousand years, it commenced to act in a nervous manner, contracted itself, and leaped over the papers like a startled frog. One would have imagined that it had suddenly been brought into contact with a galvanic battery. I could distinctly hear the dry sound made by its little heel, hard as the hoof of a gazelle.

I became rather discontented with my acquisition, inasmuch as I wished my paper-weights to be of a sedentary disposition, and thought it very unnatural that feet should walk about without legs, and I commenced to experience a feeling closely akin to fear.

Suddenly I saw the folds of my bed-curtain stir, and heard a bumping sound, like that caused by some person hopping on one foot across the floor. I must confess I became alternately hot and cold, that I felt a strange wind chill my back, and that my suddenly rising hair caused my night-cap to execute a leap of several yards.

The bed-curtains opened and I beheld the strangest figure imaginable before me.

It was a young girl of a very deep coffee-brown complexion, like the bayadère Amani, and possessing the purest Egyptian type of perfect beauty. Her eyes were almond shaped and oblique, with eyebrows so black that they seemed blue; her nose was exquisitely chiselled, almost Greek in its delicacy of outline; and she might indeed have been taken for a Corinthian statue of bronze but for the prominence of her cheek-bones and the slightly African fulness of her lips, which compelled one to recognise her as belonging beyond all doubt to the hieroglyphic race which dwelt upon the banks of the Nile.

Her arms, slender and spindle-shaped like those of very young girls, were encircled by a peculiar kind of metal bands and bracelets of glass beads; her hair was all twisted into little cords, and she wore upon her bosom a little idol-figure of green paste, bearing a whip with seven lashes, which proved it to be an image of Isis; her brow was adorned with a shining

plate of gold, and a few traces of paint relieved the coppery
tint of her cheeks.

As for her costume, it was very odd indeed.

Fancy a *pagne,* or skirt, all formed of little strips of material bedizened with red and black hieroglyphics, stiffened
with bitumen, and apparently belonging to a freshly unban-
daged mummy.

In one of those sudden flights of thought so common in
dreams I heard the hoarse falsetto of the bric-à-brac dealer,
repeating like a monotonous refrain the phrase he had uttered in his shop with so enigmatical an intonation:

"Old Pharaoh will not be well pleased He loved his daughter, the dear man!"

One strange circumstance, which was not at all calculated
to restore my equanimity, was that the apparition had but
one foot; the other was broken off at the ankle!

She approached the table where the foot was starting and
fidgeting about more than ever, and there supported herself
upon the edge of the desk. I saw her eyes fill with pearly
gleaming tears.

Although she had not as yet spoken, I fully comprehended
the thoughts which agitated her. She looked at her foot—for
it was indeed her own—with an exquisitely graceful expression of coquettish sadness, but the foot leaped and ran hither
and thither, as though impelled on steel springs.

Twice or thrice she extended her hand to seize it, but
could not succeed.

Then commenced between the Princess Hermonthis and
her foot—which appeared to be endowed with a special life
of its own—a very fantastic dialogue in a most ancient Coptic tongue, such as might have been spoken thirty centuries
ago in the syrinxes of the land of Ser. Luckily I understood
Coptic perfectly well that night.

The Princess Hermonthis cried, in a voice sweet and vi-
brant as the tones of a crystal bell:

"Well, my dear little foot, you always flee from me, yet I always took good care of you. I bathed you with perfumed water in a bowl of alabaster; I smoothed your heel with pumice-stone mixed with palm-oil; your nails were cut with golden scissors and polished with a hippopotamus tooth; I was careful to select *tatbebs* for you, painted and embroidered and turned up at the toes, which were the envy of all the young girls in Egypt. You wore on your great toe rings bearing the device of the sacred Scarabæus, and you supported one of the lightest bodies that a lazy foot could sustain."

The foot replied in a pouting and chagrined tone:

"You know well that I do not belong to myself any longer. I have been bought and paid for. The old merchant knew what he was about. He bore you a grudge for having refused to espouse him. This is an ill turn which he has done you. The Arab who violated your royal coffin in the subterranean pits of the necropolis of Thebes was sent thither by him. He desired to prevent you from being present at the reunion of the shadowy nations in the cities below. Have you five pieces of gold for my ransom?"

"Alas, no! My jewels, my rings, my purses of gold and silver were all stolen from me," answered the Princess Hermonthis with a sob.

"Princess," I then exclaimed, "I never retained anybody's foot unjustly. Even though you have not got the five louis which it cost me, I present it to you gladly. I should feel unutterably wretched to think that I were the cause of so amiable a person as the Princess Hermonthis being lame."

I delivered this discourse in a royally gallant, troubadour tone which must have astonished the beautiful Egyptian girl.

She turned a look of deepest gratitude upon me, and her eyes shone with bluish gleams of light.

She took her foot, which surrendered itself willingly this time, like a woman about to put on her little shoe, and adjusted it to her leg with much skill.

This operation over, she took a few steps about the room, as though to assure herself that she was really no longer lame.

"Ah, how pleased my father will be! He who was so unhappy because of my mutilation, and who from the moment of my birth set a whole nation at work to hollow me out a tomb so deep that he might preserve me intact until that last day when souls must be weighed in the balance of Amenthi! Come with me to my father. He will receive you kindly, for you have given me back my foot."

I thought this proposition natural enough. I arrayed myself in a dressing-gown of large-flowered pattern, which lent me a very Pharaonic aspect, hurriedly put on a pair of Turkish slippers, and informed the Princess Hermonthis that I was ready to follow her.

Before starting, Hermonthis took from her neck the little idol of green paste, and laid it on the scattered sheets of paper which covered the table.

"It is only fair," she observed, smilingly, "that I should replace your paper-weight."

She gave me her hand, which felt soft and cold, like the skin of a serpent, and we departed.

We passed for some time with the velocity of an arrow through a fluid and grayish expanse, in which half-formed silhouettes flitted swiftly by us, to right and left.

For an instant we saw only sky and sea.

A few moments later obelisks commenced to tower in the distance; pylons and vast flights of steps guarded by sphinxes became clearly outlined against the horizon.

We had reached our destination.

The princess conducted me to a mountain of rose-coloured granite, in the face of which appeared an opening so narrow and low that it would have been difficult to distinguish it from the fissures in the rock, had not its location been marked by two stelae wrought with sculptures.

Hermonthis kindled a torch and led the way before me.

We traversed corridors hewn through the living rock. Their walls, covered with hieroglyphics and paintings of allegorical processions, might well have occupied thousands of arms for thousands of years in their formation. These corridors of interminable length opened into square chambers, in the midst of which pits had been contrived, through which we descended by cramp-irons or spiral stairways. These pits again conducted us into other chambers, opening into other corridors, likewise decorated with painted sparrow-hawks, serpents coiled in circles, the symbols of the *tau* and *pedum*—prodigious works of art which no living eye can ever examine—interminable legends of granite which only the dead have time to read through all eternity.

At last we found ourselves in a hall so vast, so enormous, so immeasurable, that the eye could not reach its limits. Files of monstrous columns stretched far out of sight on every side, between which twinkled livid stars of yellowish flame; points of light which revealed further depths incalculable in the darkness beyond.

The Princess Hermonthis still held my hand, and graciously saluted the mummies of her acquaintance.

My eyes became accustomed to the dim twilight, and objects became discernible.

I beheld the kings of the subterranean races seated upon thrones—grand old men, though dry, withered, wrinkled like parchment, and blackened with naphtha and bitumen—all wearing *pshents* of gold, and breastplates and gorgets glittering with precious stones, their eyes immovably fixed like the eyes of sphinxes, and their long beards whitened by the snow of centuries. Behind them stood their peoples, in the stiff and constrained posture enjoined by Egyptian art, all eternally preserving the attitude prescribed by the hieratic code. Behind these nations, the cats, ibixes, and crocodiles contemporary with them—rendered monstrous of aspect by their swathing bands—mewed, flapped their wings, or extended their jaws in a saurian giggle.

All the Pharaohs were there—Cheops, Chephrenes, Psammetichus, Sesostris, Amenotaph—all the dark rulers of the pyramids and syrinxes. On yet higher thrones sat Chronos and Xixouthros, who was contemporary with the deluge, and Tubal Cain, who reigned before it.

The beard of King Xixouthros had grown seven times around the granite table upon which he leaned, lost in deep reverie, and buried in dreams.

Further back, through a dusty cloud, I beheld dimly the seventy-two pre-adamite kings, with their seventy-two peoples, for ever passed away.

After permitting me to gaze upon this bewildering spectacle a few moments, the Princess Hermonthis presented me to her father Pharaoh, who favoured me with a most gracious nod.

"I have found my foot again! I have found my foot!" cried the princess, clapping her little hands together with every sign of frantic joy. "It was this gentleman who restored it to me."

The races of Kemi, the races of Nahasi—all the black, bronzed, and copper-coloured nations repeated in chorus:

"The Princess Hermonthis has found her foot again!"

Even Xixouthros himself was visibly affected.

He raised his heavy eyelids, stroked his moustache with his fingers, and turned upon me a glance weighty with centuries.

"By Oms, the dog of Hell, and Tmei, daughter of the Sun and of Truth, this is a brave and worthy lad!" exclaimed Pharaoh, pointing to me with his sceptre, which was terminated with a lotus-flower.

"What recompense do you desire?"

Filled with that daring inspired by dreams in which nothing seems impossible, I asked him for the hand of the Princess

Hermonthis. The hand seemed to me a very proper antithetic recompense for the foot.

Pharaoh opened wide his great eyes of glass in astonishment at my witty request.

"What country do you come from, and what is your age?"

"I am a Frenchman, and I am twenty-seven years old venerable Pharaoh."

"Twenty-seven years old, and he wishes to espouse the Princess Hermonthis who is thirty centuries old!" cried out at once all the Thrones and all the Circles of Nations.

Only Hermonthis herself did not seem to think my request unreasonable.

"If you were even only two thousand years old," replied the ancient king, "I would willingly give you the princess, but the disproportion is too great; and, besides, we must give our daughters husbands who will last well. You do not know how to preserve yourselves any longer. Even those who died only fifteen centuries ago are already no more than a handful of dust. Behold, my flesh is solid as basalt, my bones are bars of steel!

"I will be present on the last day of the world with the same body and the same features which I had during my lifetime. My daughter Hermonthis will last longer than a statue of bronze.

"Then the last particles of your dust will have been scattered abroad by the winds, and even Isis herself, who was able to find the atoms of Osiris, would scarce be able to recompose your being.

"See how vigorous I yet remain, and how mighty is my grasp," he added, shaking my hand in the English fashion with a strength that buried my rings in the flesh of my fingers.

He squeezed me so hard that I awoke, and found my friend Alfred shaking me by the arm to make me get up.

"Oh, you everlasting sleeper! Must I have you carried out into the middle of the street, and fireworks exploded in your ears? It is afternoon. Don't you recollect your promise to take me with you to see M. Aguado's Spanish pictures?"

"God! I forgot all, all about it," I answered, dressing myself hurriedly. "We will go there at once. I have the permit lying there on my desk."

I started to find it, but fancy my astonishment when I beheld, instead of the mummy's foot I had purchased the evening before, the little green paste idol left in its place by the Princess Hermonthis!

SOME ODD FACTS ABOUT THE TILED HOUSE,
BEING AN AUTHENTIC NARRATIVE OF THE GHOST OF A HAND
Joseph Sheridan Le Fanu
(*The House by the Church-Yard*, 1861)

I'm sure she believed every word she related, for old Sally was veracious. But all this was worth just so much as such talk commonly is—marvels, fabulae, what our ancestors called winter's tales—which gathered details from every narrator and dilated in the act of narration. Still it was not quite for nothing that the house was held to be haunted. Under all this smoke there smouldered just a little spark of truth—an authenticated mystery, for the solution of which some of my readers may possibly suggest a theory, though I confess I can't.

Miss Rebecca Chattesworth, in a letter dated late in the autumn of 1753, gives a minute and curious relation of occurrences in the Tiled House, which, it is plain, although at starting she protests against all such fooleries, she has heard with a peculiar sort of interest, and relates it certainly with an awful sort of particularity.

I was for printing the entire letter, which is really very singular as well as characteristic. But my publisher meets me with his *veto*; and I believe he is right. The worthy old lady's letter *is*, perhaps, too long; and I must rest content with a few hungry notes of its tenor.

That year, and somewhere about the 24th October, there broke out a strange dispute between Mr. Alderman Harper, of High Street, Dublin, and my Lord Castlemallard, who,

in virtue of his cousinship to the young heir's mother, had
undertaken for him the management of the tiny estate on
which the Tiled or Tyled House—for I find it spelt both
ways—stood.

This Alderman Harper had agreed for a lease of the house
for his daughter, who was married to a gentleman named
Prosser. He furnished it and put up hangings, and otherwise
went to considerable expense. Mr. and Mrs. Prosser came
there some time in June, and after having parted with a good
many servants in the interval, she made up her mind that she
could not live in the house, and her father waited on Lord
Castlemallard and told him plainly that he would not take
out the lease because the house was subjected to annoyances
which he could not explain. In plain terms, he said it was
haunted, and that no servants would live there more than a
few weeks, and that after what his son-in-law's family had
suffered there, not only should he be excused from taking a
lease of it, but that the house itself ought to be pulled down
as a nuisance and the habitual haunt of something worse
than human malefactors.

Lord Castlemallard filed a bill in the Equity side of the
Exchequer to compel Mr. Alderman Harper to perform his
contract, by taking out the lease. But the Alderman drew
an answer, supported by no less than seven long affidavits,
copies of all which were furnished to his lordship, and with
the desired effect; for rather than compel him to place them
upon the file of the court, his lordship struck, and consented
to release him.

I am sorry the cause did not proceed at least far enough
to place upon the records of the court the very authentic and
unaccountable story which Miss Rebecca relates.

The annoyances described did not begin till the end of
August, when, one evening, Mrs. Prosser, quite alone, was
sitting in the twilight at the back parlour window, which was
open, looking out into the orchard, and plainly saw a hand

stealthily placed upon the stone window-sill outside, as if by some one beneath the window, at her right side, intending to climb up. There was nothing but the hand, which was rather short, but handsomely formed, and white and plump, laid on the edge of the window-sill; and it was not a very young hand, but one aged, somewhere about forty, as she conjectured. It was only a few weeks before that the horrible robbery at Clondalkin had taken place, and the lady fancied that the hand was that of one of the miscreants who was now about to scale the windows of the Tiled House. She uttered a loud scream and an ejaculation of terror, and at the same moment the hand was quietly withdrawn.

Search was made in the orchard, but no indications of any person's having been under the window, beneath which, ranged along the wall, stood a great column of flower-pots, which it seemed must have prevented any one's coming within reach of it.

The same night there came a hasty tapping, every now and then, at the window of the kitchen. The women grew frightened, and the servant-man, taking firearms with him, opened the back-door, but discovered nothing. As he shut it, however, he said, "a thump came on it," and a pressure as of somebody striving to force his way in, which frightened *him*; and though the tapping went on upon the kitchen window panes, he made no further explorations.

About six o'clock on the Saturday evening following, the cook, "an honest, sober woman, now aged nigh sixty years," being alone in the kitchen, saw, on looking up, it is supposed, the same fat but aristocratic-looking hand laid with its palm against the glass, near the side of the window, and this time moving slowly up and down, pressed all the while against the glass, as if feeling carefully for some inequality in its surface. She cried out, and said something like a prayer, on seeing it. But it was not withdrawn for several seconds after.

After this, for a great many nights, there came at first a low, and afterwards an angry rapping, as it seemed with a set of clenched knuckles at the back-door. And the servant-man would not open it, but called to know who was there; and there came no answer, only a sound as if the palm of the hand was placed against it, and drawn slowly from side to side with a sort of soft, groping motion.

All this time, sitting in the back parlour, which, for the time, they used as a drawing-room, Mr. and Mrs. Prosser were disturbed by rappings at the window, sometimes very low and furtive, like a clandestine signal, and at others sudden and so loud as to threaten the breaking of the pane.

This was all at the back of the house, which looked upon the orchard, as you know. But on a Tuesday night, at about half-past nine, there came precisely the same rapping at the hall-door, and went on, to the great annoyance of the master and terror of his wife, at intervals, for nearly two hours.

After this, for several days and nights, they had no annoyance whatsoever, and began to think that nuisance had expended itself. But on the night of the 13th September, Jane Easterbrook, an English maid, having gone into the pantry for the small silver bowl in which her mistress's posset was served, happening to look up at the little window of only four panes, observed through an auger-hole which was drilled through the window-frame, for the admission of a bolt to secure the shutter, a white pudgy finger—first the tip, and then the two first joints introduced, and turned about this way and that, crooked against the inside, as if in search of a fastening which its owner designed to push aside. When the maid got back into the kitchen we are told "she fell into 'a swounde,' and was all the next day very weak."

Mr. Prosser being, I've heard, a hard-headed and conceited sort of fellow, scouted the ghost, and sneered at the fears of his family. He was privately of opinion that the whole affair was a practical joke or a fraud, and waited an opportunity of catching the rogue *flagrante delicto.* He did not long keep this theory to himself, but let it out by degrees with no stint of oaths and threats, believing that some domestic traitor held the thread of the conspiracy.

Indeed it was time something were done; for not only his servants, but good Mrs. Prosser herself, had grown to look unhappy and anxious, and kept at home from the hour of sunset, and would not venture about the house after nightfall, except in couples.

The knocking had ceased for about a week; and one night, Mrs. Prosser being in the nursery, her husband, who was in the parlour, heard it begin very softly at the hall-door. The air was quite still, which favoured his hearing distinctly. This was the first time there had been any disturbance at that side of the house, and the character of the summons also was changed.

Mr. Prosser, leaving the parlour-door open, it seems, went quietly into the hall. The sound was that of beating on the outside of the stout door, softly and regularly, "with the flat of the hand." He was going to open it suddenly, but changed his mind; and went back very quietly, and on to the head of the kitchen stair, where was a "strong closet" over the pantry, in which he kept his firearms, swords, and canes.

Here he called his man-servant, whom he believed to be honest; and with a pair of loaded pistols in his own coat-pockets, and giving another pair to him, he went as lightly as he could, followed by the man, and with a stout walking-cane in his hand, forward to the door.

Everything went as Mr. Prosser wished. The besieger of his house, so far from taking fright at their approach, grew more impatient; and the sort of patting which had aroused his attention at first, assumed the rhythm and emphasis of a series of double-knocks.

Mr. Prosser, angry, opened the door with his right arm across, cane in hand. Looking, he saw nothing; but his arm was jerked up oddly, as it might be with the hollow of a hand, and something passed under it, with a kind of gentle squeeze. The servant neither saw nor felt anything, and did not know why his master looked back so hastily, cutting with his cane, and shutting the door with so sudden a slam.

From that time Mr. Prosser discontinued his angry talk and swearing about it, and seemed nearly as averse from the subject as the rest of his family. He grew, in fact, very uncomfortable, feeling an inward persuasion that when, in answer to the summons, he had opened the hall-door, he had actually given admission to the besieger.

He said nothing to Mrs. Prosser, but went up earlier to his bed-room, "where he read a while in his Bible, and said his prayers." I hope the particular relation of this circumstance does not indicate its singularity. He lay awake a good while, it appears; and as he supposed, about a quarter past twelve he heard the soft palm of a hand patting on the outside of the bed-room door, and then brushed slowly along it.

Up bounced Mr. Prosser, very much frightened, and locked the door, crying, "Who's there?" but receiving no answer but the same brushing sound of a soft hand drawn over the panels, which he knew only too well.

In the morning the housemaid was terrified by the impression of a hand in the dust of the "little parlour" table, where they had been unpacking delft and other things the day before. The print of the naked foot in the sea-sand did not frighten Robinson Crusoe half so much. They were by this time all nervous, and some of them half crazed, about the hand.

Mr. Prosser went to examine the mark, and made light of it, but, as he swore afterwards, rather to quiet his servants than from any comfortable feeling about it in his own mind; however, he had them all, one by one, into the room, and made each place his or her hand, palm downward, on the same table, thus taking a similar impression from every person in the house, including himself and his wife; and his "affidavit" deposed that the formation of the hand so impressed differed altogether from those of the living inhabitants of the house, and corresponded exactly with that of the hand seen by Mrs. Prosser and by the cook.

Whoever or whatever the owner of that hand might be, they all felt this subtle demonstration to mean that it was declared he was no longer out of doors, but had established himself in the house.

And now Mrs. Prosser began to be troubled with strange and horrible dreams, some of which, as set out in detail, in Aunt Rebecca's long letter, are really very appalling nightmares. But one night, as Mr. Prosser closed his bedchamber door, he was struck somewhat by the utter silence of the room, there being no sound of breathing, which seemed unaccountable to him, as he knew his wife was in bed, and his ears were particularly sharp.

There was a candle burning on a small table at the foot of the bed, beside the one he held in one hand, a heavy ledger connected with his father-in-law's business being under his arm. He drew the curtain at the side of the bed, and saw Mrs. Prosser lying, as for a few seconds he mortally feared, dead, her face being motionless, white, and covered with a cold dew; and on the pillow, close beside her head, and just within the curtains, was the same white, fattish hand, the wrist resting on the pillow, and the fingers extended towards her temple with a slow, wavy motion.

Mr. Prosser, with a horrified jerk, pitched the leger right at the curtains behind which the owner of the hand might be supposed to stand. The hand was instantaneously and smoothly snatched away, the curtains made a great wave, and

Mr. Prosser got round the bed in time to see the closet-door, which was at the other side, drawn close by the same white, puffy hand, as he believed.

He drew the door open with a fling, and stared in; but the closet was empty, except for the clothes hanging from the pegs on the wall, and the dressing-table and looking-glass facing the windows. He shut it sharply, and locked it, and felt for a minute, he says, "as if he were like to lose his wits;" then, ringing at the bell, he brought the servants, and with much ado they recovered Mrs. Prosser from a sort of "trance," in which, he says, from her looks, she seemed to have suffered "the pains of death;" and Aunt Rebecca adds, "from what she told me of her visions, with her own lips, he might have added, 'and of hell also.'"

But the occurrence which seems to have determined the crisis was the strange sickness of their eldest child, a little girl aged between two and three years. It lay awake, seemingly in paroxysms of terror, and the doctors who were called in set down the symptoms to incipient water on the brain. Mrs. Prosser used to sit up with the nurse, by the nursery fire, much troubled in mind about the condition of her child.

Its bed was placed sideways along the wall, with its head against the door of a press or cupboard, which, however, did not shut quite close. There was a little valance, about a foot deep, round the top of the child's bed, and this descended within some ten or twelve inches of the pillow on which it lay.

They observed that the little creature was quieter whenever they took it up and held it on their laps. They had just replaced it, as it seemed to have grown quite sleepy and tranquil, but it was not five minutes in its bed when it began to scream in one of its frenzies of terror; at the same moment the nurse for the first time detected, and Mrs. Prosser equally plainly saw, following the direction of her eyes, the real cause of the child's sufferings.

Protruding through the aperture of the press, and shrouded in the shade of the valance, they plainly saw the white fat hand, palm downwards, presented towards the head of the child. The mother uttered a scream, and snatched the child from its little bed, and she and the nurse ran down to the lady's sleeping-room, where Mr. Prosser was in bed, shutting the door as they entered; and they had hardly done so, when a gentle tap came to it from the outside.

There is a great deal more, but this will suffice. The singularity of the narrative seems to me to be this, that it describes the ghost of a hand, and no more. The person to whom that hand belonged never once appeared; nor was it a hand separated from a body, but only a hand so manifested and introduced, that its owner was always, by some crafty accident, hidden from view.

In the year 1819, at a college breakfast, I met a Mr. Prosser—a thin, grave, but rather chatty old gentleman, with very white hair, drawn back into a pigtail—and he told us all, with a concise particularity, a story of his cousin, James Prosser, who, when an infant, had slept for some time in what his mother said was a haunted nursery in an old house near Chapelizod, and who, whenever he was ill, over-fatigued, or in anywise feverish, suffered all through his life as he had done from a time he could scarce remember, from a vision of a certain gentleman, fat and pale, every curl of whose wig, every button and fold of whose laced clothes, and every feature and line of whose sensual, benignant, and unwholesome face, was as minutely engraven upon his memory as the dress and lineaments of his own father's portrait, which hung before him every day at breakfast, dinner, and supper.

Mr. Prosser mentioned this as an instance of a curiously monotonous, individualized, and persistent nightmare, and hinted the extreme horror and anxiety with which his cousin, of whom he spoke in the past tense as "poor Jemmie," was at any time induced to mention it.

I hope the reader will pardon me for loitering so long in the Tiled House, but this sort of lore has always had a charm for me; and people, you know, especially old people, will talk of what most interests themselves, too often forgetting that others may have had more than enough of it.

INTERLUDE

A Gruesome Gift
(Buffalo, New York, *Courier,* December 29, 1892)

Rochester, Dec. 28.—A loud scream of horror and fear, followed by a prolonged fainting spell, greeted the arrival of a Christmas present by mail on the morning of the 25th, the recipient being Miss Estelle Robinson of this city, who resides with a married sister on the outskirts of the town. The gift that caused this consternation was an odd and ghastly one in the shape of a human hand, perfectly embalmed, and mounted to serve as a paper weight. The hand, which is in an admirable state of preservation, looking as if it had just been severed from the arm, is evidently that of a man, and is sinewy and shapely, and would really be beautiful, viewed as a work of art, could the ghastliness of the thing be forgotten.

On the third finger is a broad band of gold, but which could not be removed. This, Miss Robinson reluctantly admitted, appeared to be the ring presented by her years ago to a young man to whom she was at the time engaged to be married, and who she now believes has taken this unique and abhorrent manner of returning the gift to her. But it is thought by the young lady's friends that the gentleman lost the member by accident, and, having the ring on at the time, returned both to her.

The young man to whom Miss Robinson is convinced the hand belonged was living in New York a year or two ago, but his present whereabouts are unknown to her. The ring she gave him bore an inscription on the inside, but the lady refused to have the band filed off for the purpose of identifying it. Indeed, so great is her horror of the object that she refuses to look at it, and had requested that it be at once interred. The gift was accompanied by a plain visiting card on which was printed by a typewriter the greetings of the season. The address was also typewritten.

The friends of the young lady are indignant with the sender, whoever he may be, as the shock to the nerves has made her seriously ill ever since with hysteria.

MRS. CORBET'S AMPUTATED TOE
Alexander Leighton
(1863)

The authority I have for venturing so far on the domain of belief, which every one guards with so much care, even while he permits most suspicious-looking squatters thereon, as to claim attention to the all but unbelievable story I am here to relate, was the late Professor John Lizars, who related it, in the outline, to me some years before his death. I do not deny that, even like as I am to the credulous Mylus,—*omnia audiens,*—I might, during the recital, have looked like Pyrrho,—*credens nihil,*—but it is just as likely that I might have allowed my look of incredulity to compose itself among the gravities that hang about the lower part of the face when he assured me he had seen the object itself in the room where it was said to be—moreover, that he had got some of his anatomical knowledge from it. However all that may be, it is certain that Lieutenant-Colonel Corbet, an officer who had been in India, lived in Hyndford's Close for a good many years, and along with him Mrs. Corbet, a beauty whom he had picked up in Bombay. Like other people who have passed a pretty long time in the East, they did not—as the author of the "Castes of Edinburgh" says of our Indian refugees in general—fit in very well with our people, insomuch as while they remembered the dark slaves they ruled in India, they could never exactly forget that the folks hereaway are generally white; while those whom they could not but admit to be of that hue were apt to view the somewhat dignified couple as being tinged with the colour of gold, in other words, with that of a bad liver. Yet withal they lived in good society—and, what was of more importance, they were—so far as testified to by the wise who know more of the insides of other people's houses than the fools do who live in them—very happy; a state of matters which generally excludes the wry-mouthed genius of scandal.

But, as our story does not hang by the domestic happiness of the Colonel and his wife, we may be excused from dwelling on the beauties of conjugal love; the more by reason that, as the thing is fashionable, there is more of pretension to it than of reality. Nor blessed and perfect as conjugal happiness may be, is it, alas! exclusive of visits from the angry gods, who, as Plutarch tells us, have woolly, that is, soft feet; and the softer, one would think, the less they are expected. And so in the case of our happy couple. Somehow or other, our Colonel, like most others whose livers are not so sound as that ruling organ of the human body ought to be, was most ingenious in devising remedies for ailments; and, what is really not more wonderful, he was equally expert at finding out those ailments, whether they existed or not. To give you an instance: he carried about with him, as regularly as a man does a snuff-box, out of which he generously supplies his friends, a nostrum that the most of the ailments of mankind arise from crudities in the blood, which again are the consequence of an over-accumulation of muscular force; so that if people had just the sense, which is possessed by engine-men when they let off their superabundant steam, to work off that energy, they would seldom or ever be out of sorts. Being of the tribe of theorists, it was of no account to tell him that the hard-working people had ailments as well as the lazy or slothful. He was not bound to believe what he had no wish to believe; and, therefore, he stuck to his therapeutic remedy of exercising himself every forenoon with a pair of dumb-bells, each weighing some five or six pounds avoirdupois. If he had not been a theorist, the difficulty he had in working these heavy weights might have told him that he had not much overflowing energy to work off. It was enough that he thought he had, and so he toiled for a whole hour at a time, more like a pentathlete of old than a modern gentleman who enjoyed the privilege of living at his ease. Nor was it of any avail that his wife, who saw in his spare body, indexed by a saffron-coloured face, that he had no strength to throw away, remonstrated with him on the absurdity of weakening, with the view of strengthening himself. What has reason to do with theory? and don't theorists know that reason is a mole-eyed baggage, who cannot see an inch beyond the narrow line of a poor limited experience?

So the affair went on; and we go on so far with it as to say that no man could have told how far it would have gone, had it not been for an accident—so called by mortals, for there are no accidents in nature, even where the woolly-footed powers seem to break in and play the deuce. And how innocently it occurred! Simply by Mrs. Corbet trying, in a good-humoured way, and after a little badinage, to take one of the weights out of her husband's hand. A most unfortunate effort, the weight of lead fell with a crash on the lady's toes, and a scream from the sufferer resounded through the whole house. The servants rushed in, and Mrs. Corbet was laid upon the arm-chair, in a condition approaching to a faint. On taking off the stocking, it was found that the injury was inflicted on the small toe of the left foot, which was crushed so seriously as to render it doubtful whether the bone was not broken. Probably if a doctor had been there at the moment, and before the small member began to swell, he might have decided the point; but it was not till three hours afterwards that Dr. James Russel called, and by that time

the injured part had become so swollen and irritable, that
skilly as the doctor was, he could not made himself sure on
the point; so that, with a little top-dressing, the toe was left
to develop itself according to its own temper, or rather that
of the old leech, the *vis medicatrix*. Meanwhile the swelling
diminished the pain; a result to which a little brandy contributed so much—that being always something more than
its real virtue would seem to warrant.

Apparently there was nothing to fear from an accident
of so common a character; that is to say if the interesting
patient—who by the way carried the blood of a Georgian
mother in veins which, in their pale blue lines, could not
be concealed by the fair silken skin of that famous people—
had been in her constitution perfectly normal; but there are
diathetic conditions which no doctor is bound to know, for
the simple reason that he has seldom any means of knowing them till they are evolved, and then it is generally too
late. Days passed, but without bringing those pathological
changes which are looked for or expected in consequence of
nature's comparative uniformity. On the contrary, the entire
foot became swollen to nearly the double of its natural size,
and as further time passed Dr. Russel waxed more certain
in his early suspicion that the bone had been broken at the
joint; an opinion which, when communicated to the Colonel, produced an effect as divergent from the normal as the
consequences of the injury themselves threatened to be. Nor
was the reason here so recondite as the peccant secret of the
obdurate toe, for he had from the beginning blamed himself as being the cause of the accident; and this would not
have been very formidable to him if his feelings had allowed
him—as they never do in such cases—to make the rational
distinction between acts that are voluntary and those that are
not So he murmured and tormented himself, with the usual
result of an increase of his pain; unless we are to take into
account the anxious duty of a continual attendance on the

patient, whose every look and sign he watched, as if his fate in the place of punishment depended upon the vibration of a nerve in her pale but beautiful face. Then, even if he had had the power of making the proper distinction, and thus saving him from the self-imputation of any designed harm to one so inexpressibly dear to him, he was met by the subtlety of his own creation, that the angry power who had imposed the misfortune had purposely selected him as the medium of the infliction, for the reason that he was in some secret way obnoxious to Heaven.

So far perhaps in anticipation, yet necessary in order to enable us to understand the effects produced upon one so formed by the condition of the invalid, who shewed no signs of improvement. On the contrary, she became daily worse, till at length the doctor was alarmed by a dark spot, which gave indications of gangrene. There was now no time to be lost in speculation about the condition of the bone, whether fractured or not. The toe was amputated; but the remedy came too late. That dreaded power, deadness or mortification, which we are so apt to view as a negative, was to shew its stem activities in its antagonism of darkness to light, of silence to sound, of stillness to motion, of ugliness to beauty, of coldness to heat, of death to life. The insidious enemy had got beyond the line of amputation, and had gathered its energies for the reduction of that fair form to base matter. As yet, no communication of the danger was made to her; and, as we all know that mortification generally involves a relief from pain, we are not to wonder that the patient viewed the change as a token of convalescence. We are sometimes led to think that Nature, usually so beneficent to man, often wears the Myrtean crown of the tyrant, insomuch as she is often cruelest, even by way of refinement, when she appears most kindly. And here the husband was the victim. In the forenoon, he had got the intelligence of the fatal change; and the self-imputed conviction that he was the cause of the calamity wrought on his heart at the very moment when, sitting by the bed and holding her hand, he was obliged to encounter the light of the false hope which shone in her eye. The day passed amidst the quietude of a solemnity in which all participated, except her on whom all attention was fixed; for the silence which destroys many friendships is not that silence which is enforced by the hovering presence of "the shadow feared of man." The night wore on till nearly twelve. The wax-taper had been renewed, so as to last till the first beam should come with the paean of the opening morn, wherein Nature would again give evidence of her refined mode of torturing poor mortals. The small light, meanwhile, glimmered on the pale but beautiful face of the victim, as that was presented to the anxious eye of the husband. That look of peace, if not pleasure, would have been to him as a *lumen fausti minis*, replete with all joy, had he been ignorant of the fatal secret. As it was, it scathed him even more than he could have experienced from an expression of the greatest pain. Nor was even this all: he was fated to hear the words of playfulness breaking the silence of the chamber of death. As he held her hand in his, she said—

"George, do you know what I was thinking last night?"

"No," replied he sorrowfully, as he met the happy look.

"Of course not," she proceeded. "I was afraid to tell you at the time; for I may now admit to you, that I was under a fear I was to die: but, when I am free from all pain, and hope to be soon well again, I may state it to you now for our amusement, especially as in this gloom and silence we require something to cheer us."

"Well?" groaned the Colonel

"You know," continued the invalid, "that Edinburgh has always been famous for stories of dead bodies being taken out of the graves."

"I do not believe one half of them, Isabella," replied he.

"But I believe them all," said she. "When I was under the fear of death, (how glad I am that that fear is gone!) a thought haunted me that my body might be stolen; and, do you know, I was so frightened that I intended to request of you as a great favour, that you would provide means for watching my grave? I can smile now at my intention, but wasn't it a strange whim?"

And a faint laugh twittered on the vocal chords, irrespective of the approach of the dark foe, which was gradually proceeding from the point of its first triumph in the left foot, and would soon silence those chords for ever.

"And I am not done yet," she continued in the same strain; "for, as I thought that as it was from one of those horrid dumb-bells with which you were killing yourself that I received my misfortune, I was to tell you, that if you allowed my body to be stolen, I would, in my disembodied spirit, appear to you during the nights of your watchfulness,—ay, and even during the day,—and scowl upon you just in the way that owls and goblins used to do in the old houses."

The Colonel could yet find no words to reply, and he shrunk from the cheerful expression of her face.

"Nor am I done yet," she continued; "for I was to tell you also that my spirit, when it appeared to you, would point down to my left foot, just as if it said, 'You will know my body amidst a hundred by the want of the toe.'"

And the laugh was even a little stronger.

"But do not look so sorrowful, my dear," she continued; "for you know all my danger is over now: ay, and I may yet live to dance one of your Scotch reels with that same foot, to the music of some of your beautiful tunes."

These strange words were the last the Colonel heard; and this strange play of light in the face he had worshipped, as well for its Eastern beauty as for its indicial manifestations of the love which really existed in her heart towards him,—

so like, that light, to the phosphorescence which gleams at
night from decaying organisms, with still beauty on the surface,—was the last symptom he witnessed of her naturally
buoyant spirit. He was exhausted; and the nurse came to
take his place, with that impassable calmness which befits
her kind for scenes sufficient to drive husbands and wives
mad, yea, and would have that effect if mortals were not
mad already; and sure it is, that some may even modulate
a groan and a laugh into the paradox, that if man were not
mad, he could not live. He rose, and retired to his bedroom;
there probably to wring his hands, or go through some of the
other contortions whereby wretched man tries to repress the
agonies of the spirit.

Meanwhile, the patient, after that strange manifestation
of a deluded hope, was fast undergoing the unleavening process and with all that regularity, too, which is shewn in the
circulation of the blood—every drop of which, as it left the
infected part, carried to the heart the means of stilling it for
ever. True as it is that the *nunc fluens* with all of us is ever
in continual progress towards the *nunc permanens* of eternity: her moments were charged as it were with the periods
of years; and we thus see the difference between the process
of taking down from that of building up—how slowly the
threads are added one after another to the mysterious texture
of life, yet how rapidly unwinded. Before the next midnight,
Mrs. Corbet was dead; and, in a few days more, this child of
the sunny regions of the East lay under the cold turf in the
churchyard of the Canongate. Of such things in their external aspect we have an amount of knowledge, but of the effects which are produced by them on the inner lives of those
who are left behind we know comparatively nothing. Man
may weave poetry, and think he is expressing his feelings, so
that others may know the workings of his spirit; but he pro-
duces only a specimen of art, where the words form a picture,
and where the words too are taken for the things they cannot

represent; so that to those who never experienced such a condition of the mind as that to which the bereaved husband was reduced, a description would effect no more than an endeavour to convey to one who never saw a tree the form of the blasted oak by shewing a few of its withered leaves.

Nor for the space of a month could Colonel Corbet have any precise knowledge of the state of his own mind, where every energy was resolved into images of the past, leaving the external senses dead or inoperative. Among the ancients, as Cicero tells us, it was held to be ominous to speak of the dead; a maxim which modern experience would induce us to reverse, insomuch as we have no better sign of a coming recovery from grief than is afforded by a disposition to speak of the departed. It would seem that we ease the heart by transferring its energy to the tongue. It is the unspoken brooding thought that makes ravage of the heart; yet, in the case of our bereaved husband, it might be said, all this dark brooding was for the time foregone only the normal condition of ordinary mortal grief. But there was to be a change. We will say nothing as yet of a certain peculiarity of his mind existing theretofore, whereby that change could be explained according to well-authenticated principles of psychology, or rather we should say, physiology, if the matter does not lie between the two; but we may state, what will doubtless produce surprise, that, amidst all his thoughts, he had never recurred to the extraordinary statement made by his wife on the evening of the day preceding her death. We may account for this on the supposition that, whatever impression these words of hers had made upon him at the moment, the effect was due to the false hope in which she had indulged when evidently dying, rather than to the weak words she so lightly uttered. We have said that his grief was normal; nor do we need to qualify our expression more than by stating that the aggravation produced by the conviction that he was the means through which she had met her death, was more a temporary triumph when the reason was taken captive by the feelings than a haunting produced by the conscience.

There was to be a change; and that was ushered in by a strange phenomenon. One morning, when lying in bed, his eye sought the window, where the breaking light of the early dawn was bringing out faintly the green of the curtain, which had been drawn on the previous evening. The look was only a listless one, as if he wished to augur the time of the morning; nor, indeed, could he see much even of what the room contained, for the partial light seemed to be drunk up by the curtains, leaving the apartment itself nearly as dark as it was before. While his eye was so occupied, it seemed as if some nebulous object had come between him and the drapery; and of this he could be the more apprised by the apparent darkening of the illuminated damask to an extent co-ordinate with the interrupting medium, whatever it might be. Even yet, his look was listless; for, with all his fanciful conviction of having been the cause of his wife's death, he was not a superstitious man, if he was not more independent of a belief in supernaturals than most people even with sound livers. But that listlessness began to give way to a sharpening of the eye, as he saw the face of Mrs. Corbet slowly evolving from the vapoury medium. At first he could observe only the general contour; but gradually, and as it were line by line, the features became more and more distinct; and, indeed, so apparently palpable, that the seer (for we think the word appropriate) actually made an exclamation, and held out his hand to touch it. This distinct condition of the object lasted only for a moment or two, and seemed to depend somewhat upon a sympathy with the action of the eye; for as he began to strain that organ, in order to make himself more sure of the reality of his vision, the face seemed to respond in a diminution of its distinctness—recovering again its former marked line and angles as he relaxed the intensity of his gaze. A moment or two more, and the green curtain, embued with the dawn light, recovered its apparency where that had been excluded. The figure was gone, and had left the Colonel opening and shutting his eyes, as if he would test by an experiment what he considered to be an illusion.

On throwing himself again back on the pillow from which he had partially raised himself, he began to think whether he had not been *inter res commentitias et frivolas quænus quam sunt—*

> "Things unreal, and phantoms vain,
> Which morbid minds spew forth as fumes
> That circling rise, and take on lying forms;"

and he would have been well contented if he could have rested on this conclusion; but even while he was making the effort, the words of his wife flashed across his mind with a rapidity and vivacity as if derived from a reaction of the force by which they had been so long excluded: *"If you allow my body to be stolen, I will, in my disembodied spirit, appear to you during the nights of your watchfulness."* He repeated them with trembling lips, over and over again, as if he now felt it a duty to remember them. And did she not further say, that *her spirit would scowl upon him as the cause of her death?* This, too, he remembered, but he did not forget that the words were said in playfulness; and then there was the fact that the said spirit, if spirit it was, did *not* look angry at him; so that, after all, it might be that a troubled mind and a coincidence casual, however strange, had more to do with the affair than any supernatural agency.

This conclusion, upon which he latterly came to lean, was at least philosophical, and perhaps he might have remained satisfied if he could have assured himself that there would be no recurrence of the vision. This, of course, he could not do, and having fallen asleep he awoke to a nervousness, if not unqualified misery, which hung about him throughout the whole day. He could not assure himself that he was not the object of an unfavourable attention on the part of some superior power. He did not know that even the sturdiest sceptic, when he comes to deliberate on the great question of special interpositions from above, is lost; for reason is only a temporary friend, who leaves you when the mind becomes clouded by adversity, while the instinct, which is always pointing to occult powers, clings to you for ever, even as a quality of the spirit. Yea, proud and supercilious philosophy is forced to admit, that where there are so many blanks in the links of the chain of secondary causes, there is room and verge enough for more than the subtle finger of a Deity. Of these considerations the Colonel knew nothing—he had simply an experience to deal with; and so it is with a great part of mankind—they have an inner life, the workings of which are exclusive of postulates, and premises, and formulas, and make them recusants to philosophy. Yet, withal, if there had been no repetition of his vision, our seer would have in time again lapsed into the rational mourner over the beloved dead. Nor was the test very long delayed. In the evening, after he had lain down on the sofa, and just before the bringing in of the candles, when the twilight hung between the light of day and the darkness of night, the vision repeated itself in the distinct form and features of his wife. There could be no mistake: even the changed conditions of the apparition (a word as philosophical as it is superstitious) imparted certainty, if assurance had been wanted. On the former occasion it had appeared as if against the light which faintly tinted the green hangings of the bedroom window; now it seemed invested with a light of its own, only a little stronger than the crepuscle which lingered in the dining-room—representing, as near as possible, the appearance of her face at that midnight hour when, in the light of the wax taper, she made the remarkable, however frivolous, communication to him. There was another difference which he had time and power to mark as he lay as it were enchanted, with his eye fixed and his mouth open: the face was not of that placid character which it had exhibited before—it was stern and severe, relaxing gradually into softness, only to assume again the more enduring expression; but, withal, there was again the apparent tendency to appear the less distinct the more he strained his eyes.

Entranced as he was, this latter peculiarity was not passed unnoticed by the Colonel, though he had neither power nor inclination to try to account for it; nor could he tell, as he suddenly rose from the couch, whether he did so with a view to test further the endurance of the vision under a changed condition of his own nerves, or to try to escape from what truly terrified him. Having got to his feet, he stepped into the middle of the room, and bracing himself, as a military man, of course not without even yet a remnant of courage forcing itself through his superstition, he began to walk from the side board to the window. He even affected not to look for it, but to cast his eye in various directions; yet his efforts were unavailing: somehow or other the organ would steady itself, and then it was further steadied, even to being riveted, by the vision, which thus seemed to accompany him. That by moving his arms and waving them to and fro, he satisfied himself that it was impalpable and intangible, afforded him but small relief, for it only assured him that he could not by any physical energy drive it away, besides proving the spiritual character of his visitant. At this moment the servant brought in the candles; and whether it was that ghosts do not like the light and make off at its approach, or that they have not points of reflection whereby they can appear by borrowed rays, sure it is that the vision was no more seen that evening.

Notwithstanding of this interruption, the Colonel continued his walk along the room. He was disturbed, anxious, and tremulous. The prior arguments he had used for the purpose of satisfying himself that there was no mysterious final cause in the phenomenon were discharged. The conviction settled deeper and firmer that he was obnoxious to powers who had taken his wife under their protection, and his failure of duty in not taking means to watch her grave added its remorse to the self-imputation that he had caused her death. He was, in short, under the influence of that feeling of awe—sufficient to make the boldest of us quake—that he was a particular object selected by divine power for a particular retribution. Like him who slept below the tripod of Apollo, he knew that he had the gods for his masters, and was able by their inspiration to divine his own ruin. Yet, could he not ward off his impending fate by a late repentance and an obedience to the angry spirit who had visited him. While still engaged in these thoughts the door opened, and there entered a young man, who, as a student-assistant to Dr. Russel, was present at the amputation of the toe. His name was Davidson, and the object of his visit now was to bring some medicines which the doctor had prescribed for his widower patient The presence of the student presented an opportunity, suggested by the thoughts which had been passing through his mind.

"Stop," he said, as the young man was about to depart, after laying down the parcel; "you may do me more good than these drugs, which, alas I cannot minister to the mind."

"Whatever I can," replied Davidson, in something like wonder at being thus selected as a doctor on moral ailments, of which he had but small experience during the time he had been in the world.

"Is it true," said the Colonel, as he fixed his somewhat nervous eye on the student's face, "that dead bodies are stolen from the churchyards in this country?"

"I am not just the person you should ask," replied Davidson. "You know I study anatomy myself, and we must get our knowledge somehow; besides, I am afraid to alarm you."

"Alarm me!" cried the Colonel. "What do you mean? Have you any reason to suspect anything in regard to Mrs. Corbet?"

"Not particularly," was the answer, in a tone which indicated that the interrogated had no particular desire to set the Colonel's suspicions to rest.

"Not particularly!" rejoined the questioner, as he laid his hand on the student's arm. "The words are not satisfactory. Have you any reason," he continued, in a voice which betrayed emotion, "for your halting answer? Have you ever seen the body in any of the rooms?"

"One cannot say," replied the youth, with the same calm pertinacity; "they are so changed you know."

"Yes," said the Colonel, as he tried to keep down his voice; "but there is an unmistakable mark in the case we are speaking of. You were present at the amputation?"

"The small toe of the left foot—I mean the want of it," rejoined the student, "would be a good mark if one went for the purpose of identification; but, you know, we don't go to identify subjects, and then the small toe is so very small an affair, that one is apt to overlook it."

"At least," cried the Colonel, somewhat impatiently, "you have met no such body?"

"I think not," was the reply, but with a smile, which the Colonel no doubt thought very inopportune. "If there had been six toes in place of four, one might have been more certain; and I need not say that if there had been seven, one would have been more certain still, and—"

But the Colonel, suspecting the student was proceeding to the *eight,* which probably he had no intention of, stopped him, with a request to the effect that if he should meet with any body which appeared to be that of Mrs. Corbet, he would lose no time in communicating to him the fact.

"That would be as nearly as possible a matter of course," replied Davidson, with still more of a smile on his sinister face; "but, in the meantime, you should keep an eye upon the green tumulus in the Canongate, and if you find that the turf, especially about the head of the grave, has been disturbed, we might be led to expect something in the rooms."

"I intend to visit the spot to-morrow," said the Colonel; and, with a deep heaving of the breast, "I have delayed that duty too long."

"You had better pay a visit to that quarter to-night," added the youth.

"There is no moon," rejoined the Colonel. "I could see nothing in the dark."

"There is such a thing as a lantern," was the quick reply; "and, after all, it is perhaps as well if you can avoid the sexton. These gentry are our best friends."

"I will perform the duty," said the Colonel, speaking perhaps as much to himself as to the student. "It is imperative."

"At what hour?" asked the youth—a question a little more particular than the answers he had given to the Colonel's interrogation, but the Colonel, concerned with deeper thoughts, did not mark the difference.

"About ten," he replied; "but how am I to get entry?"

"Over the low north wall," was the reply.

And the youth, having thus so far satisfied the Colonel, and perhaps to some extent himself, went away, leaving the solitary occupant of the room under the fear that that solitude would be interfered with by the same bodiless companion who had taken the trouble of visiting him twice that day; but whether it was that, as he lay on the sofa, he gazed with more earnestness into the empty space about him than was consistent with the modesty of these susceptible creatures, or that now he had resolved on conciliating the angry spirit by obedience, certain it is that he did not see the image again that night. The intermediate hours were solemn and heavy, nor had he any wish even to try to lighten them, for he was in that selfishness of misery which throws its gloom over all thoughts that are happy, so as to assimilate them to its own condition. So at half-past nine he made ready his lantern,—an article then much in use,—and wrapping himself up in a large cloak, proceeded to the burying-ground, which he had not visited since that day—known to many of earth's mourners as the true *dies iræ* which engulphs the happiness of a life—on which he committed his wife's body to the earth. Nor was he long in getting to the side of the "little hillock," which has in its bosom a story more wonderful than that which might be told by the mountains "earth-quake-born." Having made sure of the object, which he knew from the relation it held to a white marble headstone of another grave by the side, he sat down on a tablet covered with green mould, and began to direct the light of the lantern to the tumulus. The beam was made to traverse the joining of the sods, in order that he might discover whether any crevice gave indication of external disturbance. And thus amid the darkness and silence, with bent head and peering eyes he was engaged in this piety of grief for the best part of a quarter of an hour. Regaining his upright position, he got into meditation. He was in the midst of the dead—many of them in their new shrouds, those marriage dresses of death's brides not yet soiled. Even his wife would yet have undergone little change, and thus he conjured up to the eye of his fancy all those children of mortality, who, a little time before, were, as he himself was now, instinct with life, lying extended in their small habitations silent and motionless; yet the consciousness of the presence of these was as nothing to the awe which overshaded him as he thought that the place and the hour were propitious to another visit from his spiritual monitor. He felt unnerved, and even took the precaution of turning the light of the lantern upon his own face, as if thereby he might shut out the lesser light of the apparition; but the moment his face shone amid the darkness, he was startled by the sound of a voice, which behoved to be sepulchral among so many graves. The sound was distinctly articulate, and the words, "Colonel Corbet."

When a man hears his name pronounced as a salutation, he will naturally doubtless turn his eye to the source of the

sound; and so would the Colonel on the instant, if it had
not been that he was doing his best by holding the lantern to
his face to keep away the object of his dread, and somehow
or other he confusedly mixed up the party, whoever it might
be, that had pronounced the words and the apparition of his
wife. A very little power of thinking would have satisfied
him that if Mrs. Corbet's spirit chose to address her husband, she would have used the same kind of voice which was
her natural and peculiar gift when alive, and that the voice
he had heard was not at all in that key, if indeed it did not
very clearly come from a man; but then it just happened that
he had not the power of comparison, and then, we all know,
the effect of fear in the transmutation of appearances is not
more than in that of sounds. So he felt himself in that most
unsoldier-like attitude of being irresolute—inclined to turn
the lantern, yet terrified that by so doing he would reveal the
apparition he so much dreaded. Even as he thus stood in a
position sufficiently ridiculous, he was soon resolved.

"Colonel Corbet," repeated the voice, "your wife's no
aneath thae sods."

Mrs. Corbet did not speak Scotch, and so the lantern was
turned on the object—no other than a man standing on the
other side of the grave. The light brought him out in all his
perfections—a raw-boned cadaverous-looking fellow, who
could hardly have had a more grim and death-like look if he
had at that time come out of the grave on which he stood.
He had a peculiar squint, too, which gave him a leering look,
even when, as at present, he intended to be very serious; but
if he had been as villainous-looking as a solitary ghoul, who
invites no one to his feasts of dead bodies, he was at least a
being with real flesh and bones; and therefore the Colonel
was no longer afraid, however stunned he might have been by
the ominous announcement

"Who are you, and what do you mean?" was accordingly
the somewhat firm question.

"As to wha I am," replied the man; "ye may ken that when we're better acquaint; and as to what I mean, what, in the name o' a' that's gude and holy, can be plainer than the words I hae spoken—ay, just thae words—Mrs. Corbet's no aneath thae sods?"

"Where is she then?" was the natural question.

"I'm no just inclined to answer that question," was the reply, accompanied by a kind of laugh, which could have sounded better nowhere than among these graves. "But, hooly, sir, I dinna mean to say that the secret is so dead close as never by ony means to be revealed; but I am modest, and if you havena' forgotten your Latin, you might understand me when I say, *Edinæ venalia sunt omnia.*"

"You mean," said the Colonel, "that I may know where the body of my wife is if I will pay for the information?'

"Weel, you have helped my bashfulness," said the man; "and if you will meet me at the Tron the morn's night at nine o'clock, you will hear what you will hear, and see what you will see."

And with these words the man disappeared, no doubt to find his way out as quickly as possible.

Some little time elapsed before the Colonel could recover himself from his confusion, and he seemed to be rejected of heaven not to be accepted on earth, with only the problematical relief that if the body was actually stolen, he might, by redeeming it, appease the angry manes of his wife; and with some thoughts of this kind passing through his mind, he turned his steps homewards—lighting his path over the graves by his lantern, the glimmering of which would no doubt be noticed by some sly ghosts shading themselves behind the head-stones; nor when he got home could he banish from his mind the augury that, according to the old Greek saying, he was doomed either to act a tragedy or go mad. The discovery he seemed to have made satisfied him that the visions he had seen were not only veritable but justified, insomuch as he had not only caused the death of his wife, but, by his supineness and disregard of her injunctions, allowed her body to be taken out of the grave—the circumstance of all others which had filled her with the greatest apprehension. Nor had he been able to shake himself free from these thoughts up to the time when he went to bed; and as for accomplishing such a feat there, he had no great chance, even though he tossed himself in his own blankets, as if he wanted to inflict upon himself a punishment more usually conferred by others without the special consent of the culprit. It is not unlikely that he thus did himself some service, for he left himself little leisure, and certainly he had no inclination, for witnessing a vision in the dead hours of the night.

The next day was passed in similar nervousness and apprehension—feelings which were by no means allayed by the nonappearance of his expected monitor. At nine he was at his post at the Tron. The night was again dark, and the glimmering lamps at the heads of the timber posts looked as if a little of the wood at the tops had been charred and ignited into dull embers. The people were passing and repassing like shadows in Hades—that is to say, they presented that appearance to the gloomy mind of the Colonel, who now saw everything through the clouded medium of his own mind. Presently, as he stood in the middle of the street, some one whispered in his ear, "Follow me, but see that nane follow ye."

And the Colonel forthwith put himself in motion, following in the rear of the whisperer, who, as he could easily see, was his amiable friend of the churchyard. Their course was first up the High Street, next down Libberton's Wynd, then across the Cowgate, thence far up another close leading to Brown Square, and, lastly, up a kind of entry towards a house standing by itself. As yet there was no conversation, nor even when the man mounted two or three steps which led to the door of that house did he utter a word. It seemed to be

understood that the Colonel was to follow whithersoever he
was led. The door was opened by the man by means of a key
which he took from his pocket, and, proceeding inwards, he
was followed by the Colonel. The man, without yet opening
his mouth, put his hand on the shoulder of his companion as
a sign for him to stand, and then proceeded to lock the door
inside; after which act of apparent precaution, he opened an
inner door and entered, the Colonel following—not by sight,
for it was pitch dark, but simply by the ear as it conveyed
to him the motions of his leader. They were now in a room,
at least so the Colonel thought, and taking a step forward
he came against some object which seemed to be suspended
from the roof, for it moved, and seemed to oscillate backward and forward, giving forth at same time a crepitation of
dry bones rattling in chains.

"Never mind that," said his leader; "stand steddy till I
strike a licht."

And by and by the sound was heard of the flint upon the
steel: rasp—rasp—a spark—phroo, phroo—whew-w—"The
deil's in the tinder"—phroo—"There noo."

And a blue light from the sulphur at the end of the spunk
flashed through the room, shewing to the Colonel a small
apartment with two prepared skeletons suspended from the
roof, one of which—that impinged upon by the Colonel in
the dark—being still in motion, and crepitating during its
oscillation. Not a word passed yet from the man who was
busy getting the light from the match transferred to a candle, which, having with some difficulty got it ignited, he
placed in a candlestick, which again he placed in the sole
of the window. All this time the Colonel was no doubt in
great amazement. He was, moreover, shocked by the sight of
the suspended objects, each of which seemed from its empty
sockets to look down upon him in grim dissatisfaction; yet
he was under the conviction that this was a mere ante-room,
from which he would be led to another, where the body he

was doubtless brought to see would be presented him—to stun and terrify him, yea, to horrify him!

So far he was mistaken. The man, after deliberately putting away the tinder-box in a press in the wall, proceeded to take up the candle, and coming round to where the Colonel stood, he took hold of one of the suspended forms, and twirling it round so that its face might confront them, he pointed to the *patella* or knee-pan.

"Read ye thae words there," said he, "and see if ye ken wha *that is.*"

And he essayed pretty successfully a laugh.

The Colonel's eye was meanwhile fixed on the spot, where he read, in pretty legible letters, "Mrs. Col. Corbet, died 9th Sept 18—"

It was sometime before he seemed to gather up thought enough to enable him to understand the meaning of the words, and, as he bent his body and gazed with staring eyes, the man seemed inclined to question his perception.

"An auld friend wi' a new face?" said he drawlingly.

But the addition was not needed. The perceptive power had vindicated itself—the Colonel staggered as if he would have fallen; and it is more than likely he would, if there had not been a long seat behind upon which he sank under the influence of a spasm. He clutched the empty space about him, breathed laboriously, and turned more than once a harebrained look at the object, averting again his eyes and trembling violently. All which indications of misery had no more effect upon "the broken student," as he afterwards turned out to be, than the crackle of the suspended bones.

"And you see the sma' tae o' the left foot is a wanting."

Words the truth of which he pointed out by taking hold of the left foot of the figure, and which again threw the Colonel into another fit of laborious breathing—a condition, however engrossing, not now incompatible with an effort to fix his eye on that part pointed out by the man.

"Good God!" he at length exclaimed. "Is all that true? Is it possible that that is *my* Isabella?"

"Your Isabella!" replied the man. "No; she belongs now to Mr. M—, the proprietor of the dissecting-rooms; and valuable property she is, for there's no a finer specimen of the genus *homo* in Edinburgh."

"But you are a Christian," cried the Colonel, as he awakened more completely to the reality of his extraordinary position. "And since you have brought me here to witness this terrible spectacle, you can surely put me on some way and means to get possession of these bones, and get them buried." And as these words did not seem to remove the apathy of the man, (probably more affected than real,) he clutched him by the neck of the coat. "I demand of you," he cried, more loudly than the man relished, "to know whether you have authority to give me up the bones of my wife."

"Canny, sir," was the reply; "ye 'll mak naething by anger, and I will befriend you if I can; but," in a low voice, "there maun be money—money:" and whether it was that the broken student thought that some words of Latin would help a scene which was more like an incantation than a mercantile bargain, or that the reduced man was proud of the learning that had done him no good, he added what, certainly, the Colonel did not understand, *Tu mulierem amabas, missa est. Ego pecuniam dedisti.*"

"Money!" rejoined the Colonel; "I will give any money."

"Then, it's a' richt," said the man. "She's worth fifty guineas, and, if you agree, she shall be at your house within, say, twenty-four hours."

"Ten o'clock to-morrow night," said the Colonel.

"Exactly—settled—completed—dune," drawled the man; "and I can assure you, sir, she's a gude bargain at the money."

With these words this extraordinary meeting terminated.

The Colonel, as if anxious to get out of sight of the object of his purchase, hurried out as fast as a nervous groping

would permit, and in a short time was in his own house
extended upon the sofa, and in a state of mind which, with
so few examples of an analogous kind to help our sympathies,
it is almost impossible to conceive. To assure himself that he
had so far gained his point was, in reality, next to nothing,
for he was conscious that the horror entertained by his wife
of being exhumed was no doubt founded on the desecration
of the body, and that had been accomplished in a way which
had probably never occurred to her; yet, even in the worst
cases of crime or culpable negligence, there is a grain of comfort in duty done, even at the eleventh hour; and with this
small amelioration of his racked feelings he retired to bed.

Next night, precisely at ten o'clock, a knock, probably
expected by at least one individual of the family, was heard
at the door of the house in Hyndford Close; nor was it long
in being responded to. The door was opened by the Colonel
himself, and there stood the broken student with a large box
on his shoulders, which, having carried into a dark room, he
deposited upon the floor. There were very few words spoken.

Probably they were not needed, where the occasion neither required the solemnity of set sentences, nor suited the
expression of light thoughts. The money was promptly paid,
and the recipient having wished the Colonel joy of his bargain, departed with as much rapidity as probably the Colonel
wanted. So far all was as favourable as the Colonel could
wish; and seeing that there is, at least, one skeleton in every
house, and that one is generally considered to be enough,
it behoved him to get the supernumerary disposed of in the
only one way suited to our customs and our individual feelings. Next day, accordingly, he bent his steps to the house
of the sexton of the churchyard from which the body had
been taken. Having found the redoubted Andrew Gemmel
in, he recounted to him, with appropriate solemnity, his story, beginning with that part where he first encountered the

broken student. During the recital, he watched the face of the sexton, where he found solemnity the ruling expression up to the end of the narrative; but why, at that point, Andrew should have permitted that most grave of all faces to gather itself into a smile, was one mystery more added to a story which was mystery all over.

"And now, sir," said Andrew, "I will finish your story for you, for I see it wants an end."

And calling his man, he asked the Colonel to accompany him to the burying-ground. Nor did he say another word until they came to the desecrated grave, where, having given the necessary commands to his assistant, the two began to take off the turf, and thereafter to remove the earth. The grave was not a deep one, and a very short time only was required to get down to the coffin. This was laid bare, and Andrew having applied his screw-driver with all the tact of a joiner, the lid was taken off. The covering of the face was next removed, and there, with the Colonel looking down with staring eyes, lay Mrs. Corbet in all the calmness and placidity of death.

"Now, sir," said Andrew, "there is the end of your story."

The Colonel might now see somewhat more into the mystery, but he was entranced by the object which, in its still unsullied whiteness, lay in the dark hole before and beneath him. Old Chaos was busy tugging at those Caucasian lines of beauty, so like what the fading moonbeams shew on the sculptured face of Parian stone which genius has made instinct with life. It is vain to talk of thought in such situations. The charm wrought by the great wizard Nature is complete without more of incantation than a look. Yet this fixedness of anguish must obey the eternal law of motion: "Man must think;" and so recovering himself, as from a fearful dream, he started, and put the question to Andrew, so replete again with the grotesque *bizarrerie* of life—

"And what am I to do with the box of bones?"

"Just return them to Sandy Mackay," was the answer; "but as for your getting back your £50, you may as well try to make calf'sfoot jelly out of your purchase."

And so, too, the Colonel probably thought, but the loss of £50 was nothing in an account of debit and credit against the other world, or at least one spirit therein, and that account was fated to undergo a further diminution of balance against him; for in the evening he was visited by Dr. Russel, who, on hearing the detail of all these strange circumstances, assured his patient that the vision he had seen was merely the consequence of a deranged stomach. Nay, the Colonel himself recollected that when he was in India he was troubled with *musca volitantes,*—a symptom very often indicative of a tendency to that projection into space of images on the retina, which generally goes under the name of *monomania,* and is supposed, by Hibbert, to be the ground-work of most of our stories of apparitions.

The events of this day were not yet finished. About nine o'clock, two young men met in the tavern kept by Mrs. Gowans in the High Street. One of them was no other than the student Davidson, the other Sandy Mackay; who, to account for his learning and no less his squalidness, we may as well say had been a student at the Edinburgh University, from which he had been expelled, or, as they call it, broken, for some grievous misdemeanour,—a consummation which necessitated his becoming a kind of scullion-assistant at the dissecting-rooms in the place called "Society," with a pittance which he tried to eke out by occasionally procuring a *subject.* The two were clearly bent on a jollification, for they had before them each a large jug of ale, into which they had just dipt when Davidson began a certain count and reckoning:—

"I'll thank you, Sandy, for the £25," said Davidson, as he stretched forth his hand.

"Na," replied Sandy; "you forget the £5 I paid to Begbie for the auld frame of Luckie Corner, the woman who murdered Bell Gellatly. Besides, ye're importunate. It's *partitio non præfocatio*. I will divide fairly; £22, 10s. is just your share."

"Well, I'm content," said the other.

And Sandy began to count the money, laughing the while, and punning on the old maxim of the Stoics—*Quod utile honestum.*

"Can you tell me," said he, "why this is honestly won?"

"Because it is *utile,*" was the reply.

Whereat Sandy laughed again, adding thereafter, with a sigh and a smile, "But it will do me nae gude,—*mendici pera nunquam impletur*. There's nae keeping fou o' a beggar's wallet. There's your half."

"And you've made the skeleton all right at the rooms?" said Davidson, as he pocketed the cash.

"Ou ay," was the answer; "I've joined the tae, and rubbed out the letters on the knee-pan. Here's to ye."

THE FLAYED HAND
Guy De Maupassant
(1875)

One evening about eight months ago I met with some college comrades at the lodgings of our friend Louis R. We drank punch and smoked, talked of literature and art, and made jokes like any other company of young men. Suddenly the door flew open, and one who had been my friend since boyhood burst in like a hurricane.

"Guess where I come from?" he cried.

"I bet on the Mabille," responded one. "No," said another, "you are too gay; you come from borrowing money, from burying a rich uncle, or from pawning your watch." "You are getting sober," cried a third, "and, as you scented the punch in Louis' room, you came up here to get drunk again."

"You are all wrong," he replied. "I come from P., in Normandy, where I have spent eight days, and whence I have brought one of my friends, a great criminal, whom I ask permission to present to you."

With these words he drew from his pocket a long, black hand, from which the skin had been stripped. It had been severed at the wrist. Its dry and shriveled shape, and the narrow, yellowed nails still clinging to the fingers, made it frightful to look upon. The muscles, which showed that its first owner had been possessed of great strength, were bound in place by a strip of parchment-like skin.

"Just fancy," said my friend, "the other day they sold the effects of an old sorcerer, recently deceased, well known in all the country. Every Saturday night he used to go to witch gatherings on a broomstick; he practised the white magic and the black, gave blue milk to the cows, and made them wear tails like that of the companion of Saint Anthony. The old scoundrel always had a deep affection for this hand, which, he said, was that of a celebrated criminal, executed in 1736 for having thrown his lawful wife head first into a well—for which I do not blame him—and then hanging in the belfry the priest who had married him. After this double exploit he went away, and, during his subsequent career, which was brief but exciting, he robbed twelve travelers, smoked a score of monks in their monastery, and made a seraglio of a convent."

"But what are you going to do with this horror?" we cried.

"Eh! parbleu! I will make it the handle to my door-bell and frighten my creditors."

"My friend," said Henry Smith, a big, phlegmatic Englishman, "I believe that this hand is only a kind of Indian meat, preserved by a new process; I advise you to make bouillon of it."

"Rail not, messieurs," said, with the utmost sang froid, a medical student who was three-quarters drunk, "but if you follow my advice, Pierre, you will give this piece of human debris Christian burial, for fear lest its owner should come to demand it. Then, too, this hand has acquired some bad habits, for you know the proverb, 'Who has killed will kill.'"

"And who has drank will drink," replied the host as he poured out a big glass of punch for the student, who emptied it at a draught and slid dead drunk under the table. His sudden dropping out of the company was greeted with a burst of laughter, and Pierre, raising his glass and saluting the hand, cried:

"I drink to the next visit of thy master."

Then the conversation turned upon other subjects, and shortly afterward each returned to his lodgings.

About two o'clock the next day, as I was passing Pierre's door, I entered and found him reading and smoking.

"Well, how goes it?" said I. "Very well," he responded. "And your hand?" "My hand? Did you not see it on the bell-pull? I put it there when I returned home last night. But, apropos of this, what do you think? Some idiot, doubtless to play a stupid joke on me, came ringing at my door towards midnight. I demanded who was there, but as no one replied, I went back to bed again, and to sleep."

At this moment the door opened and the landlord, a fat and extremely impertinent person, entered without saluting us.

"Sir," said he, "I pray you to take away immediately that carrion which you have hung to your bell-pull. Unless you do this I shall be compelled to ask you to leave."

"Sir," responded Pierre, with much gravity, "you insult a hand which does not merit it. Know you that it belonged to a man of high breeding?"

The landlord turned on his heel and made his exit, without speaking. Pierre followed him, detached the hand and affixed it to the bell-cord hanging in his alcove.

"That is better," he said. "This hand, like the 'Brother, all must die,' of the Trappists, will give my thoughts a serious turn every night before I sleep."

At the end of an hour I left him and returned to my own apartment.

I slept badly the following night, was nervous and agitated, and several times awoke with a start. Once I imagined, even, that a man had broken into my room, and I sprang up and searched the closets and under the bed. Towards six o'clock in the morning I was commencing to doze at last, when a loud knocking at my door made me jump from my couch. It was my friend Pierre's servant, half dressed, pale and trembling.

"Ah, sir!" cried he, sobbing, "my poor master. Someone has murdered him."

I dressed myself hastily and ran to Pierre's lodgings. The house was full of people disputing together, and everything was in a commotion. Everyone was talking at the same time, recounting and commenting on the occurrence in all sorts of ways. With great difficulty I reached the bed-room, made myself known to those guarding the door and was permitted to enter. Four agents of police were standing in the middle of the apartment, pencils in hand, examining every detail, conferring in low voices and writing from time to time in their note-books. Two doctors were in consultation by the bed on which lay the unconscious form of Pierre. He was not dead, but his face was fixed in an expression of the most awful terror. His eyes were open their widest, and the dilated pupils seemed to regard fixedly, with unspeakable horror, something unknown and frightful. His hands were clinched. I raised the quilt, which covered his body from the chin downward, and saw on his neck, deeply sunk in the flesh, the marks of fingers. Some drops of blood spotted his shirt. At that moment one thing struck me. I chanced to notice that the shriveled hand was no longer attached to the bell-cord. The doctors had doubtless removed it to avoid the comments of those entering the chamber where the wounded man lay, because the appearance of this hand was indeed frightful. I did not inquire what had become of it.

I now clip from a newspaper of the next day the story of the crime with all the details that the police were able to procure:

"A frightful attempt was made yesterday on the life of young M. Pierre B., student, who belongs to one of the best families in Normandy. He returned home about ten o'clock in the evening, and excused his valet, Bouvin, from further attendance upon him, saying that he felt fatigued and was going to bed. Towards midnight Bouvin was suddenly awakened by the furious ringing of his master's bell. He was afraid, and lighted a lamp and waited. The bell was silent about a minute, then rang again with such vehemence that the domestic, mad with fright, flew from his room to awaken the concierge, who ran to summon the police, and, at the end of about fifteen minutes, two policemen forced open the door. A horrible sight met their eyes. The furniture was overturned, giving evidence of a fearful struggle between the victim and his assailant. In the middle of the room, upon his back, his body rigid, with livid face and frightfully dilated eyes, lay, motionless, young Pierre B., bearing upon his neck the deep imprints of five fingers. Dr. Bourdean was called immediately, and his report says that the aggressor must have been possessed of prodigious strength and have had an extraordinarily thin and sinewy hand, because the fingers left in the flesh of the victim five holes like those from a pistol ball, and had penetrated until they almost met. There is no clue to the motive of the crime or to its perpetrator. The police are making a thorough investigation."

The following appeared in the same newspaper next day:

"M. Pierre B., the victim of the frightful assault of which we published an account yesterday, has regained consciousness after two hours of the most assiduous care by Dr. Bourdean. His life is not in danger, but it is strongly feared that he has lost his reason. No trace has been found of his assailant."

My poor friend was indeed insane. For seven months I visited him daily at the hospital where we had placed him, but he did not recover the light of reason. In his delirium strange words escaped him, and, like all madmen, he had one fixed idea: he believed himself continually pursued by a specter. One day they came for me in haste, saying he was worse, and when I arrived I found him dying. For two hours he remained very calm, then, suddenly, rising from his bed in spite of our efforts, he cried, waving his arms as if a prey to the most awful terror: "Take it away! Take it away! It strangles me! Help! Help!" Twice he made the circuit of the room, uttering horrible screams, then fell face downward, dead.

As he was an orphan I was charged to take his body to the
little village of P., in Normandy, where his parents were buried. It was the place from which he had arrived the evening
he found us drinking punch in Louis R.'s room, when he
had presented to us the flayed hand. His body was inclosed
in a leaden coffin, and four days afterwards I walked sadly
beside the old curé, who had given him his first lessons, to
the little cemetery where they dug his grave. It was a beautiful day, and sunshine from a cloudless sky flooded the earth.
Birds sang from the blackberry bushes where many a time
when we were children we had stolen to eat the fruit. Again
I saw Pierre and myself creeping along behind the hedge and
slipping through the gap that we knew so well, down at the
end of the little plot where they bury the poor. Again we
would return to the house with cheeks and lips black with
the juice of the berries we had eaten. I looked at the bushes;
they were covered with fruit; mechanically I picked some and
bore it to my mouth. The curé had opened his breviary, and
was muttering his prayers in a low voice. I heard at the end
of the walk the spades of the grave-diggers who were opening
the tomb. Suddenly they called out, the curé closed his book,
and we went to see what they wished of us. They had found
a coffin; in digging a stroke of the pickaxe had started the
cover, and we perceived within a skeleton of unusual stature,
lying on its back, its hollow eyes seeming yet to menace and
defy us. I was troubled, I know not why, and almost afraid.

"Hold!" cried one of the men, "look there! One of the rascal's hands has been severed at the wrist. Ah, here it is!" and
he picked up from beside the body a huge withered hand,
and held it out to us.

"See," cried the other, laughing, "see how he glares at
you, as if he would spring at your throat to make you give
him back his hand."

"Go," said the curé, "leave the dead in peace, and close
the coffin. We will make poor Pierre's grave elsewhere."

The next day all was finished, and I returned to Paris, after having left fifty francs with the old curé for masses to be said for the repose of the soul of him whose sepulchre we had troubled.

THE HAND

Guy de Maupassant

(1883)

All were crowding around M. Bermutier, the judge, who was giving his opinion about the Saint-Cloud mystery. For a month this inexplicable crime had been the talk of Paris. Nobody could make head or tail of it.

M. Bermutier, standing with his back to the fireplace, was talking, citing the evidence, discussing the various theories, but arriving at no conclusion.

Some women had risen, in order to get nearer to him, and were standing with their eyes fastened on the clean-shaven face of the judge, who was saying such weighty things. They were shaking and trembling, moved by fear and curiosity, and by the eager and insatiable desire for the horrible, which haunts the soul of every woman. One of them, paler than the others, said during a pause:

"It's terrible. It verges on the supernatural. The truth will never be known."

The judge turned to her:

"True, madame, it is likely that the actual facts will never be discovered. As for the word 'supernatural' which you have just used, it has nothing to do with the matter. We are in the presence of a very cleverly conceived and executed crime, so well enshrouded in mystery that we cannot disentangle it from the involved circumstances which surround it. But once I had to take charge of an affair in which the uncanny seemed to play a part. In fact, the case became so confused that it had to be given up."

Several women exclaimed at once:

"Oh! Tell us about it!"

M. Bermutier smiled in a dignified manner, as a judge should, and went on:

"Do not think, however, that I, for one minute, ascribed anything in the case to supernatural influences. I believe only in normal causes. But if, instead of using the word 'supernatural' to express what we do not understand, we were simply to make use of the word 'inexplicable,' it would be much better. At any rate, in the affair of which I am about to tell you, it is especially the surrounding, preliminary circumstances which impressed me. Here are the facts:

"I was, at that time, a judge at Ajaccio, a little white city on the edge of a bay which is surrounded by high mountains.

"The majority of the cases which came up before me concerned vendettas. There are some that are superb, dramatic, ferocious, heroic. We find there the most beautiful causes for revenge of which one could dream, enmities hundreds of years old, quieted for a time but never extinguished; abominable stratagems, murders becoming massacres and almost deeds of glory. For two years I heard of nothing but the price of blood, of this terrible Corsican prejudice which compels revenge for insults meted out to the offending person and all his descendants and relatives. I had seen old men, children, cousins murdered; my head was full of these stories.

"One day I learned that an Englishman had just hired a little villa at the end of the bay for several years. He had brought with him a French servant, whom he had engaged on the way at Marseilles.

"Soon this peculiar person, living alone, only going out to hunt and fish, aroused a widespread interest. He never spoke to any one, never went to the town, and every morning he would practice for an hour or so with his revolver and rifle.

"Legends were built up around him. It was said that he was some high personage, fleeing from his fatherland for political reasons; then it was affirmed that he was in hiding after having committed some abominable crime. Some particularly horrible circumstances were even mentioned.

"In my judicial position I thought it necessary to get some information about this man, but it was impossible to learn anything. He called himself Sir John Rowell.

"I therefore had to be satisfied with watching him as closely as I could, but I could see nothing suspicious about his actions.

"However, as rumors about him were growing and becoming more widespread, I decided to try to see this stranger myself, and I began to hunt regularly in the neighborhood of his grounds.

"For a long time I watched without finding an opportunity. At last it came to me in the shape of a partridge which I shot and killed right in front of the Englishman. My dog fetched it for me, but, taking the bird, I went at once to Sir John Rowell and, begging his pardon, asked him to accept it.

"He was a big man, with red hair and beard, very tall, very broad, a kind of calm and polite Hercules. He had nothing of the so-called British stiffness, and in a broad English accent he thanked me warmly for my attention. At the end of a month we had had five or six conversations.

"One night, at last, as I was passing before his door, I saw him in the garden, seated astride a chair, smoking his pipe. I bowed and he invited me to come in and have a glass of beer. I needed no urging.

"He received me with the most punctilious English courtesy, sang the praises of France and of Corsica, and declared that he was quite in love with this country.

"Then, with great caution and under the guise of a vivid interest, I asked him a few questions about his life and his plans. He answered without embarrassment, telling me that he had travelled a great deal in Africa, in the Indies, in America. He added, laughing:

"'I have had many adventures.'

"Then I turned the conversation on hunting, and he gave me the most curious details on hunting the hippopotamus, the tiger, the elephant and even the gorilla.

"I said:

"'Are all these animals dangerous?'

"He smiled:

"'Oh, no! Man is the worst.'

"And he laughed a good broad laugh, the wholesome laugh of a contented Englishman.

"'I have also frequently been man-hunting.'

"Then he began to talk about weapons, and he invited me to come in and see different makes of guns.

"His parlor was draped in black, black silk embroidered in gold. Big yellow flowers, as brilliant as fire, were worked on the dark material.

"He said:

"'It is a Japanese material.'

"But in the middle of the widest panel a strange thing attracted my attention. A black object stood out against a square of red velvet. I went up to it; it was a hand, a human hand. Not the clean white hand of a skeleton, but a dried black hand, with yellow nails, the muscles exposed and traces of old blood on the bones, which were cut off as clean as though it had been chopped off with an axe, near the middle of the forearm.

"Around the wrist, an enormous iron chain, riveted and soldered to this unclean member, fastened it to the wall by a ring, strong enough to hold an elephant in leash.

"I asked:

"'What is that?'

"The Englishman answered quietly:

"'That is my best enemy. It comes from America, too. The bones were severed by a sword and the skin cut off with a sharp stone and dried in the sun for a week.'

"I touched these human remains, which must have belonged to a giant. The uncommonly long fingers were attached by enormous tendons which still had pieces of skin hanging to them in places. This hand was terrible to see; it made one think of some savage vengeance.

"I said:

"'This man must have been very strong.'

"The Englishman answered quietly:

"'Yes, but I was stronger than he. I put on this chain to hold him.'

"I thought that he was joking. I said:

"'This chain is useless now, the hand won't run away.'

"Sir John Rowell answered seriously:

"'It always wants to go away. This chain is needed.'

"I glanced at him quickly, questioning his face, and I asked myself:

"'Is he an insane man or a practical joker?'

"But his face remained inscrutable, calm and friendly. I turned to other subjects, and admired his rifles.

"However, I noticed that he kept three loaded revolvers in the room, as though constantly in fear of some attack.

"I paid him several calls. Then I did not go any more. People had become used to his presence; everybody had lost interest in him.

"A whole year rolled by. One morning, toward the end of November, my servant awoke me and announced that Sir John Rowell had been murdered during the night.

"Half an hour later I entered the Englishman's house, together with the police commissioner and the captain of the gendarmes. The servant, bewildered and in despair, was crying before the door. At first I suspected this man, but he was innocent.

"The guilty party could never be found.

"On entering Sir John's parlor, I noticed the body, stretched out on its back, in the middle of the room.

"His vest was torn, the sleeve of his jacket had been pulled off, everything pointed to, a violent struggle.

"The Englishman had been strangled! His face was black, swollen and frightful, and seemed to express a terrible fear. He held something between his teeth, and his neck, pierced by five or six holes which looked as though they had been made by some iron instrument, was covered with blood.

"A physician joined us. He examined the finger marks on the neck for a long time and then made this strange announcement:

"'It looks as though he had been strangled by a skeleton.'

"A cold chill seemed to run down my back, and I looked over to where I had formerly seen the terrible hand. It was no longer there. The chain was hanging down, broken.

"I bent over the dead man and, in his contracted mouth, I found one of the fingers of this vanished hand, cut—or rather sawed off by the teeth down to the second knuckle.

"Then the investigation began. Nothing could be discovered. No door, window or piece of furniture had been forced. The two watch dogs had not been aroused from their sleep.

"Here, in a few words, is the testimony of the servant:

"For a month his master had seemed excited. He had received many letters, which he would immediately burn.

"Often, in a fit of passion which approached madness, he had taken a switch and struck wildly at this dried hand riveted to the wall, and which had disappeared, no one knows how, at the very hour of the crime.

"He would go to bed very late and carefully lock himself in. He always kept weapons within reach. Often at night he would talk loudly, as though he were quarrelling with some one.

"That night, somehow, he had made no noise, and it was only on going to open the windows that the servant had found Sir John murdered. He suspected no one.

"I communicated what I knew of the dead man to the judges and public officials. Throughout the whole island a minute investigation was carried on. Nothing could be found out.

"One night, about three months after the crime, I had a terrible nightmare. I seemed to see the horrible hand running over my curtains and walls like an immense scorpion or spider. Three times I awoke, three times I went to sleep again; three times I saw the hideous object galloping round my room and moving its fingers like legs.

"The following day the hand was brought me, found in the cemetery, on the grave of Sir John Rowell, who had been buried there because we had been unable to find his family. The first finger was missing.

"Ladies, there is my story. I know nothing more."

The women, deeply stirred, were pale and trembling. One of them exclaimed:

"But that is neither a climax nor an explanation! We will be unable to sleep unless you give us your opinion of what had occurred."

The judge smiled severely:

"Oh! Ladies, I shall certainly spoil your terrible dreams. I simply believe that the legitimate owner of the hand was not dead, that he came to get it with his remaining one. But I don't know how. It was a kind of vendetta."

One of the women murmured:

"No, it can't be that."

And the judge, still smiling, said:

"Didn't I tell you that my explanation would not satisfy you?"

LET LOOSE
Mary Cholmondeley
(1890)

The dead abide with us! Though stark and cold
Earth seems to grip them, they are with us still.

Some years ago I took up architecture, and made a tour through Holland, studying the buildings of that interesting country. I was not then aware that it is not enough to take up art. Art must take you up, too. I never doubted but that my passing enthusiasm for her would be returned. When I discovered that she was a stern mistress, who did not immediately respond to my attentions, I naturally transferred them to another shrine. There are other things in the world besides art. I am now a landscape gardener.

But at the time of which I write I was engaged in a violent flirtation with architecture. I had one companion on this expedition, who has since become one of the leading architects of the day. He was a thin, determined-looking man with a screwed-up face and heavy jaw, slow of speech, and absorbed in his work to a degree which I quickly found tiresome. He was possessed of a certain quiet power of overcoming obstacles which I have rarely seen equalled. He has since become my brother-in-law, so I ought to know; for my parents did not like him much and opposed the marriage, and my sister did not like him at all, and refused him over and over again; but, nevertheless, he eventually married her.

I have thought since that one of his reasons for choosing me as his travelling companion on this occasion was because he was getting up steam for what he subsequently termed "an alliance with my family", but the idea never entered my head at the time. A more careless man as to dress I have rarely met, and yet, in all the heat of July in Holland, I noticed that he never appeared without a high, starched collar, which had not even fashion to commend it at that time.

I often chaffed him about his splendid collars, and asked him why he wore them, but without eliciting any response. One evening, as we were walking back to our lodgings in Middeburg, I attacked him for about the thirtieth time on the subject.

"Why on earth do you wear them?" I said.

"You have, I believe, asked me that question many times," he replied, in his slow, precise utterance; "but always on occasions when I was occupied. I am now at leisure, and I will tell you."

And he did.

I have put down what he said, as nearly in his own words as I can remember them.

Ten years ago, I was asked to read a paper on English Frescoes at the Institute of British Architects. I was determined to make the paper as good as I could, down to the slightest details, and I consulted many books on the subject, and studied every fresco I could find. My father, who had been an architect, had left me, at his death, all his papers and notebooks on the subject of architecture. I searched them diligently, and found in one of them a slight unfinished sketch of nearly fifty years ago that specially interested me. Underneath was noted, in his clear, small hand—*Frescoed east wall of crypt. Parish Church. Wet Waste-on-the-Wolds, Yorkshire (via Pickering).*

The sketch had such a fascination for me that I decided to go there and see the fresco for myself. I had only a very vague idea as to where Wet Waste-on-the-Wolds was, but I was ambitious for the success of my paper; it was hot in London, and I set off on my long journey not without a certain degree of pleasure, with my dog Brian, a large nondescript brindled creature, as my only companion.

I reached Pickering, in Yorkshire, in the course of the afternoon, and then began a series of experiments on local lines which ended, after several hours, in my finding myself deposited at a little out-of-the-world station within nine or ten miles of Wet Waste. As no conveyance of any kind was to be had, I shouldered my portmanteau, and set out on a long white road that stretched away into the distance over the bare, treeless wold. I must have walked for several hours, over a waste of moorland patched with heather, when a doctor passed me, and gave me a lift to within a mile of my destination. The mile was a long one, and it was quite dark by the time I saw the feeble glimmer of lights in front of me, and found that I had reached Wet Waste. I had considerable difficulty in getting any one to take me in; but at last I persuaded the owner of the public-house to give me a bed, and, quite tired out, I got into it as soon as possible, for fear he should change his mind, and fell asleep to the sound of a little stream below my window.

I was up early next morning, and inquired directly after breakfast the way to the clergyman's house, which I found was close at hand. At Wet Waste everything was close at hand. The whole village seemed composed of a straggling row of one-storeyed grey stone houses, the same colour as the stone walls that separated the few fields enclosed from the surrounding waste, and as the little bridges over the beck that ran down one side of the grey wide street. Everything was grey. The church, the low tower of which I could see at a little distance, seemed to have been built of the same stone; so was the parsonage when I came up to it, accompanied on my way by a mob of rough, uncouth children, who eyed me and Brian with half-defiant curiosity.

The clergyman was at home, and after a short delay I was admitted. Leaving Brian in charge of my drawing materials, I followed the servant into a low panelled room, in which, at a latticed window, a very old man was sitting. The morning light fell on his white head bent low over a litter of papers and books.

"Mr. er—?" he said, looking up slowly, with one finger keeping his place in a hook.

"Blake."

"Blake," he repeated after me, and was silent.

I told him that I was an architect; that I had come to study a fresco in the crypt of his church, and asked for the keys.

"The crypt," he said, pushing up his spectacles and peering hard at me. "The crypt has been closed for thirty years. Ever since—" and he stopped short.

"I should be much obliged for the keys," I said again.

He shook his head.

"No," he said. "No one goes in there now."

"It is a pity," I remarked, "for I have come a long way with that one object"; and I told him about the paper I had been asked to read, and the trouble I was taking with it.

He became interested. "Ah!" he said, laying down his pen, and removing his finger from the page before him, "I can understand that. I also was young once, and fired with ambition. The lines have fallen to me in somewhat lonely places, and for forty years I have held the cure of souls in this place, where, truly, I have seen but little of the world, though I myself may be not unknown in the paths of literature. Possibly you may have read a pamphlet, written by myself, on the Syrian version of the Three Authentic Epistles of Ignatius?"

"Sir," I said, "I am ashamed to confess that I have not time to read even the most celebrated books. My one object in life is my art. *Ars longa, vita brevis,* you know."

"You are right, my son," said the old man, evidently disappointed, but looking at me kindly. "There are diversities of gifts, and if the Lord has entrusted you with a talent, look to it. Lay it not up in a napkin."

I said I would not do so if he would lend me the keys of the crypt. He seemed startled by my recurrence to the subject and looked undecided.

"Why not?" he murmured to himself. "The youth appears a good youth. And superstition! What is it but distrust in God!"

He got up slowly, and taking a large bunch of keys out of his pocket, opened with one of them an oak cupboard in the corner of the room.

"They should be here," he muttered, peering in; "but the dust of many years deceives the eye. See, my son, if among these parchments there be two keys; one of iron and very large, and the other steel, and of a long thin appearance."

I went eagerly to help him, and presently found in a back drawer two keys tied together, which he recognised at once.

"Those are they," he said. "The long one opens the first door at the bottom of the steps which go down against the outside wall of the church hard by the sword graven in the wall. The second opens (but it is hard of opening and of shutting) the iron door within the passage leading to the crypt itself. My son, is it necessary to your treatise that you should enter this crypt?"

I replied that it was absolutely necessary.

"Then take them," he said, "and in the evening you will bring them to me again."

I said I might want to go several days running, and asked if he would not allow me to keep them till I had finished my work; but on that point he was firm.

"Likewise," he added, "be careful that you lock the first door at the foot of the steps before you unlock the second, and lock the second also while you are within. Furthermore, when you come out lock the iron inner door as well as the wooden one."

I promised I would do so, and, after thanking him, hurried away, delighted at my success in obtaining the keys. Finding Brian and my sketching materials waiting for me in the porch, I eluded the vigilance of my escort of children by taking the narrow private path between the parsonage and the church which was close at hand, standing in a quadrangle of ancient yews.

The church itself was interesting, and I noticed that it must have arisen out of the ruins of a previous building, judging from the number of fragments of stone caps and arches, bearing traces of very early carving, now built into the walls. There were incised crosses, too, in some places, and one especially caught my attention, being flanked by a large sword. It was in trying to get a nearer look at this that I stumbled, and, looking down, saw at my feet a flight of narrow stone steps green with moss and mildew. Evidently this was the entrance to the crypt. I at once descended the steps, taking care of my footing, for they were damp and slippery in the extreme.

Brian accompanied me, as nothing would induce him to remain behind. By the time I had reached the bottom of the stairs, I found myself almost in darkness, and I had to strike a light before I could find the keyhole and the proper key to fit into it. The door, which was of wood, opened inwards fairly easily, although an accumulation of mould and rubbish on the ground outside showed it had not been used for many years. Having got through it, which was not altogether an easy matter, as nothing would induce it to open more than about eighteen inches, I carefully locked it behind me, although I should have preferred to leave it open, as there is

to some minds an unpleasant feeling in being locked in anywhere, in case of a sudden exit seeming advisable.

I kept my candle alight with some difficulty, and after
groping my way down a low and of course exceedingly dank
passage, came to another door. A toad was squatting against
it, who looked as if he had been sitting there about a hundred years. As I lowered the candle to the floor, he gazed at
the light with unblinking eyes, and then retreated slowly
into a crevice in the wall, leaving against the door a small
cavity in the dry mud which had gradually silted up round
his person. I noticed that this door was of iron, and had a
long bolt, which, however, was broken.

Without delay, I fitted the second key into the lock, and
pushing the door open after considerable difficulty, I felt
the cold breath of the crypt upon my face. I must own I
experienced a momentary regret at locking the second door
again as soon as I was well inside, but I felt it my duty to
do so. Then, leaving the key in the lock, I seized my candle
and looked round. I was standing in a low vaulted chamber
with groined roof, cut out of the solid rock. It was difficult
to see where the crypt ended, as further light thrown on any
point only showed other rough archways or openings, cut in
the rock, which had probably served at one time for family
vaults.

A peculiarity of the Wet Waste crypt, which I had not noticed in other places of that description, was the tasteful arrangement of skulls and bones which were packed about four
feet high on either side. The skulls were symmetrically built
up to within a few inches of the top of the low archway on
my left, and the shin bones were arranged in the same manner on my right. *But the fresco!* I looked round for it in vain.
Perceiving at the further end of the crypt a very low and very
massive archway, the entrance to which was not filled up
with bones, I passed under it, and found myself in a second
smaller chamber. Holding my candle above my head, the first

object its light fell upon was—the fresco, and at a glance I saw that it was unique. Setting down some of my things with a trembling hand on a rough stone shelf hard by, which had evidently been a credence table, I examined the work more closely. It was a reredos over what had probably been the altar at the time the priests were proscribed. The fresco belonged to the earliest part of the fifteenth century, and was so perfectly preserved that I could almost trace the limits of each day's work in the plaster, as the artist had dashed it on and smoothed it out with his trowel. The subject was the Ascension, gloriously treated. I can hardly describe my elation as I stood and looked at it, and reflected that this magnificent specimen of English fresco painting would be made known to the world by myself. Recollecting myself at last, I opened my sketching bag, and, lighting all the candles I had brought with me, set to work.

Brian walked about near me, and though I was not otherwise than glad of his company in my rather lonely position, I wished several times I had left him behind. He seemed restless, and even the sight of so many bones appeared to exercise no soothing effect upon him. At last, however, after repeated commands, he lay down, watchful but motionless, on the stone floor.

I must have worked for several hours, and I was pausing to rest my eyes and hands, when I noticed for the first time the intense stillness that surrounded me. No sound from me reached the outer world. The church clock which had clanged out so loud and ponderously as I went down the steps, had not since sent the faintest whisper of its iron tongue down to me below. All was silent as the grave. This *was* the grave. Those who had come here had indeed gone down into silence. I repeated the words to myself, or rather they repeated themselves to me.

Gone down into silence.

I was awakened from my reverie by a faint sound. I sat still and listened. Bats occasionally frequent vaults and underground places.

The sound continued, a faint, stealthy, rather unpleasant sound. I do not know what kinds of sounds bats make, whether pleasant or otherwise. Suddenly there was a noise as of something falling, a momentary pause—and then—an almost imperceptible but distant jangle as of a key.

I had left the key in the lock after I had turned it, and I now regretted having done so. I got up, took one of the candles, and went back into the larger crypt—for though I trust I am not so effeminate as to be rendered nervous by hearing a noise for which I cannot instantly account; still, on occasions of this kind, I must honestly say I should prefer that they did not occur. As I came towards the iron door, there was another distinct (I had almost said hurried) sound. The impression on my mind was one of great haste. When I reached the door, and held the candle near the lock to take out the key, I perceived that the other one, which hung by a short string to its fellow, was vibrating slightly. I should have preferred not to find it vibrating, as there seemed no occasion for such a course; but I put them both into my pocket, and turned to go back to my work. As I turned, I saw on the ground what had occasioned the louder noise I had heard, namely, a skull which had evidently just slipped from its place on the top of one of the walls of bones, and had rolled almost to my feet. There, disclosing a few more inches of the top of an archway behind, was the place from which it had been dislodged. I stooped to pick it up, but fearing to displace any more skulls by meddling with the pile, and not liking to gather up its scattered teeth, I let it lie, and went back to my work, in which I was soon so completely absorbed that I was only roused at last by my candles beginning to burn low and go out one after another.

Then, with a sigh of regret, for I had not nearly finished, I turned to go. Poor Brian, who had never quite reconciled himself to the place, was beside himself with delight. As I opened the iron door he pushed past me, and a moment later I heard him whining and scratching, and I had almost added, beating, against the wooden one. I locked the iron door, and hurried down the passage as quickly as I could, and almost before I had got the other one ajar there seemed to be a rush past me into the open air, and Brian was bounding up the steps and out of sight. As I stopped to take out the key, I felt quite deserted and left behind. When I came out once more into the sunlight, there was a vague sensation all about me in the air of exultant freedom.

It was already late in the afternoon, and after I had sauntered back to the parsonage to give up the keys, I persuaded the people of the public-house to let me join in the family meal, which was spread out in the kitchen. The inhabitants of Wet Waste were primitive people, with the frank, unabashed manner that flourishes still in lonely places, especially in the wilds of Yorkshire; but I had no idea that in these days of penny posts and cheap newspapers such entire ignorance of the outer world could have existed in any corner, however remote, of Great Britain.

When I took one of the neighbour's children on my knee—a pretty little girl with the palest aureole of flaxen hair I had ever seen—and began to draw pictures for her of the birds and beasts of other countries, I was instantly surrounded by a crowd of children, and even grown-up people, while others came to their doorways and looked on from a distance, calling to each other in the strident unknown tongue which I have since discovered goes by the name of "Broad Yorkshire".

The following morning, as I came out of my room, I perceived that something was amiss in the village. A buzz of voices reached me as I passed the bar, and in the next house

I could hear through the open window a high-pitched wail of lamentation.

The woman who brought me my breakfast was in tears, and in answer to my questions, told me that the neighbour's child, the little girl whom I had taken on my knee the evening before, had died in the night.

I felt sorry for the general grief that the little creature's death seemed to arouse, and the uncontrolled wailing of the poor mother took my appetite away.

I hurried off early to my work, calling on my way for the keys, and with Brian for my companion descended once more into the crypt, and drew and measured with an absorption that gave me no time that day to listen for sounds real or fancied. Brian, too, on this occasion seemed quite content, and slept peacefully beside me on the stone floor. When I had worked as long as I could, I put away my books with regret that even then I had not quite finished, as I had hoped to do. It would be necessary to come again for a short time on the morrow. When I returned the keys late that afternoon, the old clergyman met me at the door, and asked me to come in and have tea with him.

"And has the work prospered?" he asked, as we sat down in the long, low room, into which I had just been ushered, and where he seemed to live entirely.

I told him it had, and showed it to him.

"You have seen the original, of course?" I said.

"Once," he replied, gazing fixedly at it. He evidently did not care to be communicative, so I turned the conversation to the age of the church.

"All here is old," he said. "When I was young, forty years ago, and came here because I had no means of mine own, and was much moved to marry at that time, I felt oppressed that all was so old; and that this place was so far removed from the world, for which I had at times longings grievous to be borne; but I had chosen my lot, and with it I was forced to be content. My son, marry not in youth, for love, which truly in that season is a mighty power, turns away the heart from study, and young children break the back of ambition. Neither marry in middle life, when a woman is seen to be but a woman and her talk a weariness, so you will not be burdened with a wife in your old age."

I had my own views on the subject of marriage, for I am of opinion that a well-chosen companion of domestic tastes and docile and devoted temperament may be of material assistance to a professional man. But, my opinions once formulated, it is not of moment to me to discuss them with others, so I changed the subject, and asked if the neighbouring villages were as antiquated as Wet Waste.

"Yes, all about here is old," he repeated. "The paved road leading to Dyke Fens is an ancient pack road, made even in the time of the Romans. Dyke Fens, which is very near here, a matter of but four or five miles, is likewise old, and forgotten by the world. The Reformation never reached it. It stopped here. And at Dyke Fens they still have a priest and a bell, and bow down before the saints. It is a damnable heresy, and weekly I expound it as such to my people, showing them true doctrines; and I have heard that this same priest has so far yielded himself to the Evil One that he has preached against me as withholding gospel truths from my flock; but I take no heed of it, neither of his pamphlet touching the Clementine Homilies, in which he vainly contradicts that which I have plainly set forth and proven beyond doubt, concerning the word *Asaph.*"

The old man was fairly off on his favourite subject, and it was some time before I could get away. As it was, he followed me to the door, and I only escaped because the old clerk hobbled up at that moment, and claimed his attention.

The following morning I went for the keys for the third and last time. I had decided to leave early the next day. I was tired of Wet Waste, and a certain gloom seemed to my fancy to be gathering over the place. There was a sensation of trouble in the air, as if, although the day was bright and clear, a storm were coming.

This morning, to my astonishment, the keys were refused to me when I asked for them. I did not, however, take the refusal as, final—I make it a rule never to take a refusal as final—and after a short delay I was shown into the room where, as usual, the clergyman was sitting, or rather, on this occasion, was walking up and down.

"My son," he said with vehemence, "I know wherefore you have come, but it is of no avail. I cannot lend the keys again."

I replied that, on the contrary, I hoped he would give them to me at once.

"It is impossible," he repeated. "I did wrong, exceeding wrong. I will never part with them again."

"Why not?"

He hesitated, and then said slowly:

"The old clerk, Abraham Kelly, died last night." He paused, and then went on: "The doctor has just been here to tell me of that which is a mystery to him. I do not wish the people of the place to know it, and only to me he has mentioned it, but he has discovered plainly on the throat of the old man, and also, but more faintly on the child's, marks as of strangulation. None but he has observed it, and he is at a loss how to account for it. I, alas! can account for it but in one way, but in one way!"

I did not see what all this had to do with the crypt, but to humour the old man, I asked what that way was.

"It is a long story, and, haply, to a stranger it may appear but foolishness, but I will even tell it; for I perceive that unless I furnish a reason for withholding the keys, you will not cease to entreat me for them.

"I told you at first when you inquired of me concerning the crypt, that it had been closed these thirty years, and so it was. Thirty years ago a certain Sir Roger Despard departed this life, even the Lord of the manor of Wet Waste and Dyke Fens, the last of his family, which is now, thank the Lord, extinct. He was a man of a vile life, neither fearing God nor regarding man, nor having compassion on innocence, and the Lord appeared to have given him over to the tormentors even in this world, for he suffered many things of his vices, more especially from drunkenness, in which seasons, and they were many, he was as one possessed by seven devils, being an abomination to his household and a root of bitterness to all, both high and low.

"And, at last, the cup of his iniquity being full to the brim, he came to die, and I went to exhort him on his deathbed; for I heard that terror had come upon him, and that evil imaginations encompassed him so thick on every side, that few of them that were with him could abide in his presence. But when I saw him I perceived that there was no place of repentance left for him, and he scoffed at me and my superstition, even as he lay dying, and swore there was no God and no angel, and all were damned even as he was. And the next day, towards evening, the pains of death came upon him, and he raved the more exceedingly, inasmuch as he said he was being strangled by the Evil One. Now on his table was his hunting knife, and with his last strength he crept and laid hold upon it, no man withstanding him, and swore a great oath that if he went down to burn in hell, he would leave one of his hands behind on earth, and that it would never rest until it had drawn blood from the throat of another and strangled him, even as he himself was being strangled. And he cut off his own right hand at the wrist, and no man dared go near him to stop him, and the blood went through the floor, even down to the ceiling of the room below, and thereupon he died.

"And they called me in the night, and told me of his oath, and I counselled that no man should speak of it, and I took

the dead hand, which none had ventured to touch, and I laid
it beside him in his coffin; for I thought it better he should
take it with him, so that he might have it, if haply some
day after much tribulation he should perchance be moved to
stretch forth his hands towards God. But the story got spread
about, and the people were affrighted, so, when he came to
be buried in the place of his fathers, he being the last of his
family, and the crypt likewise full, I had it closed, and kept
the keys myself, and suffered no man to enter therein any
more; for truly he was a man of an evil life, and the devil is
not yet wholly overcome, nor cast chained into the lake of
fire. So in time the story died out, for in thirty years much
is forgotten. And when you came and asked me for the keys,
I was at the first minded to withhold them; but I thought it
was a vain superstition, and I perceived that you do but ask a
second time for what is first refused; so I let you have them,
seeing it was not an idle curiosity, but a desire to improve
the talent committed to you, that led you to require them."

The old man stopped, and I remained silent, wondering
what would be the best way to get them just once more.

"Surely, sir," I said at last, "one so cultivated and deeply
read as yourself cannot be biased by an idle superstition."

"I trust not," he replied, "and yet—it is a strange thing
that since the crypt was opened two people have died, and
the mark is plain upon the throat of the old man and visible
on the young child. No blood was drawn, but the second
time the grip was stronger than the first. The third time,
perchance—"

"Superstition such as that," I said with authority, "is an
entire want of faith in God. You once said so yourself."

I took a high moral tone which is often efficacious with
conscientious, humble-minded people.

He agreed, and accused himself of not having faith as a
grain of mustard seed; but even when I had got him so far as
that, I had a severe struggle for the keys. It was only when

I finally explained to him that if any malign influence had been let loose the first day, at any rate, it was out now for good or evil, and no further going or coming of mine could make any difference, that I finally gained my point. I was young, and he was old; and, being much shaken by what had occurred, he gave way at last, and I wrested the keys from him.

I will not deny that I went down the steps that day with a vague, indefinable repugnance, which was only accentuated by the closing of the two doors behind me. I remembered then, for the first time, the faint jangling of the key and other sounds which I had noticed the first day, and how one of the skulls had fallen. I went to the place where it still lay. I have already said these walls of skulls were built up so high as to be within a few inches of the top of the low archways that led into more distant portions of the vault. The displacement of the skull in question had left a small hole just large enough for me to put my hand through. I noticed for the first time, over the archway above it, a carved coat-of-arms, and the name, now almost obliterated, of Despard. This, no doubt, was the Despard vault. I could not resist moving a few more skulls and looking in, holding my candle as near the aperture as I could. The vault was full. Piled high, one upon another, were old coffins, and remnants of coffins, and strewn bones. I attribute my present determination to be cremated to the painful impression produced on me by this spectacle. The coffin nearest the archway alone was intact, save for a large crack across the lid. I could not get a ray from my candle to fall on the brass plates, but I felt no doubt this was the coffin of the wicked Sir Roger. I put back the skulls, including the one which had rolled down, and carefully finished my work. I was not there much more than an hour, but I was glad to get away.

If I could have left Wet Waste at once I should have done so, for I had a totally unreasonable longing to leave the place; but I found that only one train stopped during the day at the

station from which I had come, and that it would not be possible to be in time for it that day.

Accordingly I submitted to the inevitable, and wandered
about with Brian for the remainder of the afternoon and until late in the evening, sketching and smoking. The day was
oppressively hot, and even after the sun had set across the
burnt stretches of the wolds, it seemed to grow very little
cooler. Not a breath stirred. In the evening, when I was tired
of loitering in the lanes, I went up to my own room, and after
contemplating afresh my finished study of the fresco, I suddenly set to work to write the part of my paper bearing upon
it. As a rule, I write with difficulty, but that evening words
came to me with winged speed, and with them a hovering
impression that I must make haste, that I was much pressed
for time. I wrote and wrote, until my candles guttered out
and left me trying to finish by the moonlight, which, until I
endeavoured to write by it, seemed as clear as day.

I had to put away my MS., and, feeling it was too early
to go to bed, for the church clock was just counting out ten,
I sat down by the open window and leaned out to try and
catch a breath of air. It was a night of exceptional beauty;
and as I looked out my nervous haste and hurry of mind
were allayed. The moon, a perfect circle, was—if so poetic an
expression be permissible—as it were, sailing across a calm
sky. Every detail of the little village was as clearly illuminated by its beams as if it were broad day; so, also, was the
adjacent church with its primeval yews, while even the wolds
beyond were dimly indicated, as if through tracing paper.

I sat a long time leaning against the window-sill. The
heat was still intense. I am not, as a rule, easily elated or
readily cast down; but as I sat that light in the lonely village
on the moors, with Brian's head against my knee, how, or
why, I know not, a great depression gradually came upon me.

My mind went back to the crypt and the countless dead
who had been laid there. The sight of the goal to which all

human life, and strength, and beauty, travel in the end, had
not affected me at the time, but now the very air about me
seemed heavy with death.

What was the good, I asked myself, of working and toil-
ing, and grinding down my heart and youth in the mill of
long and strenuous effort, seeing that in the grave folly and
talent, idleness and labour lie together, and are alike forgotten? Labour seemed to stretch before me till my heart ached
to think of it, to stretch before me even to the end of life,
and then came, as the recompense of my labour—the grave.
Even if I succeeded, if, after wearing my life threadbare with
toil, I succeeded, what remained to me in the end? The grave.
A little sooner, while the hands and eyes were still strong to
labour, or a little later, when all power and vision had been
taken from them; sooner or later only—*the grave.*

I do not apologise for the excessively morbid tenor of
these reflections, as I hold that they were caused by the lunar
effects which I have endeavoured to transcribe. The moon in
its various quarterings has always exerted a marked influence
on what I may call the sub-dominant, namely, the poetic side
of my nature.

I roused myself at last, when the moon came to look ill
upon me where I sat, and, leaving the window open, I pulled
myself together and went to bed.

I fell asleep almost immediately, but I do not fancy I
could have been asleep very long when I was wakened by Brian. He was growling in a low, muffled tone, as he sometimes
did in his sleep, when his nose was buried in his rug. I called
out to him to shut up; and as he did not do so, turned in
bed to find my match box or something to throw at him. The
moonlight was still in the room, and as I looked at him I saw
him raise his head and evidently wake up. I admonished him,
and was just on the point of falling asleep when he began
to growl again in a low, savage manner that waked me most

effectually. Presently he shook himself and got up, and began prowling about the room. I sat up in bed and called to him, but he paid no attention. Suddenly I saw him stop short in the moonlight; he showed his teeth, and crouched down, his eyes following something in the air. I looked at him in horror. Was he going mad? His eyes were glaring, and his head moved slightly as if he were following the rapid movements of an enemy. Then, with a furious snarl, he suddenly sprang from the ground, and rushed in great leaps across the room towards me, dashing himself against the furniture, his eyes rolling, snatching and tearing wildly in the air with his teeth. I saw he had gone mad. I leaped out of bed, and rushing at him, caught him by the throat. The moon had gone behind a cloud; but in the darkness I felt him turn upon me, felt him rise up, and his teeth close in my throat. I was being strangled. With all the strength of despair, I kept my grip of his neck, and, dragging him across the room, tried to crush in his head against the iron rail of my bedstead. It was my only chance. I felt the blood running down my neck. I was suffocating. After one moment of frightful struggle, I beat his head against the bar and heard his skull give way. I felt him give one strong shudder, a groan, and then I fainted away.

When I came to myself I was lying on the floor, surrounded by the people of the house, my reddened hands still clutching Brian's throat. Someone was holding a candle towards me, and the draught from the window made it flare and waver. I looked at Brian. He was stone dead. The blood from his battered head was trickling slowly over my hands. His great jaw was fixed in something that—in the uncertain light—I could not see.

They turned the light a little.

"Oh, God!" I shrieked. "There! Look! Look!"

"He's off his head," said some one, and I fainted again.

I was ill for about a fortnight without regaining consciousness, a waste of time of which even now I cannot think without poignant regret. When I did recover consciousness, I found I was being carefully nursed by the old clergyman and the people of the house. I have often heard the unkindness of the world in general inveighed against, but for my part I can honestly say that I have received many more kindnesses than I have time to repay. Country people especially are remarkably attentive to strangers in illness.

I could not rest until I had seen the doctor who attended me, and had received his assurance that I should be equal to reading my paper on the appointed day. This pressing anxiety removed, I told him of what I had seen before I fainted the second time. He listened attentively, and then assured me, in a manner that was intended to be soothing, that I was suffering from an hallucination, due, no doubt, to the shock of my dog's sudden madness.

"Did you see the dog after it was dead?" I asked.

He said he did. The whole jaw was covered with blood and foam; the teeth certainly seemed convulsively fixed, but the case being evidently one of extraordinarily virulent hydrophobia, owing to the intense heat, he had had the body buried immediately.

My companion stopped speaking as we reached our lodgings, and went upstairs. Then, lighting a candle, he slowly turned down his collar.

"You see I have the marks still," he said, "but I have no fear of dying of hydrophobia. I am told such peculiar scars could not have been made by the teeth of a dog. If you look closely you see the pressure of the five fingers. That is the reason why I wear high collars."

THE MIDDLE TOE OF THE RIGHT FOOT
Ambrose Bierce
(1890)

1

It is well known that the old Manton house is haunted. In all the rural district near about, and even in the town of Marshall, a mile away, not one person of unbiased mind entertains a doubt of it; incredulity is confined to those opinionated persons who will be called "cranks" as soon as the useful word shall have penetrated the intellectual demesne of the Marshall *Advance*. The evidence that the house is haunted is of two kinds: the testimony of disinterested witnesses who have had ocular proof, and that of the house itself. The former may be disregarded and ruled out on any of the various grounds of objection which may be urged against it by the ingenious; but facts within the observation of all are material and controlling.

In the first place, the Manton house has been unoccupied by mortals for more than ten years, and with its outbuildings is slowly falling into decay—a circumstance which in itself the judicious will hardly venture to ignore. It stands a little way off the loneliest reach of the Marshall and Harriston road, in an opening which was once a farm and is still disfigured with strips of rotting fence and half covered with brambles overrunning a stony and sterile soil long unacquainted with the plow. The house itself is in tolerably good condition, though badly weather-stained and in dire need of attention from the glazier, the smaller male population of the region having attested in the manner of its kind its disapproval of dwelling without dwellers. It is two stories in height, nearly square, its front pierced by a single doorway flanked on each side by a window boarded up to the very top. Corresponding windows above, not protected, serve to admit light and rain to the rooms of the upper floor. Grass and weeds grow pretty rankly all about, and a few shade trees, somewhat the worse for wind, and leaning all in one direction, seem to be making a concerted effort to run away. In short, as the Marshall town humorist explained in the columns of the *Advance,* "the proposition that the Manton house is badly haunted is the only logical conclusion from the premises." The fact that in this dwelling Mr. Manton thought it expedient one night some ten years ago to rise and cut the throats of his wife and two small children, removing at once to another part of the country, has no doubt done its share in directing public attention to the fitness of the place for supernatural phenomena.

To this house, one summer evening, came four men in a wagon. Three of them promptly alighted, and the one who had been driving hitched the team to the only remaining post of what had been a fence. The fourth remained seated in the wagon. "Come," said one of his companions, approaching him, while the others moved away in the direction of the dwelling—"this is the place."

The man addressed did not move. "By God!" he said harshly, "this is a trick, and it looks to me as if you were in it."

"Perhaps I am," the other said, looking him straight in the face and speaking in a tone which had something of contempt in it. "You will remember, however, that the choice of place was with your own assent left to the other side. Of course if you are afraid of spooks—"

"I am afraid of nothing," the man interrupted with another oath, and sprang to the ground. The two then joined the others at the door, which one of them had already opened with some difficulty, caused by rust of lock and hinge. All entered. Inside it was dark, but the man who had unlocked the door produced a candle and matches and made a light. He then unlocked a door on their right as they stood in the passage. This gave them entrance to a large, square room that the candle but dimly lighted. The floor had a thick carpeting of dust, which partly muffled their footfalls. Cobwebs were in the angles of the walls and depended from the ceiling like strips of rotting lace, making undulatory movements in the disturbed air. The room had two windows in adjoining sides, but from neither could anything be seen except the rough inner surfaces of boards a few inches from the glass. There was no fireplace, no furniture; there was nothing: besides the cobwebs and the dust, the four men were the only objects there which were not a part of the structure.

Strange enough they looked in the yellow light of the candle. The one who had so reluctantly alighted was especially spectacular—he might have been called sensational. He was of middle age, heavily built, deep chested and broad shouldered. Looking at his figure, one would have said that he had a giant's strength; at his features, that he would use it like a giant. He was clean shaven, his hair rather closely cropped and gray. His low forehead was seamed with wrinkles above the eyes, and over the nose these became vertical. The heavy black brows followed the same law, saved from meeting only by an upward turn at what would otherwise have been the point of contact. Deeply sunken beneath these, glowed in the obscure light a pair of eyes of uncertain color, but obviously enough too small. There was something forbidding in their expression, which was not bettered by the cruel mouth and wide jaw. The nose was well enough, as noses go; one does not expect much of noses. All that was sinister in the man's face seemed accentuated by an unnatural pallor—he appeared altogether bloodless.

The appearance of the other men was sufficiently commonplace: they were such persons as one meets and forgets that he met. All were younger than the man described, between whom and the eldest of the others, who stood apart, there was apparently no kindly feeling. They avoided looking at each other.

"Gentlemen," said the man holding the candle and keys, "I believe everything is right. Are you ready, Mr. Rosser?"

The man standing apart from the group bowed and smiled.

"And you, Mr. Grossmith?"

The heavy man bowed and scowled.

"You will be pleased to remove your outer clothing."

Their hats, coats, waistcoats and neckwear were soon removed and thrown outside the door, in the passage. The man with the candle now nodded, and the fourth man—he who had urged Grossmith to leave the wagon—produced from the pocket of his overcoat two long, murderous-looking bowie-knives, which he drew now from their leather scabbards.

"They are exactly alike," he said, presenting one to each of the two principals—for by this time the dullest observer would have understood the nature of this meeting. It was to be a duel to the death.

Each combatant took a knife, examined it critically near the candle and tested the strength of blade and handle across his lifted knee. Their persons were then searched in turn, each by the second of the other.

"If it is agreeable to you, Mr. Grossmith," said the man holding the light, "you will place yourself in that corner."

He indicated the angle of the room farthest from the door, whither Grossmith retired, his second parting from him with a grasp of the hand which had nothing of cordiality in it. In the angle nearest the door Mr. Rosser stationed himself, and after a whispered consultation his second left him, joining the other near the door. At that moment the candle was suddenly extinguished, leaving all in profound darkness. This may have been done by a draught from the opened door; whatever the cause, the effect was startling.

"Gentlemen," said a voice which sounded strangely unfamiliar in the altered condition affecting the relations of the senses—"gentlemen, you will not move until you hear the closing of the outer door."

A sound of trampling ensued, then the closing of the inner door; and finally the outer one closed with a concussion which shook the entire building.

A few minutes afterward a belated farmer's boy met a light wagon which was being driven furiously toward the town of Marshall. He declared that behind the two figures on the front seat stood a third, with its hands upon the bowed shoulders of the others, who appeared to struggle vainly to free themselves from its grasp. This figure, unlike the others, was clad in white, and had undoubtedly boarded the wagon as it passed the haunted house. As the lad could boast a considerable former experience with the supernatural thereabouts his word had the weight justly due to the testimony of an expert. The story (in connection with the next day's events) eventually appeared in the *Advance,* with some slight literary embellishments and a concluding intimation that the gentlemen referred to would be allowed the use of the paper's columns for their version of the night's adventure. But the privilege remained without a claimant.

2

The events that led up to this "duel in the dark" were simple enough. One evening three young men of the town of Marshall were sitting in a quiet corner of the porch of the village hotel, smoking and discussing such matters as three educated young men of a Southern village would naturally find interesting. Their names were King, Sancher and Rosser. At a little distance, within easy hearing, but taking no part in the conversation, sat a fourth. He was a stranger to the others. They merely knew that on his arrival by the stage-coach that afternoon he had written in the hotel register the name Robert Grossmith. He had not been observed to speak to anyone except the hotel clerk. He seemed, indeed, singularly fond of his own company—or, as the *personnel* of the *Advance* expressed it, "grossly addicted to evil associations." But then it should be said in justice to the stranger that the *personnel* was himself of a too convivial disposition fairly to judge one differently gifted, and had, moreover, experienced a slight rebuff in an effort at an "interview."

"I hate any kind of deformity in a woman," said King, "whether natural or—acquired. I have a theory that any physical defect has its correlative mental and moral defect."

"I infer, then," said Rosser, gravely, "that a lady lacking the moral advantage of a nose would find the struggle to become Mrs. King an arduous enterprise."

"Of course you may put it that way," was the reply; "but, seriously, I once threw over a most charming girl on learning quite accidentally that she had suffered amputation of a toe. My conduct was brutal if you like, but if I had married that girl I should have been miserable for life and should have made her so."

"Whereas," said Sancher, with a light laugh, "by marrying a gentleman of more liberal views she escaped with a parted throat."

"Ah, you know to whom I refer. Yes, she married Manton, but I don't know about his liberality; I'm not sure but he cut her throat because he discovered that she lacked that excellent thing in woman, the middle toe of the right foot."

"Look at that chap!" said Rosser in a low voice, his eyes fixed upon the stranger.

That chap was obviously listening intently to the conversation.

"Damn his impudence!" muttered King—"what ought we to do?"

"That's an easy one," Rosser replied, rising. "Sir," he continued, addressing the stranger, "I think it would be better if you would remove your chair to the other end of the veranda. The presence of gentlemen is evidently an unfamiliar situation to you."

The man sprang to his feet and strode forward with clenched hands, his face white with rage. All were now standing. Sancher stepped between the belligerents.

"You are hasty and unjust," he said to Rosser; "this gentleman has done nothing to deserve such language."

But Rosser would not withdraw a word. By the custom of the country and the time there could be but one outcome to the quarrel.

"I demand the satisfaction due to a gentleman," said the stranger, who had become more calm. "I have not an acquaintance in this region. Perhaps you, sir," bowing to Sancher, "will be kind enough to represent me in this matter."

Sancher accepted the trust—somewhat reluctantly it must be confessed, for the man's appearance and manner were not at all to his liking. King, who during the colloquy had hardly removed his eyes from the stranger's face and had not spoken a word, consented with a nod to act for Rosser, and the upshot of it was that, the principals having retired, a meeting was arranged for the next evening. The nature of the arrangements has been already disclosed. The duel with knives in a dark room was once a commoner feature of Southwestern life than it is likely to be again. How thin a veneering of "chivalry" covered the essential brutality of the code under which such encounters were possible we shall see.

3

In the blaze of a midsummer noonday the old Manton house was hardly true to its traditions. It was of the earth, earthy. The sunshine caressed it warmly and affectionately, with evident disregard of its bad reputation. The grass greening all the expanse in its front seemed to grow, not rankly, but with a natural and joyous exuberance, and the weeds blossomed quite like plants. Full of charming lights and shadows and populous with pleasant-voiced birds, the neglected shade trees no longer struggled to run away, but bent reverently beneath their burdens of sun and song. Even in the glassless upper windows was an expression of peace and contentment, due to the light within. Over the stony fields the visible heat danced with a lively tremor incompatible with the gravity which is an attribute of the supernatural.

Such was the aspect under which the place presented itself to Sheriff Adams and two other men who had come out from Marshall to look at it. One of these men was Mr. King, the sheriff's deputy; the other, whose name was Brewer, was a brother of the late Mrs. Manton. Under a beneficent law of the State relating to property which has been for a certain period abandoned by an owner whose residence cannot be ascertained, the sheriff was legal custodian of the Manton farm and appurtenances thereunto belonging. His present visit was in mere perfunctory compliance with some order of a court in which Mr. Brewer had an action to get possession of the property as heir to his deceased sister. By a mere coincidence, the visit was made on the day after the night that Deputy King had unlocked the house for another and very different purpose. His presence now was not of his own choosing: he had been ordered to accompany his superior and at the moment could think of nothing more prudent than simulated alacrity in obedience to the command.

Carelessly opening the front door, which to his surprise was not locked, the sheriff was amazed to see, lying on the floor of the passage into which it opened, a confused heap of men's apparel. Examination showed it to consist of two hats, and the same number of coats, waistcoats and scarves, all in a remarkably good state of preservation, albeit somewhat defiled by the dust in which they lay. Mr. Brewer was equally astonished, but Mr. King's emotion is not of record. With a new and lively interest in his own actions the sheriff now unlatched and pushed open a door on the right, and the three entered. The room was apparently vacant—no; as their eyes became accustomed to the dimmer light something was visible in the farthest angle of the wall. It was a human figure—that of a man crouching close in the corner. Something in the attitude made the intruders halt when they had barely passed the threshold. The figure more and more clearly defined itself. The man was upon one knee, his back in the angle of the wall, his shoulders elevated to the level of his ears, his hands before his face, palms outward, the fingers spread and crooked like claws; the white face turned upward on the retracted neck had an expression of unutterable fright, the mouth half open, the eyes incredibly expanded. He was stone dead. Yet, with the exception of a bowie-knife, which had evidently fallen from his own hand, not another object was in the room.

In thick dust that covered the floor were some confused footprints near the door and along the wall through which it opened. Along one of the adjoining walls, too, past the boarded-up windows, was the trail made by the man himself in reaching his corner. Instinctively in approaching the body the three men followed that trail. The sheriff grasped one of the outthrown arms; it was as rigid as iron, and the application of a gentle force rocked the entire body without altering the relation of its parts. Brewer, pale with excitement, gazed intently into the distorted face. "God of mercy!" he suddenly cried, "it is Manton!"

"You are right," said King, with an evident attempt at calmness: "I knew Manton. He then wore a full beard and his hair long, but this is he."

He might have added: "I recognized him when he challenged Rosser. I told Rosser and Sancher who he was before we played him this horrible trick. When Rosser left this dark room at our heels, forgetting his outer clothing in the excitement, and driving away with us in his shirt sleeves— all through the discreditable proceedings we knew whom we were dealing with, murderer and coward that he was!"

But nothing of this did Mr. King say. With his better light he was trying to penetrate the mystery of the man's death. That he had not once moved from the corner where he had been stationed; that his posture was that of neither attack nor defense; that he had dropped his weapon; that he had obviously perished of sheer horror of something that he saw—these were circumstances which Mr. King's disturbed intelligence could not rightly comprehend.

Groping in intellectual darkness for a clew to his maze of doubt, his gaze, directed mechanically downward in the way of one who ponders momentous matters, fell upon some- thing which, there, in the light of day and in the presence of living companions, affected him with terror. In the dust of years that lay thick upon the floor—leading from the door by which they had entered, straight across the room to within a yard of Manton's crouching corpse—were three parallel lines of footprints—light but definite impressions of bare feet, the outer ones those of small children, the inner a woman's. From the point at which they ended they did not return; they pointed all one way. Brewer, who had observed them at the same moment, was leaning forward in an attitude of rapt attention, horribly pale.

"Look at that!" he cried, pointing with both hands at the nearest print of the woman's right foot, where she had ap- parently stopped and stood. "The middle toe is missing—it was Gertrude!"

Gertrude was the late Mrs. Manton, sister to Mr. Brewer.

THE HAUNTED HAND
Henry Seton Merriman
(1894)

"Can you get it under?"

"Possibly," answered the Captain rather curtly. He was curt even to his interlocutor—a privileged person on board—a tall, fair man, with hair that was almost colourless, and manners subtly suggestive of velvet over steel.

They both stepped back a little from the forward hatch. The decks were getting too hot, despite the water that ran towards the scuppers. It was very unfortunate that the *Mahanaddy's* cargo should have ignited on this particular voyage—when the Persian Mission was on board, and the whole Press agog for their arrival at Plymouth. The Captain was mentally vowing that if he had any influence whatever with the directors, and if the good old ship pulled through this, the *Mahanaddy* should never carry that cursed Egyptian cotton again.

In the meantime they were pounding through the Bay of Biscay in a grey, warm gale of wind, such as dries the skin and sets the nerve to tingle. They were heading straight for Ushant—they were racing with the fire that burnt inside the good ship like some fell disease. And she, as if she had sense and knew her danger, lifted her great black prow to the horizon, and strained forwards through the hissing sea. The spray thrown up by the cut-water dried immediately on her hot sides, leaving the brine on the black paint. Between the planks the pitch exuded, black and glistening like jet. It stuck to the boots of the men and officers, who worked like souls possessed—tired, worn, and dirty.

"And if you don't get it under?" said the fair man softly—he spoke as if his listener was in pain, needing gentle treatment.

The Captain glanced over the rail to the wild sea, which seemed to gloat over their trouble, and shrugged his shoulders significantly.

"It is awkward," admitted the other—and he smiled softly.

As has been previously mentioned he was a privileged person. He was the second in command of the Persian Mission, and it was whispered in certain circles that he was second to none in that particular form of diplomacy which was his—namely, the management of Oriental potentates. His chief was below, in his stateroom, penning one of those perfectly-worded literary despatches for which he was famed. It seemed likely that this particular production was destined to be picked up in a bottle by a sardine fisher of the Morbihan—the work of a vanished hand—but that in the estimation of the writer was no reason why it should not be worthy of his reputation. So he sat in the cabin of what seemed to be a doomed ship, and addressed his rounded periods to Her Majesty's Secretary for Foreign Affairs.

"How are they getting on aft?" said the Captain suddenly.

"Pretty well. The ladies have found it all out, though. They see through our blandishments. They know that it is touch and go."

The Captain turned aside to give an order to one of the quarter masters, and, when that was executed, there was nothing more to be done. All that human brain could devise, human hands had executed. The hatches were battened and covered deep in soaked canvas. The bulkheads were screwed close—the decks were kept constantly under water. The question now was whether the fire could be smothered or not, and the answer was with Fate.

"I wish," said the Captain, "that you would go aft and keep up their hearts."

The fair man laughed.

"How?" he said. "Give them a meal?"

"Can't give them any more meals, they have just had lunch."

"Well," said the diplomat, "I will order tea—it is a good thing to die on."

"No—spin them a yarn or something. Distract their attention. It will be settled one way or the other in half-an-hour."

"All right," turning on his heel, "I'll tell them a little story." He lounged aft to where the ladies—there were only five of them—sat in a group, and drew forward a chair and seated himself, crossing one leg over the other, and drawing up reflectively a creaseless black sock. He made no pretence of concealment out of respect for the ladies, seeming to take it for granted that they all (including three young girls) must know that somewhere the sock ends and the leg begins.

"I have," he said, "been telling the Captain a little story—an improving tale with no moral. They lead a slow and monotonous life, these mariners; I do my best to relieve the dreariness of it."

"Tell us the story," said the Great Lady. She guessed that no questions were to be asked.

"It is," he explained, "a horrible tale! A blood-curdling little narrative which will sound nasty in the daylight."

The three young girls drew in their chairs, while the men smiled, serenely sure of their own nerves.

"The sort of tale," continued the narrator, "to haunt you. It haunts me—not the whole of me—only that hand."

He raised in the air his right arm, and contemplated, reflectively, a frail, brown-fingered hand.

"That hand," he added with a vague smile, "is haunted. It has a special ghost of its own. I sometimes wake up in the night, and the ghost is there.

"They," and he slowly curved his fingers, "have hold of it."

After a little pause, the haunted hand returned to the black sock.

"It was years ago," he began, "when I" (with an imperceptible glance towards the Great Lady) "was at the bottom of the tree. I was attaché in a great city. The peace of Europe was hanging by a thread—not only in the newspapers. A secret treaty was in course of completion between England and another Power. A draft of this treaty was sent to my chief. We had it at the Embassy, and it was rather a white elephant to us, because we suspected that its presence in the house was known to the Government of the country to which we were accredited. While it was in the house the chief asked us all to remain at home in the evening, for we all lived under one roof.

"We dined with him every night. He was a bachelor—a dried up little man with a mind like a magnet. He was the very calmest little man I have ever dealt with, just the man for the place; for there was no very stable Government in the country at that time, and he had to keep four or five parties in a good humour.

"After a long dinner on the third evening we played pool, and went on playing very late, long after the servants had gone to bed.

"It was the chief who heard the sound of stealthy keys being thrust into the lock of the front door, which was immediately below his dressing-room, whither he had gone to get change for a five—for a large coin.

"He came back to the billiard-room looking a little calmer than usual.

"'You chaps,' he said, putting on his coat, 'there is someone trying to force the front door. There is a light in the hall. Shall we go down and watch the operations?'

"We, knowing him too well to take this for a joke, laid aside our cues and followed him without waiting to put on our coats.

"We all crept downstairs and stood on the mat in the dim light of the lowered gas. Five of us—listening to the operations of the skilled workman on the other side of the door.

"This, after the manner of the doors of that country, had no bolts, but only a large lock and chain in one piece with the handle.

"After trying several keys, the idea of opening the door by unlocking it was apparently abandoned. Presently the evil-looking point of a centre-bit emerged from the woodwork of the massive panel with a sound like a dog eating biscuits. The chief motioned us to stand aside, for it was only natural to suppose that an eye would be applied to the hole when completed. Owing to the thickness of the woodwork the limit of vision through the aperture could only be small, and by crouching down we easily made ourselves invisible.

"In a marvellously short space of time there was a hole as large as that saucer in the door.

"We five crouched around it, watching it like terriers at a rat-hole.

"Then an idea struck me—a rare occurrence—and I crept back to the hat-stand, where a leather dog-leash hung beside the chief's top hat.

"He gave a little nod as I drew the thong towards me; for he read thoughts as other men read print.

"I passed the noose end through the steel swivel, and, crawling on my knees to the door, held the loop, thus made, round the hole. I was just in time. The man outside had apparently been delaying in order to turn up his sleeve. He was in no hurry; and we wondered afterwards what had become of the police guard specially told off to watch the British Embassy.

"A dirty hand—essentially the hand of toil—came through, inside my slip knot. This was followed by a bare white arm.

I felt inclined to laugh, and my two hands, outstretched to hold the dog-leash in place, shook visibly.

"The elbow came through and curved, while the dirty fingers crept over the mechanism of the lock and chain with the intelligence of a perfect knowledge.

"A little further until the muscles of the upper arm were visible—then I drew the noose tight, cutting deep into the sinews. Like cats, four pairs of hands pounced upon the hand and arm, holding it against the woodwork, while the grey fingers worked convulsively. We drew the arm through—right up to the shoulder; and they held it in place while I made fast the stout dog-leash to the two bolts of the knocker which jutted out at the top of the door.

"'A neat job!' said the chief, as we stood back and contemplated the twitching white arm. 'A very neat job. There is no hurry,' he added, beginning leisurely to unchain the door.

"It happened that I was of an athletic turn of mind in those days, and when I proposed opening the door my colleagues stepped back and ceded to me the place of honour.

"I opened it with a jerk and thrust out my hand—*that* hand—to where I knew his throat must be.

"My fingers seemed to go right through it. I grasped something that felt like a chain in a tangle of warm, wet seaweed. I had clutched his spine!

"His companions had for their own protection cut the throat of this poor hired expert. They had done it so effectually that the head was only retained by the vertebral column. In his agony he had grasped the bell with his right hand, and his rigid fingers still held to the handle. He was crucified face foremost against the door."

There was a pause, and the fair man looked round with his grave smile, which was, curiously enough, no longer meaningless and placid, but very wise with the Wisdom of Life, and not of Books.

"And so," he said, "my hand is haunted. It sometimes wakes up at night grasping a chain in a tangle of warm and dripping seaweed!"

"Ladies," said the Captain, "after so exciting a story it may scarcely interest you to know it, but the fire has been got under."

THE SKELETON HAND
Agnes Macleod
(1894)

I am about to relate some events which took place in the
early part of this century, in a remote little fishing village on
the south coast of Devonshire. The occurrences are in themselves so remarkable that they have been well known to the
present generation of inhabitants; but as things get altered in
oral transmission through many persons, it has been thought
well to place this record in writing.

Near the village of Jodziel, in a pretty little cottage on
the top of the bright red sandstone cliff which overhangs the
village, lived two maiden sisters, the Misses Rutson. Their
father, a sea-captain, had died a year before the events I am
about to relate occurred. Their mother had died in giving
birth to the younger sister, Anne, who was now a most beautiful girl of eighteen. The Misses Rutson were very devotedly
attached to one another, and were much beloved by the village neighbours. The hamlet being a very sequestered one,
they seldom saw any one from the outer world except occasionally sailors, who would stroll along the cliff from Plymouth or from other fishing villages along the coast. In the
autumn of 1813 a pressgang visited South Devon and made
their headquarters for some time in the village of Jodziel.
The captain, a certain Captain Sinclair by name—a coarse
brutal fellow in appearance—was very much struck by the
extraordinary beauty of Miss Anne. He forced himself upon

her, and continued paying her the most distasteful attentions, which the gentle girl did her very utmost to check,
but in vain. The day before Captain Sinclair left Jodziel,
he made a formal offer of marriage to Miss Anne, which in
the presence of her sister she immediately and decisively declined. Captain Sinclair flew into the most violent passion,
swore he had never been thwarted yet by any woman, and
that she should belong to him or never marry at all. Anne
was so much upset by the terrible scene, and by Captain
Sinclair's outrageous language, that her sister was very glad
when an invitation from an aunt residing in London gave
Anne a few weeks' much-needed change. Mrs. Travers was
the only near relative remaining to the Misses Rutson, and
owing to various circumstances the sisters had seen but little
of their aunt, though with Maurice Travers, her only son,
they were better acquainted. Maurice's regiment had been
quartered for the summer of 1813 at Plymouth, and he had
frequently been over to see his cousins, and many a pleasant
summer day had they spent wandering along the beautiful
Devonshire coast. Miss Rutson had not been slow to perceive
that stronger attractions than those of mere scenery brought
the young officer so constantly to their cottage, and she was
not therefore very much surprised at receiving one morning,
about three weeks after Anne's departure from home, a letter
announcing her engagement to her cousin, Maurice Travers,
and her immediate return to Jodziel. It was decided that the
marriage should take place early in the following May, and I
will now quote one or two passages from Miss Rutson's diary
at this time.

"*May* 1.—Such a horrid meeting we have just had. Anne
and I had been for a stroll along the shore when we noticed a
little boat which lay drawn up under a rock at some distance,
when Anne's eyes, which are keener than mine, caught sight
of the name painted in gold letters. 'Ah, sister, come away,'
she cried; 'it is a boat from the *Raven*. I thought Captain

Sinclair was not to be in these waters again; he told me he was to sail for the West Indies last month.' We turned, and were hurriedly retracing our steps towards the house when we heard a cry of *Stop!* I looked at Anne; she was deadly white. 'Run on quick,' I cried; 'I will speak to him.' My heart was beating so fast I could run no longer; besides, I felt it might be well to hear what Captain Sinclair had to say, so I drew myself together and waited. Presently he appeared clambering up the side of the cliff, his swarthy face purple with excitement. 'Where is she?' he gasped. 'I have come back to fetch her; I could not sail without her, my own beautiful Anne!'—'Recollect yourself, sir,' I cried indignantly. 'How dare you speak of my sister in this free manner! She has told you most clearly, and that in my presence, that she looks on your pursuit of her as odious, and she begs, both for her own sake and yours, that you will never attempt to see her again.' 'Do you think I will be daunted by such a speech from a foolish girl?' he answered scornfully; 'no, no, she shall be mine yet, whether she will or no.' 'You are mistaken,' I replied as calmly as I could; 'next Monday she marries our first cousin, Maurice Travers, and will be at peace from your hated persecutions.'

"I shall never forget his scowl of fury as he turned from me and dashed down the cliff, shouting as he did so, 'She shall be mine!' When I got home, feeling very nervous and shaken, who should I find just starting out to seek me but Maurice, who had come three days earlier than we expected him. An hour before I should have felt very cross at having my last quiet hours with Anne so much curtailed, but now I was only too thankful to feel we had a protector near us. He went out after hearing my story, but could see no trace of either boat or its owner.

"*May* 2.—To my great relief the *Raven*, with Captain Sinclair on board, has left Plymouth this morning for the West Indies. Maurice had business at Plymouth, and he took the opportunity of making inquiries concerning the *Raven*, which was, he found, in the very act of putting to sea. I feel, oh, so thankful and relieved.

"*May 4.*—How shall I ever begin to write the events of this most dreadful day! Such a brilliant sunshiny morning, quite like summer, and my darling came down looking like one of the sweet white roses which were just coming into bloom around the windows. I plucked a beautiful spray of them, and she put them in her white satin waistband just before starting for church. I have those roses by me now as I write, but, O my darling! where are you? The wedding was a very quiet one. After the ceremony we had the clergyman and doctor, with their wives and their children, to lunch, and presently Anne rose and said she would go and change her dress. I was going to follow her, but she stopped me with one of her sweet kisses and said, 'Let me have a few moments alone in the old room to say goodbye to it all.' I let her go—when did I ever thwart her in anything? She went, and Maurice began romping with the children, and we ladies cut slices of wedding-cake, to be taken round to village favourites next day, and still Anne did not call. Once, indeed, I had fancied I heard her voice; but when I had gone up stairs her door was locked, and she had not answered my gentle tap, so I came down again, not wishing to intrude upon her privacy. At length, however, Maurice became impatient, and said I must go and fetch her down, or they would never be in time to catch the coach at Plymouth. The door was still locked. When I got up-stairs I knocked, first gently, then more loudly. I was not frightened at first, for there was a door-window in the room leading down a little flight of steps into the garden, and I thought she had gone down these to take a last look at her flowers, so I called to Maurice to run round to the garden, for she must be there. I remained listening at the bedroom door, which in a moment or two flew open, and Maurice, with a very disturbed face, stood before me. 'She has evidently been in the garden,' he said, 'for the door on to the outside steps was open; but there is no one there now.' I made no answer, but flew past him into the bedroom. It needed but a glance to show my darling had gone straight through the room; her gloves and handkerchief were thrown on a chair by the window, and her pale-blue travelling-dress lay undisturbed upon the bed. I ran hastily through the room and garden, which was empty; the gate on to the cliff was ajar, and we noticed (but not till later) that there must have been a struggle at the spot, for some of the lilac boughs were torn down, as if some one had held fast by them and been dragged forcibly away. Maurice and the rest of the party followed me on to the cliff, for the alarm had now become general; for a little while we ran wildly, calling her dear name, but presently Maurice came to me, and drawing my arm within his own, led me back towards the house. 'Some one must be here to receive her when she comes home,' he said gently, and here his lips grew white. 'It might be well to have her bed ready in case—' He was out of the room without finishing his sentence. It was needless; the same horrible fear had already seized on me. The cliff, the terrible cliff; I cannot go on writing, my heart is too heavy.

"*Twelve o'clock.*—They have come back, and, O God! the only trace of her is the spray of white roses I picked for her this morning. They were found on the top of the cliff about half a mile from here. I think they are a message from my darling to me, for they were not trampled on or crushed; she must have taken them carefully and purposely from her belt; they shall never, never leave me.

"*May* 11.—It is a week since that dreadful day, and not the smallest clue to her disappearance. Poor Maurice is half mad with grief; he has sought for her high and low, and spent all the little sum destined for their wedding journey on these vain researches. Now he wanders along the cliff up and down, up and down, the whole of the long day, and then he comes and sits opposite to me with his elbows on his knees, till I tell him it is time for bed, when he goes without a word; but I hear him pacing his room half the night.

"*May* 31.—Maurice has had to join his regiment for foreign service. I am glad: he would have gone mad had he remained inactive here.

"*Sept.* 3.—I have been very ill, but Patty assures me there has not been a trace of any clue during my long time of blessed unconsciousness, and now the terrible aching void is again here. O my darling, my darling, come back!

"*Sept.* 6.—Why should I go on writing? my life henceforth is only waiting."

After this comes a long break of fully twenty years in the diary; then in an aged and trembling character occurs the following entry:—

"*May 4,* 1835.—I don't know what impels me once more to pen this diary; possibly this wild hurricane of wind which is making the house rock like a boat has upset me, but I feel so glad and satisfied, as if my long waiting were nearly over. I have just been up-stairs to see that all is in order for my darling. We have kept everything aired and prepared for her these thirty years, so that she should find all comfortable when she comes home at last. My poor darling, she will only find Patty and me to welcome her. Let me think, this is nearly twenty years ago since we heard of Maurice's death at Waterloo. Oh what a fearful crash! and how that rumbling noise goes on sounding as if the cliff had given way."

Here the diary abruptly terminates; but the remainder of the tragic story is yet told in that little Devonshire village. The violence of the storm had in very truth caused a subsidence in the cliff, and in doing so had brought to light a skeleton on which yet hung some tattered remnants of what had once been white satin, and from whose bony fingers rolled a tarnished wedding-ring. The bones were collected with tender care and brought to the house of the unhappy sister. She received them without much apparent surprise, directed they should be laid on "Miss Anne's bed up-stairs," and as soon as the men had left the house, went and laid herself upon the bed also, where her faithful maid Patty, coming to see after her an hour later, found her stone-dead, and held tight in her dead grasp was a pair of white gloves and a lace pocket-handkerchief.

The two sisters were laid to rest in one grave, and it was not till after the funeral was over that it was discovered that, through some inadvertence, one of the skeleton hands had not been placed in the coffin with the rest of the body.

At first there was some talk of reopening the grave, but the old maid Patty entreated so earnestly to be allowed to retain the hand that she at last succeeded in carrying her point. A glass case was made by Mrs. Patty's order, and in it the poor hand was placed; and when Mrs. Patty went down to the inn to spend her last remaining years with her daughter the landlady, the case was placed on a shelf close to the old woman's seat, and many a time would she recount the sad story to the sailors who frequented the village inn.

In the spring of 1837 a larger number than usual were gathered round the fireside of the Blue Dragon. A fearful storm, accompanied by violent gusts of hail, swept round the house. Suddenly the door burst open, and a young man entered, half dragging, half supporting an old man, bent and shrunk with age and infirmity. "Here you are, sir," he said to the old man; "this is the Blue Dragon. You won't find a snugger berth between here and Plymouth;" so saying, he thrust the old man into a chair by the fire, and continued, half aside to the company, "Found the old cove wander-ing about the cliffs, and thought he would be blown over, so offered to guide him here. I think he is a little—" and he tapped his forehead significantly. The rest of the party turned round curiously to gaze at the stranger, who, seeming to wake from some reverie, proceeded to order something hot both for himself and his self-constituted guide. The hot gin-and-water seemed further to rouse him, and he began asking a few questions concerning the country and neighbourhood; but in the very act of speaking his attention was suddenly arrested by the sight of the glass case and skeleton hand. He sprang from his chair with a savage cry of mingled terror and dismay. "The hand," he cried, "the hand! why does it point at me? I never meant, O God!—" and he fell down in a fit, rolling and gasping on the floor, and shrieking wildly at intervals, "The hand, the hand!" They raised the wretched man from the floor and laid him on a bed, whilst the doctor was hurriedly summoned. Meanwhile the sufferer continued disjointed mutterings, till, becoming exhausted, he sank into a stupor. On the doctor's arrival, however, he once more roused himself, and asked in a quieter and more composed manner whose the hand was. On being told, he trembled violently, but said: "I am Captain Sinclair; I knew the wedding-day; I told my ship to sail without me from Plymouth, saying I would rejoin her at Falmouth. I meant to bring Anne with me; I hid in the garden, she came into it alone, I rushed forward, threw a shawl I had ready over her head, and carried her away; she resisted with all her might, but I was a strong man, and her cries were stifled by the shawl. Of course I could not get along very fast, and presently I heard voices of those in search of her. She heard them also, and made another frantic effort to free herself. My strength was nearly exhausted, but mad with rage and disappointment, I drew my knife from my belt and stabbed her to the heart, crying fiercely, 'I have kept my oath, you shall never be another's.' Then I hurled the body down the cliff, where I saw it catch in a crevice of the rock. O God!" he cried, shuddering and covering his face with his hands, "I see it now,—that dreadful scene, the blue waves dancing beneath the brilliant sunshine, and that white shapeless mass caught in the frowning cliff with one arm sticking stiffly upwards. I rolled down one or two stones, endeavouring to conceal it; and when I left the spot, all I could see was a hand pointing at me." Here the miserable wretch broke off with a deep groan. In a moment more he sprang up with another wild shout of "The hand, the bloody hand!" and so shrieking, his body fell lifeless to the ground. . . . The skeleton hand in the adjoining room was dropping blood.

THE STORY OF THE BROWN HAND
Sir Arthur Conan Doyle
(1899)

Everyone knows that Sir Dominick Holden, the famous Indian surgeon, made me his heir, and that his death changed me in an hour from a hard-working and impecunious young man to a well-to-do landed proprietor. Many know also that there were at least five people between the inheritance and me, and that Sir Dominick's selection appeared to be altogether arbitrary and whimsical. I can assure them, however, that they are quite mistaken, and that, although I only knew Sir Dominick in the closing years of his life, there were, none the less, very real reasons why he should show his goodwill towards me. As a matter of fact, though I say it myself, no man ever did more for another than I did for my Indian uncle. I cannot expect the story to be believed, but it is so singular that I should feel that it was a breach of duty if I did not put it upon record—so here it is, and your belief or incredulity is your own affair.

Sir Dominick Holden, C.B., K.C.S.I., and I don't know what besides, was the most distinguished Indian surgeon of his day. In the Army originally, he afterwards settled down into civil practice in Bombay, and visited, as a consultant, every part of India. His name is best remembered in connection with the Oriental Hospital, which he founded and supported. The time came, however, when his iron constitution began to show signs of the long strain to which he had

157

subjected it, and his brother practitioners (who were not, perhaps, entirely disinterested upon the point) were unanimous in recommending him to return to England. He held on so long as he could, but at last he developed nervous symptoms of a very pronounced character, and so came back, a broken man, to his native county of Wiltshire. He bought a considerable estate with an ancient manor-house upon the edge of Salisbury Plain, and devoted his old age to the study of Comparative Pathology, which had been his learned hobby all his life, and in which he was a foremost authority.

We of the family were, as may be imagined, much excited by the news of the return of this rich and childless uncle to England. On his part, although by no means exuberant in his hospitality, he showed some sense of his duty to his relations, and each of us in turn had an invitation to visit him. From the accounts of my cousins it appeared to be a melancholy business, and it was with mixed feelings that I at last received my own summons to appear at Rodenhurst. My wife was so carefully excluded in the invitation that my first impulse was to refuse it, but the interests of the children had to be considered, and so, with her consent, I set out one October afternoon upon my visit to Wiltshire, with little thought of what that visit was to entail.

My uncle's estate was situated where the arable land of the plains begins to swell upwards into the rounded chalk hills which are characteristic of the county. As I drove from Dinton Station in the waning light of that autumn day, I was impressed by the weird nature of the scenery. The few scattered cottages of the peasants were so dwarfed by the huge evidences of prehistoric life, that the present appeared to be a dream and the past to be the obtrusive and masterful reality. The road wound through the valleys, formed by a succession of grassy hills, and the summit of each was cut and carved into the most elaborate fortifications, some circular, and some square, but all on a scale which has defied

the winds and the rains of many centuries. Some call them
Roman and some British, but their true origin and the reasons for this particular tract of country being so interlaced
with entrenchments have never been finally made clear. Here
and there on the long, smooth, olive-coloured slopes there
rose small, rounded barrows or tumuli. Beneath them lie the
cremated ashes of the race which cut so deeply into the hills,
but their graves tell us nothing save that a jar full of dust
represents the man who once laboured under the sun.

It was through this weird country that I approached my
uncle's residence of Rodenhurst, and the house was, as I
found, in due keeping with its surroundings. Two broken
and weather-stained pillars, each surmounted by a mutilated
heraldic emblem, flanked the entrance to a neglected drive. A
cold wind whistled through the elms which lined it, and the
air was full of the drifting leaves. At the far end, under the
gloomy arch of trees, a single yellow lamp burned steadily.
In the dim half-light of the coming night I saw a long, low
building stretching out two irregular wings, with deep eaves,
a sloping gambrel roof, and walls which were criss-crossed
with timber balks in the fashion of the Tudors. The cheery
light of a fire flickered in the broad, latticed window to the
left of the low-porched door, and this, as it proved, marked
the study of my uncle, for it was thither that I was led by his
butler in order to make my host's acquaintance.

He was cowering over his fire, for the moist chill of an
English autumn had set him shivering. His lamp was unlit,
and I only saw the red glow of the embers beating upon
a huge, craggy face, with a Red Indian nose and cheek,
and deep furrows and seams from eye to chin, the sinister
marks of hidden volcanic fires. He sprang up at my entrance
with something of an old-world courtesy and welcomed me
warmly to Rodenhurst. At the same time I was conscious,
as the lamp was carried in, that it was a very critical pair of
light-blue eyes which looked out at me from under shaggy

eyebrows, like scouts beneath a bush, and that this outland-
ish uncle of mine was carefully reading off my character with
all the ease of a practised observer and an experienced man
of the world.

For my part I looked at him, and looked again, for I had
never seen a man whose appearance was more fitted to hold
one's attention. His figure was the framework of a giant, but
he had fallen away until his coat dangled straight down in a
shocking fashion from a pair of broad and bony shoulders.
All his limbs were huge yet emaciated, and I could not take
my gaze from his knobby wrists, and long, gnarled hands.
But his eyes—those peering, light-blue eyes—they were the
most arrestive of any of his peculiarities. It was not their
colour alone, nor was it the ambush of hair in which they
lurked; but it was the expression which I read in them. For
the appearance and bearing of the man were masterful, and
one expected a certain corresponding arrogance in his eyes,
but instead of that I read the look which tells of a spirit
cowed and crushed, the furtive, expectant look of the dog
whose master has taken the whip from the rack. I formed
my own medical diagnosis upon one glance at those critical
and yet appealing eyes. I believed that he was stricken with
some mortal ailment, that he knew himself to be exposed to
sudden death, and that he lived in terror of it. Such was my
judgment—a false one, as the event showed; but I mention it
that it may help you to realize the look which I read in his
eyes.

My uncle's welcome was, as I have said, a courteous one,
and in an hour or so I found myself seated between him and
his wife at a comfortable dinner, with curious, pungent del-
icacies upon the table, and a stealthy, quick-eyed Oriental
waiter behind his chair. The old couple had come round to
that tragic imitation of the dawn of life when husband and
wife, having lost or scattered all those who were their inti-
mates, find themselves face to face and alone once more,

their work done, and the end nearing fast. Those who have reached that stage in sweetness and love, who can change their winter into a gentle, Indian summer, have come as victors through the ordeal of life. Lady Holden was a small, alert woman with a kindly eye, and her expression as she glanced at him was a certificate of character to her husband. And yet, though I read a mutual love in their glances, I read also mutual horror, and recognized in her face some reflection of that stealthy fear which I had detected in his. Their talk was sometimes merry and sometimes sad, but there was a forced note in their merriment and a naturalness in their sadness which told me that a heavy heart beat upon either side of me.

We were sitting over our first glass of wine, and the servants had left the room, when the conversation took a turn which produced a remarkable effect upon my host and hostess. I cannot recall what it was which started the topic of the supernatural, but it ended in my showing them that the abnormal in psychical experiences was a subject to which I had, like many neurologists, devoted a great deal of attention. I concluded by narrating my experiences when, as a member of the Psychical Research Society, I had formed one of a committee of three who spent the night in a haunted house. Our adventures were neither exciting nor convincing, but, such as it was, the story appeared to interest my auditors in a remarkable degree. They listened with an eager silence, and I caught a look of intelligence between them which I could not understand. Lady Holden immediately afterwards rose and left the room.

Sir Dominick pushed the cigar-box over to me, and we smoked for some little time in silence. That huge, bony hand of his was twitching as he raised it with his cheroot to his lips, and I felt that the man's nerves were vibrating like fiddle-strings. My instincts told me that he was on the verge of some intimate confidence, and I feared to speak lest I should interrupt it. At last he turned towards me with a spasmodic gesture like a man who throws his last scruple to the winds.

"From the little that I have seen of you it appears to me, Dr. Hardacre," said he, "that you are the very man I have wanted to meet."

"I am delighted to hear it, sir."

"Your head seems to be cool and steady. You will acquit me of any desire to flatter you, for the circumstances are too serious to permit of insincerities. You have some special knowledge upon these subjects, and you evidently view them from that philosophical standpoint which robs them of all vulgar terror. I presume that the sight of an apparition would not seriously discompose you?"

"I think not, sir."

"Would even interest you, perhaps?"

"Most intensely."

"As a psychical observer, you would probably investigate it in as impersonal a fashion as an astronomer investigates a wandering comet?"

"Precisely."

He gave a heavy sigh.

"Believe me, Dr. Hardacre, there was a time when I could have spoken as you do now. My nerve was a byword in India. Even the Mutiny never shook it for an instant. And yet you see what I am reduced to—the most timorous man, perhaps, in all this county of Wiltshire. Do not speak too bravely upon this subject, or you may find yourself subjected to as long-drawn a test as I am—a test which can only end in the madhouse or the grave."

I waited patiently until he should see fit to go farther in his confidence. His preamble had, I need not say, filled me with interest and expectation.

"For some years, Dr. Hardacre," he continued, "my life and that of my wife have been made miserable by a cause which is so grotesque that it borders upon the ludicrous. And yet familiarity has never made it more easy to bear—on the contrary, as time passes my nerves become more worn and shattered by the constant attrition. If you have no physical fears, Dr. Hardacre, I should very much value your opinion upon this phenomenon which troubles us so."

"For what it is worth my opinion is entirely at your service. May I ask the nature of the phenomenon?"

"I think that your experiences will have a higher evidential value if you are not told in advance what you may expect to encounter. You are yourself aware of the quibbles of unconscious cerebration and subjective impressions with which a scientific sceptic may throw a doubt upon your statement. It would be as well to guard against them in advance."

"What shall I do, then?"

"I will tell you. Would you mind following me this way?" He led me out of the dining-room and down a long passage until we came to a terminal door. Inside there was a large, bare room fitted as a laboratory, with numerous scientific instruments and bottles. A shelf ran along one side, upon which there stood a long line of glass jars containing pathological and anatomical specimens.

"You see that I still dabble in some of my old studies," said Sir Dominick. "These jars are the remains of what was once a most excellent collection, but unfortunately I lost the greater part of them when my house was burned down in Bombay in '92. It was a most unfortunate affair for me—in more ways than one. I had examples of many rare conditions, and my splenic collection was probably unique. These are the survivors."

I glanced over them, and saw that they really were of a very great value and rarity from a pathological point of view: bloated organs, gaping cysts, distorted bones, odious parasites—a singular exhibition of the products of India.

"There is, as you see, a small settee here," said my host. "It was far from our intention to offer a guest so meagre an accommodation, but since affairs have taken this turn, it would be a great kindness upon your part if you would consent to spend the night in this apartment. I beg that you will not hesitate to let me know if the idea should be at all repugnant to you."

"On the contrary," I said, "it is most acceptable."

"My own room is the second on the left, so that if you should feel that you are in need of company a call would always bring me to your side."

"I trust that I shall not be compelled to disturb you."

"It is unlikely that I shall be asleep. I do not sleep much. Do not hesitate to summon me."

And so with this agreement we joined Lady Holden in the drawing-room and talked of lighter things.

It was no affectation upon my part to say that the prospect of my night's adventure was an agreeable one. I have no pretence to greater physical courage than my neighbours, but familiarity with a subject robs it of those vague and undefined terrors which are the most appalling to the imaginative mind. The human brain is capable of only one strong emotion at a time, and if it be filled with curiosity or scientific enthusiasm, there is no room for fear. It is true that I had my uncle's assurance that he had himself originally taken this point of view, but I reflected that the break-down of his nervous system might be due to his forty years in India as much as to any psychical experiences which had befallen him. I at least was sound in nerve and brain, and it was with something of the pleasurable thrill of anticipation with which the sportsman takes his position beside the haunt of his game that I shut the laboratory door behind me, and partially undressing, lay down upon the rug-covered settee.

It was not an ideal atmosphere for a bedroom. The air was heavy with many chemical odours, that of methylated spirit predominating. Nor were the decorations of my chamber very sedative. The odious line of glass jars with their relics of disease and suffering stretched in front of my very eyes. There was no blind to the window, and a three-quarter moon streamed its white light into the room, tracing a silver square with filigree lattices upon the opposite wall. When I had extinguished my candle this one bright patch in the midst of the general gloom had certainly an eerie and discomposing aspect. A rigid and absolute silence reigned throughout the old house, so that the low swish of the branches in the garden came softly and smoothly to my ears. It may have been the hypnotic lullaby of this gentle susurrus, or it may have been the result of my tiring day, but after many dozings and many efforts to regain my clearness of perception, I fell at last into a deep and dreamless sleep.

I was awakened by some sound in the room, and I instantly raised myself upon my elbow on the couch. Some hours had passed, for the square patch upon the wall had slid downwards and sideways until it lay obliquely at the end of my bed. The rest of the room was in deep shadow. At first I could see nothing, presently, as my eyes became accustomed to the faint light, I was aware, with a thrill which all my scientific absorption could not entirely prevent, that something was moving slowly along the line of the wall. A gentle, shuffling sound, as of soft slippers, came to my ears, and I dimly discerned a human figure walking stealthily from the direction of the door. As it emerged into the patch of moonlight I saw very clearly what it was and how it was employed. It was a man, short and squat, dressed in some sort of dark grey gown, which hung straight from his shoulders to his feet. The moon shone upon the side of his face, and I saw that it was chocolate-brown in colour, with a ball of black hair like a woman's at the back of his head. He walked slowly, and his eyes were cast upwards towards the line of bottles which contained those gruesome remnants of humanity. He seemed to examine each jar with attention, and then to pass on to the next. When he had come to the end of the line, immediately opposite my bed, he stopped, faced me, threw up his hands with a gesture of despair, and vanished from my sight.

I have said that he threw up his hands, but I should have said his arms, for as he assumed that attitude of despair I observed a singular peculiarity about his appearance. He had only one hand! As the sleeves drooped down from the up-flung arms I saw the left plainly, but the right ended in a knobby and unsightly stump. In every other way his appearance was so natural, and I had both seen and heard him so clearly, that I could easily have believed that he was an Indian servant of Sir Dominick's who had come into my room in search of something. It was only his sudden disappearance which suggested anything more sinister to me. As it was I sprang from my couch, lit a candle, and examined the whole room carefully. There were no signs of my visitor, and I was forced to conclude that there had really been something outside the normal laws of Nature in his appearance. I lay awake for the remainder of the night, but nothing else occurred to disturb me.

I am an early riser, but my uncle was an even earlier one, for I found him pacing up and down the lawn at the side of the house. He ran towards me in his eagerness when he saw me come out from the door.

"Well, well!" he cried. "Did you see him?"

"An Indian with one hand?"

"Precisely."

"Yes, I saw him"—and I told him all that occurred. When I had finished, he led the way into his study.

"We have a little time before breakfast," said he. "It will suffice to give you an explanation of this extraordinary affair—so far as I can explain that which is essentially inexplicable. In the first place, when I tell you that for four years I have never passed one single night, either in Bombay, aboard ship, or here in England without my sleep being broken by this fellow, you will understand why it is that I am a wreck of my former self. His programme is always the same. He appears by my bedside, shakes me roughly by the shoulder, passes from my room into the laboratory, walks slowly along the line of my bottles, and then vanishes. For more than a thousand times he has gone through the same routine."

"What does he want?"

"He wants his hand."

"His hand?"

"Yes, it came about in this way. I was summoned to Peshawur for a consultation some ten years ago, and while there I was asked to look at the hand of a native who was passing through with an Afghan caravan. The fellow came from some mountain tribe living away at the back of beyond somewhere on the other side of Kaffiristan. He talked a bastard Pushtoo, and it was all I could do to understand him. He was suffering from a soft sarcomatous swelling of one of the metacarpal joints, and I made him realize that it was only by losing his hand that he could hope to save his life. After much persuasion he consented to the operation, and he asked me, when it was over, what fee I demanded. The poor fellow was almost a beggar, so that the idea of a fee was absurd, but I answered in jest that my fee should be his hand, and that I proposed to add it to my pathological collection.

"To my surprise he demurred very much to the suggestion, and he explained that according to his religion it was an all-important matter that the body should be reunited after death, and so make a perfect dwelling for the spirit. The belief is, of course, an old one, and the mummies of the Egyptians arose from an analogous superstition. I answered him that his hand was already off, and asked him how he intended to preserve it. He replied that he would pickle it in salt and carry it about with him. I suggested that it might be safer in my keeping than in his, and that I had better means than salt for preserving it. On realizing that I really intended to carefully keep it, his opposition vanished instantly. 'But remember, sahib,' said he, 'I shall want it back when I am dead.' I laughed at the remark, and so the matter ended. I returned to my practice, and he no doubt in the course of time was able to continue his journey to Afghanistan.

"Well, as I told you last night, I had a bad fire in my house at Bombay. Half of it was burned down, and, amongst other things, my pathological collection was largely destroyed. What you see are the poor remains of it. The hand of the hillman went with the rest, but I gave the matter no particular thought at the time. That was six years ago.

"Four years ago—two years after the fire—I was awakened one night by a furious tugging at my sleeve. I sat up under the impression that my favourite mastiff was trying to arouse me. Instead of this, I saw my Indian patient of long ago, dressed in the long, grey gown which was the badge of his people. He was holding up his stump and looking reproachfully at me. He then went over to my bottles, which at that time I kept in my room, and he examined them carefully, after which he gave a gesture of anger and vanished. I realized that he had just died, and that he had come to claim my promise that I should keep his limb in safety for him.

"Well, there you have it all, Dr. Hardacre. Every night at the same hour for four years this performance has been repeated. It is a simple thing in itself, but it has worn me out like water dropping on a stone. It has brought a vile insomnia with it, for I cannot sleep now for the expectation of his coming. It has poisoned my old age and that of my wife, who has been the sharer in this great trouble. But there is the breakfast gong, and she will be waiting impatiently to know how it fared with you last night. We are both much indebted to you for your gallantry, for it takes something from the weight of our misfortune when we share it, even for a single night, with a friend, and it reassures us to our sanity, which we are sometimes driven to question."

This was the curious narrative which Sir Dominick confided to me—a story which to many would have appeared to be a grotesque impossibility, but which, after my experience of the night before, and my previous knowledge of such things, I was prepared to accept as an absolute fact. I thought deeply over the matter, and brought the whole range of my reading and experience to bear over it. After breakfast, I surprised my host and hostess by announcing that I was returning to London by the next train.

"My dear doctor," cried Sir Dominick in great distress, "you make me feel that I have been guilty of a gross breach of hospitality in intruding this unfortunate matter upon you. I should have borne my own burden."

"It is, indeed, that matter which is taking me to London," I answered; "but you are mistaken, I assure you, if you think that my experience of last night was an unpleasant one to me. On the contrary, I am about to ask your permission to return in the evening and spend one more night in your laboratory. I am very eager to see this visitor once again."

My uncle was exceedingly anxious to know what I was about to do, but my fears of raising false hopes prevented me from telling him. I was back in my own consulting-room a little after luncheon, and was confirming my memory of a passage in a recent book upon occultism which had arrested my attention when I read it.

"In the case of earth-bound spirits," said my authority, "some one dominant idea obsessing them at the hour of death is sufficient to hold them in this material world. They are the amphibia of this life and of the next, capable of passing from one to the other as the turtle passes from land to water. The causes which may bind a soul so strongly to a life which its body has abandoned are any violent emotion. Avarice, revenge, anxiety, love, and pity have all been known to have this effect. As a rule it springs from some unfulfilled wish, and when the wish has been fulfilled the material bond relaxes. There are many cases upon record which show the singular persistence of these visitors, and also their disappearance when their wishes have been fulfilled, or in some cases when a reasonable compromise has been effected."

"A reasonable compromise effected"—those were the words which I had brooded over all the morning, and which I now verified in the original. No actual atonement could be made here—but a reasonable compromise! I made my way as fast as a train could take me to the Shadwell Seamen's Hospital, where my old friend Jack Hewett was house-surgeon. Without explaining the situation I made him understand what it was that I wanted.

"A brown man's hand!" said he, in amazement. "What in the world do you want that for?"

"Never mind. I'll tell you some day. I know that your wards are full of Indians."

"I should think so. But a hand—" He thought a little, and then struck a bell.

"Travers," said he to a student-dresser, "what became of the hands of the Lascar which we took off yesterday? I mean the fellow from the East India Dock who got caught in the steam winch."

"They are in the *post-mortem* room, sir."

"Just pack one of them in antiseptics and give it to Dr. Hardacre."

And so I found myself back at Rodenhurst before dinner with this curious outcome of my day in town. I still said nothing to Sir Dominick, but I slept that night in the laboratory, and I placed the Lascar's hand in one of the glass jars at the end of my couch.

So interested was I in the result of my experiment that sleep was out of the question. I sat with a shaded lamp beside me and waited patiently for my visitor. This time I saw him clearly from the first. He appeared beside the door, nebulous for an instant, and then hardening into as distinct an outline as any living man. The slippers beneath his grey gown were red and heelless, which accounted for the low, shuffling sound which he made as he walked. As on the previous night he passed slowly along the line of bottles until he paused before that which contained the hand. He reached up to it, his whole figure quivering with expectation, took it down, examined it eagerly, and then, with a face which was convulsed with fury and disappointment, he hurled it down on the floor. There was a crash which resounded throughout the house, and when I looked up the mutilated Indian had disappeared. A moment later my door flew open and Sir Dominick rushed in.

"You are not hurt?" he cried.

"No—but deeply disappointed."

He looked in astonishment at the splinters of glass, and the brown hand lying upon the floor.

"Good God!" he cried. "What is this?"

I told him my idea and its wretched sequel. He listened intently, but shook his head.

"It was well thought of," said he, "but I fear that there is no such easy end to my sufferings. But one thing I now insist upon. It is that you shall never again upon any pretext occupy this room. My fears that something might have happened to you—when I heard that crash have been the most acute of all the agonies which I have undergone. I will not expose myself to a repetition of it."

He allowed me, however, to spend the remainder of the night where I was, and I lay there worrying over the problem and lamenting my own failure. With the first light of morning there was the Lascar's hand still lying upon the floor to remind me of my fiasco. I lay looking at it—and as I lay suddenly an idea flew like a bullet through my head and brought me quivering with excitement out of my couch. I raised the grim relic from where it had fallen. Yes, it was indeed so. The hand was the left hand of the Lascar.

By the first train I was on my way to town, and hurried at once to the Seamen's Hospital. I remembered that both hands of the Lascar had been amputated, but I was terrified lest the precious organ which I was in search of might have been already consumed in the crematory. My suspense was soon ended. It had still been preserved in the *post-mortem* room. And so I returned to Rodenhurst in the evening with my mission accomplished and the material for a fresh experiment.

But Sir Dominick Holden would not hear of my occupying the laboratory again. To all my entreaties he turned a deaf ear. It offended his sense of hospitality, and he could no longer permit it. I left the hand, therefore, as I had done its fellow the night before, and I occupied a comfortable bedroom in another portion of the house, some distance from the scene of my adventures.

But in spite of that my sleep was not destined to be uninterrupted. In the dead of night my host burst into my room, a lamp in his hand. His huge, gaunt figure was enveloped in a loose dressing-gown, and his whole appearance might certainly have seemed more formidable to a weak-nerved man than that of the Indian of the night before. But it was not his entrance so much as his expression which amazed me. He had turned suddenly younger by twenty years at the least. His eyes were shining, his features radiant, and he waved one hand in triumph over his head. I sat up astounded, staring sleepily at this extraordinary visitor. But his words soon drove the sleep from my eyes.

"We have done it! We have succeeded!" he shouted. "My dear Hardacre, how can I ever in this world repay you?"

"You don't mean to say that it is all right?"

"Indeed I do. I was sure that you would not mind being awakened to hear such blessed news."

"Mind! I should think not indeed. But is it really certain?"

"I have no doubt whatever upon the point. I owe you such a debt, my dear nephew, as I have never owed a man before, and never expected to. What can I possibly do for you that is commensurate? Providence must have sent you to my rescue. You have saved both my reason and my life, for another six months of this must have seen me either in a cell or a coffin. And my wife—it was wearing her out before my eyes. Never could I have believed that any human being could have lifted this burden off me." He seized my hand and wrung it in his bony grip.

"It was only an experiment—a forlorn hope—but I am delighted from my heart that it has succeeded. But how do you know that it is all right? Have you seen something?"

He seated himself at the foot of my bed.

"I have seen enough," said he. "It satisfies me that I shall be troubled no more. What has passed is easily told. You know that at a certain hour this creature always comes to me. To-night he arrived at the usual time, and aroused me with even more violence than is his custom. I can only surmise that his disappointment of last night increased the bitterness of his anger against me. He looked angrily at me, and then went on his usual round. But in a few minutes I saw him, for the first time since this persecution began, return to my chamber. He was smiling. I saw the gleam of his white teeth through the dim light. He stood facing me at the end of my bed, and three times he made the low Eastern salaam which is their solemn leave-taking. And the third time that he bowed he raised his arms over his head, and I saw his two hands outstretched in the air. So he vanished, and, as I believe, for ever."

So that is the curious experience which won me the affection
and the gratitude of my celebrated uncle, the famous Indian
surgeon. His anticipations were realised, and never again was
he disturbed by the visits of the restless hillman in search of
his lost member. Sir Dominick and Lady Holden spent a very
happy old age, unclouded, so far as I know, by any trouble,
and they finally died during the great influenza epidemic
within a few weeks of each other. In his lifetime he always
turned to me for advice in everything which concerned that
English life of which he knew so little; and I aided him also
in the purchase and development of his estates. It was no
great surprise to me, therefore, that I found myself eventually promoted over the heads of five exasperated cousins, and
changed in a single day from a hard-working country doctor
into the head of an important Wiltshire family. I, at least,
have reason to bless the memory of the man with the brown
hand, and the day when I was fortunate enough to relieve
Rodenhurst of his unwelcome presence.

INTERLUDE

Woman's Ghastly Hand Saves Engineer's Life
(Charlotte, North Carolina, *News,* February 7, 1902)

Cumberland, Md., Feb. 7.—A strange story has reached here from Hoffman mine, in the Georges Creek region, to the effect that the engineer at the mine, Stralter, had his life saved in a mysterious manner. Stralter had started to enter the mine for the purpose of setting the points for the headings, when he was pushed back by a woman's hand.

Stralter then went to another room, where some miners were at work, to whom he related his strange experience. The old miners present laughed at the story, and while they were doing so a crash was heard. Going to the room that Stralter had been warned not to enter, all were surprised to discover that the roof had caved in. The men hesitated before returning to work.

THE MONKEY'S PAW
W. W. Jacobs
(1901)

1

Without, the night was cold and wet, but in the small parlour of Laburnam Villa the blinds were drawn and the fire burned brightly. Father and son were at chess, the former, who possessed ideas about the game involving radical changes, putting his king into such sharp and unnecessary perils that it even provoked comment from the white-haired old lady knitting placidly by the fire.

"Hark at the wind," said Mr. White, who, having seen a fatal mistake after it was too late, was amiably desirous of preventing his son from seeing it.

"I'm listening," said the latter, grimly surveying the board as he stretched out his hand. "Check."

"I should hardly think that he'd come tonight," said his father, with his hand poised over the board.

"Mate," replied the son.

"That's the worst of living so far out," bawled Mr. White, with sudden and unlooked-for violence; "of all the beastly, slushy, out-of-the-way places to live in, this is the worst. Pathway's a bog, and the road's a torrent. I don't know what people are thinking about. I suppose because only two houses in the road are let, they think it doesn't matter."

"Never mind, dear," said his wife, soothingly; "perhaps you'll win the next one." Mr. White looked up sharply, just

177

in time to intercept a knowing glance between mother and
son. The words died away on his lips, and he hid a guilty grin
in his thin grey beard.

"There he is," said Herbert White, as the gate banged to
loudly and heavy footsteps came toward the door.

The old man rose with hospitable haste, and opening the
door, was heard condoling with the new arrival. The new
arrival also condoled with himself, so that Mrs. White said,
"Tut, tut!" and coughed gently as her husband entered the
room, followed by a tall, burly man, beady of eye and rubi-
cund of visage.

"Sergeant-Major Morris," he said, introducing him.

The sergeant-major shook hands, and taking the proffered seat by the fire, watched contentedly while his host got
out whiskey and tumblers and stood a small copper kettle on
the fire.

At the third glass his eyes got brighter, and he began to
talk, the little family circle regarding with eager interest this
visitor from distant parts, as he squared his broad shoulders
in the chair and spoke of wild scenes and doughty deeds; of
wars and plagues and strange peoples.

"Twenty-one years of it," said Mr. White, nodding at his
wife and son. "When he went away he was a slip of a youth
in the warehouse. Now look at him."

"He don't look to have taken much harm," said Mrs.
White, politely.

"I'd like to go to India myself," said the old man, "just to
look round a bit, you know."

"Better where you are," said the sergeant-major, shaking
his head. He put down the empty glass, and sighing softly,
shook it again.

"I should like to see those old temples and fakirs and
jugglers," said the old man. "What was that you started telling me the other day about a monkey's paw or something,
Morris?"

"Nothing," said the soldier, hastily. "Leastways nothing worth hearing."

"Monkey's paw?" said Mrs. White, curiously.

"Well, it's just a bit of what you might call magic, perhaps," said the sergeant-major, offhandedly.

His three listeners leaned forward eagerly. The visitor absent-mindedly put his empty glass to his lips and then set it down again. His host filled it for him.

"To look at," said the sergeant-major, fumbling in his pocket, "it's just an ordinary little paw, dried to a mummy."

He took something out of his pocket and proffered it. Mrs. White drew back with a grimace, but her son, taking it, examined it curiously. "And what is there special about it?" inquired Mr. White as he took it from his son, and having examined it, placed it upon the table.

"It had a spell put on it by an old fakir," said the sergeant-major, "a very holy man. He wanted to show that fate ruled people's lives, and that those who interfered with it did so to their sorrow. He put a spell on it so that three separate men could each have three wishes from it."

His manner was so impressive that his hearers were conscious that their light laughter jarred somewhat.

"Well, why don't you have three, sir?" said Herbert White, cleverly.

The soldier regarded him in the way that middle age is wont to regard presumptuous youth. "I have," he said, quietly, and his blotchy face whitened.

"And did you really have the three wishes granted?" asked Mrs. White.

"I did," said the sergeant-major, and his glass tapped against his strong teeth.

"And has anybody else wished?" persisted the old lady.

"The first man had his three wishes. Yes," was the reply; "I don't know what the first two were, but the third was for death. That's how I got the paw."

His tones were so grave that a hush fell upon the group.

"If you've had your three wishes, it's no good to you now, then, Morris," said the old man at last. "What do you keep it for?"

The soldier shook his head. "Fancy, I suppose," he said, slowly. "I did have some idea of selling it, but I don't think I will. It has caused enough mischief already. Besides, people won't buy. They think it's a fairy tale; some of them, and those who do think anything of it want to try it first and pay me afterward."

"If you could have another three wishes," said the old man, eyeing him keenly, "would you have them?"

"I don't know," said the other. "I don't know."

He took the paw, and dangling it between his forefinger and thumb, suddenly threw it upon the fire. White, with a slight cry, stooped down and snatched it off.

"Better let it burn," said the soldier, solemnly.

"If you don't want it, Morris," said the other, "give it to me."

"I won't," said his friend, doggedly. "I threw it on the fire. If you keep it, don't blame me for what happens. Pitch it on the fire again like a sensible man."

The other shook his head and examined his new possession closely. "How do you do it?" he inquired.

"Hold it up in your right hand and wish aloud," said the sergeant-major, "but I warn you of the consequences."

"Sounds like the Arabian Nights," said Mrs. White, as she rose and began to set the supper. "Don't you think you might wish for four pairs of hands for me?"

Her husband drew the talisman from pocket, and then all three burst into laughter as the sergeant-major, with a look of alarm on his face, caught him by the arm. "If you must wish," he said, gruffly, "wish for something sensible."

Mr. White dropped it back in his pocket, and placing chairs, motioned his friend to the table. In the business of supper the talisman was partly forgotten, and afterward the three sat listening in an enthralled fashion to a second instalment of the soldier's adventures in India.

"If the tale about the monkey's paw is not more truthful than those he has been telling us," said Herbert, as the door closed behind their guest, just in time for him to catch the last train, "we sha'nt make much out of it."

"Did you give him anything for it, father?" inquired Mrs. White, regarding her husband closely.

"A trifle," said he, colouring slightly. "He didn't want it, but I made him take it. And he pressed me again to throw it away."

"Likely," said Herbert, with pretended horror. "Why, we're going to be rich, and famous and happy. Wish to be an emperor, father, to begin with; then you can't be hen-pecked." He darted round the table, pursued by the maligned Mrs. White armed with an antimacassar.

Mr. White took the paw from his pocket and eyed it dubiously. "I don't know what to wish for, and that's a fact," he said, slowly. "It seems to me I've got all I want."

"If you only cleared the house, you'd be quite happy, wouldn't you?" said Herbert, with his hand on his shoulder. "Well, wish for two hundred pounds, then; that'll just do it."

His father, smiling shamefacedly at his own credulity, held up the talisman, as his son, with a solemn face, somewhat marred by a wink at his mother, sat down at the piano and struck a few impressive chords.

"I wish for two hundred pounds," said the old man distinctly.

A fine crash from the piano greeted the words, interrupted by a shuddering cry from the old man. His wife and son ran toward him.

"It moved," he cried, with a glance of disgust at the object as it lay on the floor. "As I wished, it twisted in my hand like a snake."

"Well, I don't see the money," said his son as he picked it up and placed it on the table, "and I bet I never shall."

"It must have been your fancy, father," said his wife, regarding him anxiously.

He shook his head. "Never mind, though; there's no harm done, but it gave me a shock all the same."

They sat down by the fire again while the two men finished their pipes. Outside, the wind was higher than ever, and the old man started nervously at the sound of a door banging upstairs. A silence unusual and depressing settled upon all three, which lasted until the old couple rose to retire for the night.

"I expect you'll find the cash tied up in a big bag in the middle of your bed," said Herbert, as he bade them goodnight, "and something horrible squatting up on top of the wardrobe watching you as you pocket your ill-gotten gains."

He sat alone in the darkness, gazing at the dying fire, and seeing faces in it. The last face was so horrible and so simian that he gazed at it in amazement. It got so vivid that, with a little uneasy laugh, he felt on the table for a glass containing a little water to throw over it. His hand grasped the monkey's paw, and with a little shiver he wiped his hand on his coat and went up to bed.

2

In the brightness of the wintry sun next morning as it streamed over the breakfast table he laughed at his fears. There was an air of prosaic wholesomeness about the room which it had lacked on the previous night, and the dirty, shrivelled little paw was pitched on the sideboard with a carelessness which betokened no great belief in its virtues.

"I suppose all old soldiers are the same," said Mrs. White. "The idea of our listening to such nonsense! How could wishes be granted in these days? And if they could, how could two hundred pounds hurt you, father?"

"Might drop on his head from the sky," said the frivolous Herbert.

"Morris said the things happened so naturally," said his father, "that you might if you so wished attribute it to coincidence."

"Well, don't break into the money before I come back," said Herbert as he rose from the table. "I'm afraid it'll turn you into a mean, avaricious man, and we shall have to disown you."

His mother laughed, and following him to the door, watched him down the road; and returning to the breakfast table, was very happy at the expense of her husband's credulity. All of which did not prevent her from scurrying to the door at the postman's knock, nor prevent her from referring somewhat shortly to retired sergeant-majors of bibulous habits when she found that the post brought a tailor's bill.

"Herbert will have some more of his funny remarks, I expect, when he comes home," she said, as they sat at dinner.

"I dare say," said Mr. White, pouring himself out some beer; "but for all that, the thing moved in my hand; that I'll swear to."

"You thought it did," said the old lady soothingly.

"I say it did," replied the other. "There was no thought about it; I had just—What's the matter?"

His wife made no reply. She was watching the mysterious movements of a man outside, who, peering in an undecided fashion at the house, appeared to be trying to make up his mind to enter. In mental connection with the two hundred pounds, she noticed that the stranger was well dressed, and wore a silk hat of glossy newness. Three times he paused at the gate, and then walked on again. The fourth time he stood with his hand upon it, and then with sudden resolution flung it open and walked up the path. Mrs. White at the same moment placed her hands behind her, and hurriedly unfastening the strings of her apron, put that useful article of apparel beneath the cushion of her chair.

She brought the stranger, who seemed ill at ease, into the room. He gazed at her furtively, and listened in a preoccupied fashion as the old lady apologized for the appearance of the room, and her husband's coat, a garment which he usually reserved for the garden. She then waited as patiently as her sex would permit, for him to broach his business, but he was at first strangely silent.

"I—was asked to call," he said at last, and stooped and picked a piece of cotton from his trousers. "I come from 'Maw and Meggins.'"

The old lady started. "Is anything the matter?" she asked, breathlessly. "Has anything happened to Herbert? What is it? What is it?"

Her husband interposed. "There, there, mother," he said, hastily. "Sit down, and don't jump to conclusions. You've not brought bad news, I'm sure, sir;" and he eyed the other wistfully.

"I'm sorry—" began the visitor.

"Is he hurt?" demanded the mother, wildly.

The visitor bowed in assent. "Badly hurt," he said, quietly, "but he is not in any pain."

"Oh, thank God!" said the old woman, clasping her hands. "Thank God for that! Thank—"

She broke off suddenly as the sinister meaning of the assurance dawned upon her and she saw the awful confirmation of her fears in the other's perverted face. She caught her breath, and turning to her slower-witted husband, laid her trembling old hand upon his. There was a long silence. "He was caught in the machinery," said the visitor at length in a low voice.

"Caught in the machinery," repeated Mr. White, in a dazed fashion, "yes."

He sat staring blankly out at the window, and taking his wife's hand between his own, pressed it as he had been wont to do in their old courting-days nearly forty years before.

"He was the only one left to us," he said, turning gently to the visitor. "It is hard."

The other coughed, and rising, walked slowly to the window. "The firm wished me to convey their sincere sympathy with you in your great loss," he said, without looking round. "I beg that you will understand I am only their servant and merely obeying orders."

There was no reply; the old woman's face was white, her eyes staring, and her breath inaudible; on the husband's face was a look such as his friend the sergeant might have carried into his first action.

"I was to say that Maw and Meggins disclaim all responsibility," continued the other. "They admit no liability at all, but in consideration of your son's services, they wish to present you with a certain sum as compensation."

Mr. White dropped his wife's hand, and rising to his feet, gazed with a look of horror at his visitor. His dry lips shaped the words, "How much?"

"Two hundred pounds," was the answer.

Unconscious of his wife's shriek, the old man smiled faintly, put out his hands like a sightless man, and dropped, a senseless heap, to the floor.

3

In the huge new cemetery, some two miles distant, the old people buried their dead, and came back to a house steeped in shadow and silence. It was all over so quickly that at first they could hardly realize it, and remained in a state of expectation as though of something else to happen—something else which was to lighten this load, too heavy for old hearts to bear.

But the days passed, and expectation gave place to resignation—the hopeless resignation of the old, sometimes miscalled, apathy. Sometimes they hardly exchanged a word, for now they had nothing to talk about, and their days were long to weariness.

It was about a week after that the old man, waking suddenly in the night, stretched out his hand and found himself alone. The room was in darkness, and the sound of subdued weeping came from the window. He raised himself in bed and listened.

"Come back," he said, tenderly. "You will be cold."

"It is colder for my son," said the old woman, and wept afresh.

The sound of her sobs died away on his ears. The bed was warm, and his eyes heavy with sleep. He dozed fitfully, and then slept until a sudden wild cry from his wife awoke him with a start.

"The paw!" she cried wildly. "The monkey's paw!"

He started up in alarm. "Where? Where is it? What's the matter?"

She came stumbling across the room toward him. "I want it," she said, quietly. "You've not destroyed it?"

"It's in the parlour, on the bracket," he replied, marvelling. "Why?"

She cried and laughed together, and bending over, kissed his cheek.

"I only just thought of it," she said, hysterically. "Why didn't I think of it before? Why didn't you think of it?"

"Think of what?" he questioned.

"The other two wishes," she replied, rapidly. "We've only had one."

"Was not that enough?" he demanded, fiercely.

"No," she cried, triumphantly; "we'll have one more. Go down and get it quickly, and wish our boy alive again."

The man sat up in bed and flung the bedclothes from his quaking limbs. "Good God, you are mad!" he cried, aghast.

"Get it," she panted; "get it quickly, and wish— Oh, my boy, my boy!"

Her husband struck a match and lit the candle. "Get back to bed," he said, unsteadily. "You don't know what you are saying."

"We had the first wish granted," said the old woman, feverishly; "why not the second?"

"A coincidence," stammered the old man.

"Go and get it and wish," cried his wife, quivering with excitement.

The old man turned and regarded her, and his voice shook. "He has been dead ten days, and besides he—I would not tell you else, but—I could only recognize him by his clothing. If he was too terrible for you to see then, how now?"

"Bring him back," cried the old woman, and dragged him toward the door. "Do you think I fear the child I have nursed?"

He went down in the darkness, and felt his way to the parlour, and then to the mantelpiece. The talisman was in its place, and a horrible fear that the unspoken wish might bring his mutilated son before him ere he could escape from the room seized upon him, and he caught his breath as he found that he had lost the direction of the door. His brow cold with sweat, he felt his way round the table, and groped along the wall until he found himself in the small passage with the unwholesome thing in his hand.

Even his wife's face seemed changed as he entered the room. It was white and expectant, and to his fears seemed to have an unnatural look upon it. He was afraid of her.

"*Wish!*" she cried, in a strong voice.

"It is foolish and wicked," he faltered.

"*Wish!*" repeated his wife.

He raised his hand. "I wish my son alive again." The talisman fell to the floor, and he regarded it fearfully. Then he sank trembling into a chair as the old woman, with burning eyes, walked to the window and raised the blind.

He sat until he was chilled with the cold, glancing occasionally at the figure of the old woman peering through the window. The candle-end, which had burned below the rim of the china candlestick, was throwing pulsating shadows on the ceiling and walls, until, with a flicker larger than the rest, it expired. The old man, with an unspeakable sense of relief at the failure of the talisman, crept back to his bed, and a minute or two afterward the old woman came silently and apathetically beside him.

Neither spoke, but lay silently listening to the ticking of the clock. A stair creaked, and a squeaky mouse scurried noisily through the wall. The darkness was oppressive, and after lying for some time screwing up his courage, he took the box of matches, and striking one, went downstairs for a candle.

At the foot of the stairs the match went out, and he paused to strike another; and at the same moment a knock, so quiet and stealthy as to be scarcely audible, sounded on the front door.

The matches fell from his hand and spilled in the passage. He stood motionless, his breath suspended until the knock was repeated. Then he turned and fled swiftly back to his room, and closed the door behind him. A third knock sounded through the house.

"What's that?" cried the old woman, starting up.

"A rat," said the old man in shaking tones—"a rat. It passed me on the stairs."

His wife sat up in bed listening. A loud knock resounded through the house.

"It's Herbert!" she screamed. "It's Herbert!"

She ran to the door, but her husband was before her, and catching her by the arm, held her tightly.

"What are you going to do?" he whispered hoarsely.

"It's my boy; it's Herbert!" she cried, struggling mechanically. "I forgot it was two miles away. What are you holding me for? Let go. I must open the door."

"For God's sake don't let it in," cried the old man, trembling.

"You're afraid of your own son," she cried, struggling. "Let me go. I'm coming, Herbert; I'm coming."

There was another knock, and another. The old woman with a sudden wrench broke free and ran from the room. Her husband followed to the landing, and called after her appealingly as she hurried downstairs. He heard the chain rattle back and the bottom bolt drawn slowly and stiffly from the socket. Then the old woman's voice, strained and panting.

"The bolt," she cried, loudly. "Come down. I can't reach it."

But her husband was on his hands and knees groping wildly on the floor in search of the paw. If he could only find it before the thing outside got in. A perfect fusillade of knocks reverberated through the house, and he heard the scraping of a chair as his wife put it down in the passage against the door. He heard the creaking of the bolt as it came slowly back, and at the same moment he found the monkey's paw, and frantically breathed his third and last wish.

The knocking ceased suddenly, although the echoes of it were still in the house. He heard the chair drawn back, and the door opened. A cold wind rushed up the staircase, and a long loud wail of disappointment and misery from his wife gave him courage to run down to her side, and then to the gate beyond. The street lamp flickering opposite shone on a quiet and deserted road.

THE MUMMY HAND: A STORY OF CHRISTMAS EVE
As Narrated by Eustace Ormerod
Adeline Sergeant
(1901)

Yes, it is rather an odd story, and I never can help thinking of it at Christmas time. But my wife says there is something uncanny about it, so I don't usually refer to it in her presence. Women are a little sensitive and nervous about these things. But I will tell you what happened if you like. And a very odd experience I had, on Christmas Eve, when I was in Upper Egypt.

I had had rather a run of ill-luck. I was engaged to Mabel, but her father was doing his best to break off the engagement, because I was such a bad match for her.

To begin with, I had scarcely any money, except what I made by illustrations for papers and magazines, and old Sir John did not take a very high view of the artistic profession. Then my health had broken down, and the doctor said I ought to winter in a warm climate—which did not look very well for the future, did it?

Old Sir John was quite kind and paternal, but inexorable, too. "My dear boy," he said to me, "I like you immensely, and Mabel likes you, too, but as long as you are a pauper and an invalid, it is not much good proposing to marry her, for I think too well of you to suppose that you want to live upon my money."

It is a little hard to listen to a statement of that kind, but I had to swallow it, because I did not want to quarrel with

Sir John, and I knew that Mabel would be true to me. So I said good-bye to them both, and made my way to the office of the paper for which I worked.

The editor was Wilkins, an awfully kind chap. I told him the whole story, and he said a great many pleasant things to me about my work, and told me that he would consult with the directors, and see whether there was not some permanent post that they could offer me.

He was as good as his word. The very next day I got a proposal from him that I should go out to Egypt, at the expense of the paper, and visit the scene of some recent excavations, making sketches as I went, of temples, statues, sarcophagi, or anything that struck me an interesting.

They proposed to utilise these sketches partly in the paper, for a set of articles on the buried cities of Egypt, and partly for a handbook on Egyptian antiquities that somebody or other connected with the firm was going to bring out. Anyway, he said that they would pay me handsomely for the job, that I could take my own time over it, and so forth, and that they would not grudge any reasonable expense. They also intimated that if I acquitted myself well, I count upon permanent employment as one of the staff.

This was good news for me, and I closed with their offer immediately. I saw Mabel once, and said good-bye to her, then started immediately, for the November fogs were coming on, and I had a nasty cough that I wanted to get rid of.

I knew noshing at that time of Egyptian history or hieroglyphics, and I can assure you that I had never heard the name of Mr. Flinders Petrie. So I had my work cut out for me, even on the voyage, to get up the subject.

I need not dwell upon my difficulties, nor upon the steps I took to start my expedition. I reported myself to a bigwig, and got as much information as I could about the recent discoveries. Thanks to the introductions I had brought, I lost very little time in getting to work, and by the middle of

December I was comfortably established in my own dahabee-ah, and had got some distance up the Nile.

I must tell you—though without wishing to boast—that I have always had rather a knack at languages. I can usually become pretty fluent in a new tongue in two or three months time, and Arabic was not entirely new to me, because, you know, my father was something of an Oriental scholar and I had learnt various Eastern languages from him. So that it was not altogether remarkable that I should soon put myself into communication with any Arabs that I came across, and more particularly with the Bedouin tribes upon the river banks.

They soon learnt to understand the interest I took in old tombs and temples. And, of course, I did my best to ingratiate myself with them, because I thought it very likely that they might know of places upon which no Englishman's eye had rested and the discovery of which might add to the value of my work, and also to my reputation.

It was also lucky for me that on one or two occasions I was able to give some assistance to a boy, who turned out to be the favourite son of one of the sheiks—in point of saved the young monkey from being gobbled up by a crocodile, and the sheik's gratitude was boundless, or so at least it seemed to me. I may as well add that in considering the matter afterwards I thought a good deal of deliberate calculation mixed up with it.

He came to me one day, and after the usual greetings, the cup of coffee and the chibouk which were handed to him, he intimated that he had something special to say. Would I like to go with him to a city partially buried beneath the sand, which no Englishman had ever seen? I asked him a good many questions about it, and what he said distinctly raised my curiosity.

"It is the City of the Princess," said the Sheik, with a face like a mask, and which sedulously avoided mine.

He was a handsome old man, brown, and lithe, and slender, as Arabs generally are, but of great statute, and considerable strength. His features were regular and delicate; he wore no beard, and his arched eyebrows and fine dark eyes lent a rather peculiar character to his face. He had very beautiful hands. I used to watch the movement of the long, slender fingers, as if I were fascinated by them—and yet I hardly knew why. I had already received hints from Cairo that old Sheik Muhammed was not altogether to be trusted, and indeed I believed him to be the most thorough-going scoundrel and cut-throat on the banks of the Nile. But he had the supple grace of a tiger, and I shall never forget the velvety softness of his eyes. He sat cross-legged before me, on a carpet, his white robes and turban immaculately clean, his demeanor as cool and dignified as that of an emperor. Yet he looked more like a sage and a poet than a Bedouin sheik.

"Why do you call it the City of the Princess?" I inquired.

He bowed gravely, touching his forehead, and chest. "She was the daughter of a great king," he said. "It was by her orders that the city was built. And her tomb is in the midst."

"Her tomb—does that still exist? Can you take me to see it?" I cried.

"If the Effendi has no fears," said Sheik Muhammed, "I can show him the place where the Princess used to lie."

"Does she not lie there now?" I asked. "Who then has broken open her tomb? You say no Englishman has been there before."

The sheik simply shook his head. "In this land there are many thieves," he observed, "and perhaps the body was removed to a place of greater safety. But the Effendi shall see, and judge for himself."

It is needless to say that I consented with alacrity. Such a chance was not to be despised: I should see what no other Englishman had seen, and I might make valuable and important discoveries. I waited, with impatience, until the moment came for setting out upon my expedition to the buried city.

The sand of Egypt is as the waves of the sea, it over-
throws and submerges the works of man, and shews merely
the smooth, unbroken surface above them; where no one can
discern, or even guess, at the existence of the things that
have been lost. As we journeyed over the vast expanse I wondered how it was possible for my guides to know their way,
or for their eye to distinguish any landmark by which our
destination could be known, for, as the sheik had explained
to me, we were not going to look for ruin visible to the eye of
man, but for some subterranean passages and buried cities,
which had not seen the light of day for hundreds of years.

We had set out at dawn, but the sun was high before we
paused at what looked to me like a flat, round stone, buried in the sand, and shaded by one or two palm trees. The
ground, by its verdure, showed the presence of underground
water-springs.

I looked on with deepest interest while my escorts formed
their camp, and then removed the stone from its place. As
I had expected, I saw that it covered the entrance to some
underground building, for there were stone steps, and above
them a domed roof, and a passage, into which the sun's rays
penetrated only a little way.

The sheik, who was accompanied only by two of his sons,
and one or two of his most trustworthy servants, looked at
me with triumph in his eye. "Did I not tell you," he said,
"and now, if the Effendi chooses, I will show him the burial
place of the Princess. Will the Effendi follow, or—"—with
an unmistakable touch of scorn in his voice—"is the Effendi
afraid?"

For I must be confessed that I had hesitated, as a breath
of chill, dank air came from the vault, like a foreshadowing
of death. But at the sheik's question my courage returned
to me, and I haughtily begged him to hold his peace and go
forward.

I shall never forget the curious sensations produced in me by that expedition. One of the servants went first, holding a lantern, and then came the sheik, and then myself, while one of the sheik's sons brought up the rear. But for the light of the lamp we should not have been able to see a step before us. The steps went down for some distance, and were succeeded by a level passage. But that also went down until we seemed to be descending into the very bowels of the earth. Worse than that, the walls narrowed on each side, until I almost thought that it would be impossible to proceed. The lithe figures of the Arabs hopped easily from the narrow steps, but I, a tall and broad-shouldered Englishman, had considerable difficulty in squeezing myself along the passage. Once or twice I almost came to a full stop. But it occurred to me that there was nothing to be done but to go forward. One could never turn in that narrow passage. It was a case of going further or being wedged for ever in the darkness. At last, to my unspeakable relief, the passage widened until it opened out into a large hall or chamber, supported by pillars and illuminated by dim radiance, which must have come from the outer day, although I failed to see the shafts which must have communicated with the outer world.

But what surprised me was that there seemed to be no outlet from the chamber. Looking round it I saw no door or passage, except the one by which we had come. But the Sheik smiled at my bewilderment. "Look up," he said, "on your right side, to the East. Look up!"

He look the lantern from the Arab's hand and hung it aloft, so that I could see a great opening high in the wall, and as the light streamed into it I could see that it was a vast and magnificent chamber adorned with brilliant wall paintings, with carved images of sphinxes and colossi, and with some great objects in the middle of the chamber, which I could not at first make out. "What is it?" I asked, pointing to the black central mass.

"It is the tomb," he said briefly. "Look, I will show you."

And to my surprise he put his foot into a small crevice or cleft in the rock, and swung himself up to the opening, with the lightness and dexterity which only an Arab could have shown. Then standing aloft in the large dim chamber, his white robes making him a noticeable object, even in the semi-obscurity, he looked more like a phantasmal form, some presiding genius of the place, than mere human flesh and blood. The Arabs clambered after him with lighted torches, which they held high above their heads, thus enabling him to see the wonders of the place.

There was an enormous sarcophagus of rose granite, supported on a great marble slab, with granite pillars: it was here no doubt that the body of the Egyptian Princess reposed—a mummied body, wrapped with spices in linen clothes, which I ardently desired to unroll, in order that I might add some scrap of knowledge to the great sum-total of Egyptian archaeology.

But disappointment awaited me. I tried in vain to swing myself up to the opening in the inner chamber, as the Arabs had done. I was too big and heavy for the operation. The crevices which had afforded foothold to the Arabs did not suffice for me, and even when two of the men supported me, and the others tried to pull me up by my arms, it was found that the attempt was impossible. The only way was to come there again, with ropes and other implements, so that I might for myself examine the chamber, and all that it contained.

The Arabs were evidently disappointed with the result of our visit. Evidently they had wanted me to examine the sarcophagus, but I told them I would do so in the course of a couple of days, and that in the meantime if they would keep silence they should be handsomely rewarded.

There was certainly nothing more to be done that day, and we determined to make our way to the upper earth again.

I took some hasty notes of the place where we stood, and of the different things I could see, not falling to remark that the great stone coffin had already been, to some extent, tampered with, for its great cover had been removed and partially broken. But the contents of the sarcophagus I was assured were still intact, and I was consoled with the thought of opening for myself the gilded mummy case, and removing the poor mummied body from its swaddling bands.

I went back to my dahabeeah in a state of wild excitement, and occupied myself for some hours in getting ready or sending messages for the implements that I thought I should require. On the second day, however, I received a shock. My movements had evidently not been unobserved. The Government had got wind of my private researches—so at least I supposed, for here was an official letter from the Director of the Museum in Cairo stating that he was on his way to join me, as he thought that some valuable Egyptian remains were to be discovered near the village beside which my boat was anchored.

Now, I know very well that all antiquities belonged to the Egyptian Government, and may not be carried out of the country, and that everyone who could be proved to be defrauding the Government in this matter was liable to punishment. Of course, I had not meant to appropriate anything that I might find, but I did want to have the honour and glory of my discoveries all to myself, and I was very much annoyed that M. Bougier should in any way anticipate me. But there was nothing to be done. He might arrive at almost any moment, and would certainly not be later than the following day.

I sat and fumed secretly while I gave all the necessary orders for the entertainment of a guest. In the dusk of the evening the Sheik Muhammed sent word that he wished to come on board and speak to me. I received him with all the ceremony which he considered proper to his position, and as we sat opposite to each other drinking coffee and smoking in our respective modes—for he preferred a narghilek, while I restricted myself to the customary cigar—he entered, after some preamble, upon the subject of conversation he wished to make. "The Effendi has had a letter!"

"True," I answered, oracularly.

"The letter is from the Great One in the City, who has control over everything that is ancient in this country. He comes soon, and will demand tribute."

"How the devil do you know?" I asked, rather forgetting my manners in my surprise. The glimmer of a triumphant smile passed across the handsome old face.

"Pardon, Effendi, but all the people know it. The letter was carried to Effendi by a messenger, who has seen letters of the same kind at other times. It is of the blue colour, and it has the name of the Great Man in writing upon it. If the Effendi looks at it he will see that it is so. We all know the look of that covering and the signature."

I hastily withdrew the director's epistle from my pocket and looked at the envelope. It was a blue, official-looking document, and the director had carefully inscribed his signature outside.

Possibly he had no idea that the Arabs knew it just as well as an Englishman or a Frenchman would have done.

"Well—you cannot have read it!" I exclaimed.

"No, Effendi. But we know when a letter of that kind comes, the Great One follows. He will be here to-morrow or the next day. Is it not so?"

"Yes, you are right!" I said, thinking it no use to deny what was so well known. "And what of that?"

"It is just this. Effendi, that the coming of the Master means ruin to my house. The Effendi does not know the methods of the Great One. He will come and ask questions, and he will frighten those of my household, and force them to tell things that they should not: also, he searches our houses and ourselves, and if he finds but a mummy finger, or a tarnished ornament of no value, or a little carbon stone, he sends us to the Black Prison, and deprives us of our goods. Now the Effendi knows that there are always small things that even the children pick up in the sands, and some of them may have been brought by chance into my tent, and therefore, if the Great Lord comes and searches me and my house, behold I am a doomed man, and a price will be put upon my head."

"Not quite so bad as all that," I said. "There will be a fine, I suppose, and perhaps imprisonment. I don't know. But you will get off lightly, I think. Besides, why don't you clear out all those curiosities, and make a present of them to the Government if you are afraid they will be discovered?"

The old man's eyes twinkled. I was somewhat inexperienced in Oriental wiles, but it struck me that Sheik Muhammed was bent upon concealing something valuable for himself, and I hardly knew whether to aid and abet him or to side with the director, who was certainly very much in my way. I fell back upon my generalities. "We must all obey the law," I said. "The things belong to the Government, who will give you a fair price for your labour in digging. But if you keep and sell them to strangers, most assuredly, Sheik, you will be put in goal and suffer great loss beside."

The sheik said nothing. His hands had been folded in the large, white garment which he wore, but he now slid them out of the folds and exposed them to my view. On one of the long, brown fingers, I at once observed, there gleamed a jewel of extraordinary size and lustre; it seemed to be a blood-red ruby, set in dim gold. Without a word he quietly slipped it off his finger and held it out to me upon his flat, thin palm.

"What is it?" I exclaimed. "What a magnificent ring! Why, it's ancient! Where did you find it?"

He made no immediate answer, but motioned to me to take the ring. "It is for the Effendi. The Effendi can keep it for himself."

"Antica?" I said, using the word that every Arabian knows. "If I take it I must give it up to M. Bougier." But I took it from the sheik's hand and tried it on, conscious at the same time of a sudden flash of triumph from the sheik's brilliant, dark eyes. Though what he had to triumph about I could not exactly see.

"It is yours, Effendi," he said, in a low voice. "But do not show it to the Great Man from Cairo. Keep it safely, for it is worth much gold."

"That is impossible," I said, gazing at the jewel as though it fascinated me, for I could not accept such a valuable gift, and I had not enough money to purchase it.

"Keep it then for a little while. Keep it until their visit is overpassed, and then we will speak of barter."

"Oh, now I understand!" I cried, bursting into hearty laughter. "The fact is, you want me to conceal this ring from the eyes of the officials, because you know very well you have stolen it. It would be very convenient for you, I have no doubt, if I kept it concealed until the director had gone back to Cairo, and then presented it to you again."

I spoke in English, but I think the sheik understood me, although he sat grave and immovable. "Where did you find it?" I asked curiously, in Arabic.

"Where we went together, in the chamber of the dead Princess."

"You have not meddled with the sarcophagus, have you?" I cried.

"Allah, forbid. I have left it for the Effendim and their servants. But the ring has virtues. Without it no one can open the door which leads to the secret chamber. Unless the Effendi will keep it safe we cannot go to see the chamber again."

I began to understand. The ring was a bribe, most assuredly. I was to conceal it, and return it to the old sheik when the director had returned to Cairo, and as my reward, I should be shown the sarcophagus, and be allowed to explore its hidden treasures. Under these circumstances what should I do?

It flashed across my mind that it I refused to keep the ring, or presented it to the Government officials I should lose the sheik's friendship, and with it probably every chance of making discoveries in that part of Egypt. With the loss of this chance went also a certain amount of any chance of winning Sir John's consent to my marriage with Mabel. I really could not afford to sacrifice the old sheik's protection for the sake of a scruple, and yet it was hardly fair or honest to defraud the Government of what was its due.

"I should like to examine the ring a little," I said "For the present I will keep it, and return it to you later on. I should like to find out what these hieroglyphics mean," I said, and I pointed to some characters roughly inscribed on the inside of the little circlet.

Not a muscle of the sheik's face changed, although he must have thought that he had secured a tremendous triumph. He went on in a bolder tone, "There is one other thing, Effendi. One of my house has found an ancient mummy, such as the English love to take away to their own country. We dare not keep it because of the search which will shortly be in our house. But if the Effendi would but buy it for himself—"

"The mummy, as well as the ring," I observed. "How much more? No, I don't want any mummies, Sheik. Why don't you bury it in the ground until the director has gone, if you want to get off free?"

It was a very improper statement to make, no doubt, and the old man's eyes twinkled shrewdly.

"It is difficult to do it without many knowing," he said, "and I fear me lest we should be betrayed. But if the Effendi will allow me to bring it to his boat he can see if there is some little corner where it can be kept safe from prying eyes. It is only a small mummy, Effendi—and it is not quite complete: it is only partially unwound—and if the Effendi would but keep it a little while—"

I laughed, in spite of myself. "I have no room for it," I said, "and I should like to know what the director would say if he found me concealing a valuable mummy. No, no. Be content, Sheik. I have got your ring, but really I cannot take the mummy too."

But perhaps there was something in my face that told of yielding, for at night, when the darkness had fallen, and I was sitting alone in my cabin writing up my journal, the sheik himself reappeared, with two of his sons, informing me in the humblest of tones that they had found a hiding place for the mummy, if I would but let it remain. And when I inquired the nature of this hiding place. I was quietly shown the upper bunk in my sleeping apartment, which had hitherto stood empty, and was a receptacle for all kinds of rubbish.

Certainly no one would think of hunting there for curiosities, and the men's ingenuity was so great that I at last consented to allow their precious burden to be deposited there. And early next morning M. Bougier arrived.

I entertained M Bougier at dinner. He was a clever, amiable little Frenchman, full of anecdotes, and very inquisitive concerning my relations with the Arabs in the neighborhood. Especially was he anxious to know whether I thought the Sheik Muhammed had made any recent discoveries. I was pleased to be able to state that I did not know. It was a rather illusive answer, I am afraid, because I implied that I did not know whether the sheik's discoveries were recent or not. Only I did not take the director into my confidence respecting the buried city, the mummy in my bunk, or the wonderful ring. He would know about all these things, no doubt, in good time, but I was not going to betray the sheik's confidence.

We spent a very pleasant evening together, and he did not leave me until late. It must be confessed that I was rather glad to get rid of him, as my thoughts wandered incessantly to the concealed treasures in my cabin. I was restlessly

anxious to know that the ring was safe, and went so far at last as to take the ring from its hiding place and conceal it in my pocket. I should have worn it if I had not been afraid of attracting M. Bougier's attention. But when he was gone I took it out and slipped it over my fourth finger, as it was too small for any of the others. There was something about it that fascinated me. I wished with all my heart that I could afford to buy it, and that it was fair for me to do so. I knew very well that I should have to advise Sheik Muhammed to report his treasures to the Director, or if not should ultimately be obliged to do so myself. But at present I very much wished to put off the evil day.

Moved by new, strange impulses for which I could scarcely account, I took the candle and let its rays fall upon the covered shelf which contained the sheik's mummy. I wondered vaguely why he attached so much importance to it. Finally, I took off the covering and made a superficial examination of the mummied figure. It had been partially unrolled, and I could make out that the mummy was that of a young woman, slight and small. But evidently, from the nature of the wrappings and the spices employed, a person of distinction. I speedily made another discovery which startled me a little. The right hand had been severed from the body, but not taken away. It lay amongst the wrappings, long, brown, and ghastly, and it struck me that one of the fingers had also been mutilated. Though of this, in the dim light, I could not be sure. I resolved to ask the sheik for the full history of this mummy, and why the hand had been severed from the arm. The full significance of it did not strike me at the time. But I came to see it afterwards that it was easy to conjecture why the sheik or one of his family had committed this outrage upon the dead.

I recovered the mummy, put the ring in a box, which I locked for greater security, and went to bed. I think I never had a worse night. I woke continually, and dreamt frightful dreams at intervals. The air seemed curiously thick, and there were strange rustlings, probably caused by the presence of some lizard or scorpion which had crawled into the boat.

At last I lighted a candle and read till morning. Then, feeling strangely weary and unrefreshed, got up and joined M. Bougier, who was holding a sort of bit-de-justice on the river bank.

"Ciel! It is the twenty-fourth!" he ejaculated, as he made his last note towards the close of the sitting. "It is the eve of Noel! And we are far away from all Christian festivities! You, Mr. Ormerod, will be able, I hope, to furnish a Christmas dinner. I will supply the wine, which I brought from Cairo. Is it a bargain?"

"It is, indeed," I said with satisfaction. "I was thinking that my Christmas Day would be a somewhat dreary one, but in your company, M. Bougier, I shall no doubt spend a very agreeable time."

"Very well," said Bougier, in extremely good humour. "Then you dine with me tonight, my friend, and I dine with you tomorrow, Christmas Day. That is so, is it not?"

He gave me a very good dinner that evening on board the dahabeeah, and I came back to my own boat in good spirts, though by no means unduly excited. I mention this fact because a kind friend has now and then suggested that I had dined too freely. I can assure you that I, Eustace Ormerod, was never more sane, more clear-headed, or light-hearted, than I was that Christmas Eve, when I looked at the dim, glimmering waters of the Nile, and thought of the Christmas bells that were ringing out across the cold Northern lands, and of the girl that I knew was waiting for me at home.

"I wish I could send her a Christmas gift," I said to myself. "By the way, that ring of the sheik's would please her
immensely. I wonder if I could get Muhammed to sell it at
a low price, and Bougier to wink at my keeping it. It is too
small for a man; it is evidently meant for a woman's hand."
So saying, I unlocked the box, took out the ring, admired it
and held it up to the light, then put it as I had done before
on the little finger of my left hand. But this time I did not
take it off again. I looked upon it as a possible gift to Mabel,
and I pleased myself with the idea of wearing it first.

I fell asleep in my berth almost immediately. But in a
short time I awoke just as I had done on the previous night
with the sensation of having had a horrible dream, of which
I could not remember the details. I said some angry words to
myself on the subject of these bad nights, and then composed
myself to sleep again. But this time I did not lose consciousness. I dreamt, and yet I was awake, for I knew that what I
saw was not all a dream. It seemed to me that the air was full
of a strange presence. That some hungry, malignant creature
was going to and fro in the room, not speaking or crying out,
but full of a deliberate enmity towards myself, and a determination to take my life. Once or twice the thing seemed to
come near me, then drew back as if afraid. I knew, in a vague
way, that it waited for me to sleep, and I tried with a growing
horror, which I cannot express, to awake myself thoroughly,
and to drive away from me this creature of darkness to the
realm to which it belonged. But I was paralysed. I could not
move hand or foot. The terror of a sort of nightmare was
upon me, and I was absolutely helpless.

The thing certainly came nearer. It hovered over me.
It almost brushed my face. Then it seemed to take shape
and form. I knew it, only my eyelids were shut—and I saw
beside me for one dazzling moment a young and beautiful
girl, with long almond eyes, full of passion and fire, red lips,
and brown shapely limbs, on which glimmered costly robes,

jewels, and flowers. I felt the scent of the rich blossoms over-power my faculties. Yet mixed with it there was a strange, rank odour, like that of corruption, and death. Yet the girl's glowing face, the lithe yet rounded figure breathed nothing but life and energy! It would have been the most beautiful vision I ever beheld, had the face possessed any softness or tenderness of expression, but it was disfigured by terror and by hate. It seemed to me that she sought of something that she could not find and that she was determined to avenge herself on me as upon an enemy. Her slender brown fingers closed upon my throat, and then at that moment I knew that one of the fingers was bleeding and broken, and that there was a strange red circlet about the slender wrist.

I knew no more. I did not come to myself for some hours, and I believe I narrowly escaped brain fever. It seems at that supreme moment of my nightmare, if so it may be called, I uttered a strange, stifled cry, which brought Said, the most faithful servant that I ever possessed, to my side. He said that I seemed to be in convulsions, with my hands tearing at my throat, and my face almost black; and there were strange discoloured marks such as could only be made by clutching fingers upon the flesh.

He told me that M. Bougier had doctored me to the best of his ability, and that the old sheik had manifested every sign of alarm and distress when he heard that I had been taken ill. He had also demanded back from Said the precious mummy which he had conveyed to my cabin. But Said, with an infinite reverence for things in his master's apartment, had refused to let him touch the mummy figure, which still, therefore, reposed upon the empty berth opposite my own.

As soon as I was able, although still feeling very weak. I crawled out of my bunk and lifted the coverings with which the mummy was hidden. "But someone has been here," I ejaculated, involuntarily, "or you, Said, have rearranged the wrappings." Said swore that he had not touched the figure, and also that he had not admitted anyone into the cabin. But all the draperies and wrappings had been rearranged, and lay in straight, stiff folds about the figure, almost as if the swathing was complete. The hands were entirely hidden, but my curiosity impelled me to remove some of the easily-loosened bandages, and then I saw—what I had vaguely expected to see—that upon one of the slender brown fingers of the mummy's hand was the ruby ring which I myself had worn when I went to sleep on Christmas Eve.

I sent for M. Bougier and confided to him the whole story. With his help we partially unrolled the mummy, and found it in a very good state of preservation.

The face was especially perfect. It was that of a young girl, whose beauty it was easy to conjecture had been very great, and it seemed to me that it was the face of the woman who had hovered over me, with cruel, clutching fingers, in my dreams.

"She was of Royal race," said M. Bougier. "The hieroglyphics tell us that, and here is a papyrus roll, which we may be able to decipher. I remember hearing some tradition of this Princess. She died of grief, because of her lover's death, and was buried with his ring upon her hand. You must have heard this story, my friend, and you dreamt that she came back from the dead to take back her ring."

"I did not dream at all," I answered, somewhat angrily. "She—it—the Thing, whatever it was, was here, and I saw it."

"Ah, well," said the little Frenchman placidly, "there is no saying. We dream wonderful things sometimes. It strikes me this mummy was taken from the sarcophagus that you saw in the buried city. The Sheik wanted to steal a march upon us all. I should like to arrest him and hear what he has to say."

But Sheik Muhammed had fled. He had scented danger as soon as he knew that I was ill, and he and his family were never seen again. Nor could we recover a clue to the buried city, which still, therefore, remains unexplored. I entreated Bougier to let the dead Egyptian Princess keep her ring, and he, with some reluctance, consented. But I couldn't persuade him to abandon the idea of adding the mummy to the other exhibits in his museum. She lies there to this day, in a glass case, duly ticketed and labelled, but with her lover's ring still safe upon her mummy hand, and perhaps with this she is content.

But although I have been a happy and successful man for many years, and have married the girl I loved, and spent many a joyous Christmas in my own English home, I shall never forget the weird experiences of the gruesome Christmas Eve upon the Nile. And upon my throat I still carry, and shall carry as long as I live, the marks of that murderous mummy hand.

A DEAD FINGER
Sabine Baring-Gould
(1904)

1

Why the National Gallery should not attract so many visitors as, say, the British Museum, I cannot explain. The latter does not contain much that, one would suppose, appeals to the interest of the ordinary sightseer. What knows such of pre-historic flints and scratched bones? Of Assyrian sculpture? Of Egyptian hieroglyphics? The Greek and Roman statuary is cold and dead. The paintings in the National Gallery glow with colour, and are instinct with life. Yet, somehow, a few listless wanderers saunter yawning through the National Gallery, whereas swarms pour through the halls of the British Museum, and talk and pass remarks about the objects there exposed, of the date and meaning of which they have not the faintest conception.

I was thinking of this problem, and endeavouring to un-ravel it, one morning whilst sitting in the room for English masters at the great collection in Trafalgar Square. At the same time another thought forced itself upon me. I had been through the rooms devoted to foreign schools, and had then come into that given over to Reynolds, Morland, Gainsbor-ough, Constable, and Hogarth. The morning had been for a while propitious, but towards noon a dense umber-tinted fog had come on, making it all but impossible to see the pic-tures, and quite impossible to do them justice. I was tired, and so seated myself on one of the chairs, and fell into the consideration first of all of—why the National Gallery is not as popular as it should be; and secondly, how it was that the British School had no beginnings, like those of Italy and the Netherlands. We can see the art of the painter from its first initiation in the Italian peninsula, and among the Flemings. It starts on its progress like a child, and we can trace every stage of its growth. Not so with English art. It springs to life in full and splendid maturity. Who were there before Reynolds and Gainsborough and Hogarth? The great names of those portrait and subject painters who have left their canvases upon the walls of our country houses were those of foreigners—Holbein, Kneller, Van Dyck, and Lely for portraits, and Monnoyer for flower and fruit pieces. Landscapes, figure subjects were all importations, none home-grown. How came that about? Was there no limner that was native? Was it that fashion trampled on home-grown pictorial beginnings as it flouted and spurned native music?

Here was food for contemplation. Dreaming in the brown fog, looking through it without seeing its beauties, at Hogarth's painting of Lavinia Fenton as Polly Peachum, without wondering how so indifferent a beauty could have captivated the Duke of Bolton and held him for thirty years, I was recalled to myself and my surroundings by the strange conduct of a lady who had seated herself on a chair near me, also discouraged by the fog, and awaiting its dispersion.

I had not noticed her particularly. At the present moment I do not remember particularly what she was like. So far as I can recollect she was middle-aged, and was quietly yet well dressed. It was not her face nor her dress that attracted my attention and disturbed the current of my thoughts; the effect I speak of was produced by her strange movements and behaviour.

She had been sitting listless, probably thinking of nothing at all, or nothing in particular, when, in turning her eyes round, and finding that she could see nothing of the paintings, she began to study me. This did concern me greatly. A cat may look at the king; but to be contemplated by a lady is a compliment sufficient to please any gentleman. It was not gratified vanity that troubled my thoughts, but the consciousness that my appearance produced—first of all a startled surprise, then undisguised alarm, and, finally, indescribable horror.

Now a man can sit quietly leaning on the head of his umbrella, and glow internally, warmed and illumined by the consciousness that he is being surveyed with admiration by a lovely woman, even when he is middle-aged and not fashionably dressed; but no man can maintain his composure when he discovers himself to be an object of aversion and terror.

What was it? I passed my hand over my chin and upper lip, thinking it not impossible that I might have forgotten to shave that morning, and in my confusion not considering that the fog would prevent the lady from discovering neglect in this particular, had it occurred, which it had not. I am a little careless, perhaps, about shaving when in the country; but when in town, never.

The next idea that occurred to me was—a smut. Had a London black, curdled in that dense pea-soup atmosphere, descended on my nose and blackened it? I hastily drew my silk handkerchief from my pocket, moistened it, and passed it over my nose, and then each cheek. I then turned my eyes into the corners and looked at the lady, to see whether by this means I had got rid of what was objectionable in my personal appearance.

Then I saw that her eyes, dilated with horror, were riveted, not on my face, but on my leg.

My leg! What on earth could that harmless member have in it so terrifying? The morning had been dull; there had been rain in the night, and I admit that on leaving my hotel

I had turned up the bottoms of my trousers. That is a proceeding not so uncommon, not so outrageous as to account for the stony stare of this woman's eyes.

If that were all I would turn my trousers down.

Then I saw her shrink from the chair on which she sat to one further removed from me, but still with her eyes fixed on my leg—about the level of my knee. She had let fall her umbrella, and was grasping the seat of her chair with both hands, as she backed from me.

I need hardly say that I was greatly disturbed in mind and feelings, and forgot all about the origin of the English schools of painters, and the question why the British Museum is more popular than the National Gallery.

Thinking that I might have been spattered by a hansom whilst crossing Oxford Street, I passed my hand down my side hastily, with a sense of annoyance, and all at once touched something cold, clammy, that sent a thrill to my heart, and made me start and take a step forward. At the same moment, the lady, with a cry of horror, sprang to her feet, and with raised hands fled from the room, leaving her umbrella where it had fallen.

There were other visitors to the Picture Gallery besides ourselves, who had been passing through the saloon, and they turned at her cry, and looked in surprise after her.

The policeman stationed in the room came to me and asked what had happened. I was in such agitation that I hardly knew what to answer. I told him that I could explain what had occurred little better than himself. I had noticed that the lady had worn an odd expression, and had behaved in most extraordinary fashion, and that he had best take charge of her umbrella, and wait for her return to claim it.

This questioning by the official was vexing, as it prevented me from at once and on the spot investigating the cause of her alarm and mine—hers at something she must have seen on my leg, and mine at something I had distinctly felt creeping up my leg.

The numbing and sickening effect on me of the touch of the object I had not seen was not to be shaken off at once. Indeed, I felt as though my hand were contaminated, and that I could have no rest till I had thoroughly washed the hand, and, if possible, washed away the feeling that had been produced.

I looked on the floor, I examined my leg, but saw nothing. As I wore my overcoat, it was probable that in rising from my seat the skirt had fallen over my trousers and hidden the thing, whatever it was. I therefore hastily removed my overcoat and shook it, then I looked at my trousers. There was nothing whatever on my leg, and nothing fell from my overcoat when shaken.

Accordingly I reinvested myself, and hastily left the Gallery; then took my way as speedily as I could, without actually running, to Charing Cross Station and down the narrow way leading to the Metropolitan, where I went into Faulkner's bath and hairdressing establishment, and asked for hot water to thoroughly wash my hand and well soap it. I bathed my hand in water as hot as I could endure it, employed carbolic soap, and then, after having a good brush down, especially on my left side where my hand had encountered the object that had so affected me, I left. I had entertained the intention of going to the Princess's Theatre that evening, and of securing a ticket in the morning; but all thought of theatre-going was gone from me. I could not free my heart from the sense of nausea and cold that had been produced by the touch. I went into Gatti's to have lunch, and ordered something, I forget what, but, when served, I found that my appetite was gone. I could eat nothing; the food inspired me with disgust. I thrust it from me untasted, and, after drinking a couple of glasses of claret, left the restaurant, and returned to my hotel.

Feeling sick and faint, I threw my overcoat over the sofa-back, and cast myself on my bed.

I do not know that there was any particular reason for my doing so, but as I lay my eyes were on my great-coat.

The density of the fog had passed away, and there was light again, not of first quality, but sufficient for a Londoner to swear by, so that I could see everything in my room, though through a veil, darkly.

I do not think my mind was occupied in any way. About the only occasions on which, to my knowledge, my mind is actually passive or inert is when crossing the Channel in *The Foam* from Dover to Calais, when I am always, in every weather, abjectly seasick—and thoughtless. But as I now lay on my bed, uncomfortable, squeamish, without knowing why—I was in the same inactive mental condition. But not for long.

I saw something that startled me.

First, it appeared to me as if the lappet of my overcoat pocket were in movement, being raised. I did not pay much attention to this, as I supposed that the garment was sliding down on to the seat of the sofa, from the back, and that this displacement of gravity caused the movement I observed. But this I soon saw was not the case. That which moved the lappet was something in the pocket that was struggling to get out. I could see now that it was working its way up the inside, and that when it reached the opening it lost balance and fell down again. I could make this out by the projections and indentations in the cloth; these moved as the creature, or whatever it was, worked its way up the lining.

"A mouse," I said, and forgot my seediness; I was interested. "The little rascal! However did he contrive to seat himself in my pocket? and I have worn that overcoat all the morning!" But no—it was not a mouse. I saw something white poke its way out from under the lappet; and in another moment an object was revealed that, though revealed, I could not understand, nor could I distinguish what it was.

Now roused by curiosity, I raised myself on my elbow. In doing this I made some noise, the bed creaked. Instantly the something dropped on the floor, lay outstretched for a moment, to recover itself, and then began, with the motions of a maggot, to run along the floor.

There is a caterpillar called "The Measurer," because, when it advances, it draws its tail up to where its head is and then throws forward its full length, and again draws up its extremity, forming at each time a loop; and with each step measuring its total length. The object I now saw on the floor was advancing precisely like the measuring caterpillar. It had the colour of a cheese-maggot, and in length was about three and a half inches. It was not, however, like a caterpillar, which is flexible throughout its entire length, but this was, as it seemed to me, jointed in two places, one joint being more conspicuous than the other. For some moments I was so completely paralysed by astonishment that I remained motionless, looking at the thing as it crawled along the carpet—a dull green carpet with darker green, almost black, flowers in it.

It had, as it seemed to me, a glossy head, distinctly marked; but, as the light was not brilliant, I could not make out very clearly, and, moreover, the rapid movements prevented close scrutiny.

Presently, with a shock still more startling than that produced by its apparition at the opening of the pocket of my great-coat, I became convinced that what I saw was a finger, a human forefinger, and that the glossy head was no other than the nail.

The finger did not seem to have been amputated. There was no sign of blood or laceration where the knuckle should be, but the extremity of the finger, or root rather, faded away

to indistinctness, and I was unable to make out the root of
the finger.

I could see no hand, no body behind this finger, nothing
whatever except a finger that had little token of warm life in
it, no coloration as though blood circulated in it; and this
finger was in active motion creeping along the carpet towards a wardrobe that stood against the wall by the fireplace.

I sprang off the bed and pursued it.

Evidently the finger was alarmed, for it redoubled its
pace, reached the wardrobe, and went under it. By the time
I had arrived at the article of furniture it had disappeared. I
lit a vesta match and held it beneath the wardrobe, that was
raised above the carpet by about two inches, on turned feet,
but I could see nothing more of the finger.

I got my umbrella and thrust it beneath, and raked forwards and backwards, right and left, and raked out flue, and
nothing more solid.

2

I packed my portmanteau next day and returned to my home
in the country. All desire for amusement in town was gone,
and the faculty to transact business had departed as well.

A languor and qualms had come over me, and my head
was in a maze. I was unable to fix my thoughts on anything.
At times I was disposed to believe that my wits were desert-
ing me, at others that I was on the verge of a severe illness.
Anyhow, whether likely to go off my head or not, or take to
my bed, home was the only place for me, and homeward I
sped, accordingly. On reaching my country habitation, my
servant, as usual, took my portmanteau to my bedroom, un-
strapped it, but did not unpack it. I object to his throwing
out the contents of my Gladstone bag; not that there is anything in it he may not see, but that he puts my things where I
cannot find them again. My clothes—he is welcome to place
them where he likes and where they belong, and this latter

he knows better than I do; but, then, I carry about with me
other things than a dress suit, and changes of linen and flan-
nel. There are letters, papers, books—and the proper desti-
nations of these are known only to myself. A servant has a
singular and evil knack of putting away literary matter and
odd volumes in such places that it takes the owner half a day
to find them again. Although I was uncomfortable, and my
head in a whirl, I opened and unpacked my own portmanteau. As I was thus engaged I saw something curled up in my
collar-box, the lid of which had got broken in by a boot-heel
impinging on it. I had pulled off the damaged cover to see if
my collars had been spoiled, when something curled up inside suddenly rose on end and leapt, just like a cheese-jump-
er, out of the box, over the edge of the Gladstone bag, and
scurried away across the floor in a manner already familiar
to me.

I could not doubt for a moment what it was—here was
the finger again. It had come with me from London to the
country.

Whither it went in its run over the floor I do not know, I
was too bewildered to observe.

Somewhat later, towards evening, I seated myself in my
easy-chair, took up a book, and tried to read. I was tired with
the journey, with the knocking about in town, and the dis-
comfort and alarm produced by the apparition of the finger.
I felt worn out. I was unable to give my attention to what I
read, and before I was aware was asleep. Roused for an instant
by the fall of the book from my hands, I speedily relapsed
into unconsciousness. I am not sure that a doze in an arm-
chair ever does good. It usually leaves me in a semi-stupid
condition and with a headache. Five minutes in a horizontal
position on my bed is worth thirty in a chair. That is my
experience. In sleeping in a sedentary position the head is a
difficulty; it drops forward or lolls on one side or the other,
and has to be brought back into a position in which the line

to the centre of gravity runs through the trunk, otherwise
the head carries the body over in a sort of general capsize out
of the chair on to the floor.

I slept, on the occasion of which I am speaking, pretty
healthily, because deadly weary; but I was brought to waking, not by my head falling over the arm of the chair, and my
trunk tumbling after it, but by a feeling of cold extending
from my throat to my heart. When I awoke I was in a diago-
nal position, with my right ear resting on my right shoulder,
and exposing the left side of my throat, and it was here—
where the jugular vein throbs—that I felt the greatest intensity of cold. At once I shrugged my left shoulder, rubbing
my neck with the collar of my coat in so doing. Immediately
something fell off, upon the floor, and I again saw the finger.

My disgust—horror, were intensified when I perceived
that it was dragging something after it, which might have
been an old stocking, and which I took at first glance for
something of the sort.

The evening sun shone in through my window, in a brilliant golden ray that lighted the object as it scrambled along.
With this illumination I was able to distinguish what the
object was. It is not easy to describe it, but I will make the
attempt.

The finger I saw was solid and material; what it drew
after it was neither, or was in a nebulous, protoplasmic condition. The finger was attached to a hand that was curdling
into matter and in process of acquiring solidity; attached to
the hand was an arm in a very filmy condition, and this arm
belonged to a human body in a still more vaporous, imma-
terial condition. This was being dragged along the floor by
the finger, just as a silkworm might pull after it the tangle
of its web. I could see legs and arms, and head, and coat-tail
tumbling about and interlacing and disentangling again in
a promiscuous manner. There were no bone, no muscle, no
substance in the figure; the members were attached to the

trunk, which was spineless, but they had evidently no functions, and were wholly dependent on the finger which pulled
them along in a jumble of parts as it advanced.

In such confusion did the whole vaporous matter seem,
that I think—I cannot say for certain it was so, but the impression left on my mind was—that one of the eyeballs was
looking out at a nostril, and the tongue lolling out of one of
the ears.

It was, however, only for a moment that I saw this germ-
body; I cannot call by another name that which had not
more substance than smoke. I saw it only so long as it was
being dragged athwart the ray of sunlight. The moment it
was pulled jerkily out of the beam into the shadow beyond, I
could see nothing of it, only the crawling finger.

I had not sufficient moral energy or physical force in me
to rise, pursue, and stamp on the finger, and grind it with
my heel into the floor. Both seemed drained out of me. What
became of the finger, whither it went, how it managed to
secrete itself, I do not know. I had lost the power to inquire.
I sat in my chair, chilled, staring before me into space.

"Please, sir," a voice said, "there's Mr. Square below, electrical engineer."

"Eh?" I looked dreamily round.

My valet was at the door.

"Please, sir, the gentleman would be glad to be allowed
to go over the house and see that all the electrical apparatus
is in order."

"Oh, indeed! Yes—show him up."

3

I had recently placed the lighting of my house in the hands
of an electrical engineer, a very intelligent man, Mr. Square,
for whom I had contracted a sincere friendship.

He had built a shed with a dynamo out of sight, and had
entrusted the laying of the wires to subordinates, as he had

been busy with other orders and could not personally watch every detail. But he was not the man to let anything pass unobserved, and he knew that electricity was not a force to be played with. Bad or careless workmen will often insufficiently protect the wires, or neglect the insertion of the lead which serves as a safety-valve in the event of the current being too strong. Houses may be set on fire, human beings fatally shocked, by the neglect of a bad or slovenly workman.

The apparatus for my mansion was but just completed, and Mr. Square had come to inspect it and make sure that all was right.

He was an enthusiast in the matter of electricity, and saw for it a vast perspective, the limits of which could not be predicted.

"All forces," said he, "are correlated. When you have force in one form, you may just turn it into this or that, as you like. In one form it is motive power, in another it is light, in another heat. Now we have electricity for illumination. We employ it, but not as freely as in the States, for propelling vehicles. Why should we have horses drawing our buses? We should use only electric trams. Why do we burn coal to warm our shins? There is electricity, which throws out no filthy smoke as does coal. Why should we let the tides waste their energies in the Thames? in other estuaries? There we have Nature supplying us—free, gratis, and for nothing—with all the force we want for propelling, for heating, for lighting. I will tell you something more, my dear sir," said Mr. Square. "I have mentioned but three modes of force, and have instanced but a limited number of uses to which electricity may be turned. How is it with photography? Is not electric light becoming an artistic agent? I bet you," said he, "before long it will become a therapeutic agent as well."

"Oh, yes; I have heard of certain impostors with their life-belts."

Mr. Square did not relish this little dig I gave him. He winced, but returned to the charge. "We don't know how to direct it aright, that is all," said he. "I haven't taken the matter up, but others will, I bet; and we shall have electricity used as freely as now we use powders and pills. I don't believe in doctors' stuffs myself. I hold that disease lays hold of a man because he lacks physical force to resist it. Now, is it not obvious that you are beginning at the wrong end when you attack the disease? What you want is to supply force, make up for the lack of physical power, and force is force wherever you find it—here motive, there illuminating, and so on. I don't see why a physician should not utilise the tide rushing out under London Bridge for restoring the feeble vigour of all who are languid and a prey to disorder in the Metropolis. It will come to that, I bet, and that is not all. Force is force, everywhere. Political, moral force, physical force, dynamic force, heat, light, tidal waves, and so on—all are one, all is one. In time we shall know how to galvanise into aptitude and moral energy all the limp and crooked consciences and wills that need taking in hand, and such there always will be in modern civilisation. I don't know how to do it. I don't know how it will be done, but in the future the priest as well as the doctor will turn electricity on as his principal, nay, his only agent. And he can get his force anywhere, out of the running stream, out of the wind, out of the tidal wave.

"I'll give you an instance," continued Mr. Square, chuckling and rubbing his hands, "to show you the great possibilities in electricity, used in a crude fashion. In a certain great city away far west in the States, a go-ahead place, too, more so than New York, they had electric trams all up and down and along the roads to everywhere. The union men working for the company demanded that the non-unionists should be turned off. But the company didn't see it. Instead, it turned off the union men. It had up its sleeve a sufficiency of the others, and filled all places at once. Union men didn't like it, and passed word that at a given hour on a certain day every wire was to be cut. The company knew this by means of its spies, and turned on, ready for them, three times the power into all the wires. At the fixed moment, up the poles went the strikers to cut the cables, and down they came a dozen times quicker than they went up, I bet. Then there came wires to the hospitals from all quarters for stretchers to carry off the disabled men, some with broken legs, arms, ribs; two or three had their necks broken. I reckon the company was wonderfully merciful—it didn't put on sufficient force to make cinders of them then and there; possibly opinion might not have liked it. Stopped the strike, did that. Great moral effect—all done by electricity."

In this manner Mr. Square was wont to rattle on. He interested me, and I came to think that there might be something in what he said—that his suggestions were not mere nonsense. I was glad to see Mr. Square enter my room, shown in by my man. I did not rise from my chair to shake his hand, for I had not sufficient energy to do so. In a languid tone I welcomed him and signed to him to take a seat. Mr. Square looked at me with some surprise.

"Why, what's the matter?" he said. "You seem unwell. Not got the 'flue, have you?"

"I beg your pardon?"

"The influenza. Every third person is crying out that he has it, and the sale of eucalyptus is enormous, not that eucalyptus is any good. Influenza microbes indeed! What care they for eucalyptus? You've gone down some steps of the ladder of life since I saw you last, squire. How do you account for that?"

I hesitated about mentioning the extraordinary circumstances that had occurred; but Square was a man who would not allow any beating about the bush. He was downright and straight, and in ten minutes had got the entire story out of me.

"Rather boisterous for your nerves that—a crawling finger," said he. "It's a queer story taken on end."

Then he was silent, considering.

After a few minutes he rose, and said: "I'll go and look
at the fittings, and then I'll turn this little matter of yours
over again, and see if I can't knock the bottom out of it, I'm
kinder fond of these sort of things."

Mr. Square was not a Yankee, but he had lived for some
time in America, and affected to speak like an American. He
used expressions, terms of speech common in the States, but
had none of the Transatlantic twang. He was a man absolutely without affectation in every other particular; this was his
sole weakness, and it was harmless.

The man was so thorough in all he did that I did not expect his return immediately. He was certain to examine every
portion of the dynamo engine, and all the connections and
burners. This would necessarily engage him for some hours.
As the day was nearly done, I knew he could not accomplish
what he wanted that evening, and accordingly gave orders
that a room should be prepared for him. Then, as my head
was full of pain, and my skin was burning, I told my servant
to apologise for my absence from dinner, and tell Mr. Square
that I was really forced to return to my bed by sickness, and
that I believed I was about to be prostrated by an attack of
influenza.

The valet—a worthy fellow, who has been with me for
six years—was concerned at my appearance, and urged me to
allow him to send for a doctor. I had no confidence in the
local practitioner, and if I sent for another from the nearest
town I should offend him, and a row would perhaps ensue, so
I declined. If I were really in for an influenza attack, I knew
about as much as any doctor how to deal with it. Quinine,
quinine—that was all. I bade my man light a small lamp,
lower it, so as to give sufficient illumination to enable me to

find some lime-juice at my bed head, and my pocket-handkerchief, and to be able to read my watch. When he had done
this, I bade him leave me.

I lay in bed, burning, racked with pain in my head, and
with my eyeballs on fire.

Whether I fell asleep or went off my head for a while I
cannot tell. I may have fainted. I have no recollection of
anything after having gone to bed and taken a sip of lime-
juice that tasted to me like soap—till I was roused by a sense
of pain in my ribs—a slow, gnawing, torturing pain, waxing
momentarily more intense. In half-consciousness I was partly dreaming and partly aware of actual suffering. The pain
was real; but in my fancy I thought that a great maggot was
working its way into my side between my ribs. I seemed to
see it. It twisted itself half round, then reverted to its former
position, and again twisted itself, moving like a bradawl, not
like a gimlet, which latter forms a complete revolution.

This, obviously, must have been a dream, hallucination
only, as I was lying on my back and my eyes were directed
towards the bottom of the bed, and the coverlet and blankets and sheet intervened between my eyes and my side. But
in fever one sees without eyes, and in every direction, and
through all obstructions.

Roused thoroughly by an excruciating twinge, I tried to
cry out, and succeeded in throwing myself over on my right
side, that which was in pain. At once I felt the thing withdrawn that was awling—if I may use the word—in between
my ribs.

And now I saw, standing beside the bed, a figure that
had its arm under the bedclothes, and was slowly removing
it. The hand was leisurely drawn from under the coverings
and rested on the eider-down coverlet, with the forefinger
extended.

The figure was that of a man, in shabby clothes, with a
sallow, mean face, a retreating forehead, with hair cut after

the French fashion, and a moustache, dark. The jaws and
chin were covered with a bristly growth, as if shaving had
been neglected for a fortnight. The figure did not appear to
be thoroughly solid, but to be of the consistency of curd,
and the face was of the complexion of curd. As I looked at
this object it withdrew, sliding backward in an odd sort of
manner, and as though overweighted by the hand, which was
the most substantial, indeed the only substantial portion of
it. Though the figure retreated stooping, yet it was no longer
huddled along by the finger, as if it had no material existence. If the same, it had acquired a consistency and a solidity which it did not possess before.

How it vanished I do not know, nor whither it went. The
door opened, and Square came in.

"What!" he exclaimed with cheery voice; "influenza is it?"

"I don't know—I think it's that finger again."

4

"Now, look here," said Square, "I'm not going to have that
cuss at its pranks any more. Tell me all about it."

I was now so exhausted, so feeble, that I was not able to
give a connected account of what had taken place, but Square
put to me just a few pointed questions and elicited the main
facts. He pieced them together in his own orderly mind, so
as to form a connected whole. "There is a feature in the
case," said he, "that strikes me as remarkable and important.
At first—a finger only, then a hand, then a nebulous figure
attached to the hand, without backbone, without consistency. Lastly, a complete form, with consistency and with backbone, but the latter in a gelatinous condition, and the entire
figure overweighted by the hand, just as hand and figure
were previously overweighted by the finger. Simultaneously
with this compacting and consolidating of the figure, came
your degeneration and loss of vital force and, in a word,
of health. What you lose, that object acquires, and what it

acquires, it gains by contact with you. That's clear enough, is it not?"

"I dare say. I don't know. I can't think."

"I suppose not; the faculty of thought is drained out of you. Very well, I must think for you, and I will. Force is force, and see if I can't deal with your visitant in such a way as will prove just as truly a moral dissuasive as that employed on the union men on strike in—never mind where it was. That's not to the point."

"Will you kindly give me some lime-juice?" I entreated.

I sipped the acid draught, but without relief. I listened to Square, but without hope. I wanted to be left alone. I was weary of my pain, weary of everything, even of life. It was a matter of indifference to me whether I recovered or slipped out of existence.

"It will be here again shortly," said the engineer. "As the French say, *l'appetit vient en mangeant*. It has been at you thrice, it won't be content without another peck. And if it does get another, I guess it will pretty well about finish you."

Mr. Square rubbed his chin, and then put his hands into his trouser pockets. That also was a trick acquired in the States, an inelegant one. His hands, when not actively occupied, went into his pockets, inevitably they gravitated thither. Ladies did not like Square; they said he was not a gentleman. But it was not that he said or did anything "off colour," only he spoke to them, looked at them, walked with them, always with his hands in his pockets. I have seen a lady turn her back on him deliberately because of this trick.

Standing now with his hands in his pockets, he studied my bed, and said contemptuously: "Old-fashioned and bad, fourposter. Oughtn't to be allowed, I guess; unwholesome all the way round."

I was not in a condition to dispute this. I like a fourposter with curtains at head and feet; not that I ever draw

them, but it gives a sense of privacy that is wanting in one of
your half-tester beds.

If there is a window at one's feet, one can lie in bed without the glare in one's eyes, and yet without darkening the
room by drawing the blinds. There is much to be said for a
fourposter, but this is not the place in which to say it.

Mr. Square pulled his hands out of his pockets and began
fiddling with the electric point near the head of my bed,
attached a wire, swept it in a semicircle along the floor, and
then thrust the knob at the end into my hand in the bed.

"Keep your eye open," said he, "and your hand shut and
covered. If that finger comes again tickling your ribs, try it
with the point. I'll manage the switch, from behind the curtain."

Then he disappeared.

I was too indifferent in my misery to turn my head and
observe where he was. I remained inert, with the knob in my
hand, and my eyes closed, suffering and thinking of nothing
but the shooting pains through my head and the aches in my
loins and back and legs.

Some time probably elapsed before I felt the finger again
at work at my ribs; it groped, but no longer bored. I now
felt the entire hand, not a single finger, and the hand was
substantial, cold, and clammy. I was aware, how, I know not,
that if the finger-point reached the region of my heart, on
the left side, the hand would, so to speak, sit down on it,
with the cold palm over it, and that then immediately my
heart would cease to beat, and it would be, as Square might
express it, "gone coon" with me.

In self-preservation I brought up the knob of the electric
wire against the hand—against one of the ringers, I think—
and at once was aware of a rapping, squealing noise. I turned
my head languidly, and saw the form, now more substantial
than before, capering in an ecstasy of pain, endeavouring

fruitlessly to withdraw its arm from under the bedclothes, and the hand from the electric point.

At the same moment Square stepped from behind the curtain, with a dry laugh, and said: "I thought we should fix him. He has the coil about him, and can't escape. Now let us drop to particulars. But I shan't let you off till I know all about you."

The last sentence was addressed, not to me, but to the apparition.

Thereupon he bade me take the point away from the hand of the figure—being—whatever it was, but to be ready with it at a moment's notice. He then proceeded to catechise my visitor, who moved restlessly within the circle of wire, but could not escape from it. It replied in a thin, squealing voice that sounded as if it came from a distance, and had a querulous tone in it. I do not pretend to give all that was said. I cannot recollect everything that passed. My memory was affected by my illness, as well as my body. Yet I prefer giving the scraps that I recollect to what Square told me he had heard.

"Yes—I was unsuccessful, always was. Nothing answered with me. The world was against me. Society was. I hate Society. I don't like work neither, never did. But I like agitating against what is established. I hate the Royal Family, the landed interest, the parsons, everything that is, except the people—that is, the unemployed. I always did. I couldn't get work as suited me. When I died they buried me in a cheap coffin, dirt cheap, and gave me a nasty grave, cheap, and a service rattled away cheap, and no monument. Didn't want none. Oh! there are lots of us. All discontented. Discontent! That's a passion, it is—it gets into the veins, it fills the brain, it occupies the heart; it's a sort of divine cancer that takes possession of the entire man, and makes him dissatisfied with everything, and hate everybody. But we must have our share of happiness at some time. We all crave for it in one way or other. Some think there's a future state of blessedness and so have hope, and look to attain to it, for hope is a cable and anchor that attaches to what is real. But when you have no hope of that sort, don't believe in any future state, you must look for happiness in life here. We didn't get it when we were alive, so we seek to procure it after we are dead. We can do it, if we can get out of our cheap and nasty coffins. But not till the greater part of us is mouldered away. If a finger or two remains, that can work its way up to the surface, those cheap deal coffins go to pieces quick enough. Then the only solid part of us left can pull the rest of us that has gone to nothing after it. Then we grope about after the living. The well-to-do if we can get at them—the honest working poor if we can't—we hate them too, because they are content and happy. If we reach any of these, and can touch them, then we can draw their vital force out of them into ourselves, and recuperate at their expense. That was about what I was going to do with you. Getting on famous. Nearly solidified into a new man; and given another chance in life. But I've missed it this time. Just like my luck. Miss everything. Always have, except misery and disappointment. Get plenty of that."

"What are you all?" asked Square. "Anarchists out of employ?"

"Some of us go by that name, some by other designations, but we are all one, and own allegiance to but one monarch— Sovereign discontent. We are bred to have a distaste for manual work; and we grow up loafers, grumbling at everything and quarrelling with Society that is around us and the Providence that is above us."

"And what do you call yourselves now?"

"Call ourselves? Nothing; we are the same, in another condition, that is all. Folk called us once Anarchists, Nihilists, Socialists, Levellers, now they call us the Influenza. The learned talk of microbes, and bacilli, and bacteria. Microbes, bacilli, and bacteria be blowed! We are the Influenza; we the social failures, the generally discontented, coming up out of our cheap and nasty graves in the form of physical disease. We are the Influenza."

"There you are, I guess!" exclaimed Square triumphantly. "Did I not say that all forces were correlated? If so, then all negations, deficiencies of force are one in their several man-ifestations. Talk of Divine discontent as a force impelling to progress! Rubbish, it is a paralysis of energy. It turns all it absorbs to acid, to envy, spite, gall. It inspires nothing, but rots the whole moral system. Here you have it—moral, so-cial, political discontent in another form, nay aspect—that is all. What Anarchism is in the body Politic, that Influenza is in the body Physical. Do you see that?"

"Ye-e-s-e-s," I believe I answered, and dropped away into the land of dreams.

I recovered. What Square did with the Thing I know not, but believe that he reduced it again to its former negative and self-decomposing condition.

THE BEAST WITH FIVE FINGERS
W. F. Harvey
(1919)

When I was a little boy I once went with my father to call on
Adrian Borlsover. I played on the floor with a black spaniel
while my father appealed for a subscription. Just before we
left my father said, "Mr. Borlsover, may my son here shake
hands with you? It will be a thing to look back upon with
pride when he grows to be a man."

I came up to the bed on which the old man was lying and
put my hand in his, awed by the still beauty of his face. He
spoke to me kindly, and hoped that I should always try to
please my father. Then he placed his right hand on my head
and asked for a blessing to rest upon me. "Amen!" said my
father, and I followed him out of the room, feeling as if I
wanted to cry. But my father was in excellent spirits.

"That old gentleman, Jim," said he, "is the most wonderful man in the whole town. For ten years he has been quite
blind."

"But I saw his eyes," I said. "They were ever so black and
shiny; they weren't shut up like Nora's puppies. Can't he see
at all?"

And so I learnt for the first time that a man might have
eyes that looked dark and beautiful and shining without being able to see.

"Just like Mrs. Tomlinson has big ears," I said, "and can't
hear at all except when Mr. Tomlinson shouts."

"Jim," said my father, "it's not right to talk about a lady's ears. Remember what Mr. Borlsover said about pleasing me and being a good boy."

That was the only time I saw Adrian Borlsover. I soon forgot about him and the hand which he laid in blessing on my head. But for a week I prayed that those dark tender eyes might see.

"His spaniel may have puppies," I said in my prayers, "and he will never be able to know how funny they look with their eyes all closed up. Please let old Mr. Borlsover see."

Adrian Borlsover, as my father had said, was a wonderful man. He came of an eccentric family. Borlsovers' sons, for some reason, always seemed to marry very ordinary women, which perhaps accounted for the fact that no Borlsover had been a genius, and only one Borlsover had been mad. But they were great champions of little causes, generous patrons of odd sciences, founders of querulous sects, trustworthy guides to the bypath meadows of erudition.

Adrian was an authority on the fertilization of orchids. He had held at one time the family living at Borlsover Conyers, until a congenital weakness of the lungs obliged him to seek a less rigorous climate in the sunny south coast watering-place where I had seen him. Occasionally he would relieve one or other of the local clergy. My father described him as a fine preacher, who gave long and inspiring sermons from what many men would have considered unprofitable texts. "An excellent proof," he would add, "of the truth of the doctrine of direct verbal inspiration."

Adrian Borlsover was exceedingly clever with his hands. His penmanship was exquisite. He illustrated all his scientific papers, made his own woodcuts, and carved the reredos that is at present the chief feature of interest in the church at Borlsover Conyers. He had an exceedingly clever knack in cutting silhouettes for young ladies and paper pigs and

cows for little children, and made more than one complicat-
ed wind instrument of his own devising.

When he was fifty years old Adrian Borlsover lost his
sight. In a wonderfully short time he had adapted himself to
the new conditions of life. He quickly learned to read Braille.
So marvelous indeed was his sense of touch that he was still
able to maintain his interest in botany. The mere passing of
his long supple fingers over a flower was sufficient means for
its identification, though occasionally he would use his lips.
I have found several letters of his among my father's correspondence. In no case was there anything to show that he
was afflicted with blindness and this in spite of the fact that
he exercised undue economy in the spacing of lines. Towards
the close of his life the old man was credited with powers of
touch that seemed almost uncanny: it has been said that he
could tell at once the color of a ribbon placed between his
fingers. My father would neither confirm nor deny the story.

Adrian Borlsover was a bachelor. His elder brother George
had married late in life, leaving one son, Eustace, who lived
in the gloomy Georgian mansion at Borlsover Conyers,
where he could work undisturbed in collecting material for
his great book on heredity.

Like his uncle, he was a remarkable man. The Borlsovers
had always been born naturalists, but Eustace possessed in a
special degree the power of systematizing his knowledge. He
had received his university education in Germany, and then,
after post-graduate work in Vienna and Naples, had traveled
for four years in South America and the East, getting together a huge store of material for a new study into the processes
of variation.

He lived alone at Borlsover Conyers with Saunders his
secretary, a man who bore a somewhat dubious reputation in
the district, but whose powers as a mathematician, combined
with his business abilities, were invaluable to Eustace.

Uncle and nephew saw little of each other. The visits of Eustace were confined to a week in the summer or autumn: long weeks, that dragged almost as slowly as the bath-chair in which the old man was drawn along the sunny sea front. In their way the two men were fond of each other, though their intimacy would doubtless have been greater had they shared the same religious views. Adrian held to the old-fashioned evangelical dogmas of his early manhood; his nephew for many years had been thinking of embracing Buddhism. Both men possessed, too, the reticence the Borlsovers had always shown, and which their enemies sometimes called hypocrisy. With Adrian it was a reticence as to the things he had left undone; but with Eustace it seemed that the curtain which he was so careful to leave undrawn hid something more than a half-empty chamber.

Two years before his death Adrian Borlsover developed, unknown to himself, the not uncommon power of automatic writing. Eustace made the discovery by accident. Adrian was sitting reading in bed, the forefinger of his left hand tracing the Braille characters, when his nephew noticed that a pencil the old man held in his right hand was moving slowly along the opposite page. He left his seat in the window and sat down beside the bed. The right hand continued to move, and now he could see plainly that they were letters and words which it was forming.

"Adrian Borlsover," wrote the hand, "Eustace Borlsover, George Borlsover, Francis Borlsover Sigismund Borlsover, Adrian Borlsover, Eustace Borlsover, Saville Borlsover. B, for Borlsover. Honesty is the Best Policy. Beautiful Belinda Borlsover."

"What curious nonsense!" said Eustace to himself.

"King George the Third ascended the throne in 1760," wrote the hand. "Crowd, a noun of multitude; a collection of individuals—Adrian Borlsover, Eustace Borlsover."

"It seems to me," said his uncle, closing the book, "that you had much better make the most of the afternoon sunshine and take your walk now." "I think perhaps I will," Eustace answered as he picked up the volume. "I won't go far, and when I come back I can read to you those articles in *Nature* about which we were speaking."

He went along the promenade, but stopped at the first shelter, and seating himself in the corner best protected from the wind, he examined the book at leisure. Nearly every page was scored with a meaningless jungle of pencil marks: rows of capital letters, short words, long words, complete sentences, copy-book tags. The whole thing, in fact, had the appearance of a copy-book, and on a more careful scrutiny Eustace thought that there was ample evidence to show that the handwriting at the beginning of the book, good though it was, was not nearly so good as the handwriting at the end.

He left his uncle at the end of October, with a promise to return early in December. It seemed to him quite clear that the old man's power of automatic writing was developing rapidly, and for the first time he looked forward to a visit that combined duty with interest.

But on his return he was at first disappointed. His uncle, he thought, looked older. He was listless too, preferring others to read to him and dictating nearly all his letters. Not until the day before he left had Eustace an opportunity of observing Adrian Borlsover's new-found faculty.

The old man, propped up in bed with pillows, had sunk into a light sleep. His two hands lay on the coverlet, his left hand tightly clasping his right. Eustace took an empty manuscript book and placed a pencil within reach of the fingers of the right hand. They snatched at it eagerly; then dropped the pencil to unloose the left hand from its restraining grasp.

"Perhaps to prevent interference I had better hold that hand," said Eustace to himself, as he watched the pencil. Almost immediately it began to write.

"Blundering Borlsovers, unnecessarily unnatural, extraordinarily eccentric, culpably curious."

"Who are you?" asked Eustace, in a low voice.

"Never you mind," wrote the hand of Adrian.

"Is it my uncle who is writing?"

"Oh, my prophetic soul, mine uncle."

"Is it anyone I know?"

"Silly Eustace, you'll see me very soon."

"When shall I see you?"

"When poor old Adrian's dead."

"Where shall I see you?"

"Where shall you not?"

Instead of speaking his next question, Borlsover wrote it. "What is the time?"

The fingers dropped the pencil and moved three or four times across the paper. Then, picking up the pencil, they wrote:

"Ten minutes before four. Put your book away, Eustace. Adrian mustn't find us working at this sort of thing. He doesn't know what to make of it, and I won't have poor old Adrian disturbed. *Au revoir.*"

Adrian Borlsover awoke with a start.

"I've been dreaming again," he said; "such queer dreams of leaguered cities and forgotten towns. You were mixed up in this one, Eustace, though I can't remember how. Eustace, I want to warn you. Don't walk in doubtful paths. Choose your friends well. Your poor grandfather—"

A fit of coughing put an end to what he was saying, but Eustace saw that the hand was still writing. He managed unnoticed to draw the book away. "I'll light the gas," he said, "and ring for tea." On the other side of the bed curtain he saw the last sentences that had been written.

"It's too late, Adrian," he read. "We're friends already; aren't we, Eustace Borlsover?"

On the following day Eustace Borlsover left. He thought his uncle looked ill when he said good-by, and the old man spoke despondently of the failure his life had been.

"Nonsense, uncle!" said his nephew. "You have got over your difficulties in a way not one in a hundred thousand would have done. Every one marvels at your splendid perseverance in teaching your hand to take the place of your lost sight. To me it's been a revelation of the possibilities of education."

"Education," said his uncle dreamily, as if the word had started a new train of thought, "education is good so long as you know to whom and for what purpose you give it. But with the lower orders of men, the base and more sordid spirits, I have grave doubts as to its results. Well, good-by, Eustace, I may not see you again. You are a true Borlsover, with all the Borlsover faults. Marry, Eustace. Marry some good, sensible girl. And if by any chance I don't see you again, my will is at my solicitor's. I've not left you any legacy, because I know you're well provided for, but I thought you might like to have my books. Oh, and there's just one other thing. You know, before the end people often lose control over themselves and make absurd requests. Don't pay any attention to them, Eustace. Good-by!" and he held out his hand. Eustace took it. It remained in his a fraction of a second longer than he had expected, and gripped him with a virility that was surprising. There was, too, in its touch a subtle sense of intimacy.

"Why, uncle!" he said, "I shall see you alive and well for many long years to come."

Two months later Adrian Borlsover died.

Eustace Borlsover was in Naples at the time. He read the obituary notice in the *Morning Post* on the day announced for the funeral.

"Poor old fellow!" he said. "I wonder where I shall find room for all his books."

The question occurred to him again with greater force when three days later he found himself standing in the library at Borlsover Conyers, a huge room built for use, and not for beauty, in the year of Waterloo by a Borlsover who was an ardent admirer of the great Napoleon. It was arranged on the plan of many college libraries, with tall, projecting bookcases forming deep recesses of dusty silence, fit graves for the old hates of forgotten controversy, the dead passions of forgotten lives. At the end of the room, behind the bust of some unknown eighteenth-century divine, an ugly iron corkscrew stair led to a shelf-lined gallery. Nearly every shelf was full.

"I must talk to Saunders about it," said Eustace. "I suppose that it will be necessary to have the billiard-room fitted up with book cases."

The two men met for the first time after many weeks in the dining-room that evening.

"Hullo!" said Eustace, standing before the fire with his hands in his pockets. "How goes the world, Saunders? Why these dress togs?" He himself was wearing an old shooting-jacket. He did not believe in mourning, as he had told his uncle on his last visit; and though he usually went in for quiet-colored ties, he wore this evening one of an ugly red, in order to shock Morton the butler, and to make them thrash out the whole question of mourning for themselves in the servants' hall. Eustace was a true Borlsover. "The world," said Saunders, "goes the same as usual, confoundedly slow. The dress togs are accounted for by an invitation from Captain Lockwood to bridge."

"How are you getting there?"

"I've told your coachman to drive me in your carriage. Any objection?"

"Oh, dear me, no! We've had all things in common for far too many years for me to raise objections at this hour of the day."

"You'll find your correspondence in the library," went on Saunders. "Most of it I've seen to. There are a few private letters I haven't opened. There's also a box with a rat, or something, inside it that came by the evening post. Very likely it's the six-toed albino. I didn't look, because I didn't want to mess up my things but I should gather from the way it's jumping about that it's pretty hungry."

"Oh, I'll see to it," said Eustace, "while you and the Captain earn an honest penny."

Dinner over and Saunders gone, Eustace went into the library. Though the fire had been lit the room was by no means cheerful.

"We'll have all the lights on at any rate," he said, as he turned the switches. "And, Morton," he added, when the butler brought the coffee, "get me a screwdriver or something to undo this box. Whatever the animal is, he's kicking up the deuce of a row. What is it? Why are you dawdling?"

"If you please, sir, when the postman brought it he told me that they'd bored the holes in the lid at the post-office. There were no breathin' holes in the lid, sir, and they didn't want the animal to die. That is all, sir."

"It's culpably careless of the man, whoever he was," said Eustace, as he removed the screws, "packing an animal like this in a wooden box with no means of getting air. Confound it all! I meant to ask Morton to bring me a cage to put it in. Now I suppose I shall have to get one myself."

He placed a heavy book on the lid from which the screws had been removed, and went into the billiard-room. As he came back into the library with an empty cage in his hand he heard the sound of something falling, and then of something scuttling along the floor.

"Bother it! The beast's got out. How in the world am I to find it again in this library!"

To search for it did indeed seem hopeless. He tried to follow the sound of the scuttling in one of the recesses where the animal seemed to be running behind the books in the shelves, but it was impossible to locate it. Eustace resolved to go on quietly reading. Very likely the animal might gain confidence and show itself. Saunders seemed to have dealt in his usual methodical manner with most of the correspondence. There were still the private letters.

What was that? Two sharp clicks and the lights in the hideous candelabra that hung from the ceiling suddenly went out.

"I wonder if something has gone wrong with the fuse," said Eustace, as he went to the switches by the door. Then he stopped. There was a noise at the other end of the room, as if something was crawling up the iron corkscrew stair. "If it's gone into the gallery," he said, "well and good." He hastily turned on the lights, crossed the room, and climbed up the stair. But he could see nothing. His grandfather had placed a little gate at the top of the stair, so that children could run and romp in the gallery without fear of accident. This Eustace closed, and having considerably narrowed the circle of his search, returned to his desk by the fire.

How gloomy the library was! There was no sense of intimacy about the room. The few busts that an eighteenth-century Borlsover had brought back from the grand tour, might have been in keeping in the old library. Here they seemed out of place. They made the room feel cold, in spite of the heavy red damask curtains and great gilt cornices.

With a crash two heavy books fell from the gallery to the floor; then, as Borlsover looked, another and yet another.

"Very well; you'll starve for this, my beauty!" he said. "We'll do some little experiments on the metabolism of rats deprived of water. Go on! Chuck them down! I think I've got the upper hand." He turned once again to his correspondence. The letter was from the family solicitor. It spoke of his uncle's death and of the valuable collection of books that had been left to him in the will.

"There was one request," he read, "which certainly came as a surprise to me. As you know, Mr. Adrian Borlsover had left instructions that his body was to be buried in as simple a manner as possible at Eastbourne. He expressed a desire that there should be neither wreaths nor flowers of any kind, and hoped that his friends and relatives would not consider it necessary to wear mourning. The day before his death we received a letter canceling these instructions. He wished his body to be embalmed (he gave us the address of the man we were to employ—Pennifer, Ludgate Hill), with orders that his right hand was to be sent to you, stating that it was at your special request. The other arrangements as to the funeral remained unaltered."

"Good Lord!" said Eustace; "what in the world was the old boy driving at? And what in the name of all that's holy is that?"

Someone was in the gallery. Someone had pulled the cord attached to one of the blinds, and it had rolled up with a snap. Someone must be in the gallery, for a second blind did the same. Someone must be walking round the gallery, for one after the other the blinds sprang up, letting in the moonlight.

"I haven't got to the bottom of this yet," said Eustace, "but I will do before the night is very much older," and he hurried up the corkscrew stair. He had just got to the top when the lights went out a second time, and he heard again the scuttling along the floor. Quickly he stole on tiptoe in the dim moonshine in the direction of the noise, feeling as he went for one of the switches. His fingers touched the metal knob at last. He turned on the electric light.

About ten yards in front of him, crawling along the floor, was a man's hand. Eustace stared at it in utter astonishment. It was moving quickly, in the manner of a geometer caterpillar, the fingers humped up one moment, flattened out the next; the thumb appeared to give a crab-like motion to the whole. While he was looking, too surprised to stir, the hand disappeared round the corner. Eustace ran forward. He no longer saw it, but he could hear it as it squeezed its way behind the books on one of the shelves. A heavy volume had been displaced. There was a gap in the row of books where it had got in. In his fear lest it should escape him again, he seized the first book that came to his hand and plugged it into the hole. Then, emptying two shelves of their contents, he took the wooden boards and propped them up in front to make his barrier doubly sure.

"I wish Saunders was back," he said; "one can't tackle this sort of thing alone." It was after eleven, and there seemed little likelihood of Saunders returning before twelve. He did not dare to leave the shelf unwatched, even to run downstairs to ring the bell. Morton the butler often used to come round about eleven to see that the windows were fastened, but he might not come. Eustace was thoroughly unstrung. At last he heard steps down below.

"Morton!" he shouted; "Morton!"

"Sir?"

"Has Mr. Saunders got back yet?"

"Not yet, sir."

"Well, bring me some brandy, and hurry up about it. I'm up here in the gallery, you duffer."

"Thanks," said Eustace, as he emptied the glass. "Don't go to bed yet, Morton. There are a lot of books that have fallen down by accident; bring them up and put them back in their shelves."

Morton had never seen Borlsover in so talkative a mood as on that night. "Here," said Eustace, when the books had been put back and dusted, "you might hold up these boards for me, Morton. That beast in the box got out, and I've been chasing it all over the place."

"I think I can hear it chawing at the books, sir. They're not valuable, I hope? I think that's the carriage, sir; I'll go and call Mr. Saunders."

It seemed to Eustace that he was away for five minutes, but it could hardly have been more than one when he returned with Saunders. "All right, Morton, you can go now. I'm up here, Saunders."

"What's all the row?" asked Saunders, as he lounged forward with his hands in his pockets. The luck had been with him all the evening. He was completely satisfied, both with himself and with Captain Lockwood's taste in wines. "What's the matter? You look to me to be in an absolute blue funk."

"That old devil of an uncle of mine," began Eustace—"oh, I can't explain it all. It's his hand that's been playing old Harry all the evening. But I've got it cornered behind these books. You've got to help me catch it."

"What's up with you, Eustace? What's the game?"

"It's no game, you silly idiot! If you don't believe me take out one of those books and put your hand in and feel."

"All right," said Saunders; "but wait till I've rolled up my sleeve. The accumulated dust of centuries, eh?" He took off his coat, knelt down, and thrust his arm along the shelf.

"There's something there right enough," he said. "It's got a funny stumpy end to it, whatever it is, and nips like a crab. Ah, no, you don't!" He pulled his hand out in a flash. "Shove in a book quickly. Now it can't get out."

"What was it?" asked Eustace.

"It was something that wanted very much to get hold of me. I felt what seemed like a thumb and forefinger. Give me some brandy."

"How are we to get it out of there?"

"What about a landing net?"

"No good. It would be too smart for us. I tell you, Saunders, it can cover the ground far faster than I can walk. But I think I see how we can manage it. The two books at the end of the shelf are big ones that go right back against the wall. The others are very thin. I'll take out one at a time, and you slide the rest along until we have it squashed between the end two."

It certainly seemed to be the best plan. One by one, as they took out the books, the space behind grew smaller and smaller. There was something in it that was certainly very much alive. Once they caught sight of fingers pressing outward for a way of escape. At last they had it pressed between the two big books.

"There's muscle there, if there isn't flesh and blood," said Saunders, as he held them together. "It seems to be a hand right enough, too. I suppose this is a sort of infectious hallucination. I've read about such cases before."

"Infectious fiddlesticks!" said Eustace, his face white with anger; "bring the thing downstairs. We'll get it back into the box."

It was not altogether easy, but they were successful at last. "Drive in the screws," said Eustace, "we won't run any risks. Put the box in this old desk of mine. There's nothing in it that I want. Here's the key. Thank goodness, there's nothing wrong with the lock."

"Quite a lively evening," said Saunders. "Now let's hear more about your uncle."

They sat up together until early morning. Saunders had no desire for sleep. Eustace was trying to explain and to forget: to conceal from himself a fear that he had never felt before—the fear of walking alone down the long corridor to his bedroom.

"Whatever it was," said Eustace to Saunders on the following morning, "I propose that we drop the subject. There's nothing to keep us here for the next ten days. We'll motor up to the Lakes and get some climbing."

"And see nobody all day, and sit bored to death with each other every night. Not for me thanks. Why not run up to town? Run's the exact word in this case, isn't it? We're both in such a blessed funk. Pull yourself together Eustace, and let's have another look at the hand."

"As you like," said Eustace; "there's the key." They went into the library and opened the desk. The box was as they had left it on the previous night.

"What are you waiting for?" asked Eustace.

"I am waiting for you to volunteer to open the lid. However, since you seem to funk it, allow me. There doesn't seem to be the likelihood of any rumpus this morning, at all events." He opened the lid and picked out the hand.

"Cold?" asked Eustace.

"Tepid. A bit below blood-heat by the feel. Soft and supple too. If it's the embalming, it's a sort of embalming I've never seen before. Is it your uncle's hand?"

"Oh, yes, it's his all right," said Eustace. "I should know those long thin fingers anywhere. Put it back in the box, Saunders. Never mind about the screws. I'll lock the desk, so that there'll be no chance of its getting out. We'll compromise by motoring up to town for a week. If we get off soon after lunch we ought to be at Grantham or Stamford by night."

"Right," said Saunders; "and to-morrow— Oh, well, by to-morrow we shall have forgotten all about this beastly thing."

If when the morrow came they had not forgotten, it was certainly true that at the end of the week they were able to tell a very vivid ghost story at the little supper Eustace gave on Hallow E'en.

"You don't want us to believe that it's true, Mr. Borlsover? How perfectly awful!"

"I'll take my oath on it, and so would Saunders here; wouldn't you, old chap?"

"Any number of oaths," said Saunders. "It was a long thin hand, you know, and it gripped me just like that."

"Don't Mr. Saunders! Don't! How perfectly horrid! Now tell us another one, do. Only a really creepy one, please!"

"Here's a pretty mess!" said Eustace on the following day as he threw a letter across the table to Saunders. "It's your affair, though. Mrs. Merrit, if I understand it, gives a month's notice."

"Oh, that's quite absurd on Mrs. Merrit's part," Saunders replied. "She doesn't know what she's talking about. Let's see what she says."

> "Dear Sir," he read, "this is to let you know that I must give you a month's notice as from Tuesday the 13th. For a long time I've felt the place too big for me, but when Jane Parfit, and Emma Laidlaw go off with scarcely as much as an 'if you please,' after frightening the wits out of the other girls, so that they can't turn out a room by themselves or walk alone down the stairs for fear of treading on half-frozen toads or hearing it run along the passages at night, all I can say is that it's no place for me. So I must ask you, Mr. Borlsover, sir, to find a new housekeeper that has no objection to large and lonely houses, which some people do say, not that I believe them for a minute, my poor mother always having been a Wesleyan, are haunted.
>
> "Yours faithfully, Elizabeth Merrit.
>
> "P. S.—I should be obliged if you would give my respects to Mr. Saunders. I hope that he won't run no risks with his cold."

"Saunders," said Eustace, "you've always had a wonderful way with you in dealing with servants. You mustn't let poor old Merrit go."

"Of course she shan't go," said Saunders. "She's probably only angling for a rise in salary. I'll write to her this morning."

"No; there's nothing like a personal interview. We've had enough of town. We'll go back to-morrow, and you must work your cold for all it's worth. Don't forget that it's got on to the chest, and will require weeks of feeding up and nursing."

"All right. I think I can manage Mrs. Merrit."

But Mrs. Merrit was more obstinate than he had thought. She was very sorry to hear of Mr. Saunders's cold, and how he lay awake all night in London coughing; very sorry indeed. She'd change his room for him gladly, and get the south room aired. And wouldn't he have a basin of hot bread and milk last thing at night? But she was afraid that she would have to leave at the end of the month.

"Try her with an increase of salary," was the advice of Eustace.

It was no use. Mrs. Merrit was obdurate, though she knew of a Mrs. Handyside who had been housekeeper to Lord Gargrave, who might be glad to come at the salary mentioned.

"What's the matter with the servants, Morton?" asked Eustace that evening when he brought the coffee into the library. "What's all this about Mrs. Merrit wanting to leave?"

"If you please, sir, I was going to mention it myself. I have a confession to make, sir. When I found your note asking me to open that desk and take out the box with the rat, I broke the lock as you told me, and was glad to do it, because I could hear the animal in the box making a great noise, and I thought it wanted food. So I took out the box, sir, and got a cage, and was going to transfer it, when the animal got away."

"What in the world are you talking about? I never wrote any such note."

"Excuse me, sir, it was the note I picked up here on the floor on the day you and Mr. Saunders left. I have it in my pocket now."

It certainly seemed to be in Eustace's handwriting. It was written in pencil, and began somewhat abruptly.

"Get a hammer, Morton," he read, "or some other tool, and break open the lock in the old desk in the library. Take out the box that is inside. You need not do anything else. The lid is already open. Eustace Borlsover."

"And you opened the desk?"

"Yes, sir; and as I was getting the cage ready the animal hopped out."

"What animal?"

"The animal inside the box, sir."

"What did it look like?"

"Well, sir, I couldn't tell you," said Morton nervously; "my back was turned, and it was halfway down the room when I looked up."

"What was its color?" asked Saunders; "black?"

"Oh, no, sir, a grayish white. It crept along in a very funny way, sir. I don't think it had a tail."

"What did you do then?"

"I tried to catch it, but it was no use. So I set the rat-traps and kept the library shut. Then that girl Emma Laidlaw left the door open when she was cleaning, and I think it must have escaped."

"And you think it was the animal that's been frightening the maids?"

"Well, no, sir, not quite. They said it was—you'll excuse me, sir—a hand that they saw. Emma trod on it once at the bottom of the stairs. She thought then it was a half-frozen toad, only white. And then Parfit was washing up the dishes in the scullery. She wasn't thinking about anything in particular. It was close on dusk. She took her hands out of the water and was drying them absent-minded like on the roller towel, when she found that she was drying someone else's hand as well, only colder than hers."

"What nonsense!" exclaimed Saunders.

"Exactly, sir; that's what I told her; but we couldn't get her to stop."

"You don't believe all this?" said Eustace, turning suddenly towards the butler.

"Me, sir? Oh, no, sir! I've not seen anything."

"Nor heard anything?"

"Well, sir, if you must know, the bells do ring at odd times, and there's nobody there when we go; and when we go round to draw the blinds of a night, as often as not somebody's been there before us. But as I says to Mrs. Merrit, a young monkey might do wonderful things, and we all know that Mr. Borlsover has had some strange animals about the place."

"Very well, Morton, that will do."

"What do you make of it?" asked Saunders when they were alone. "I mean of the letter he said you wrote."

"Oh, that's simple enough," said Eustace. "See the paper it's written on? I stopped using that years ago, but there were a few odd sheets and envelopes left in the old desk. We never fastened up the lid of the box before locking it in. The hand got out, found a pencil, wrote this note, and shoved it through a crack on to the floor where Morton found it. That's plain as daylight."

"But the hand couldn't write?"

"Couldn't it? You've not seen it do the things I've seen," and he told Saunders more of what had happened at Eastbourne.

"Well," said Saunders, "in that case we have at least an explanation of the legacy. It was the hand which wrote unknown to your uncle that letter to your solicitor, bequeathing itself to you. Your uncle had no more to do with that request than I. In fact, it would seem that he had some idea of this automatic writing, and feared it."

"Then if it's not my uncle, what is it?"

"I suppose some people might say that a disembodied spirit had got your uncle to educate and prepare a little body for it. Now it's got into that little body and is off on its own."

"Well, what are we to do?"

"We'll keep our eyes open," said Saunders, "and try to catch it. If we can't do that, we shall have to wait till the bally clockwork runs down. After all, if it's flesh and blood, it can't live for ever."

For two days nothing happened. Then Saunders saw it sliding down the banister in the hall. He was taken unawares, and lost a full second before he started in pursuit, only to find that the thing had escaped him. Three days later, Eustace, writing alone in the library at night, saw it sitting on an open book at the other end of the room. The fingers crept over the page, feeling the print as if it were reading; but before he had time to get up from his seat, it had taken the alarm and was pulling itself up the curtains. Eustace watched it grimly as it hung on to the cornice with three fingers, flicking thumb and forefinger at him in an expression of scornful derision.

"I know what I'll do," he said. "If I only get it into the open I'll set the dogs on to it."

He spoke to Saunders of the suggestion.

"It's jolly good idea," he said; "only we won't wait till we find it out of doors. We'll get the dogs. There are the two terriers and the under-keeper's Irish mongrel that's on to rats like a flash. Your spaniel has not got spirit enough for this sort of game." They brought the dogs into the house, and the keeper's Irish mongrel chewed up the slippers, and the terriers tripped up Morton as he waited at table; but all three were welcome. Even false security is better than no security at all.

For a fortnight nothing happened. Then the hand was caught, not by the dogs, but by Mrs. Merrit's gray parrot. The bird was in the habit of periodically removing the pins that kept its seed and water tins in place, and of escaping through the holes in the side of the cage. When once at liberty Peter would show no inclination to return, and would often be about the house for days. Now, after six consecutive weeks of captivity, Peter had again discovered a new means of unloosing his bolts and was at large, exploring the tapestried forests of the curtains and singing songs in praise of liberty from cornice and picture rail.

"It's no use your trying to catch him," said Eustace to Mrs. Merrit, as she came into the study one afternoon towards dusk with a step-ladder. "You'd much better leave Peter alone. Starve him into surrender, Mrs. Merrit, and don't leave bananas and seed about for him to peck at when he fancies he's hungry. You're far too softhearted."

"Well, sir, I see he's right out of reach now on that picture rail, so if you wouldn't mind closing the door, sir, when you leave the room, I'll bring his cage in to-night and put some meat inside it. He's that fond of meat, though it does make him pull out his feathers to suck the quills. They do say that if you cook—"

"Never mind, Mrs. Merrit," said Eustace, who was busy writing. "That will do; I'll keep an eye on the bird."

There was silence in the room, unbroken but for the continuous whisper of his pen.

"Scratch poor Peter," said the bird. "Scratch poor old Peter!"

"Be quiet, you beastly bird!"

"Poor old Peter! Scratch poor Peter, do."

"I'm more likely to wring your neck if I get hold of you." He looked up at the picture rail, and there was the hand holding on to a hook with three fingers, and slowly scratching the head of the parrot with the fourth. Eustace ran to the bell and pressed it hard; then across to the window, which he closed with a bang. Frightened by the noise the parrot shook its wings preparatory to flight, and as it did so the fingers of the hand got hold of it by the throat. There was a shrill scream from Peter as he fluttered across the room, wheeling round in circles that ever descended, borne down under the weight that clung to him. The bird dropped at last quite suddenly, and Eustace saw fingers and feathers rolled into an inextricable mass on the floor. The struggle abruptly ceased as finger and thumb squeezed the neck; the bird's eyes rolled up to show the whites, and there was a faint, half-choked gurgle. But before the fingers had time to loose their hold, Eustace had them in his own.

"Send Mr. Saunders here at once," he said to the maid who came in answer to the bell. "Tell him I want him immediately."

Then he went with the hand to the fire. There was a ragged gash across the back where the bird's beak had torn it, but no blood oozed from the wound. He noticed with disgust that the nails had grown long and discolored.

"I'll burn the beastly thing," he said. But he could not burn it. He tried to throw it into the flames, but his own hands, as if restrained by some old primitive feeling, would not let him. And so Saunders found him pale and irresolute, with the hand still clasped tightly in his fingers.

"I've got it at last," he said in a tone of triumph.

"Good; let's have a look at it."

"Not when it's loose. Get me some nails and a hammer and a board of some sort."

"Can you hold it all right?"

"Yes, the thing's quite limp; tired out with throttling poor old Peter, I should say."

"And now," said Saunders when he returned with the things, "what are we going to do?"

"Drive a nail through it first, so that it can't get away; then we can take our time over examining it."

"Do it yourself," said Saunders. "I don't mind helping you with guinea-pigs occasionally when there's something to be learned; partly because I don't fear a guinea-pig's revenge. This thing's different."

"All right, you miserable skunk. I won't forget the way you've stood by me."

He took up a nail, and before Saunders had realised what he was doing had driven it through the hand, deep into the board.

"Oh, my aunt," he giggled hysterically, "look at it now," for the hand was writhing in agonized contortions, squirming and wriggling upon the nail like a worm upon the hook.

"Well," said Saunders, "you've done it now. I'll leave you to examine it."

"Don't go, in heaven's name. Cover it up, man, cover it up! Shove a cloth over it! Here!" and he pulled off the antimacassar from the back of a chair and wrapped the board in it. "Now get the keys from my pocket and open the safe. Chuck the other things out. Oh, Lord, it's getting itself into frightful knots! and open it quick!" He threw the thing in and banged the door.

"We'll keep it there till it dies," he said. "May I burn in hell if I ever open the door of that safe again."

Mrs. Merrit departed at the end of the month. Her successor certainly was more successful in the management of the servants. Early in her rule she declared that she would stand no nonsense, and gossip soon withered and died. Eustace Borlsover went back to his old way of life. Old habits crept over and covered his new experience. He was, if anything, less morose, and showed a greater inclination to take his natural part in country society.

"I shouldn't be surprised if he marries one of these days," said Saunders. "Well, I'm in no hurry for such an event. I know Eustace far too well for the future Mrs. Borlsover to like me. It will be the same old story again: a long friendship slowly made—marriage—and a long friendship quickly forgotten."

But Eustace Borlsover did not follow the advice of his uncle and marry. He was too fond of old slippers and tobacco.

The cooking, too, under Mrs. Handyside's management was excellent, and she seemed, too, to have a heaven-sent faculty in knowing when to stop dusting.

Little by little the old life resumed its old power. Then came the burglary. The men, it was said, broke into the house by way of the conservatory. It was really little more than an attempt, for they only succeeded in carrying away a few pieces of plate from the pantry. The safe in the study was certainly found open and empty, but, as Mr. Borlsover informed the police inspector, he had kept nothing of value in it during the last six months.

"Then you're lucky in getting off so easily, sir," the man replied. "By the way they have gone about their business, I should say they were experienced cracksmen. They must have caught the alarm when they were just beginning their evening's work."

"Yes," said Eustace, "I suppose I am lucky."

"I've no doubt," said the inspector, "that we shall be able to trace the men. I've said that they must have been old hands at the game. The way they got in and opened the safe shows that. But there's one little thing that puzzles me. One of them was careless enough not to wear gloves, and I'm bothered if I know what he was trying to do. I've traced his finger-marks on the new varnish on the window sashes in every one of the downstairs rooms. They are very distinct ones too."

"Right hand or left, or both?" asked Eustace.

"Oh, right every time. That's the funny thing. He must have been a foolhardy fellow, and I rather think it was him that wrote that." He took out a slip of paper from his pocket. "That's what he wrote, sir. 'I've got out, Eustace Borlsover, but I'll be back before long.' Some gaol bird just escaped, I suppose. It will make it all the easier for us to trace him. Do you know the writing, sir?"

"No," said Eustace; "it's not the writing of anyone I know."

"I'm not going to stay here any longer," said Eustace to Saunders at luncheon. "I've got on far better during the last six months than ever I expected, but I'm not going to run the risk of seeing that thing again. I shall go up to town this afternoon. Get Morton to put my things together, and join me with the car at Brighton on the day after to-morrow. And bring the proofs of those two papers with you. We'll run over them together."

"How long are you going to be away?"

"I can't say for certain, but be prepared to stay for some time. We've stuck to work pretty closely through the summer, and I for one need a holiday. I'll engage the rooms at Brighton. You'll find it best to break the journey at Hitchin. I'll wire to you there at the Crown to tell you the Brighton address."

The house he chose at Brighton was in a terrace. He had been there before. It was kept by his old college gyp, a man of discreet silence, who was admirably partnered by an excellent cook. The rooms were on the first floor. The two bedrooms were at the back, and opened out of each other. "Saunders can have the smaller one, though it is the only one with a fireplace," he said. "I'll stick to the larger of the two, since it's got a bathroom adjoining. I wonder what time he'll arrive with the car."

Saunders came about seven, cold and cross and dirty. "We'll light the fire in the dining-room," said Eustace, "and get Prince to unpack some of the things while we are at dinner. What were the roads like?"

"Rotten; swimming with mud, and a beastly cold wind against us all day. And this is July. Dear old England!"

"Yes," said Eustace, "I think we might do worse than leave dear old England for a few months."

They turned in soon after twelve.

"You oughtn't to feel cold, Saunders," said Eustace, "when you can afford to sport a great cat-skin lined coat like this.

You do yourself very well, all things considered. Look at those gloves, for instance. Who could possibly feel cold when wearing them?"

"They are far too clumsy though for driving. Try them on and see," and he tossed them through the door on to Eustace's bed, and went on with his unpacking. A minute later he heard a shrill cry of terror. "Oh, Lord," he heard, "it's in the glove! Quick, Saunders, quick!" Then came a smacking thud. Eustace had thrown it from him. "I've chucked it into the bathroom," he gasped, "it's hit the wall and fallen into the bath. Come now if you want to help." Saunders, with a lighted candle in his hand, looked over the edge of the bath. There it was, old and maimed, dumb and blind, with a ragged hole in the middle, crawling, staggering, trying to creep up the slippery sides, only to fall back helpless.

"Stay there," said Saunders. "I'll empty a collar box or something, and we'll jam it in. It can't get out while I'm away."

"Yes, it can," shouted Eustace. "It's getting out now. It's climbing up the plug chain. No, you brute, you filthy brute, you don't! Come back, Saunders, it's getting away from me. I can't hold it; it's all slippery. Curse its claw! Shut the window, you idiot! The top too, as well as the bottom. You utter idiot! It's got out!" There was the sound of something dropping on to the hard flagstones below, and Eustace fell back fainting.

For a fortnight he was ill.

"I don't know what to make of it," the doctor said to Saunders. "I can only suppose that Mr. Borlsover has suffered some great emotional shock. You had better let me send someone to help you nurse him. And by all means indulge that whim of his never to be left alone in the dark. I would keep a light burning all night if I were you. But he must have more fresh air. It's perfectly absurd this hatred of open windows."

Eustace, however, would have no one with him but Saunders. "I don't want the other men," he said. "They'd smuggle it in somehow. I know they would."

"Don't worry about it, old chap. This sort of thing can't go on indefinitely. You know I saw it this time as well as you. It wasn't half so active. It won't go on living much longer, especially after that fall. I heard it hit the flags myself. As soon as you're a bit stronger we'll leave this place; not bag and baggage, but with only the clothes on our backs, so that it won't be able to hide anywhere. We'll escape it that way. We won't give any address, and we won't have any parcels sent after us. Cheer up, Eustace! You'll be well enough to leave in a day or two. The doctor says I can take you out in a chair to-morrow."

"What have I done?" asked Eustace. "Why does it come after me? I'm no worse than other men. I'm no worse than you, Saunders; you know I'm not. It was you who were at the bottom of that dirty business in San Diego, and that was fifteen years ago."

"It's not that, of course," said Saunders. "We are in the twentieth century, and even the parsons have dropped the idea of your old sins finding you out. Before you caught the hand in the library it was filled with pure malevolence—to you and all mankind. After you spiked it through with that nail it naturally forgot about other people, and concentrated its attention on you. It was shut up in the safe, you know, for nearly six months. That gives plenty of time for thinking of revenge."

Eustace Borlsover would not leave his room, but he thought that there might be something in Saunders's suggestion to leave Brighton without notice. He began rapidly to regain his strength.

"We'll go on the first of September," he said.

The evening of August 31st was oppressively warm. Though at midday the windows had been wide open, they had been shut an hour or so before dusk. Mrs. Prince had long since ceased to wonder at the strange habits of the gentlemen on the first floor. Soon after their arrival she had been told to take down the heavy window curtains in the two bedrooms, and day by day the rooms had seemed to grow more bare. Nothing was left lying about.

"Mr. Borlsover doesn't like to have any place where dirt can collect," Saunders had said as an excuse. "He likes to see into all the corners of the room."

"Couldn't I open the window just a little?" he said to Eustace that evening. "We're simply roasting in here, you know."

"No, leave well alone. We're not a couple of boarding-school misses fresh from a course of hygiene lectures. Get the chessboard out."

They sat down and played. At ten o'clock Mrs. Prince came to the door with a note. "I am sorry I didn't bring it before," she said, "but it was left in the letter-box."

"Open it, Saunders, and see if it wants answering."

It was very brief. There was neither address nor signature.

"Will eleven o'clock to-night be suitable for our last appointment?"

"Who is it from?" asked Borlsover.

"It was meant for me," said Saunders. "There's no answer, Mrs. Prince," and he put the paper into his pocket. "A dunning letter from a tailor; I suppose he must have got wind of our leaving."

It was a clever lie, and Eustace asked no more questions. They went on with their game.

On the landing outside Saunders could hear the grandfather's clock whispering the seconds, blurting out the quarter-hours.

"Check!" said Eustace. The clock struck eleven. At the same time there was a gentle knocking on the door; it seemed to come from the bottom panel.

"Who's there?" asked Eustace.

There was no answer.

"Mrs. Prince, is that you?"

"She is up above," said Saunders; "I can hear her walking about the room."

"Then lock the door; bolt it too. Your move, Saunders."

While Saunders sat with his eyes on the chessboard, Eustace walked over to the window and examined the fastenings. He did the same in Saunders's room and the bathroom. There were no doors between the three rooms, or he would have shut and locked them too.

"Now, Saunders," he said, "don't stay all night over your move. I've had time to smoke one cigarette already. It's bad to keep an invalid waiting. There's only one possible thing for you to do. What was that?"

"The ivy blowing against the window. There, it's your move now, Eustace."

"It wasn't the ivy, you idiot. It was someone tapping at the window," and he pulled up the blind. On the outer side of the window, clinging to the sash, was the hand.

"What is it that it's holding?"

"It's a pocket-knife. It's going to try to open the window by pushing back the fastener with the blade."

"Well, let it try," said Eustace. "Those fasteners screw down; they can't be opened that way. Anyhow, we'll close the shutters. It's your move, Saunders. I've played."

But Saunders found it impossible to fix his attention on the game. He could not understand Eustace, who seemed all at once to have lost his fear. "What do you say to some wine?" he asked. "You seem to be taking things coolly, but I don't mind confessing that I'm in a blessed funk."

"You've no need to be. There's nothing supernatural about that hand, Saunders. I mean it seems to be governed by the laws of time and space. It's not the sort of thing that vanishes into thin air or slides through oaken doors. And since that's so, I defy it to get in here. We'll leave the place in the morning. I for one have bottomed the depths of fear. Fill your glass, man! The windows are all shuttered, the door is locked and bolted. Pledge me my uncle Adrian! Drink, man! What are you waiting for?"

Saunders was standing with his glass half raised. "It can get in," he said hoarsely; "it can get in! We've forgotten. There's the fireplace in my bedroom. It will come down the chimney."

"Quick!" said Eustace, as he rushed into the other room; "we haven't a minute to lose. What can we do? Light the fire, Saunders. Give me a match, quick!"

"They must be all in the other room. I'll get them."

"Hurry, man, for goodness' sake! Look in the bookcase! Look in the bathroom! Here, come and stand here; I'll look."

"Be quick!" shouted Saunders. "I can hear something!"

"Then plug a sheet from your bed up the chimney. No, here's a match." He had found one at last that had slipped into a crack in the floor.

"Is the fire laid? Good, but it may not burn. I know—the oil from that old reading-lamp and this cotton-wool. Now the match, quick! Pull the sheet away, you fool! We don't want it now."

There was a great roar from the grate as the flames shot up. Saunders had been a fraction of a second too late with the sheet. The oil had fallen on to it. It, too, was burning.

"The whole place will be on fire!" cried Eustace, as he tried to beat out the flames with a blanket. "It's no good! I can't manage it. You must open the door, Saunders, and get help."

Saunders ran to the door and fumbled with the bolts. The key was stiff in the lock.

"Hurry!" shouted Eustace; "the whole place is ablaze!"

The key turned in the lock at last. For half a second Saunders stopped to look back. Afterwards he could never be quite sure as to what he had seen, but at the time he thought that something black and charred was creeping slowly, very slowly, from the mass of flames towards Eustace Borlsover. For a moment he thought of returning to his friend, but the noise and the smell of the burning sent him running down the passage crying, "Fire! Fire!" He rushed to the telephone to summon help, and then back to the bathroom—he should have thought of that before—for water. As he burst open the bedroom door there came a scream of terror which ended suddenly, and then the sound of a heavy fall.

This is the story which I heard on successive Saturday evenings from the senior mathematical master at a second-rate suburban school. For Saunders has had to earn a living in a way which other men might reckon less congenial than his old manner of life. I had mentioned by chance the name of Adrian Borlsover, and wondered at the time why he changed the conversation with such unusual abruptness. A week later Saunders began to tell me something of his own history; sordid enough, though shielded with a reserve I could well understand, for it had to cover not only his failings, but those of a dead friend. Of the final tragedy he was at first especially loath to speak; and it was only gradually that I was able to piece together the narrative of the preceding pages. Saunders was reluctant to draw any conclusions. At one time he thought that the fingered beast had been animated by the spirit of Sigismund Borlsover, a sinister eighteenth-century ancestor, who, according to legend, built and worshipped in the ugly pagan temple that overlooked the lake. At another time Saunders believed the spirit to belong to a man whom Eustace had once employed as a laboratory assistant, "a black-haired, spiteful little brute," he said, "who died cursing his doctor, because the fellow couldn't help him to live to settle some paltry score with Borlsover."

From the point of view of direct contemporary evidence, Saunders's story is practically uncorroborated. All the letters

mentioned in the narrative were destroyed, with the exception of the last note which Eustace received, or rather which
he would have received, had not Saunders intercepted it.
That I have seen myself. The handwriting was thin and shaky,
the handwriting of an old man. I remember the Greek "e" was
used in "appointment". A little thing that amused me at the
time was that Saunders seemed to keep the note pressed between the pages of his Bible.

I had seen Adrian Borlsover once. Saunders I learnt to
know well. It was by chance, however, and not by design,
that I met a third person of the story, Morton, the butler.
Saunders and I were walking in the Zoological Gardens one
Sunday afternoon, when he called my attention to an old
man who was standing before the door of the Reptile House.

"Why, Morton," he said, clapping him on the back, "how
is the world treating you?"

"Poorly, Mr. Saunders," said the old fellow, though his
face lighted up at the greeting. "The winters drag terribly
nowadays. There don't seem no summers or springs."

"You haven't found what you were looking for, I suppose?"

"No, sir, not yet; but I shall some day. I always told them
that Mr. Borlsover kept some queer animals."

"And what is he looking for?" I asked, when we had parted from him.

"A beast with five fingers," said Saunders. "This afternoon, since he has been in the Reptile House, I suppose it
will be a reptile with a hand. Next week it will be a monkey
with practically no body. The poor old chap is a born mate-
rialist.

"It's a queer coincidence, by the way, that you should
have known Adrian Borlsover and that you should have received a blessing at his hand. Has it brought you any luck?"

"No," I answered slowly, as I looked back over a life of
inconspicuous failure, "I don't think it has. It was his right
hand, you know."

THE CALL OF THE HAND
Louis Golding
(1919)

1

No one knew what sin Nikolai Kupreloff had committed to bring on his head so terrible a penalty. Year after year his wife and he had prayed for a child, to their ikons in the tiny basilica in the wood, and when his wife gave birth at last, it was neither a child nor children. She had given birth to two little boys, perfectly made, exquisitely proportioned, but there was a deadly thing had befallen them . . . the tiny right hand of the one was inexorably seized by the left hand of the other.

The little woodcutter's cottage of Nikolai lay deeply hidden in the great pine woods of Lower Serbia, miles from his nearest neighbour. Yet even in that wild country the fame of the intertwined children travelled far, and the wise old women from those parts came to see if herbs or chanting or any of their dark gifts might be of the least avail. They were no more useful than a real doctor who had studied at Belgrade, was practising at Monastir, and was stimulated to great interest by the account of these strange children. The case defied all the arts of black or white magic, and the interest of the episode flickered and died down.

So it was that Nikolai reconciled himself to the inevitable, and as the boys grew older he would cross himself devoutly and say: "Thank God, it might have been a thousand times worse!" They were lads of extraordinary beauty. Peter and Ivan he called them, Ivan being the lad who held so irrevocably the wrist of his brother within his fingers. In appearance they were identical—the light, tough hair and the laughing blue eyes of the Serbian Slav, sturdy, well-knit limbs, and a sterling robustness of physique. It was only their parents and themselves who knew that between them there was one slight but unmistakable mark of distinction— below the knuckle of Ivan's thumb was marked dully a little red arrow. In fact, a stranger might not have known that this abnormal bond existed between the two brothers as he saw them swinging along under the pines. "What a loving little pair!" he would exclaim, as he heard them laugh and chatter in complete harmony, and look into each other's eyes with the understanding born of flawless love.

When they were about fifteen years old their mother died, and the father Nikolai began more and more to remain behind in his cottage attending to the frugal needs of the little family, while Peter and Ivan, as the years went on, grew even more skilful in the art of woodcutting; for Peter wielding the axe in his left hand, Ivan in his right, achieved such a fine reciprocity of movement, that Nikolai would laugh in his great yellow beard and mutter: "Truly the ways of God are inscrutable, for even out of their calamity has He made a great blessing!" The passing of time only knit closer their perfect intimacy, so that they almost did not notice when their father Nikolai sickened and died. Now they were left to their cottage and their woodcutting and their complete love, the whole being crowned by the splendid physique of young foresters at twenty-one; so that life, it seemed, had nothing in store for them but long years of undivided love and content.

Yet even into their seclusion rumours came of the great world beyond. Now and again they would catch glimpses of the marvels of Salonika in the eyes of travelled men. They

would hear of a city where lovely women, infinitely more
beautiful than the queen of the tousled gypsies who flickered
from time to time along the forest paths, sang upon stages of
golden wood, in gardens full of hanging lights. They would
hear of the sea and glowing ships, and men who spoke low
musical languages uttered in countries beyond the sea.

So it was the brothers determined to leave their woodcutting behind them for a season and adventure forth into the
world of ships and songs and lovely women.

2

To Peter and Ivan Salonika was a revelation of wonders they
barely thought actual. From a little room in the street of
Johann Tschimiski they saw the multicoloured tides of cos-
mopolitan humanity sweeping down from Egnatia Street,
down Venizelos Street to the Place de la Concorde. They
would walk along the quay-side past the great hotels to the
Jardins de la Tour Blanche, and were sent into an ecstasy
of delight by the chic little women who smiled archly at
these two fair-headed lads from the up-country, who walked
along hand clasped in wrist in so naive and rustic a manner.
Yet when they entered the Theatre des Varietes at the White
Tower it seemed to them that the very portals of heaven had
opened wide. They would return in a daze of delight to their
room and recount with an almost religious fervour the beauties and enchantments of the show. Each little Spanish or
French girl who came to do her song or minuet had seemed
to them more enchanting than the last. Never a cloud of dis-
agreement came between them. There was a perfect coincidence in their tastes, and never, they felt, had their love for
each other been so sympathetic and complete as it was now.

The brothers had no large sum of money at their disposal. The time of their holiday was drawing to a close. One
evening they turned up at the theatre for the last time, their
nerves keyed up to a pitch of delighted impatience, the more

tense as the brothers knew that the next day would see them on the arduous road back to their Serbian forest. Turn followed turn with alluring consequence. Then at one stage the music ceased for some moments and there was an atmosphere of expectance in the air. It was then that a simple and delightful English girl came half-shyly from the wings. There was nothing flamboyant in her appearance or her manner. Yet at once she seemed to seize the house with the graceful and reticent winsomeness of her song. So she sang her song through, a dainty little ballad of old-world gardens and fragrant flowers and love unto death. Peter felt the fingers of Ivan tighten round his wrist. He himself had been so stirred to his depths by the gentle grace of the girl that it was with a slight feeling of resentment he realised that Ivan had been experiencing once again an identical emotion. As he involuntarily moved away his arm Ivan uttered a slight cry of impatience. He turned round and looked into Peter's eyes and found them aflame with a light deeper than mere appreciation. Peter was aware of his brother's glance and looked at Ivan in return to find his face flushed almost as if he were half-drunk.

That night for the first time in their history there occurred a slight bickering between the two. No mention of the little English actress passed between them, but each of them determined that some day, when his brother's interest had died away, he should broach the subject and the possibility of a rediscovery of the English actress at Salonika.

Next day they entrained for Monastir, and a few days later saw them installed once again in their father's cottage in the wood.

3

In proportion as the fortunes of the Kupreloff brothers increased, something that had once existed between them receded further away. The perfection of their old intimacy became a memory of the past. No longer did the most minute physical or spiritual experience of the one become automatically part of his brother's consciousness. So that now for the first time their indissoluble partnership became more and more galling.

There was no doubt of it. Everything dated from that last night at Salonika, when the English girl appeared on the stage. They would still occasionally revive something of the old fervour as they discussed from time to time their impressions of the unforgettable holiday. Yet never a word passed between them concerning the unconscious girl who had captured both their hearts. At night they would lie awake, each thinking that the other was asleep. Bitterly, definitely, they would confess to their own deep hearts: "She is mine, she is mine; I am hers for ever." And yet to each their love seemed hopeless beyond recall. There was the double sting that each of them loved the girl with an intensity reserved hitherto for his brother; but, if possible, more fatal was the despairing conviction that no girl could ever love the one of two brothers to whom the other would remain physically attached till death carried them both away. As the months passed by the friction between them increased. They were now in a position to buy land and a little livestock. But if Peter insisted upon keeping pigs, in the fashion of the majority of Serbians, Ivan would insist upon cattle. If Peter felt that he had done enough woodcutting for the day, Ivan felt that the day was only just beginning.

One night in late autumn Peter lay tossing very heavily in his sleep. Ivan lay awake, thinking, thinking for ever of the girl, his whole heart full of rancour against the brother who must for ever prevent the consummation of his love. Heavily, wearily, Peter heaved on the bed. Outside the wind was howling. The dreariness of the wind seemed to enter Peter's heart. "My little girl," he murmured, "my little girl! When shall we meet, my little girl? Never, never, never!" Ivan's forehead contracted with hate. He was filled suddenly with a tremendous loathing of his brother. "Never, never, never!" moaned Peter. Suddenly, obeying a frantic impulse, Ivan pulled with all his strength away from his brother's wrist to which Fate had so viciously fastened him. With a great scream of pain Peter half leapt from the bed.

"What's this? What do you mean?" he shouted, his voice thick with pain and sleep. "Nothing! Nothing! I couldn't help it! I was dreaming!" replied Ivan savagely, and the brothers settled down again for the night.

Night after night the same thing happened. Peter would murmur for ever in his sleep, "My little girl, when shall we meet? Never, never, never!" Ivan would lie awake, hatred surging violently through his whole body, till his eyes would see nothing but flames in the darkness of their log-built room; and the sound of the branches in the forest would begin to mutter and moan: "Have done with it, Ivan, have done with it! She is waiting for you, waiting, always waiting. Have done with it! Have done with *him*—with *him*—with *him!*"

One desolate night towards mid-winter the room was full of the miserable sleep-cries of Peter. Outside thunder ripped among the clouds. A finger of lightning came suddenly through the windows and pointed with a gesture of flame towards the open breast of Peter. A sudden and terrible thought flooded into Ivan's soul! Whatever there was of human kindness and brother-love seemed in one sinister moment to be washed away from before the onset of the flood. All the branches upon all the trees shrieked across the night. "We shall be quiet, you shall have rest. She shall be yours. Have done with him, have done with him!"

A great calm settled down upon Ivan's soul—the issue was decided, the issue which had been hovering for so long in his subconsciousness was decided at last. There was nothing left to do. The mere deed was the mere snapping of a thread.

With his eyes wide open, a terrible silence laying upon his soul, he stared into the night, waiting, waiting for the dawn.

Dawn came at last. The brothers washed and took food. There was a long way to go, far off into the woods. There was almost a tenderness in Ivan's attitude towards Peter. What mattered now? The issue was decided; the gods had taken the thing out of his hands. With their axes swinging they made their way into the woods, through a day sharp with frost. At last they arrived at the clearing where they were to continue their tree-felling. A brazier stood waiting there, and before work started they lit a fire in preparation for the midday meal. Then they picked up their axes and set to. Lustily their strokes rang through the wood. Chime rang upon chime. It was strenuous work, the work of men with strong muscles and keen eyes.

The morning went by steadily. There was no hate in Ivan's soul—only a deadly patience. He knew the moment would come. He knew when the moment came that he would act. For a few minutes they stopped and wiped their foreheads. Peter opened his shirt wide and exposed his breast to Ivan. The quick vision presented itself of Peter heaving darkly in their bed, the sudden finger of lightning, the naked breast.

"Come!" said Ivan thickly, "let us begin!"

They both took up their positions against a tree. Peter with the axe in his left hand struck against the tree. Ivan, quick as the lightning which last night had shown him his way, whirled his axe round, away from the tree, and the sharp edge went cracking through Peter's ribs, deep beyond the heart. A great fountain of blood spurted into the air. A long, feeble moan left Peter's lips. Deeper than the axe had cut, his eyes looked sorrowfully into the soul of Ivan. His weight tottered and Ivan felt himself following to the ground. There was not a moment to lose. Again the axe whirled through the air. With the whole of a strong man's strength the axe came down upon his own wrist, and down fell the body of Peter with the hand of his brother indissoluble in death round his wrist, as it had been indissoluble in life.

The thing he had brought about was too monstrous for Ivan at that moment to understand. It was only the little things that his ear and eye seized—the frightened screech of a bird in a tree, the sullen shining of the little red arrow in the thumb of his own severed hand.

Ivan felt the blood streaming from the stump of his forearm. He knew that if he did not reassert complete mastery over himself he would bleed to death. All would be vain—the call of the far girl, the murder, the last look in Peter's eyes. He staggered over to the brazier and plunged his forearm for one swift instant into the embers. Then darkness overwhelmed him and he fell backward into unutterable night.

4

It was easy enough to explain. Not the least suspicion attached itself to Ivan. People came from remote cabins and farms to sympathise with the bereaved brother. What was more likely in the world than that Ivan's axe should slide from a knot in the tree and come crashing against Peter, who, even if he could see the axe coming, could not by any human means have disengaged himself from his brother. "I always thought something like this would happen," people muttered wisely to each other, and shook their heads and crossed their breasts.

Of course they all understood how Ivan could no longer remain in the cottage consecrated by memories of his brother. So Ivan sold his accumulation of timber and his land and what little stock the brothers had bought, and it was not many weeks after his forearm was healed that the jangling train from Monastir was bearing him through the Macedonian hills upon his quest for the English girl at Salonika.

In Salonika she was nowhere to be found. Forlornly he went from music-hall to music-hall, but she was gone. He haunted even the *cafés chantants* along Egnatia Street, even the degenerate *brasseries* on the Monastir Road, where the red-costumed women stood upon improvised platforms and sang to tipsy crowds with the accompaniment of feeble violins. But there was no trace of her in the whole city. From the director at the White Tower he learned that perhaps she had proceeded to Constantinople, perhaps she had returned to Athens, whence the European artistes generally came to Salonika on their round of the greater Levantine towns.

With all the fervour and idealism of a mediaeval knight Ivan stepped upon the deck of a Messageries Maritimes boat returning to Marseilles by way of the Piraeus. When the electric train from the harbour landed him at the station in Athens a mystic conviction filled him that here in this city, some day, the English girl would be revealed to him. Ambitiously he first tried the great *Opéra,* but she was not there. The weeks lengthened into months and failure followed failure, but the mysterious foreknowledge of his race held up his weary spirits and bade him put aside despair.

When at last she appeared upon the stage of one of the lesser music-halls, it was with no great start of surprise or welcome that he recognised her arrival. It was as if a mother or a sister had slipped back into the place from which for some reason she had been absent. Her features had become engraved upon every curve of his brain. She came upon the stage and filled his life again as naturally as day fills the place of night. Life became for him a thing of meaning and splendour. He realised that at last Life was to begin.

He knew little of the half-measures and half-advances of Western civilisation. He lost no time in appearing before the girl. After only a few words of difficult apology, with a voice of low and subdued passion he told her a fragment or two of

his tale. It was a broken French that he talked—the French
of which his mother long ago had taught her boys the few
phrases she knew, and which his experiences in Salonika and
Athens during the last few months had greatly improved.

The large grey eyes of the English girl opened wide in
wonder as she listened, fascinated, to the stammering avow-
als of this tall stranger from a shadowy land. Half in fright
she drew back against the wall of her wretched little dressing-room, but, even so soon she realised that the destiny was
overwhelming her which was to bring an end to her wander-
ings. She consented shyly to his suggestion that she should
see him for a little while next night, and it was with a thrill
of delight and fear she saw his great figure waiting for her at
the gate of the Museum, as the purple Athenian dusk came
wandering down from the Acropolis and cast velvet glooms
among the pillars of Pentelican marble.

For years since her mother had died and her father had
become a confirmed drunkard, it was a very lonely life that
Mary Weston had led. She had no great talent, and she had
drifted from theatre to theatre upon the Continent, for to
her England was a place of no kindly memories. Ivan Kupreloff began to mean for her what her mother had meant before
she died and her father before he had taken to drink.

A few months had passed only. There was no escape from
Ivan. There was nothing importunate about him, but he was
irresistible. He was Life. Proudly he realised that he had con-
quered her. To world's end and Time's end she was his own.

They were married at length. Athens and all the cities she
had known, the Serbian wood and the murdered brother—
these passed utterly from their souls in the strong kiss which
united them for all days.

5

Yet not for ever was the memory of his dead life to vanish
from the heart of Ivan. Even during the times of his most

passionate love for Mary there began to invade him moments of bitter memory and regret. There was something which prevented the entire fusion with Mary towards which he yearned and ached. It was something deep in his soul. It was something which gnawed at his forearm, bit with teeth of contrition at the place where the axe had fallen and severed the hand from the wrist.

He tried to put all this futility from him. He would seize Mary more closely, look desperately into her eyes, and in the perfume of her lips and hair seek anodyne. Between them there was a sufficient store of money, small though it was, to allow them a few months of liberty, undisturbed by any thought of the future. They wandered lazily about Greece for a little time, finding in the Greek day and the immemorial hills a perfect setting for their love.

And yet ever more insistently came to him the call of the hand—the hand which had been his own and not his own, the hand which had united in so unique an embrace his brother with himself.

Again at night voices tormented him. Again, when winds were about, they called with living words: "The hand! The hand! It is calling you, calling! Answer! He wants you! Peter!" wailed the wind. "Peter! Peter!"

Lines began to draw across his forehead. With anxiety Mary saw shadows growing under his eyes, and in his eyes a hunger which grew more and more forlorn. "What is it, love?" she would murmur. "You've not slept well!"

"Nothing at all, love, nothing! All's well!" he would reply, trying with a kiss to forget the wind and the hand and the call.

"There's something you're longing for. Tell me, Ivan. Let me help you. You must."

"Nothing, Mary. I've got you. There's nothing else in the world." But the call of the hand did not abate. "Peter!" the winds wailed, "Peter! He wants you! Answer!"

The urgency of the call grew more imperious. He was sickening and growing weak. There was a hot torpidity in the dry Greek noon which shrivelled his veins. He would drag his coat down from his neck and lift his head and try to breathe the deep breath he had known in his Serbian wood. But there was no spaciousness, no great draughts of cool air in the wind, only voices: "Peter! Peter! Peter!"

"We must go somewhere. We must go away," said Mary. "We must go to Athens and see a doctor, Ivan. I'm afraid!"

"Not Athens! No!" he replied with a shudder, his temples contracting as before the hot blast from an oven. Those dry marble spaces! The dusty pepper-trees! The sweating crowds in the shops, swallowing sweet cakes like swine swallowing husks in a sty! Athens became a nightmare.

He was lying awake one night, the body of Mary curled beside him, her hair floating vaguely on the pillow in the half-light of the moon. She stirred in her sleep, and her little white hand unconsciously sought his wrist and fastened tightly round it. That moment bridged the buried time. Unescapably Mary had brought back to him the sensation of Peter lying in the grasp of his own hand. Never before was the call of the hand so imperious. Never so clearly did the wind exclaim, "Peter! He wants you! Answer!"

An irresistible love for his murdered brother overwhelmed him. He raised himself from his bed and lifted helplessly his lopped arm into the whispering room. "Coming, my brother, I am coming! Wait! Peter!" he moaned, and the wind replied: "Peter! Peter!"

He lay back in bed. He realised that the strongest claim in the world upon him was the call of the hand. As for Mary— she was nothing different from himself. For her as for him the call of the hand came dictatorially. In each other they were one, but without the hand their unity was uncompleted. The call of the hand must be obeyed. To-morrow they must leave Greece behind. To-morrow to Serbia, to-morrow the response to the hand.

Mary was not surprised when Ivan without warning explained that all their plans were altered. She was used to his unaccountable whims, the sudden mystic impulses of his Slavonic soul.

They packed up the few things which were all the impediment they possessed, and next day saw them well started on their way to Monastir, carefully skirting Athens. Arrived at Monastir, a few days elapsed before they appeared at the remote wood where Ivan was born. The cottage built by Ivan Kupreloff was not yet occupied. The strange character of its former inhabitants combined with the terrible nature of Peter's death had succeeded in keeping it empty! They obtained permission from its owner to occupy the cottage, and with a great sigh of content Ivan flung open the door where he and his brother had passed so frequently in former days.

In a little time Mary had made of the house such a palace of delight as it had not been since Ivan's mother was dead. Happily, Ivan took in large draughts of the Serbian pineland air, filling his lungs. Happily, with Mary beside him on the bed where he and Peter had lain entwined, the dark drowsy nights melted into dawn.

He made his reply to the call of the hand. Only faintly, if at all, the wind or the branches whispered "Peter! Peter!" Peter seemed to be happy at last. The severed hand seemed at last to be tranquil round the wrist of the murdered brother. Then the winds died away, and there was no sound of "Peter!"; only fitfully a swaying of twigs and a rustle of pine-needles.

So it seemed. Till summer drooped her drowsing hair. Summer became wrinkled and old. Summer went and the swift autumn came. The days shortened into the rigours of winter, the days ever contracted towards the anniversary of that red day when the axe was lifted and Peter fell. Never a moment did it occur to Ivan that now when the fatal day was approaching he might leave behind him his Serbian wood. He knew that, more tightly than ever during his living days, the wrist of Peter lay within his own hand, tight, unescapable. Mary and he lay under the thumb of that severed hand wherefrom the red arrow glowed when the night was dark and the woodfire threw leaping shadows over the log-walls. There was no gainsaying the call of the hand till the end of days. Ivan knew that never again would he leave behind his Serbian wood.

Came the night which was the anniversary of that dead, unburyable night when Peter's doom had been sealed. Again there was the rumbling of thunder, there were evil flashes of lightning that ran among the clouds. Never with so firm an embrace had Mary been clasped within his arms. Nothing in the world was so strong as his love for Mary. They had responded to the call of the hand. There was no further claim upon them. Ivan kissed her sleeping eyes and was lulled in the music of her breathing. A drowsiness came over him, and for a time he slid into sleep.

In his sleep something tightened round him, something growing so tight that it forced through the barriers of his sleep. Vaguely, faintly a half-consciousness came back to him. He was not awake. He was not asleep. He was in a borderland where the other world is not dead and this world is half-alive. Tighter grew the thing which pressed against his sleep. It was round his wrist, it was round the wrist where something had once come crashing down. What was it? What was it had come crashing down? An axe it was that had come crashing down. It was the hand of Mary growing tighter round his wrist. No, it could not be the hand of Mary. Mary had fallen from his arms. Mary was turned away from him. He could see her hands pale where she had lifted them in sleep above her head. It was not the hand of Mary growing tighter round his wrist. But it was a hand. No doubt of that. It was a hand. With a dull glow of flame a little red arrow gleamed like embers below the thumb of the hand. Where had he seen that arrow? Where and when? When his hand had fallen away from him, lopped at the wrist. It was the dead hand which was not dead. It was his own hand. It was the hand with the red arrow which had held Peter so tightly. It was the dead hand which was alive, the living hand which had arisen from the dead. Tighter round his wrist grew the pressure of the severed hand. The hand was tired of calling. The hand had come. There was no gainsaying the hand. So tight grew the clutch of the hand that his whole arm slowly lifted from his side. Irresistibly the shoulder followed the rising arm. There was no gainsaying the hand. Neither awake nor asleep, neither living nor dead, he followed the hand, he rose from the bed where Mary lay, sleeping sundered from him, his no more. Mary was alive. He was neither living nor dead. The door of the room was opened wide. Closed doors were no barrier against the hand which had arisen from the grave. Slowly, with steady feet, with wide, filmy eyes, Ivan passed through the door. Slowly through the outer door, slowly into the sound of thunder, into the gleam of lightning and the voices of winds moaning unceasingly, "Peter! Peter! He is calling you! Ivan! Peter is calling you! Follow!" and ever again unceasingly, "Peter! Peter!"

Tighter than the bonds of ice or granite hills, tight only as the bond of death, the arisen hand held the lopped wrist, drew the slow body of Ivan through the haunted night far into the wood, far through the talking trees, far to the place of that tree which had not been cut down, to the place where an axe had fallen through bones and flesh, where Peter had fallen, where Peter lay buried, not deep down; where Peter lay buried under twigs and loose earth.

Tightly round the wrist of the man neither alive nor dead clutched the resurrected hand. Nearer and nearer to the shallow grave the hand pulled down the body of Ivan. Methodically, steadily, working with no pause, the free hand of Ivan moved the twigs and the loose earth—methodically, with no pause, until at last the body of Peter lay revealed; not recognisable, dissolute beneath the change through which all men shall pass, recognisable only to those filmy eyes of Ivan, to that questing hungry soul of Ivan which had come to claim its own. Closer and closer to the dead brother the severed hand drew the body of Ivan down; so close, so close, until at last the hand clutched again and for ever that wrist to which Fate had fastened it long years ago. Alongside of his dead brother, quietly, with those eyes which neither saw nor did not see, Ivan lay down full length. Gradually the severed hand, the hand which had arisen from the dead to claim him, because the dead brother called and the severed hand called for its own, gradually the hand slipped from the lopped wrist; the wrist and the arm became one. The hand of Ivan had brought Ivan to his own. Indissolubly, Peter and Ivan lay joined together. But the death which lay cold in the heart and body of Peter passed from the clutched wrist, passed into the hand which clutched it, passed along the arm which had been severed once, and along Ivan's shoulder, until it made his eyes unseeing discs and of his heart cold stone which could beat no more.

As the grey light of dawn came emptily down the Serbian woods, the two brothers lay immortally one again, like the two babies the gods had given Nikolai Kupreloff upon a long-vanished night.

INTERLUDE

A Mysterious Hand
(Morristown, Tennessee, *Gazette,* April 28, 1875)

A short time since mention was made in the *Union and American* of a mysterious hand that had grown from a grave in Gibson county. We got our information from an article in the *Jackson Courier-Herald.* We extract from that article the following account of this wonderful phenomenon:

"Monday our city was unusually excited by the exhibition in the *Courier-Herald* office of a hand of wood which grew out of a grave near Yorkville, in Gibson county. It was brought into our office by Capt. G. S. Andrews, of that county, who gives us its history. A man named Wm. Herron was out walking with his wife one Sunday evening not long since, and in passing an old neglected graveyard near the public road, she saw a gum bush with a bunch of mistletoe on its top, and requested her husband to get it for her. He went and cut the top off the bush, and commenced breaking off the mistletoe, when to his surprise and terror he discovered that the wood underneath presented the perfect form of a human hand. Capt. Andrews, hearing of the wonderful discovery, went to the house of Mr. Herron, who, feeling rather uncomfortable over the thought that he cut it from a grave, and perhaps having some theory as to its supernatural significance, very

281

willingly let Capt. Andrews have it. There are citizens of this city to whom both Capt. Andrews and Mr. Herron are known and they are vouched for as truthful men, but the hand itself is proof enough of the truth of the statement concerning its growth on a bush. The bush from which it was cut was six feet high and the hand was on the top pointing upward, presenting the position of the minster's hand when pronouncing a benediction. It is about the size of a six year old child's hand, with long slender fingers like those of a person very much emaciated by sickness. The wood has enlarged formations on each finger and the thumb, representing and corresponding with the joints of the human hand. The most remarkable feature about it is the natural appearance of the nails. They have a kind of flesh color, and the balance of the hand, where the bark has been entirely removed, looks ghastly white. The first impression it makes upon you is the same experienced in handling a skeleton, and a large majority of those who see it, regard it with the same subdued, half superstitious awe, inspired by the presence of a corpse. Mr. Anderson says the grave from which it was cut is supposed to be the grave of a very devout Methodist minister by the name of Butcher, who was buried there many years ago."

Capt. Andrews spoke of in the above is in the city. He last night brought the mysterious hand to the *Union and American* office and placed it on exhibition. We can give no more exact description of it than we find in the above from the *Jackson Courier-Herald*. It is certainly a most wonderful growth and must be a mere freak of nature. It is possible that some human agency may have contributed to the present formation, but it must have taken years to have done it and that while the bush, of which it was part, was growing.

Capt. Andrews will be in the city for a few days. He will be at the counting room of the *Union and American* tomorrow morning, and will gladly exhibit the phenomenon to any who may wish to see it.

THE HAND
Theodore Dreiser
(1919)

Davidson could distinctly remember that it was between two and three years after the grisly event in the Monte Orte range—the sickening and yet deserved end of Mersereau, his quondam partner and fellow adventurer—that anything to be identified with Mersereau's malice toward him, and with Mersereau's probable present existence in the spirit world, had appeared in his life.

He and Mersereau had worked long together as prospectors, investors, developers of property. It was only after they had struck it rich in the Klondike that Davidson had grown so much more apt and shrewd in all commercial and financial matters, whereas Mersereau had seemed to stand still—not to rise to the splendid opportunities which then opened to him. Why, in some of those later deals it had not been possible for Davidson even to introduce his old partner to some of the moneyed men he had to deal with. Yet Mersereau had insisted, as his right, if you please, on being "in on" everything—everything!

Take that wonderful Monte Orte property, the cause of all the subsequent horror. He, Davidson—not Mersereau—had discovered or heard of the mine, and had carried it along, with old Besmer as a tool or decoy—Besmer being the ostensible factor—until it was all ready for him to take over and sell or develop. Then it was that Mersereau, having so long

been his partner, demanded a full half—a third, at least—on
the ground that they had once agreed to work together in all
these things.

Think of it! And Mersereau growing duller and less useful
and more disagreeable day by day, and year by year! Indeed,
toward the last he had threatened to expose the trick by which
jointly, seven years before, they had possessed themselves of
the Skyute Pass Mine; to drive Davidson out of public and
financial life, to have him arrested and tried—along with
himself, of course. Think of that!

But he had fixed the man—yes, he had, damn him! He
had trailed Mersereau that night to old Besmer's cabin on
the Monte Orte, when Besmer was away. Mersereau had at-
tempted to steal the diagram of the new field. Yes, just when
Mersereau thought that no one was about, and that he was
making safely away, Davidson had struck him cleanly over
the ear with that heavy rail-bolt fastened to the end of a wal-
nut stick, and the first blow had done for him.

Lord, how the bone above Mersereau's ear had sounded when it cracked! And how bloody one side of that bolt
was! Mersereau hadn't had time to do anything before he was
helpless. He hadn't died instantly, though, but had turned
over and faced Davidson with that savage, scowling face of
his and those blazing, animal eyes.

Lying half propped up on his left elbow, Mersereau had
reached out toward him with that big, rough, bony right
hand of his—the right with which he always boasted of having done so much damage on this, that, and the other occasion—had glared at him as much as to say:

"Oh, if I could only reach you just for a moment before
I go!"

Then it was that Davidson had lifted the club again. Horrified as he was, and yet determined that he must save his
own life, he had finished the task, dragging the body back to

an old fissure behind the cabin and covering it with branches,
a great pile of pine fronds, and as many as one hundred and
fifty boulders, great and small, and had left his victim. It was
a sickening job and a sickening sight, but it had to be.

Yes, having finished, he had slipped dismally away, like
a jackal, thinking of that hand in the moonlight, held up so
savagely, and that look. Nothing might have come of that,
either, if he hadn't been inclined to brood on it so much, on
the fierceness of it.

No, nothing had happened. A year had passed, and if
anything were going to turn up it surely would have done so.
Davidson had gone first to New York, later to Chicago, to
dispose of the Monte Orte claim. Then, after two years, he
came back to Mississippi to look after some sugar property
which had once belonged to him, and which he was now able
to reclaim and put in charge of his sister as a kind of home
for himself. He had none other.

But that body back there! That hand uplifted in the moonlight—to clutch him if it could! Those eyes!

JUNE, 1905

Take that first year, for instance, when he had returned to
Gatchard in Mississippi, whence both he and Mersereau had
originally come. After looking at his own property he had
gone out to a tumble-down estate of his uncle's in Issaquena
County—a leaky old slope-roofed house where, in a bedroom
on the top floor, he had had his first experience with the significance or reality of the hand.

Yes, that was where first he had really seen it pictured in
that curious, unbelievable way; only who would believe that
it was Mersereau's hand? They would say it was an accident,
chance, rain dripping down. But the hand had appeared on
the ceiling of that room just as sure as anything, after a
heavy rain-storm—it was almost a cyclone when every chink
in the old roof had seemed to leak water.

During the night, after he had climbed to the room by way of those dismal stairs with their great landing and small glass oil-lamp, and had sunk to rest, or tried to, in the heavy, wide, damp bed, thinking, as he always did those days, of the Monte Orte and Mersereau, the storm had come up. As he listened to the wind moaning outside he had heard first the scratch, scratch, scratch, of some limb, no doubt, against the wall—sounding, or so it seemed in his feverish unrest, like some one penning an indictment against him with a worn, rusty pen.

And then, the storm growing worse, he had gone to the window in a fit of irritation and self-contempt at his own nervousness, just as the lightning struck a branch of the tree nearest the window. He had retreated, feeling that it was meant for him.

But that big, knotted hand painted on the ceiling by the dripping water during the night! There it was, right over him when he awoke, outlined or painted as if with wet, gray whitewash against the wretched but normal pale-blue of the ceiling when dry. There it was—a big, open hand just like Mersereau's as he had held it up that night—huge, knotted, rough, the fingers extended as if tense and clutching. And, if you will believe it, near it was something that looked like a pen—an old, long-handled pen—to match that scratch, scratch, scratch!

"Huldah," he had inquired of the old black mammy who entered in the morning to bring him fresh water and throw open the shutters, "what does that look like to you up there—that patch on the ceiling where the rain came through?"

He wanted to reassure himself as to the character of the thing he saw—that it might not be a creation of his own feverish imagination, accentuated by the dismal character of this place.

"'Pears t' me mo' like a big han' 'an anythin' else, Marse Davi'son," commented Huldah, pausing and staring upward. "Mo' like a big fist, kinda. Dat air's a new drip come las' night, I reckon. Dis here ole place ain' gonna hang togethah much longah, less'n some repairin' be done mighty quick now. Yassir, dat air's a new drip, sho's yo' bo'n, en it come on'y las' night. I hain't never seed dat befo'."

And then he had inquired, thinking of the fierceness of the storm:

"Huldah, do you have many such storms up this way?"

"Good gracious, Marse Davi'son, we hain't seed no sech a blow en—en come three year now. I hain't seed no sech lightnin' en I doan' know when."

Wasn't that strange, that it should all come on the night when he was there?

Huldah stared idly, always ready to go slow and rest if possible, whereas he had turned irritably. To be annoyed by ideas such as this! To always be thinking of that Monte Orte affair! Why couldn't he forget it? It was Mersereau's own fault. He never would have killed the man if he hadn't been forced to it.

And to be haunted in this way, making mountains out of mole-hills, as he thought then! It must be his own miserable fancy—and yet Mersereau had looked so threateningly at him. That glance had boded something; it was too terrible not to.

Davidson might not want to think of it, but how could he stop? Mersereau might not be able to hurt him any more, at least not on this earth; but still, couldn't he? Didn't the appearance of this hand seem to indicate that he might? He was dead, of course. His body, his skeleton, was under that pile of rocks and stones, some of them as big as wash-tubs. Why worry over that, and after two years? And still—

That hand on that ceiling!

December, 1905

Then, again, take that matter of meeting Pringle in Gatchard just at that time, within the same week. It was due to Davidson's sister. She had invited Mr. and Mrs. Pringle in to meet

him one evening, without telling him that they were spiritu-
alists and might discuss spiritualism.

Clairvoyance, Pringle called it, or seeing what can't be
seen with material eyes, and clairaudience, or hearing what
can't be heard with material ears, as well as materialization,
or ghosts, and table-rapping, and the like. Table-rapping—
that damned tap-tapping that Davidson had been hearing
ever since!

It was Pringle's fault, really. Pringle had persisted in
talking. He, Davidson, wouldn't have listened, except that he
somehow became fascinated by what Pringle said concerning
what he had heard and seen in his time. Mersereau must have
been at the bottom of that, too.

At any rate, after he had listened, Davidson was sorry, for
Pringle had time to fill his mind full of those awful facts or
ideas which had since harassed him so much—all that stuff
about drunkards, degenerates, and weak people generally being followed about by vile, evil spirits and used to effect
those spirits' purposes or desires in this world. Horrible!

Wasn't it awful? Pringle—big, mushy creature that he
was, sickly and stagnant like a springless pool—insisted that
he had even seen clouds of these spirits about drunkards,
degenerates, and the like, in street-cars, on trains, and about
vile corners at night. Once, he said, he had seen just one evil
spirit—think of that!—following a certain man all the time,
at his left elbow—a dark, evil, red-eyed thing, until finally
the man had been killed in a quarrel.

Pringle described their shapes, these spirits, as varied.
They were small, dark, irregular clouds, with red or green
spots somewhere for eyes, changing in form and becoming
longish or round like a jellyfish, or even like a misshapen cat
or dog. They could take any form at will—that of a man, say,
for a little while.

Once, Pringle declared, he had seen as many as fifty about
a drunkard who was staggering down a street, all of them

trying to urge him into the nearest saloon, so that they might reexperience in some vague way the sensation of drunkenness, which at some time or other they themselves, having been drunkards in life, had enjoyed!

It would be the same with a drug fiend, or indeed with any one of weak or evil habits. They gathered about such people like flies, their red or green eyes glowing—attempting to get something from them, perhaps, if nothing more than a little sense of their old earth-life.

The whole thing was so terrible and disturbing at the time, particularly that idea of men being persuaded or influenced to murder, that Davidson could stand it no longer, and got up and left. But in his room up-stairs he meditated on it, standing before his mirror. Suddenly—would he ever forget it?—as he was taking off his collar and tie, he had heard that queer tap, tap, tap, right on his dressing-table or under it, which Pringle said ghosts made when table-rapping in answer to a call, or to give warning of their presence.

Then something said to him, almost as clearly as if he heard it:

"*This is me, Mersereau, come back at last to get you! Pringle was just an excuse of mine to let you know I was coming, and so was that hand in the Hatch house. It was mine! I will be with you from now on. Don't think I will ever leave you!*"

It frightened Davidson and made him half sick, so wrought up was he. For the first time he felt cold chills run up and down his spine—the creeps. He felt as if he could almost feel some one standing over him—Mersereau, of course—only he could not see or hear a thing, just that faint tap at first, growing louder a little later, and quite angry when he tried to ignore it.

People did live, then, after they were dead, especially evil people—people stronger than you, perhaps. They had the power to come back, to haunt, to annoy you if they didn't like anything you had done to them. No doubt Mersereau was following him in the hope of revenge, there in the spirit-world just outside this one, close at his heels, like that evil spirit attending the other man whom Pringle had described.

FEBRUARY, 1906

Take that case of the hand impressed on the soft dough and plaster of Paris, described in an article that he had picked up in the dentist's office out there in Pasadena—Mersereau's very hand, so far as he could judge. How about that for a co-incidence, picking up the magazine with that disturbing article about psychic materialization in Italy, and later in Bern, Switzerland, where the scientists were gathered to investigate that sort of thing? And just when he was trying to rid himself finally of the notion that any such thing could be!

According to that magazine article, some old crone over in Italy—spiritualist, or witch, or something—had got together a crowd of experimentalists or professors in an abandoned house on an almost deserted island off the coast of Sardinia. There they had conducted experiments with spirits, which they called materialization, getting the impression of the fingers of a hand, or of a whole hand and arm, or of a face, on a plate of glass covered with soot, the plate being locked in a small safe on the center of a table about which they sat!

Davidson couldn't understand how it was done, but done it was. There in that magazine were half a dozen pictures, re-productions of photographs of a hand, an arm, and a face—or a part of one, anyhow. And if they looked like anything, they looked exactly like Mersereau's!

There was not the least doubt of it—they were Mersereau's, intended, when they were made over there in Italy, for Da-vidson to see later there in Pasadena. Yes, they were! And looking at that sinister face reproduced in the magazine, it seemed to say, with Mersereau's old coarse sneer:

*"You see? You can't escape me! I'm showing you how much
alive I am over here, just as I was on earth. And I'll get you yet,
even if I have to go farther than Italy to do it!"*

It was amazing, the shock Davidson got out of it. It wasn't
just that alone, but the persistence and repetition of this
hand business. What could it mean? It was Mersereau's hand,
all right. As for the face, it wasn't all there—just the jaw,
mouth, cheek, left temple, and a part of the nose and eye;
but it was Mersereau, all right. He had gone clear over there
into Italy somewhere, in a lone house on an island, to get
this message of his undying hate back to Davidson. Or was
it just spirits, evil spirits, bent on annoying him because he
was nervous and sensitive now?

OCTOBER, 1906

Even crowded new hotels and new buildings weren't the protection Davidson had first thought they were. Even there
you weren't safe—not from a man like Mersereau. Take that
incident there in Los Angeles, and again in Seattle, only two
months ago now—he was always careful to take a room these
days in the best and busiest hotels—when Mersereau was able
to make that dreadful explosive or crashing sound, as if one
had burst a huge paper bag full of air, or upset a china-clos-
et full of glass and broken everything, when as a matter of
fact nothing at all had happened. It had frightened Davidson
horribly the first two or three times, believing as he did that
something fearful had happened. Finding that it was nothing—or Mersereau—he was becoming used to it now; but
other people, unfortunately, were not.

He would be—as he had been that first time—sitting in
his room perfectly still and trying to amuse himself, or not
to think, when suddenly there would be that awful crash. It
was astounding! Other people heard it, of course. They had
in Los Angeles. A maid and a porter had come running the

first time to inquire, and he had had to protest that he had heard nothing. They couldn't believe it at first, and had gone to other rooms to look. When it happened the second time, the management had protested, thinking it was a joke he was playing; and to avoid the risk of exposure he had left.

After that he could not keep a valet or nurse about him for long. Servants wouldn't stay, and managers of hotels wouldn't let him remain when such things went on. Yet he couldn't live in a private house or apartment alone, for there the noises and sights would be worse than ever.

June, 1907

Take that last old house he had been in—or ever would be in again!—at Anne Haven, which was much worse, and which proved it all. There the hand actually appeared to him, a thing as big as a washtub at first, something like smoke or shadow in a black room moving about over the bed and everywhere. Then, as he lay there, gazing at it spellbound, it condensed slowly, and he began to feel it. It was now a hand of normal size—there was no doubt of it in the world—going over him softly, without force, as a ghostly hand must, having no real physical strength, but all the time with a strange, secretive something about it, a searching, as if it were not quite sure of itself, and not quite sure that he was really there.

The hand, or so it seemed—God!—moved right up to his neck and began to feel over that as he lay there. Then it was that he guessed just what it was that Mersereau was after—he wanted to choke him to death!

It was just like a hand, the fingers and thumb made into a circle and pressed down over his throat; only it moved over him gently at first, because it really couldn't do anything yet, not having the material strength. But the intention! The sense of cruel, savage determination that went with it!

And yet, if one went to a nerve specialist or doctor about all this, as he did afterward, what did the doctor say? Davidson tried to describe how he was breaking down under the strain, how he could not eat or sleep on account of all these constant tappings and noises; but the moment he even began to hint at his experiences, especially the hand or the noises, the doctor exclaimed:

"Why, this is plain delusion! You're nervously run down, that's all that ails you—on the verge of pernicious anemia, I should say. You'll have to watch yourself as to this illusion about spirits. Get it out of your mind. There's nothing to it!"

Wasn't that just like one of these nerve specialists, bound up in their little ideas and what they knew or saw, or thought they saw?

NOVEMBER, 1907

And now take this very latest development at Battle Creek recently, where he had gone trying to recuperate on the diet there. Hadn't Mersereau, implacable demon that he was, developed this latest trick of making his food taste queer to him—unpalatable, or with an odd odor?

Davidson knew it was Mersereau, for he felt him beside him at the table whenever he sat down. Besides, he seemed to hear something—clairaudience, of course: he was beginning to develop that, too, now! It was Mersereau, of course, saying in a voice which was more like a memory of a voice than anything real—the voice of some one you could remember as having spoken in a certain way, say, ten years or more ago:

"I've fixed it so you can't eat any more, you—"

There followed a long list of vile expletives, enough in itself to sicken one.

Thereafter, in spite of anything he could do to make himself think to the contrary, knowing that the food was all right, really, Davidson found it to have an odor or a taste which disgusted him, and which he could not overcome, try as he would. The management assured him that it was all right, as he knew it was—for others. He saw them eating it.

But he couldn't—had to get up and leave, and the little he could get down he couldn't retain, or it wasn't enough for him to live on.

And Mersereau seemed always by, rejoicing in the result. Why, if it weren't for fresh fruit on the stands at times, and just plain, fresh-baked bread in bakers' windows, which he could buy and eat quickly, he might not be able to live at all. It was getting to that pass!

August, 1908

That wasn't the worst, either, bad as all that was. The worst was the fact that under the strain of all this he was slowly but surely breaking down, and that in the end Mersereau might really succeed in driving him out of life here—to do what, if anything, to him there? What? It was such an evil pack by which he was surrounded, those who lived just on the other side and hung about the earth, vile, debauched creatures, as Pringle had described them, and as Davidson had come to know for himself, fearing them and their ways so much, and really seeing them at times.

Since he had come to be so weak and sensitive, he could see them for himself— vile things that they were, swimming before his gaze in the dark whenever he chanced to let himself be in the dark, which was not often—friends of Mersereau, no doubt, and inclined to help him just for the evil of it.

For this long time now Davidson had taken to sleeping with the light on, wherever he was, only tying a handkerchief over his eyes to keep out some of the glare. Even then he could see them—queer, misshapen things, for all the world like wavy, stringy jellyfish or coils of thick, yellowish-black smoke, moving about, changing in form at times, always looking dirty or vile, somehow, and with those queer, dim, reddish or greenish glows for eyes. It was sickening!

OCTOBER, 1908

Having accomplished so much, Mersereau would by no means be content to let him go. Davidson knew that! He could talk to him occasionally now, or at least could hear him and answer back, if he chose, when he was alone and quite certain that no one was listening.

Mersereau was always saying, when Davidson would listen to him at all—which he wouldn't often—that he would get him yet, that he would make him pay, or charging him with fraud and murder.

"I'll choke you yet!" The words seemed to float in from somewhere, as if he were remembering that at some time Mersereau had said just that in his angry, savage tone—not as if he heard it; and yet he was hearing it, of course. *"I'll choke you yet! You can't escape! You may think you'll die a natural death, but you won't, and that's why I'm poisoning your food to weaken you. You can't escape! I'll get you, sick or well, when you can't help yourself, when you're sleeping. I'll choke you, just as you hit me with that club. That's why you're always seeing and feeling this hand of mine! I'm not alone. I've nearly had you many a time already, only you have managed to wriggle out so far, jumping up, but some day you won't be able to—see? Then—"*

The voice seemed to die away at times, even in the middle of a sentence, but at other times—often, often—he could hear it completing the full thought. Sometimes he would turn on the thing and exclaim:

"Oh, go to the devil!" or, "Let me alone!" or, "Shut up!" Even in a closed room and all alone, such remarks seemed strange to him, addressed to a ghost; but he couldn't resist at times, annoyed as he was. Only he took good care not to talk if any one was about.

It was getting so that there was no real place for him outside of an asylum, for often he would get up screaming at night—he had to, so sharp was the clutch on his throat—and then always, wherever he was, a servant would come in and want to know what was the matter. He would have to say that it was a nightmare—only the management always requested him to leave after the second or third time, say, or after an explosion or two. It was horrible!

He might as well apply to a private asylum or sanatorium now, having all the money he had, and explain that he had delusions—delusions! Imagine!—and ask to be taken care of. In a place like that they wouldn't be disturbed by his jumping up and screaming at night, feeling that he was being choked, as he was, or by his leaving the table because he couldn't eat the food, or by his talking back to Mersereau, should they chance to hear him, or by the noises when they occurred.

They could assign him a special nurse and a special room, if he wished—only he didn't wish to be too much alone. They could put him in charge of some one who would understand all these things, or to whom he could explain. He couldn't expect ordinary people, or hotels catering to ordinary people, to put up with him any more.

He must go and hunt up a good place somewhere where they understood such things, or at least tolerated them, and explain, and then it would all pass for the hallucinations of a crazy man—though, as a matter of fact, he wasn't crazy at all. It was all too real, only the average or so-called normal person couldn't see or hear as he could—hadn't experienced what he had.

December, 1908

"The trouble is, doctor, that Mr. Davidson is suffering from the delusion that he is pursued by one or more evil spirits—I can't quite make out which yet. He was not committed here by any court, but came of his own accord about four months ago, and we let him wander about here at will.

"One of his worst delusions, doctor, is that there is one spirit in particular who is trying to choke him to death, especially at night. Dr. Major, our superintendent, says he has tuberculosis of the throat, with occasional spasmodic contractions. He won't believe that: but whenever he tries to sleep, especially in the middle of the night, he will jump up and come running out into the hall, insisting that one of these spirits is trying to choke him to death. He really seems to believe it, for he comes out coughing and choking and feeling at his neck as if some one had been trying to strangle him. He always explains the whole matter to me as being the spirits, and asks me to not pay any attention to him unless he calls for help or rings his call-bell; and so I never think anything more of it now unless he does.

"Another of his ideas is that these same spirits do something to his food—put poison in it, or give it a bad odor or taste, so that he can't eat it. When he does find anything he can eat, he grabs it and almost swallows it whole, before, as he says, the spirits have time to do anything to it. Once, he says, he weighed more than two hundred pounds, but now he only weighs one hundred and twenty. It's pathetic, doctor!

"Dr. Major insists that it is purely a delusion, that so far as being choked is concerned, it is the tuberculosis of the throat, and that his stomach trouble comes from the same thing; but by association of ideas, or delusion, he thinks some one is trying to choke him and poison his food, when it isn't so at all. Dr. Major says that he can't imagine what could have started it. He is always trying to talk to Mr. Davidson about it; but whenever he begins to ask him questions, Mr. Davidson refuses to talk, and gets up and leaves.

"One of the peculiar things about his idea of being choked, doctor, is that when he is merely dozing he always wakes up in time, and has the power to throw it off. He claims that their strength is not equal to his own when he is awake, or even dozing, but when he's asleep their spirit is stronger than his. Sometimes, when he has had a fright like this, he will come out in the hall and down to my desk there at the lower end, and ask if he mayn't sit there by me. He says it calms him. I always tell him yes; but it won't be five minutes before he'll get up and leave again, saying that he's being annoyed, or that he won't be able to contain himself if he stays any longer, because of the remarks being made over his shoulder or in his ear.

"Often he'll say: 'Did you hear that, Miss Liggett? It's astonishing, the low, vile things that man can say at times!' When I say, 'No, I didn't hear,' he always says: 'I'm so glad!'"

"No one has ever tried to relieve him of this idea by hypnotism, I suppose?"

"Not that I know of, doctor. Dr. Major may have tried it. I have only been here three months."

"Tuberculosis is certainly the cause of the throat trouble, as Dr. Major says; and as for the stomach trouble, that comes from the same thing—natural enough under the circumstances. We may have to resort to hypnotism a little later. I'll see. In the mean time you'd better caution all who come in touch with him never to sympathize, or even to seem to believe in anything he imagines is being done to him. It will merely encourage him in his notions. And get him to take his medicine regularly; it won't cure, but it will help. Dr. Major has asked me to give especial attention to his case, and I want the conditions as near right as possible."

"Yes, sir."

JANUARY, 1909

The trouble with these doctors was that they really knew nothing of anything save what was on the surface, the little they had learned at a medical college or in practice—chiefly how certain drugs, tried by their predecessors in certain cases,

were known to act. They had no imagination whatever, even
when you tried to tell them.

Take that latest young person who was coming here now
in his good clothes and with his car, fairly bursting with
his knowledge of what he called psychiatrics, looking into
Davidson's eyes so hard and smoothing his temples and
throat—massage, he called it—saying that he had incipient
tuberculosis of the throat and stomach trouble, and utterly
disregarding things which he, Davidson, could personally see
and hear! Imagine the fellow trying to persuade him, at this
late date, that all that was wrong with him was tuberculosis, that he didn't see Mersereau standing right beside him
at times, bending over him, holding up that hand and telling him how he intended to kill him yet—that it was all an
illusion!

Imagine saying that Mersereau couldn't actually seize him
by the throat when he was asleep, or nearly so, when Davidson himself, looking at his throat in the mirror, could see the
marks of his fingers—actually his fingers!—for a moment or
so afterward. At any rate, his throat was red and sore from
being clutched as Mersereau of late was able to clutch him!
And to say, as they had said at first, that he himself was making it so by rubbing and feeling it, and then later that it was
tuberculosis!

Rot! Wasn't it enough to make one want to quit the place?
If it weren't for Miss Liggett and her devoted care, he would.
That nurse was worth her weight in gold, learning his ways
as she had, being so uniformly kind, and bearing with his
difficulties so genially. He would leave her something in his
will.

To leave this place and go elsewhere, unless he could take
her along, would be folly. And anyway, where else would
he go? Here at least were other people, patients like himself, who could understand and sympathize with him. Old

Rankin, the lawyer, for instance, who had suffered untold persecution from one living person and another, mostly politicians, was convinced that Davidson's troubles were genuine, and liked to hear about them. These two did not insist, as the doctors did, that he had slow tuberculosis of the throat, and could live a long time and overcome his troubles if he would—which he couldn't. They were merely companionable at such times as Mersereau would give him enough peace to be sociable.

The trouble was that he was growing so weak from lack of sleep and food—his inability to eat the food which his enemy bewitched and to sleep at night on account of the choking—that he couldn't last much longer. This new visiting physician was insisting that along with his throat trouble he was suffering from acute anemia, due to long undernourishment, and that only a solution of strychnine injected direct into the veins would help him.

Now that he was practically bedridden, not able to jump up as freely as before, Davidson was subject to a veritable storm of bedevilment. Not only could he see—especially toward evening, and in the very early hours of the morning—Mersereau hovering about him like a black shadow, but he could feel his enemy's hand moving over him. What was worse, behind or about him he often saw a veritable cloud of evil creatures, swimming about like fish in dark waters, and seeming to eye the procedures with satisfaction.

When food was brought to him, early or late, and in whatever form, Mersereau and they were there, close at hand, as thick as flies, even passing over and through it in an evident attempt to spoil it before he could eat it. Just to see them doing it was enough to poison it for Davidson. He could hear their voices urging Mersereau to do it.

"That's right—poison it!"

"He can't last much longer!"

"Soon he'll be weak enough so that when you grip him he will really die!"

He also heard vile phrases addressed to him by Mersereau, the iterated and reiterated words *"murderer"* and *"swindler"* and *"cheat,"* there in the middle of the night. Often he saw as many as seven dark figures, very much like Mersereau's, although different, gathered close about him, even though the light was still on. Some of them were upon his bed, and it seemed as if they were about to help Mersereau to finish him, adding their hands to his.

Behind them again was a complete circle of all those evil, swimming things with eyes, always watching—helping, probably. He had actually felt the pressure of the hand stronger than ever of late, when they were all there. Only, just before he fainted, and because he could not spring up any more, he screamed or gasped a choking gasp and held his finger on the button. Then Miss Liggett always came, lifted him up, and fixed his pillows. She assured him that it was only the inflammation of his throat, and rubbed it with alcohol, and gave him a few drops of something internally to ease it.

After all this time, and in spite of anything he could tell them, they still believed, or pretended to believe, that he was suffering from tuberculosis, and that all the rest was a delusion, a phase of insanity!

And Mersereau's skeleton still out there on the Monte Orte!

Mersereau would choke him to death, or get others to help, there was no doubt of it now; and yet they would believe that he had died of tuberculosis of the throat! Think of that!

MIDNIGHT OF FEBRUARY 16, 1909

THE GHOST OF MERSEREAU *(to Davidson, bending over)*—"Softly! Softly! He's quite asleep! He didn't think we could get him—that I could! But Miss Liggett is asleep at the end of the hall and can't come, can't hear. He's become so weak now, that he can scarcely move or groan. Strengthen my hand, you! I will grip him so tight about the neck this time that he won't get away! His cries won't help him this time! He can't cry as he once did! Now! Now!"

A Cloud of Evil Spirits *(swimming about)*—"Right! Right! Good! Good! Now! Ah!"

Davidson *(waking, choking, screaming, and feebly striking out)*—"Help! Help! H-e-l-p! Miss— Miss— H—e—l—p!"

Miss Liggett *(dozing heavily at her desk)*—"Everything is still. No one restless. I can sleep." *(Her head nods.)*

The Cloud of Evil Spirits—"Good! Good! Good! His soul at last! Here it comes! He couldn't escape this time! Ah! Good! Good! Ah!"

Mersereau *(to Davidson)*—"You murderer! At last! At last!"

3 a.m. of February 17, 1909

Miss Liggett *(at the bedside, distressed and pale)*—"He must have died some time between one and two, doctor. I left him at one o'clock, as comfortable as I could make him. He said he was feeling as well as could be expected. He's been very weak during the last few days, taking only a little gruel. Between half past one and two I thought I heard a noise, and came to see. He was lying just as you see here, except that his hands were up to his throat, as if it were hurting or choking him. I put them down for fear they would stiffen that way. In trying to call one of the other nurses just now, I found that the bell was out of order, although I know it was all right when I left, because he always made me try it. So he may have tried to ring."

Dr. Major *(turning the head and examining the throat)*—"It looks as if he had clutched at his throat rather tightly this time, I must say. Here is the mark of his thumb on this side and of his four fingers on the other. Rather deep for the little strength he had. Odd that he should have imagined that any one else was trying to choke him, when he was always pressing at his own neck! Throat tuberculosis is very painful at times. That would explain the desire to clutch at his throat."

MISS LIGGETT—"He was always believing that an evil spirit was trying to choke him, doctor."

DR. MAJOR—"Yes, I know—association of ideas. Dr. Scaim and I agree as to that. He had a bad case of chronic tuberculosis of the throat, with accompanying malnutrition, due to the effect of the throat on the stomach; and his notion about evil spirits pursuing him and trying to choke him was simply due to an innate tendency on the part of the subconscious mind to join things together—any notion, say, with any pain. If he had had a diseased leg, he would have imagined that evil spirits were attempting to saw it off, or something like that. In the same way the condition of his throat affected his stomach, and he imagined that the spirits were doing something to his food. Make out a certificate showing acute tuberculosis of the esophagus as the cause, with illusions of persecution as his mental condition. While I am here we may as well look in on Mr. Baff."

THE HAND OF SAINT URY
Gordon MacCreagh
(1951)

Young Jimmy Doak presented his advertisement at the office
of the London *Times*.

> WANTED—Research worker, experienced in
> genealogy.
>
> J. Doak, Hotel Cecil.

The girl behind the help-wanted desk smiled. Jimmy was
immediately belligerent.

"And it does not stand for Joe."

The girl looked hurt. Being English, she had no idea that
Joe Doak was an American collective cognomen assigned to
ridicule. Her smile had been an unconscious recognition of
Jimmy's handsome head with its wavy dark hair and serious
eyes. Even the just now angry mouth was no detriment to a
strong sort of attractiveness.

"And I suppose the ad is funny too?" Jimmy self-con-
sciously challenged.

"Oh, by no means," the girl said quickly. "Thousands of
Americans come to trace their family history. They're hoping
always to find an old title—or at least a family ghost."

"Gosh, are there that many of them?" Jimmy went out
grumbling. "Chasing antique families. I'd rather chase an-
tiques."

Which is just what he went and did. It was in a little lost
end of an alley off Marrowbone Road that he found a little
lost Old Curiosity Shop that might have survived right out
of Dickens, with a battered overhead sign and diamond-pane
windows and cobwebs all complete.

"Huh! Probably artificial." Jimmy had seen how spider-
webbing; was made for American movies. "But good browsing, I expect."

That was just what the proprietor expected, too. He looked
over the edge of his spectacles and invited crustily, "Just call
me if you see anything as interests you." He went on picking
at and polishing a trayful of the assorted rubbish that col-
lects in a shop of that kind. A scuffling on a broad overhead
shelf bothered him. He looked angrily through his eyebrows.
"Blarsted nuisances! They don't usually get up there." But he
did no more about it than go on with his work.

Jimmy presently brought a small jar to the counter. "What
would you want for this majolica piece?"

The old man was irritable but honest. "Well now, sir, I
wouldn't delude you on that there. 'S a matterafact I don't
believe it is genuine. You see—" The scuffling and scrabbling
overhead distracted him. "If I 'ad a 'undred bloomin' traps
I couldn't keep the bloody pests down. I thought I 'ad 'em
rid; but never 'eard 'em so bold as now." He was turning the
jar over in his hands, when forcefully shoved objects clinked
overhead and a grizzly object fell with a dry plop onto the
counter. Jimmy started back from it, grimacing sickly. The
thing was a human hand! Old and dessicate, the fingers gruesomely half-hooked, as though in some last spasm. A thin
tracery of spider-webs spanned the contorted fingertips. A
particular horror was a ring that rattled on the withered first
joint of the index finger, held in place by the thicker bent
joint. It might have been a signet or something set with two
little red stones, almost like snake eyes.

As Jimmy recoiled, the proprietor poked at it gingerly himself.

"Cawn't say as I like it myself, sir. A beastly sort of a piece, what?"

"What the hell is. it?" Jimmy asked. "I mean, where—" The shop was mustily stuffy. Jimmy took off his overcoat and dropped it on the counter. "Where did you ever get a thing like that?"

"It's supposed to be the 'and of Saint Ury, sir; though I 'ave no idea 'oo 'e ever was. That 'ole through the middle is said to be stigmata—what made 'im a saint, you know. Though if you awsk me," the man evinced all the disillusionment of an antiquarian—"I'd say somebody bloody well drove a nail through it."

Jimmy shuddered away. He left the jar there and went to examine things at the far end of the shop. But that horrid relic persisted in his vision. Almost as though some involuntary war activity of his own—shrapnel or something—had caused such a maiming that he had never known about but for which he might be indirectly to blame. He could imagine the broken thing, hating the world, and wanting to get back at him. He could find no pleasure in browsing.

"I think I'll be going," he said. "Some, other time perhaps—"

The proprietor was stuffing his rubbish amongst the other clutter of his shelves. "It's orl right, sir. Glad to 'ave you look around, sir."

Jimmy took up his coat and went. He was barely round the corner when he heard footsteps pattering after him; and there was the proprietor, panting and furious.

"You give me back that there 'and, young man," he spluttered. "Or I'll 'ave to call the police."

Jimmy recoiled. "What d'you mean, the hand? D'you think I'd touch the filthy thing?"

"You certainly did, young feller. I've seen the likes o' you before. There it was a-lyin' one minute, and the next thing you was gone and it, too. You with them big pockets." He dived at Jimmy and thrust his hands into the overcoat pockets—and there, out of one of them, he fished the horrid object.

Jimmy's stomach heaved. His mouth opened in protest; but he had to shut it again quickly to swallow his nausea.

"There we are!" The proprietor triumphed. "You bloody Yanks 'll swipe hanythink for a souvenir. Now just you pay me a pound, young man, and I'll say nothink about this."

"It's a racket!" Jimmy knew then. A damned panel-joint game. Slip something into the chump's pocket and then yelp about shoplifting.

"One pound." The proprietor held out an open hand. "Or I ups and whistles for them."

So what could Jimmy do but pay? He was here on business; he couldn't waste time in a court over a shameful charge of shoplifting. He went to his hotel more disgruntled than ever about this whole silly business. He spent a night dreaming about dried hands that crawled like hairy spiders all over his bed.

Over a fantastic breakfast of bloaters on toast and porridge he was discreetly paged—not piercingly shouted for by any brass-buttoned midget. A desk clerk bent over his table.

"A lady to see you, sir!"

"A lady? I—I don't think I know any ladies in London."

"In response to an advertisement of yours, sir."

Jimmy went rather uncertainly to the lobby. In his mind had been an idea that it was professorial men who did this sort of thing. He was quite glad that he had been wrong. A delightful picture awaited him; a girl, neatly dressed in something that showed a figure, with alert eyes in a fresh round face and a cute turned-up nose and full lips.

"I came in a hurry to be the first," she smiled at him ingenuously. "Because, frankly, I need the job, and the competition for this sort of thing is ferocious."

"Oh?" said Jimmy. "Are you—I mean, d'you know how to go about all this unpleasant business of digging up dead relatives?"

"Certainly, Mr. Doak. I have a certificate from the College of Heraldry." She fished papers out of a bag. "We are trained in all the various avenues of research. You wish, I presume, to trace your ancestry. Somewhere back from British stock, is it?"

Jimmy felt silly again. "It's just my dad. This name, you know. Like in a comic book. Well, Dad doesn't believe any human being was ever deliberately named Doak. He thinks there must be some mix-up somewhere along the line. He's heard so many wisecracks about it, it's got to be a complex."

"Surely. We understand about that. Thousands of corruptions have crept into names during the illiterate Middle Ages and they got to be written by somebody who couldn't spell the nearest way to how somebody pronounced them; and then the pronunciation grew to follow the spelling. We have old books and records about all those things."

"You do seem to know all about it. Then you'll take on the chore?"

The girl smiled confidently. "That's what I came for." And then diffidently, "Er, we usually work on a day and expense basis."

Jimmy was feeling more at ease since he knew there were other people who wished they could be called something else. "Oh, of course. You need a retaining fee or something."

The girl had two distinct dimples. "I could use it. And I shall go straight to the museum and have some information for you by tomorrow morning. You might, in the meantime, call up the paper and cancel your advertisement. Right? Cheerio."

Jimmy got a *Times* to look up the telephone number—and there the horrid story stared him in the face.

"American Accused of Shoplifting"

The rewrite man was able to see what seemed to Jimmy to be a far-fetched British humor in his shameful experience; and it was worse even than he knew. The story went on: "So badly did this queer fellow want the relic that he apparently returned that night and broke into the shop to get it. A mystery note, however, comes in, for the police report that only a single small pane of glass was broken; and the extraordinary part of it all was that the glass was pushed out from the *inside!* Almost as though the thing had loved him at first sight, and had jumped out to him of its own volition. Saintly hands, of course, have been known to accomplish miracles more astounding than that."

What a foul thought! That a thing like that should want to be friends! Jimmy had a creep all over to think of putting his hand into his pocket and finding the horny thing clasping his fingers. His next immediate reaction, naturally, was that he was a fugitive from lynx-eyed Scotland Yard. But the paper had given no description of him. He breathed easier, reflecting that the things after all, had no great value. It had remained, as its spider-webs attested, on that top shelf for who knew how many years before it jumped down to— Jimmy, too, jumped from his chair with a hunted look. It had not been rats! If it had not jumped down of its own volition, how had the foul thing crawled into his pocket? Could it be really true that there were haunts in this old country of ancient traditions?

With a mad impulse Jimmy raced to his room to hunt through his coat pockets again. No. Thank God! Jimmy, grinned sheepishly to himself. What a foolishness! But the beastly thing had made such a horrid impression on him. Why wouldn't it, getting into his pocket that way? Then Jimmy's eyes widened and he made a dash for his suitcase.

Perhaps it— That damned reporter's loathsome suggestion
that it had fallen in love with him—! He stood off to survey
each tumbled article on the bed. His breath blew from him in
a vast relief. He lit a comforting pipe and sat down to consider a reasonable theory for himself. The most reasonable one
was that the proprietor, obviously a vile-tempered old crank,
had flown into an insane rage and hurled the miserable thing
through his own window pane. And then, repenting, he had
gone out to retrieve the implement of his cunning racket, to
find that some stray cat or something had run off with it,
and he had been ashamed, then, to admit his silly rage.

"Bloody fool!" Jimmy expressed his quickly learned Angli-
cism. "And me too. This business of digging into dead men's
pasts gets a guy morbid. But, phe-ew, what an experience!"

Morning brought the girl, full of news and triumphant. "You
never even asked my name," she blamed him and herself in
the one breath. "And I was so staggered with the amount of
money you advanced that I just ran. I'm Eula Bogue." She
dimpled. "It used to be Boggs—that's how I got into this
research work. And I have lots of news. Let's sit down and
look at it."

In businesslike manner she spread sheaves of notes over
the little desk. "For just now let's never mind all the false
starts. Let's look first at what seems to be a definite lead.
It goes fascinatingly back. There seems to have been an old
Anglo-Saxon name, Dork, or Dawk, or Dock, spelled half a
dozen ways. Mostly north of England."

Jimmy whistled. "Whe-ee! As far back as that? Dad would
sure be tickled. And it could be, I suppose, that it was twisted to Doak?"

"Oh, very possibly indeed. With the illiterate Puritan
emigration from here, you know. And there's something even
more exciting. Up in Cumberlandshire there's a little place
called Dockbridge, apparently the family home town, and

there's one of those fearfully old manor houses that's been built over, and rebuilt and remodeled and its full of rats and rattly windows and a mouldy library and a housekeeper and—it's vacant!" She finished all of that in one breath.

Jimmy was thrilling in response to her enthusiasm. "You mean, we could go there and dig in the library?"

"If," she said uncertainly, "you could—I mean, all you Americans are rich, aren't you—if you could afford to rent the place for a week or so."

"Gee!" said Jimmy. "A post-grad in ancient history! I'll cable Dad we've got a hot lead. So let's go."

Dockbridge manor house was not quite as Eula had described it. The more modern part was not full of rats and even had a bathroom. It was built on a knoll and apparently at one time there had been a moat, now a sunken garden of unkempt cannas and iris and weeds. There were crumbly walls and moss-grown mounds of masonry, some of which had been rock-gardened and then left. Clearly, with the current austerity, it was too expensive to keep up and now stood hopefully for rent.

The housekeeper, a gaunt lady dressed in ghostly gray, had lived so long with the older conventions that she turned a sternly disapproving eye on so modern an intrusion as a young man and a girl.

"I'm Mrs. Medford," she introduced herself. "And I'm as good a chaperone as any. So, if the young gentleman will carry the bags, I'll show you to your rooms."

She showed them to rooms discreetly separated at the two ends of a musty right-angled corridor. She had quite clearly moved her own things into a room right at the corner.

"So that, if you need 'elp, Miss, I'll 'ear your call."

"Why, the idea!" Eula flamed scarlet around to the back of her neck.

"Oh, I down't mean from 'im, Miss. Though I wouldn't put it past 'im. We saw all about them good-lookin' Yanks during their invasion. It's just that old Sir 'arry's ghost mi-auws around moonless nights; 'im that was Prince Charlie's Marster of 'Orse when the old manor stood, what's founda-tions this is on."

Eula laughed gaily. "All my frowzy browsing"—as though she'd spent twenty years at it—"and I've never had a ghost yet."

The housekeeper's disapproval sank several notches lower. "It's you moderns as ain't no reverence. But I sees 'em!"

Jimmy stared at her. He was developing a habit of staring at these sudden surprises. Mrs. Medford seemed to be accus-tomed to surprising people. She added to this one, "You, sir, will not be 'earing the miaulin's and prowlin's on your side. You're over the old chapel. So your windows 'as the bars."

Jimmy looked his question at Eula, as though she ought to know all the conventions of old manors. The housekeeper offered the logical answer.

"Because them as don't say prayers regular goes balmy and jumps. I'll serve dinner before dark, sir and ma'am. We don't dress nowadays." She went sternly about her affairs.

"Is it an act?" Jimmy all unconsciously whispered it.

Eula giggled. "I think the poor soul has gone a little balmy herself, living alone in this mouldy old place. The library ought to yield pure gold. We'll dig tomorrow."

Even tomorrow's sun couldn't make a cheerful breakfast, be-cause the morning paper had another item by the same re-write man who dealt in humor.

NORTH LONDON DRUNKS
HAVE A NEW HEEBIE-JEEBIE
It's not pink elephants any more for a party of late home-stragglers from the Coach and Horn pub on the Lincoln Road. It's a five-legged spi-der the size of a saucer that runs along the dark gutters with the speed of a greyhound.

Well, of course, there was nothing so much to that. But Jimmy stared at the paper with a reluctant horror. For the item went on:

> Curious verification comes from two boys— models of rectitude, their parents insist—who say they saw it by dawn's gray light, scuttling along a country lane ten miles farther North in Middlesex. Only, to their juvenile imaginations, not so far removed from fairy lore—

This was the part that held Jimmy's eyes in their wide stare.

> —it looked more like a hand running on its fingertips.

"What's the matter?" Eula was alarmed at Jimmy's pallor.

He pushed the paper to her, waited while she read the item, and to her answering stare said, "Did you see the one about the Yank shoplifting a dead hand, and then the broken window?" And, as she nodded, he silently pointed his finger to his own chest.

"You? Good heavens! But you didn't, of course."

"No, I wouldn't touch the filthy thing. But—you know more about these antique incubi. What does it all mean? Why is it following me north?"

Eula was, for the first time, serious. "Why do you say 'incubi'? As though this one were hung onto you. Of course, we do have a lot of spooky legends in an old country like this—some of them accepted as authentic by professors of psychic lore—such as the Glastonbury crypt and the Monster of Glamis Castle. But a dried hand—" She closed her eyes in tight thought. "Wait a minute. Let me think. What is it about, somewhere, a 'hand of glory'?—But no. That's just black magic."

"Just black magic." Jimmy repeated it. "That's all. So what is this? A pure white symbol of grace?"

Eula made herself laugh again. "Oh, it's all rubbish! Some drunks have a D.T. and some boys read about it and let their imaginations run. This is our usual summer hysteria—to fill up space in the paper when there's no crime. You'll see."

And within a couple of days they did see. A *Times* reader-correspondent, and amateur entomologist, wrote a solemn article decrying hysteria and offered his theory that a tarantula (a large Central-American spider, he injected his educational note) might very easily have been imported with a bunch of bananas and that, like all the arachnidae, was capable of running with a considerable speed that, to people under the influence of liquor—etc., etc.

"There! You see?" said Eula. "Now perhaps you can help me with some of this mouldy reading."

The reading proved to be exciting. The library, although a muddle of volumes saved up from, it seemed, the beginning of printing, but never indexed, contained ancient tomes of incunabula, and even manuscripts.

"Priceless!" Eula mooned over the mess. "I mean, even in money. And to think that the owner never comes here, nor, I suppose, has ever opened a book."

The housekeeper stood at the door. She had an uncanny memory for having, once upon a time, dusted some volume and, if any of the old family names had appeared, remembering them.

"'E don't come," she stated like a Hecuba, "because this 'ouse gives 'im the 'orrors."

"I think," said Jimmy, "some of these books all about battle and murder and sudden death would give me the horrors if I should read them all."

"That's out of the prayer book," Mrs. Medford accused him. "Which, if you doesn't say it reverent, the Lord says the blasphemers shall perish. And if you'd a but told me you was a-'unting for old family names, I'd a told the young lady, pore thing, to look in that there book with the brown binding ate by roaches."

"Why poor thing?" Eula grimaced.

"Ah!" said Mrs. Medford.

Only that, "Aa-ah!" and she drifted grayly out.

But the book proved to be some of the 'gold mine' Eula had expected.

"Look! Oh, looky! Here's 'Ye Hystorie of ye Familye of ye Noble Sieur Armand D'Auk wyth his Battailles and his Honneurs.'"

"They sure thought up long, titles in those days," Jimmy obtusely said.

"Yes, but don't you see, Silly? There's your name! D'Auk!— Dork, Dock, Doak, and I suppose dozens of other spellings. Norman origin, not Anglo-Saxon. I expect we'll be finding your dad to be one of our oldest families."

"Golly!" said Jimmy. "Damn if I don't think it may be. Can you read that olde Englyshe stuff?"

"Of course. What the roaches haven't eaten. And—it seems there ought to be three more volumes of it. Perhaps Mrs. Medford knows where to find—we must get a ton of paper and you take the notes while I puzzle it all out."

The excitement of this find was such that they didn't read the morning paper until the afternoon. And then both looked at each other, questioning what each thought. For a sober scientist had written his screed to the *Times,* attacking with all the virulence of scientists the "insufficiently informed" opinion of a layman who dared to shoot off his mouth. A tarantula, he maintained, while capable of moving with considerable speed when attacking its food, was a creature as sedentary as a wolf-spider or a common household daddy-long-legs; that all of them spent their life span within a circumscribed radius of perhaps no more than fifty feet; that the distance of ten miles was ridiculous to the point of impossibility; and that there this thing that the boys had seen in upper Middlesex, whatever else it might be, was certainly not a tarantula; and furthermore, a tarantula was not a nocturnal hunter nor could it withstand the night temperatures of the English countryside; and, if it could, it would be in a lethargic and dormant condition.

His thorough disposal of that matter left Jimmy's dark question:—

"Then what was it? If not my—" his inadvertent slip brought a shiver. "If not that damned hand?"

Eula reassured him. "Oh, what does it matter what it was? A something. A scurrying rat, a rabbit, an anything. We've got much more exciting things here to speculate about. Look. This D'Auks whole name was The Sieur Armand D'Auk D'Auberge and—" She suddenly clapped her hands. "Why, there it is! D'Auk D'Auberge— From which, following Grimm's law of colloquial sublimation, we get Dockbridge. This very village and the manor. Now for some of his 'battailles' and his 'honneurs', and there ought to be his 'offsprynges' somewhere."

The research, while fascinating, was jarred to a standstill more than once by the morning paper that both of them avidly scanned for any follow-up on the tarantula that couldn't be a tarantula. The rewrite man was not laughing any more. He was calling it now, "The Spider Horror." There was the item about a lady, a stern and very well-balanced social worker, who was going home late from her church meeting and had been attacked by the Horror!

"I saw it in the moonlight," she related to her interviewer. "Scurrying along like a—well, like something I, for one had never seen before. So I struck at it with my umbrella and—now I cannot truthfully say that it snarled at me; but I could see its wicked little red eyes; and then it leaped at me!

At least three or four feet, the distance must have been from my umbrella end. And it caught me by the ankle and threw me down; and then I suppose—no, I have never fainted. I should say not. But then I don't know what happened. When I came to—I mean, when I could see again, it was gone."

"Did you notice," Jimmy pointed out, *"where* that happened? In Leicestershire."

"Well, so what?"

"Still coming *north!* Following!"

Eula shrank away, envisioning a dead, mummified hand's relentless coming. "But, Jimmy, it *can't* be! She saw its red eyes, she said."

"The ring!"

Eula's hand covered her lips. "D'you really think the thing is after you for some weird reason? Like a voodoo or something?"

"How should I know? I don't know anything about voodoo."

"But, coming from America, isn't that sort of in your back yard? Your Negroes, you know; and Haiti. Don't they kill chickens with their teeth and project occult 'sendings?' Little dolls and snakes and things to go and carry curses and—?"

"Helluva idea you've got of America," Jimmy growled.

"Well, I've read it somewhere. And you're the one who insists it's following you. Jimmy, I'm afraid."

"You're afraid?"

"Yes, because—I mean, if it's as real as that—not just summer hysteria—and if it can jump at a strong-minded lady who hits it with an umbrella and can catch her by the leg and throw her down, it could—" She shivered close to him.

It was Jimmy's role to comfort her. "Well, at least it didn't bite her when her strong mind went out like a weak light. After all, what can it do, wandering about the country like a homeless ghost—" He wished immediately he had not said that.

"What I mean, what gave me the willies was just looking at the beastly thing. Come on, let's lunch."

Mrs. Medford supplied a skimpy lunch. "Seein' as 'ow the hiceman didn't come, the cold chicken went bad, so I gave it to Lady Jane."

Lady Jane was her woolly poodle that yapped at flies and assiduously hunted cockroaches in baseboard corners. The skimpiness of the lunch didn't matter because Mrs. Medford banished all appetite, remarking out of nothing;

"It's a-comin' 'ome!"

Both Jimmy and Eula sat suddenly stiff in their chairs. Mrs. Medford answered their stares with, "I've read it in the paper, same's you 'ave." To which she added the shock. "And me bein' a seventh daughter, I seen it!"

"Good Lord!" Jimmy had until now been willing to accept Eula's comforting theory that he had received a gruesomely strong impression and was attaching it to similarly gruesome accounts in the newspaper. "What d'you mean, it's coming home and you've 'seen' it?"

"I don't know, sir, just what it means. All I can say is, I was a-setting with me old friend, Mrs. Shaughnessy, she being psychic (physic, she pronounced it) and all a suddent I seen it in the dark before my mind's-eye. A yuman 'and it was and it was nailed to a board! And Mrs. Shaughnessy she says, 'If you seen it, that means it must belong in your 'ouse, else why wouldn't I 'ave seen it too?'"

Jimmy, sanely unaccustomed to the jargons and hallucinations of psychics, flouted the phantasmagoria. "You've been reading the horror story in the paper and so you sat wishing for spooks and you dreamed the picture up in your imagination." And he repeated his self-encouragement. "After all, what could a thing like that do?"

"Ah!" said Mrs. Medford. "Aa-ah!"

The paper showed what it could do.

"A Mister Bill Dibbs," it reported, "of Kirk-by-Sheperd in Westmoreland, a gentleman who has had his difficulties with Lord Gravely's gamekeeper, was strolling home with two dogs and a gun—harmlessly enjoying the moonlit night, he insists—when his dogs flushed the 'Spider Horror' out of a ditch. The thing raced, he reports, along the edge of the road with incredible speed. He just happened, he says, to have had a cartridge in his gun and he would have shot the whatever it was, but for the dogs that were too close after it. They chased it into a copse and there he heard all the frenzied barking and scuffling of what might have been a rabbit hunt. Until suddenly one of the dogs let out a piercing yelp and came cringing back to him in apparent terror, as though it might have found a bear, and the other dog was ominously silent. His gun ready for emergency, he entered the shadows of the copse to investigate, and there, to his consternation, found his dog dead. 'Strangled! Choked,' Mr. Dibbs said, 'as though by some strong man.' The gamekeeper reports having found nothing more menacing than rabbits in all the surrounding woods. The local police opinion is that it is funny that all these untoward happenings always occur at night and always to unreliable people."

Jimmy's only question to all this was, "Where's Westmoreland?"

"The shire just south of Cumberland where we are." Eula clung to his arm. "Jimmy, it can't be true, is it?"

"Comin' 'ome!" Jimmy quoted. "What do you in England do about getting a gun? And who is there who can tell us

about the aims and motivations of this sort of thing? The
whole works, I mean. All these stories add up to it can't be
anything other than that brutal hand thing I saw in the store.
The 'Hand of Saint Ury', he said; and not holy stigmata,
but a nail hole. And our gray ghost woman threw her fit and
saw it nailed to a board. So, very well, who can tell us what
turned it loose. How? Why it's crawling home at night? Why
pick on this place—on me—all the way up from London. If
it gets here, what's it good for—or bad for? Who can tell us
all about the rules and regulations of the haunt union?"

Eula frowned out of the window. "There's a whole lot of
psychic investigators. I think the best would be possibly Dr.
Eugene Harries. He's one of the W. T. Stead Foundation and
a member of the Psychic Research Society. They go about
shooting holes into the ghost stories that crop up every now
and then and they publish a bulletin about their findings.
What I don't like is that every now and then, too, they find
some horrid thing that they can't laugh off."

"Let's invite him in and throw the whole thing into his
lap," said Jimmy promptly. "So we can put in a little time
on our own work on ye olde Brityshe Familyes. The deeper
we dig into the tomes, the better Dad will be pleased. Heck,
make us Doaks respectable old-timers, and I'll hold him up
to pay for our honeymoon."

"Wha-a-at?" Eula sprang away from him and put the great
old carved desk between them, her eyes wider than at any
time over Mrs. Medford's revelations.

"Well, we Doakses have to be respectable; and it would
be the only way to quell Mrs. Medford's disapproving eye."

"Good—heavens!" The shock was burning Eula all the
way up to her hair, rising like a red flame. "You Americans
are certainly sudden. Is that the way you always propose?"

"Sometimes they do it in an automobile or some such romantic spot; but I figure you Englishers, with all your haunts
and such, would have to be different."

Eula was recovering some of her composure. "Here we almost never marry our boss. We have too much work to do."

"Work to do *together*," Jimmy said. "Come on and dig. We've been neglecting the gold mine."

It turned out to be, as Jimmy awesomely said, a dynamite mine! Though, when they first found it, they were thrilled.

"Ooh, look! The Sieur D'Auk was 'Lord of ye High Justice and ye Middle and ye Low' and a 'ryghte valliante Carryer of ye Crosse'."

"Does that mean a preacher? Another Saint?"

"No, silly. A crusader. He went to slaughter paynims."

"That makes us Doakses a whole lot respectable."

"And here's your—this is jolly exciting—here's Saint Ury!"

"I don't see him."

"You're not looking at the book. He isn't in my hair. Here—Benoit De La Ceinture. Benoit of the Belt. He wasn't a saint at all. He was seneschal of ye keepe—that means post commander while ye doughtie crusader was away. And then, as understanding of Norman French died out, our old colloquial adaptation law turned Ceinture into Saint Ury."

Further investigation made him very far from a saint, and the two investigators sat looking at each other with gray faces.

The doughty crusader had come back, as crusaders did in those pre-telegraphic days, without notice and he found, as other warriors have, that his ladye faire whom he left to languish through his long absence had been more friendly than was thought proper, even in those days, with the captain of the home guard. Having the rights of the High Justice and the Middle and the Low, he flew into a right noble rage and struck off the seneschal's offending right hand and spiked it to the great oaken door of the keep for all to see how the penalties of philandering were paid, naming at the same time the child—the second of his house—"a bastarde by fulle acknowledgemente and herebye sundered from alle inheritance."

Jimmy put his own right hand over Eula's cold one. "So that's the Hand of Saint Ury. And it's coming home!" He essayed a lame joke. "Perhaps that leaves us Doaks not so awfully respectable."

"Don't joke about it," Eula shuddered. "Your line could have come from the earlier child and you'd be a descendant of D'Auk."

Jimmy did not perceive the dire import of this until Doctor Eugene Harries arrived. The doctor elaborated his theories of the case with professional obscurity.

"Interesting. Most interesting! From what you tell me, we must indubitably accept this scuttling creature of the dark as the hand of which you have traced the history. Quite clearly one of our more authentic cases."

"So all right," said Jimmy. "So it's a dead hand that was once nailed to the front door here, and it existed around somewhere and finally gathered cobwebs in an antique store. What I want to know is, what suddenly wakes it up? How? Why is it scuttling the night roads back to here? Who's it after?"

"Ah!" said the doctor, much as Mrs. Medford might. "These things are not very easy to explain. There is an old occult theory, now being almost reaccepted, that thoughts are *physical* forces; that a thought of hate can be a powerful enough force to persist after the death of its originator." He held up his hand. "A moment, please. I say the theory of thought force is being reaccepted in these modern days because you have the experiments of your own Dr. Rhine in America, who seems to have established that a concentrated thought can control so material a function as the roll of dice. In your big University of Ohio, isn't it?"

"Yes," Jimmy was closely following. "But that's a *live* thought."

"Ah!" the doctor said again. "But let us explore that liveness. A thought, an admittedly tangible force, has been created and projected into the—shall we say—surrounding ether? Where, then, is it, and for how long may it persist? To explain which very evanescent query let us consider the modern analogy of radio. A tangible impulse is projected. Where is it? It is everywhere. It can affect a properly tuned receiver at a great distance. It has been shown to circulate the earth with a certain perceptible time lapse and a diminished power that, however, can still affect a sufficiently delicately attuned receiver. Very well then; if once, we may logically assume the possibility of twice, or more, ad infinitum. Given, then, a sufficiently sensitive receiver, where, we may ask, is the point of extinction? The what you call *dead* hand is in this case the receiver, exactly attuned to the wavelength of the powerfully projected thought of hate because it was a part of the original projector."

"Sounds hideously reasonable. But that's drawing it pretty thin, isn't it?"

"Admittedly so. But, the possibility accepted, the point is not one of tenuity but of capability to affect the receiver. In the case of radio, to make it talk; which means, first, to affect *physically* a receiving element and *make it move!* To revitalize it! To make it repeat the impulse that was originally projected!"

Jimmy and Eula were both hanging on the doctor's words with a growing unease. "You mean, this hate force could affect a damned thing like that hand and make it move? Well, then, why didn't it hit it long ago? I mean, any time after it whatever way got loose off the board where it couldn't run. What suddenly tuned it in now?"

The doctor beamed benignly upon his class of two. "We have considered, so far, the analogy of diminishing, though persisting, wave lengths or impulses. Let us now consider another ancient theory of magic that has been accepted by modern science—that of transmutation. We have derided the middle-age mystics for their belief in the transmutation of baser metals into gold. But our quite latest experiments have shown that the very atomic structure of so dead a substance as a metallic ore, when bombarded by certain electronic impulses, can be transmuted to another arrangement of its nuclei; that what we have called dead matter can be vitalized to become something so devastating as a bomb."

"That one," said Jimmy, "seems to be drifting far afield."

"By no means. The principle established, who, in these days, will be bold enough to set a limit upon material or transmuting agent? The analogy is that within *you*, the descendant of this Sieur D'Auk persist the genes that create a, let us no longer say, *psychic* force—but a tangible electronic—we used to call it magnetic—emanation that bombards the dormant atomic structure of the too glibly called *dead* hand. Your presence, then, in the shop was what vitalized its implanted hate force and released it, to exhibit its present destructive manifestation."

"Hate! Hate! Hate!" It sobbed from Eula. "And I suppose you mean that this hateful thing is now scuttling along the gutters, coming home; and it somehow wickedly knows that the descendant of the man who cut it off is here and it will exact some horrible vengeance."

Dr. Harries looked at Jimmy and very soberly nodded. Jimmy asked his question for the third time, and not with any doubting scorn.

"Just what can it do?"

"We have so far," the doctor weighed the possibilities with merciless impartiality, "discussed only the material sources of its potential; and we know from the reports that it can strangle a hunting hound. We must accept the probability, then, that it could also strangle a man. If we are willing to admit the psychic sources of power—as they are today being admitted in studies of the abnormal strength displayed by lunatics—we must face the possibility that it could be deadly dangerous, not only to the object of its vengeance, but to any interference that might stand in the way of its purpose."

To Eula's close shudder against him Jimmy grunted. "Hmmm!" But his tight-mouthed expression showed that he was no longer taking this thing as lightly as he once had.

"I suppose," he asked, not very hopefully, "it's no use trying to run away? If the cursed thing can run on its fingertips under its own power it could follow anywhere. What's chances of it running out of gas?"

"We have no means of knowing," the doctor said judicially. "Records of our Society show that destructive forces from the mysterious 'other side' have been known to persist for many hundreds of years."

"That would eventually wear me out," Jimmy said. "We may as well stay here and fight it. . . . How?"

"There remains," the doctor said hopefully, "yet another consideration. You have observed that it made no attempt to harm you that first day of your meeting. It has retaliated only against those who have molested it—the umbrella woman, the poacher's dog. It is just possible, then—if I may offer a slightly embarrassing surmise—that its smuggling of itself into your pocket and the subsequent following may have been induced by motives of affection."

"Good Lord!" Jimmy's eyes boggled. "What d'you mean, affection from a foul thing like that?"

"Well, it might just be, you know, that—er—your branch of the family descended from that illegitimate offspring and that the hand, or rather its original owner, was your ancestor."

"Godamighty!" Jimmy shuddered away from the thought. "And it wants to snuggle up? Crawl out of the dark and hold hands? Get into bed on cold nights and—"

Eula shrieked. Jimmy looked quickly at her, for the moment forgetful of the impending horror. Eula shrank away from so fearful a connection.

"In any event," the doctor said, "the possibilities of this whole manifestation are so intriguing—quite one of our most authentic cases, I'm sure that, if you would invite me, I would, despite the many dangers, have to consider it my scientific duty to stay and offer such assistance as I may."

Eula caught at him, not to let him go. "Oh, please! We're so helpless and—frightened. We wouldn't know what ever to do."

It was not occurring to her that she had no inescapable part in this hideous thing, that she could pack and go.

"Would you advise," Jimmy asked, "that we should be armed?"

"By all means, and immediately. We must accept the surmise that the thing is coming here, and a force like that, if not benevolent, could be devastating, since it is a 'walker of the night'. Er, this tall lady in gray whom I have seen hovering in the background, could she be relied upon in a situation of danger involving, we must be prepared to accept, certain aspects of supra-normal horror?"

"She's one of the three Norns," Eula said. "She lives with all the horrors of this house. If she approves of you she will let you stay."

Mrs. Medford did approve of Dr. Harries as being one who could understand her "physic" manifestations. And Dr. Harries approved of her idea of sitting in séance with her friend Mrs. Shaughnessy.

"There is always a possibility," he said, "that out of these visualizations impressed upon the subconscious by wandering thought forces—spirits, as the faithful call them—one may obtain useful information, as one does also occasionally from people under hypnosis."

The séance turned out to be a distressful affair of moanings and shriekings and dire threats. Mrs. Shaughnessy first moaned and shook and went into her trance, out of which she announced that a "dark spirit" filled the room, and wanted to "get through," but not through her; it wanted to "control" someone closer to the house. Whereupon Mrs. Medford went through the moans and shudders and sat finally in a rigid coma. Till a ventral voice croaked from her.

"I'm 'ere," it said. "Not 'ere, but in this 'ouse before it was 'ere. I'm a-lookin' out a winder onto the cabbage garden; which they ain't cabbages but mossy cobblestones. And there's people an' soldiers in harmor an' lords in velvet an'—" Suddenly she shrieked. "—I see 'im! There 'e comes! Shoved along by soldiers in harmor and all a-draggin' of iron chains. I see 'im! A 'orrid great 'airy man!" She shook and groaned the anguishes of the hairy man.

"It was a horrid great hairy hand," Jimmy fitted into the picture.

Mrs. Medford shouted out of her temporary quiescence. "'E lifts them 'ands in their chains an' rattles 'is fists. A-cursin 'e is. Eatin' an drinkin,' 'e says, 'wakin' an' sleepin', livin' an' dyin', I'll be awaitin' you, Lord of the Auberge.' An' the velvet lord laughs and says 'e, 'Let the judgment of the 'igh Justice be carried out'." And then suddenly she clutched at her wrist and writhed in fearful resistance and shrieked agony again; and then she slumped down in a quivering heap of moaning and muttering semi-consciousness.

Jimmy and Eula came out of the dark room shivering, Eula unconsciously chafing her own wrist. Dr. Harries was not so much impressed.

"So many of these manifestations," he evaluated the experiment, "although the faithful insist that they are 'spirit-controlled', can be ascribed to demonstrations of the subconscious. Impressions formed in not too well balanced and sensitive minds out of reading or hearsay are portrayed with fearful reality. This phenomenon is, in fact, the explanation of visions of saints or Madonnas. Although," he was coldly judicious, "we cannot entirely dismiss the possibility that the sensitive medium, the receiving instrument, having been impressed by some wavelength from an outside source. We have witnessed, then, either a visualization of subconscious impressions or—" his acceptance of the possibility was frightening "—a reaching out of the still active hate force. We can do nothing about it until the hand is here."

It was Lady Jane who served notice that it had somewhere furtively arrived. Out of the dusk came the piercing, ki-yies of a poodle frightened to the near death, and the creature staggered, rather than ran, under a chair, there to continue its shuddering yelpings.

"So all right then," Jimmy said through tight teeth. "What can be done in the way of protection?"

He did not say, in the way of offensive fight.

"Ah!" said Dr. Harries, this time signifying meditation. "If we but knew how to immunize you—that is to say, throw some sort of an impervious blanket about you, as is accomplished by lead in our analogy of radioactive force, we might shut off your emanations from continuing to vitalize the thing."

"Well," Jimmy's, very impotence flared to anger, "I'm not doing it on purpose!"

"Of course not. Though that, too, may be an unconscious possibility; since we know that such activation can be consciously projected by such people as the so-called wizards of mediaeval history and by African witch doctors in our present. Protection is supposedly supplied by various 'magic circles' and 'holy pentagrams' and so on, although I do not attach much faith in these myself. More credible is another one of the scouted mediaeval beliefs in the potency of cold iron against what they called witchcraft—which accounts for the spiking of the hand to the door with a nail, the spiking of suicides, supposedly dissatisfied and homeless spirits, through their middles, iron coffins, and so on. Which belief has persisted into our own times in the form of iron amulets, iron crosses, whether as medals or over gravestones. Unfortunately we cannot enclose you in an iron coffin; and in order to spike down the hand again we must first catch it.

"Like catching a cobra. How about," said Jimmy grimly, "the cold iron of a gun?"

"The possibility is acceptable. Since, if such a thing could be disintegrated—say, by a shotgun at close range—while the hate force would not necessarily be dissipated, its physical medium of offense would be shattered."

Jimmy drew a long breath of almost relief. But the doctor mercilessly continued. "We might then be rid of the whole business—unless the force might still persist in some telekinetic form that could move other objects so as to, for example, push a brick off a high wall."

To Jimmy's hunted bafflement he offered the cold cheer, "The question of exactly why a brick, or even paint, falls upon the 'unlucky' person has never been sufficiently explored."

"Well, I'm going right into town," Jimmy said, "and buy a sawed-off shotgun."

"Or perhaps," Doctor Harries suggested with that chilly acceptance of the worst possible, "you might get two. And perhaps, although it is still daylight, I might accompany you as an escort."

They returned with an arsenal and, an addition, two gaunt boxer dogs.

"If they catch it scuttling about the house gutters," Jimmy told Eula, "and between them tear it apart; or eat it; I guess it'll be considerably disintegrated."

Eula's face contorted over so sickening a thought. "I suppose they would at least keep it on the run. But that poacher's dogs—"

That first night after the thing's arrival was a bedlam of scurryings and furious barkings that yielded nothing. Stealthy noises sounded in the unkempt garden. The dogs yelped their excitement after whatever it might be and galloped their great feet hither and yon like mad dray horses. At each disturbance Jimmy and the doctor stood alertly at windows that overlooked the dark grounds. They could discern the shadowy forms of the great dogs racing through moon patches, but not a thing else.

"Of course," the doctor suggested. "It could still be rats."

"Oh, rats!" Eula expressed her English idiom of disbelief.

"Perhaps we'll at least find tracks in the morning," Jimmy hoped, "and then we'll at least be sure."

Such tracks as they found besides those of the dogs were indecipherable smudges.

"Did the thing," Dr. Harries asked, "when you saw it in the shop, have long fingernails?" And he evaluated the situation so far. "We can at all events assume that the thing is nocturnal, as are nearly all of these darker forces. We may, therefore, feel safe during the day—or fairly so—if we do not venture into dark places. We know that it avoids overwhelming weight, as of two ferocious dogs; also that it is cunning enough to do so, and, as in the poacher's case, to segregate them and attack one at a time. And since it has remained furtive, has not shown itself, we must, I am sorry to say, resign ourselves to the ultimate fact that its purpose is definitely malignant and that it is intelligent enough to be deadly."

"If we could hunt it down by daylight then?" Jimmy expressed a hope. "We can't just go on, knowing that a hellish something in the shape of a great hairy hand is skulking somewhere about the grounds, waiting, for darkness to jump out at somebody and tear his throat out."

"If we could but find it. Its grizzly advantage is that it is small enough to hide in any of a thousand holes in the ancient tumbled masonry, while the hate force that activates it is powerful enough to be murderous."

Mrs. Medford knew where to find it. "It's livin' in the root-cellar!" she told them; and before they asked her, "I seen it!"

"With the 'physic' eye, I suppose," the doctor said. "But let's take our guns and go look."

The root-cellar was a dim vault of great stones behind a massive door, cool and mouldy. Holes where stones had fallen out dripped water. Bins along the walls contained potatoes and the gross turnips that country folk and cattle ate. The doctor with inadequate flashlight scrutiny surmised it to have been one of those, sunless guard-houses for prisoners in the old days of brutality and insanitation.

"Hell!" Jimmy swore. All this uncertainty and impending menace was wearing on his nerves. "There's a million hidie holes. If we could rig an extension light from the house perhaps—?"

"We would still not be able to explore all these holes. Who knows how deep they may burrow into the banks. We would need ferrets, as in a rabbit warren." And he could not refrain from adding his inevitable note of warning. "And we know it is vastly more dangerous than a rabbit."

A scuffling noise in a dim corner whirled both of them around. A choked squeak came from Jimmy's throat and spasmodically he blasted both barrels of his gun in that direction. The flash beam showed that he had very thoroughly disintegrated some onions and a rat.

"And we do know," the doctor mused as though studying a continuous theory, "that it immediately retaliates against aggression." His scientific approach, even in the face of danger, was excruciating. Acrid fumes of nitro powder drove them from the enclosed space.

"My God!" Jimmy coughed. "What a pessimist!"

"We cannot afford," the doctor rumbled, "to be optimistic about any force that operates in the darkness. It is not a mere Christian superstition that light and benevolence are compatible. All we can do is be desperately careful."

Over the late meal he suggested, "I would advise, Miss Bogue, that you sleep in the same room with our so formidable housekeeper."

Eula fluttered her wide spread fingers at the prospect. "I'd be more afraid than—"

"And I," the doctor said, "will move in with Mr. Doak. I would also suggest contiguous rooms—in this old chapel wing with the barred windows."

So it came that the four of them foregathered that night to peer down at pandemonium all round the house. A crashing of bushes, a mad galloping of feet and yelping dogs, at times both together, furiously chasing a something; and then again in separate confusion, the one in a hysteria under something too high in a bush to reach, and the other equally convinced that it had something cornered in a drain. And then the watchers witnessed a horror in the moonlight.

One of the great dogs lurched out of the shadows, coughing and choking, and staggered loose-legged across a strip of lawn. In the uncertain light it looked for a moment as though it held a limp something in its jaws and furiously shook it. But as its head writhed from side to side they could see that nothing was in its jaws; but that a something hung from its throat and was not at all limp!

Jimmy and the doctor snatched their guns and raced downstairs and out. But the dog had by that time staggered into the darkness of bush shadows. Calling brought no response. Not even from the other one!

"We had better not venture too far into the shadows," the doctor warned. "Nor leave the women alone."

At the door both stood for a moment shocked back on their heels.

"My God, we left it open!"

Within the house no worse was immediately apparent than that Mrs. Medford was shuddering back out of a swoon,

Eula chafing her hands. Water profusely splashed from the old-fashion wash-basin indicated the process of revivement.

"Gaw!" Mrs. Medford mumbled. "I seen it."

"Well, you've seen it before," Eula said crossly, "and you didn't go off like this and leave me all alone."

"Ah!" said Mrs. Medford. "But this time I seen it real. A 'orrible 'airy 'and it were."

"She could not," Doctor Harries said precisely, "have identified it in the uncertain light from these upper windows. However, since the door was momentarily unguarded, we must sit up, and together, for the rest of the night."

Jimmy was furious with everything in the world; particularly with himself for his uncontrolled nerves that had permitted the door to stand wide. "Yeh," he rasped. "Sit up and tell ghost stories." His hand nervously caressed his throat.

Eula sent him a reproachful look. "He was only warning us."

"Perhaps," said the doctor, "I have not impressed the warning sufficiently, even upon myself. Or we would not have left open that door. We shall know more in the morning."

All that they knew in the morning was that both dogs were dead; Both heavy-jawed faces contorted and tongues hanging out thickly black.

"Ye-es." The doctor hissed it slowly. "Cunning enough to have run them to exhaustion, confused them and taken one at a time. We must, while daylight lasts, make a very thorough search of every room in this house."

"And since dogs are no good," Jimmy said, "I'll go into town and hire a night watchman. Arm him, by God, with a battery of flashlights and a machine-gun."

Jimmy returned late. "Had a helluva job to find anybody who'd take the chore on. Not at old Dockbridge Manor, they popped their eyes. Why not? Well, there were 'aunts' there. Not relatives, 'black things'; and there were dead men's bones under the house. They had a legend; and so every damned yokel was scared. . . . But I got a great lout finally. He'd been a guard in the Whitehaven prison, he says, and he'd watch a graveyard if he was paid. D'you find anything in the house?"

Dr. Harries shook his head. "We found only uncertainty; more nerve-racking than discovery. There are rat holes by the dozens in the dark corners of closets and cupboards. Holes large enough through broken plaster for cats to pass. I wish to heaven, since dogs are useless, we might hire a leopard or something that could adequately see in the dark."

It was almost a relief of the uncertainty that night to be awakened by Eula's screams from the next room. Rushing in, the two found her hysterical in Mrs. Medford's arms. Mrs. Medford darkly gave the answer.

"This time she seen it! I was a-sleepin' peaceful as a babe when I up and 'eard 'er a-screechin' 'There it is!', and I says, 'where?', and whatever she seen was so 'orrible, she went off like this."

Eula, shuddering back to normalcy, clung to Jimmy, her arms about his neck. "Take me away!" she moaned. "Oh take me away, Jimmy, from this fearful place."

All the comfort that Jimmy could give was, "I could let *you* go away. But it would be no use my running too. We know it can relentlessly follow. I've got to stick it out here. Isn't that right, Doctor?"

"I'm afraid so. Flight would be only a postponement, and here we at least know the conditions. This thing must be met and—since we don't know how to immunize its power source—it must be destroyed. *If* its power is destructible. Try to tell us, if you can, just what you saw."

Eula pointed shakily to the window. "Out there. I couldn't sleep, of course; and from the bed I could see the silhouette of that tree's branches outside the window. And then suddenly it was there! Its eyes! Its wicked little red eyes. Sitting on a branch and watching!"

Puzzled, the doctor looked at Jimmy.

"The umbrella woman," Jimmy reminded him. "She said she saw eyes. Close, like a spider's, as everybody was calling it at that time. And it had a beastly ring, I think I told you, a black flat disk with two red stones."

"Hm-mm? I wonder? I just wonder now, could it be the dark mirror and the red eyes of Anubis?"

"What's the eyes of Anubis?"

"But no." The doctor shook that theory from himself. "That's an ancient Egyptian magic of terrible power. But that cannot apply here. This is black Norman hate that history has shown to be powerful enough. . . . You, my dear, you must try to get some rest. We can't have a nervous breakdown on our hands at this precarious juncture. Leave your door open. We shall sit up on watch by turns."

"I suppose," Jimmy grumbled, "we can't really blame that fool of a watchman for not spotting something as elusive as a rat climbing up a tree. It couldn't have jumped that distance, could it?"

"Twenty feet or so? I would hardly think so. At any rate there is no tree opposite this window. Have you any preference for first trick?"

"I'll take it," Jimmy said. "I couldn't sleep under drugs. I'll light me a pipe and stay up. I suppose we must definitely take it by now that the thing is not, as you gruesomely suggested, friendly. It's out for revenge."

"I'm afraid so. And I hardly like to tell you how much afraid. So—don't for a second let yourself nod. Wake me if you even hear anything."

Jimmy soon enough did. The doctor was one who had the faculty of being instantly completely awake. "What goes?"

"There's a scrabbling in the ivy outside the window," Jimmy whispered.

Doctor Harries' answer was loud. "I wish we *could* pretend it might be rats or a burglar. It's not *it* that's afraid. It seems, in fact, to have gained the window-sill. Lights! For God's sake, quick! Light!"

The old-fashioned bulb in the ceiling lit the room but not the outside. With the same impulse both men snatched up their guns and rushed to the window, directing their white flash beams through the glass. Whatever had scrabbled was not quick enough to disappear. Jimmy threw up the window before the doctor, crying, "Good God! No!" could stop him. The bright glare showed nothing. Only a rustle of retreat scuttled though the ivy.

"Ha!" The doctor found a small satisfaction. "As I thought; it functions best in the dark. Light is a certain measure of defense."

"Look!" Jimmy whispered again, hoarsely. His flash beam was directed on the window-sill.

There in the dust was an imprint! Of a hand! Of long, withered fingers and a palm—and the thin scratches of uncut nails!

From below came another flash into their eyes. The watchman's dim form bulked behind it. "Hanythink up?" he called.

"We don't know," the doctor said quickly before Jimmy might blurt out the shocking discovery and, perhaps, despite the man's boast, frighten him entirely away. "We heard something in the ivy. If you do, don't wait, but shoot at the sound."

"Hi will that, sir. Though that there ivy is a 'ome for all the vermin, rats an' sparrows an' what not, in the bloomin' county."

"So a watchman, then," Doctor Harries said, "is no better than dogs." He very firmly closed the window down.

"Why?" Jimmy could not break away from the awed whisper normal to a disturbed night. "Why didn't it break through the glass and in? It broke that shop window."

"I wonder." Dr. Harries stood with narrowed eyes. "Those were little *leaded* panes, weren't they? Could it be that it knew we were armed with weapons that could disintegrate it. Or could it be—could it just be on account of the bars of cold iron at the window? We know so little. Heavens, how little, about these darker forces. We know only that this one has a deadly potentiality."

"A dead man's hand!" Jimmy was muttering, his eyes staring out at nothing. "Supercharged with hate! Able to crawl! Able to run—to choke the life out of—"

"Here, here!" The doctor caught and shook him. "Snap out of that. Once let it crack your nerve and you're lost. Don't you see, that's just what it is hellishly trying to do? Like with the dogs; get them confused and hysterical. Come, get hold of yourself."

"*Phe-eew!*" Jimmy let go a long breath. He shook his head. "It's the damned beastliness, of it all. The something from some evil portion of the outer dark. With all the advantage on its side."

"Not quite all," the doctor encouraged him. "We have the advantage of the light. Even flash beams. I don't know why. But it has always been that the darker forces function in the dark. Which, of course, is what makes them so frightful."

Jimmy shook himself to shed the shakiness of his nerves that had been creeping up on him. "You're damn right, Doc. We dassent let go. What about the watchman down there? Ought we not perhaps to give him an inkling, at least, of what sort of thing to watch for?"

"Or rather, to watch out for. If that thing should crawl up on him unexpectedly—"

"I'll tell him first thing in the morning," said Jimmy. "Before he goes home—and let's hope then that he'll come back."

Jimmy did not tell the watchman first thing in the morning. Because there was no watchman! A sick feeling of dread crept up the fine hairs of Jimmy's back as he explored the grounds, expecting to find a limp body with a blackened face huddled somewhere under a bush or in some dim corner of tumbled masonry. He found foot tracks. Not—he thanked God—hand tracks. Big flat-footed boot marks. The man had faithfully patrolled. But he himself had completely disappeared. "Well, the hell thing can't completely dematerialize a man," he reported in. "Or is that something else we don't know?"

The doctor shook his head. "No. I'm sure that our danger is entirely physical."

"Then I suppose he saw it and emigrated out of the country."

Mrs. Medford offered her, "Aa-ah!" And, "You go an' look in the root-cellar!"

"Good heavens!" It came from all of them. "You haven't 'seen' any new horror?"

"No, sirs an' ma'am. I ain't 'ad no sights. But I knows the likes of them constable chaps. I'll bet 'e went root-cellar a-lookin' for cold beer, as most folks 'ere keeps it there account o' hice bein' irregular. Else why did 'e 'ave to leave 'is fat job at the jail? You tell me that."

"Now be careful, Jimmy." Eula sent a worried look at him, starting up.

"Hold on a minute," said the doctor, "I want to look up an idea I have in one of these old records. It won't take long—you shouldn't go alone."

But Jimmy was too tense and impatient. "I'll carry my little old 'disintegrator'," he said grimly, "and flash-light. I'm having an idea myself, and it's that the man may just possibly be needing help."

"Well, if you find anything, call," said the doctor, obviously torn between research and action.

Surely enough, Jimmy found the flat boot tracks leading to the cellar; and, as they came nearer, they seemed to have been walking on tip toe. The great door stood open. Jimmy peered down the worn, slimy steps. He called. Listened hopefully for drunken breathing. His only answer was the slow-grinding creak of the door in a buffety wind. It reminded him of a radio program. He damned it and shoved an old cobblestone under its lower edge. Leaning thus close, he saw a muddy toe mark on the very sill, and, naturally enough, on the next step.

"The fool!" he growled and he stepped on gingerly down, careful against slipping on the smooth, worn old stone slabs. Not a thing was in the cellar. It was the same dimly dank place that he had seen the first time, sourly redolent, not of stale beer, but of stored vegetables. He did not this time hysterically fire at the soft scurry of rats behind the bins. He flashed his light under them and into the darker corners. Nothing.

Though yes. A door again surely. So green and moss-grown in its equally mossy wall that it could easily be missed. The flash beam would, in fact, not have picked it out at all were it not for a lighter line all along its lintel and jambs. Jimmy stepped closer. And sure enough, the scummy growth had been scratched away by some blunt implement, as though to release old in-grown debris and free the opening. And there, by the sill, lay the implement; a sliver of broken lattice from the arbor outside.

"I wonder now," Jimmy muttered out loud. "I wonder if he could have guessed it would be in there?"

A verdigris brass knob invited his hand. The door swung easily out towards him. Within was wet darkness. He stood uncertainly and flashed his beam about. The place contained bins again—or rather, stout oaken shelves; and on the shelves, stout oaken boxes. Long narrow boxes.

A vague intuition was pressing at the back of Jimmy's mind as to what sort of storage this might be. His nose was curling, uncertainly sniffing, when he saw that one of the boxes had had its lid shoved slightly askew, and the pale whitish gleam that thrust out of the slit to reflect his flash could be nothing other than a bone.

"The old crypt, by God!" Jimmy was, with normal impulse, backing away from it when his lowered flash beam picked out the body! It was huddled limply on the floor and was unmistakable.

The watchman!

The rough homespun sleeve feebly moved. "Good Lord!" Jimmy rushed in and bent to lift the man. He was heavy. Jimmy yelled over his shoulder:

"Help here! I've found him!"

The boisterous wind must have carried his voice away. A gust of it swung the inner door shut with a slam, cutting off even the dimness from the outer one, leaving only Jimmy's flash beam in the pit blackness.

Jimmy damned. And with the hot breath of the word, chilled. Had that been a gust? He had felt no draught. He'd have to get the man out of there in a hurry. To be in a crypt at any time was a creepy enough happening. To find a blacked-out watchman there, whether drunk or wounded, was a shock to anybody's nerves. To have a charnel house's only source of light and ventilation slam shut on one was—Jimmy kept up his courage by furiously swearing.

His light on the stationary snap, he bent again awkwardly and in a frenzy of hurry to lift the man. His sawed-off shot gun in the crook of his arm, it was difficult to get a grip on so lumpy a thing as a man. And the man was— The realization came in like a blow over the heart. He was stiff!

How could his sleeve have moved then? Jimmy yelled again, futilely, for help.

And in that instant a something, violent and bone hard, dashed the flash from his hand! For a moment he could trace its spinning arc through the air and then it tinkled into the corner and was out!

Jimmy's breath ee-eeked out in a choked gasp. His stomach fell away, his blood, everything. Pit blackness and pit silence enveloped him. His knees limp, he sank down on the body he had been trying to lift. Even that relict of humanity was a comfort. Only persistence of vision seemed to function. He could see in the blackness a pale green arc of his last light.

And then another function, desperately needed, began to assert itself out of his paralysis. He could fearfully listen. He heard his pulse—like a persistent and useless little rubber hammer. So he wasn't dead of shock. He could still move. He *must* move.

He shoved himself off that dead thing on which he had fallen and hurled himself toward the door. A blow hit him in the face and rocked him dizzily back. He didn't normally curse it. He was prayerfully thankful for it. What had hit him was mouldily damp; it was the side of one of the old coffins. It oriented him, at least in direction.

He plunged to the door. It must be the door. His hands, desperately fumbling, could feel the wet panels, the straight crack of its jamb. He clawed frenziedly up and down the crack, inches on either side. Desperately back and forth and around.

And there was no knob on the inside!

Jimmy lolled limp against the door. He could feel his knees bend against it and his chest sliding slimily down the boards.

An awful sound stabbed at him with galvanizing force. A sound in itself commonplace and harmless. But here, terrifying. A stealthy scuffling.

It came from that grizzly box up there with the opened lid! Where that bone had been sticking out! The sound was a bony scratching of pointed nails!

Breath surged back to Jimmy, absurdly to *whoo-oosh!* And out of his jetty blackness he fired at the sound.

Pit silence again.

A thin hope of desperation trembled through Jimmy. Could it be possible that there was a merciful God in this hell pit and his blast had shattered the—had "disintegrated"—no other word fitted in—the whatever had made that sound up there? Jimmy's chilled consciousness refused to give it the name that it fearsomely knew.

And then his whole being shrank together once more to hear the scrabbling of fingernails again. Not rats. Rats never sounded like that. Rats softly pattered. They harmlessly scuffled. They cheerfully squeaked. Rats were inoffensive warm creatures of human homes. They were—

The scrabbling noise plopped onto the sodden floor! Jimmy madly fired in that direction. Madly listened. He was shockingly conscious of the gun-blasted air. Conscious of infinitely worse than that. For that was his all! His last defense! Nobody with a sawed-off shotgun ever carried more than the two cartridges in the barrels. With a sawed-off shotgun it was never necessary—not against anything on earth. . . .

And then Jimmy shrieked. Every breath forced fearfully from him as a something scuttled up the outside of his pants leg, over his back, and rushed coldly savagely to tear at his throat!

Jimmy clawed furiously at it. Not his most remotely dragged-in hope could call for God's mercy. This was *it!* Dried flesh and loathly coarse hair and overgrown nails! They tore at Jimmy with a savage hate.

Jimmy was able, with all the strength of his two hands, to loosen the thing's grip sufficiently so that he could at least suck in a breath to replenish the emptiness of his long-drawn shriek. The thing, quicker than any rat, let go of

Jimmy's throat, twisted itself free, and out of the empty dark slammed itself against his neck. Slammed again at his face. It didn't seem to know about the modernly developed technique of a knockout blow to the jaw. It battered at any part of the head. Coming out of the blackness, Jimmy could see nothing to ward. Every advantage was with the pent-up hate that could see in the dark. It could beat a man to a pulp at its vengeful will.

With arms and elbows, like an already beaten fighter, Jimmy tried to protect his face. Then the thing was at his throat again, as though it could tell that Jimmy was gasping from the fumes of his shots.

Jimmy's desperation gave him strength to tear the thing away. He could feel blood oozing. The thing, needing no rest, battered at his face again. It was not floating in air; it seemed to be getting its take-off from his shoulders, from his arms, even up from his chest, any place where it could momentarily settle and spring. At one time it missed its blow. Its own vicious force carried it on to slap hollowly against a coffin. It plopped to the floor.

With mad hope Jimmy jumped, both feet together, thinking to step on it. But there it was, scuttering up his pants again, a devil thing of the dark, vicious with life, savagely bent on death. Jimmy's feet stumbled over that other dead thing on the floor. Its stiff limbs tripped him. He fell. Immediately he felt the scrabbling fingers run onto his chest. His frenzied snatch this time caught it. It was strong enough, crawling on its three loose fingers, to drag his both hands remorselessly up to his throat and to dig those fingers in. Jimmy dizzily thought he could hear voices and a pounding on the door.

Hope brought him strength again. He tore the thing loose. He knew that flesh ripped with its nails. It twisted itself free. Jimmy tried to roll away from it. That was worse. On the floor it could choose any vantage point from which to fling itself at him. Jimmy heaved himself up to his knees. The thing leaped at his throat again. The light flashes of beaten nerves were sparking within Jimmy's head

But there the beast suddenly let go. Jimmy was able to suck in life-saving breaths and to flail wildly with his arms. If it were possible for the thing to be even temporarily disabled by so soft a thing as a human fist—

The light flashes had not been in his head. They were real. White beams of flash-lights. The doctor was curbing Jimmy's wild blind swings. Lifting him, hampered by Eula, who clung sobbing to him. The doctor sharply slapped her. "Snap out! Get hold of him! This place is poisonous with the fumes of all hell."

Jimmy was able to croak, "Look out! It's it! Here! It comes from everywhere!" Eula made tight-bitten noises out of her hysteria. Together the two rushed Jimmy out. The doctor kicked the door behind him. Uselessly, for they had battered the panels in. They hurried Jimmy, slipping and clawing, up the slime-green steps to God's open air. The doctor slammed that door shut.

It was Mrs. Medford who first had the courage to propose going back. After washing Jimmy off and bandaging his torn throat and after a stiff stimulant all round—that she stoutly refused—she offered her fearsome thought.

"It's 'ad its fight. It'll never be weaker than now. Lights, you say, is what scares it. If it's got to be destroyed, what I says is the time is now."

The doctor looked at the extraordinary woman. He slowly began to nod. Jimmy, his lips tightly set, nodded. Eula covered her eyes with her hands—and nodded.

They went then, with the one shotgun and a flash light each. The outer door had remained shut. In the root-cellar nothing moved. The inner door stood broken as it had been left.

"You drag it open," the doctor told Jimmy. "I'll stand by with the gun."

Within the crypt nothing moved. The lights showed only the slime puddles where Jimmy had rolled. Those, and indented scratches of fingernails. From Jimmy's throat squeaked a memory and he turned his beam up to the coffin. The white bone that he had indistinctly seen before still protruded from the chink between box and lid.

Eula screamed. The doctor half-levelled his gun and then he softly whistled. Mrs. Medford said "Aa-ah! I should ha' knowed it."

The white thing was the two bones of an arm—and they had no hand!

The doctor looked at the others, round-eyed. He pointed, thrusting with his finger. It was he who was whispering now.

"It's in there! Come home where it belongs!"

Silently, as though stalking a snake, he handed the gun to Jimmy. He made a rush to the coffin, shoved the arm bones in, and dragged the lid over to close the crack.

"Help me now," he shouted. "Help to hold it down! We don't know how strong it is."

All together, swallowing down repugnance, they grappled with the box.

"Light!" the doctor panted. "Out into the sunlight."

Inexpertly, getting in one another's way, desperately gripping down the lid, they pulley-hauled the coffin from its shelf. Shoved it sliding up the wet steps. Out into the warm summer sun.

There with an astounding courage the doctor sat his whole weight down on it. Beckoned Jimmy to add his weight. Beckoned Eula. She came, but would sit no closer to the oaken board than on Jimmy's lap.

Mrs. Medford said, "So now you've catched it. So now tell us 'ow a thing like that is kept catched."

The doctor frowned away into the distances of his dark knowledge. "I— don't—know," he said. "For the present, in bright daylight, it will not burst out. I must think. My immediate thought is—nails. *Iron* nails. I expect Mrs. Medford must know where there are some. And the next thought is, what about the unfortunate watchman?"

"We can only guess," Jimmy said. "I'd guess he saw something and tiptoed after it; and then down there—" He shivered in the warm sun and put his fingers tenderly to his throat.

"Yes, I suppose so. We must get him out and notify the authorities."

Mrs. Medford came back with a hammer and nails. "Not that them'll 'old it down for long. Not come dark."

"No. We must think of something better."

Eula, nose wrinkling, watched with a determined vindictiveness the doctor's nailing of the lid. Suddenly she pointed to where his hands smudged off some gray mold.

"Look. It was he, sure enough."

Faint Gothic letters showed. "B-n-t d- l- Cein-ure."

"Yes," Doctor Harries said. "It would make a priceless piece for some museum. But the more I've been thinking, the more convinced am I that light—fire light—will destroy this malignant force. And why not now? And here!"

"God knows there's enough of old timbers lying about." Jimmy, without any argument or question, set about collecting. Eula helped with a determined enthusiasm.

"The only thing I like about this dreadful place," she said. "Is its stock of old firewood."

In the bright sunlight, then, they hoisted the gray, mouldy coffin onto the pyre. Eula vindictively lit it, and they stood back.

The dry timbers roared up and quickly made a red furnace in the middle of which the coffin gave off a vast black smoke before its sides began to crack and long lines of fire crept along the slits and ate into its moldy interior. Eula suddenly covered her eyes and screamed. With a grim satisfaction Jimmy watched a gray spidery horror break through the burning side, scrabble madly in the furnace and then fall back. In tight-lipped silence, his every nerve taut, he watched the gray fingers turn black and curl together and glow red and disintegrate in little licking blue fires.

"That," Doctor Harries said, "I think disposes of that."

Jimmy put his arm about Eula. "At all events," he said, "I think it proves that ours was the respectable branch of us Doaks. It took to my pocket in the first place for some sort of revenge. Fancy my going into the very shop it'd been in all these years.

"From now on, how shall we spell our name?"

Eula pushed away from him. "I'll have nothing to do with anything from the past. The plain American way is all we'll ever use," she said firmly.

"Oke—Doak," retorted Jimmy, at last able to get a grin out of the business. "But how are we going to convince Dad?"